'For mo 'e things that happen on the t .....unitarian takes you 'there' - to a place w ordinary people are left to fathom the unfathomable. Goss's intimate interweaving of fact and fiction around the 2005 Kashmir earthquake disaster takes readers to places they will never forget and, God-willing, they will never have to go.'

Peter Foster, *Daily Telegraph*

'A wonderfully visual writer, whose story of those caught up in natural disaster is told with insight, honesty and compassion. A moving and exciting first novel.'

Parang Khezri, *Film-maker and social activist*

'Based around the 2005 earthquake which left a lasting trail of destruction in Kashmir, Goss's novel describes the depth of human emotions of sympathy and of hatred in a land where instability lives, and aid workers struggle not only against the hazards brought by collapsing houses and destructive avalanches but also deep cultural barriers. The novel is true to its theme and the story told with heartfelt emotion.'

Kamila Hyat, *Columnist and human rights activist*

THE
HUMANITARIAN

Andrew Goss

The Book Guild Ltd

First published in Great Britain in 2020 by
The Book Guild Ltd
9 Priory Business Park
Wistow Road, Kibworth
Leicestershire, LE8 0RX
Freephone: 0800 999 2982
www.bookguild.co.uk
Email: info@bookguild.co.uk
Twitter: @bookguild

Copyright © 2020 Andrew Goss

The right of Andrew Goss to be identified as the author of this
work has been asserted by him in accordance with the
Copyright, Design and Patents Act 1988.

All rights reserved. No part of this publication may be
reproduced, transmitted, or stored in a retrieval system, in any form or by any means,
without permission in writing from the publisher, nor be otherwise circulated in
any form of binding or cover other than that in which it is published and without
a similar condition being imposed on the subsequent purchaser.

This work is entirely fictitious and bears no resemblance to any persons living or dead.

Typeset in 12pt Adobe Jenson Pro

Printed and bound in the UK by TJ International, Padstow, Cornwall

ISBN 978 1913208 530

British Library Cataloguing in Publication Data.
A catalogue record for this book is available from the British Library.

For **Jalal** with love, to explain how his mother and
father came to be in the mountains of Pakistan.

For those 'mercenaries, missionaries and misfits'
who travel to foreign fields to help others.

For the poorest of the poor who smile,
hope and dream in the face of adversity.

And for **Claire**, with thanks for all her love and support.

*"The Game is so large that one sees
but a little at one time."*
Rudyard Kipling

Dedicated to **Abdul Waheed Khan**, whose life was taken while
striving to ensure little girls could learn to read and write.

…and in remembrance of a woman
who was loved and lost in Pakistan.

*"Even if just one person's life is changed for the better, then it is all
worthwhile."*
Afsa Ali

Although based on actual places and events, this book is a work
of fiction and any resemblance of the central characters to persons
living or dead is entirely coincidental.

However, acknowledgements are due to the following:
Frank Lyman and **Syed Latif** for their inspirational work in Pakistan.

Also to my uncle, **Heinz Bauer**, who showed me the way.

PREFACE

A DEVASTATING EARTHQUAKE strikes without warning, sweeping away the fragile infrastructure of Pakistan's Himalayan sub-ranges within a few seconds.

The earthquake claims the lives of 80,000 people, injures some 100,000, leaving more than 3.5 million without shelter. And the bitter winter is moving in.

Against this backdrop, a multi-national team of aid workers is drawn from across the world in a race against time to assist survivors under intense physical and emotional pressure. The events following the disaster, their effect on local communities and the mix of international staff thrown together in extreme circumstances, are seen through the eyes of British journalist John Cousins, the accidental 'humanitarian' of the story.

Cousins finds himself at the centre of conflicting interests played out against the highly charged disaster scenario. The events he bears witness to in the remote mountain areas are both heartbreaking and inspiring, leading him to question his own values, and the perceptions of Pakistan and the West.

It is an account which brings into focus the relationships between those affected by disaster and those humanitarian agencies seeking to assist, in a country at the very heart of East-West tensions in a part of South Asia of vital strategic importance.

Above all, it is an inspirational story set in the mountains of north-west Pakistan, highlighting the human struggle in the face of crushing adversity, which brings the wider relationship of the developed world and its poorer countries into question.

It is a story of courage, compassion and political intrigue in the wake of a devastating natural disaster.

ONE

From his vantage point on the natural outcrop which jutted from the mountainside, he sat and gazed out across the valley. Shahbaz, the shepherd boy, was eleven, but he looked younger and smaller than his years. His slight frame shivered in the freshness of the morning air. But he could already feel the soothing warmth of the low sun through the woollen blanket draped around his shoulders, as it climbed above the peaks and chased the shadows of the mountains away.

The goats Shahbaz tended were spread evenly on the slopes within his peripheral vision, contentedly chewing on scrub and grass which grew abundantly on the lower slopes, before the terrain rose sharply and the vegetation thinned to the rockier ground at higher altitude. As he sat taking in the first warmth of the clear autumn morning, his dark eyes gazed through matted, black hair at the ragged peaks opposite, capped with a dusting of snow set in stark contrast against the clear blue sky. More snow would come soon.

He squatted on his haunches, dreaming of wonderful things that were yet to touch his life, as poor shepherd boys do to while away the hours. In his hands beneath the blanket he held the small wooden cricket bat his father had given to him. He shrugged the blanket from his shoulders and looked at the bat again, running his thin brown fingers along its smooth contours.

"Perhaps it will help you play for Pakistan one day, *Beta*," his father had said, smiling as he had handed the prized item to his son. And the boy's face had lit up. He knew his father had set money aside for many weeks in order to buy the gift he knew his son would treasure. It was the same bat the boy had seen so many times in the shop at the *markaz* in the town below.

It was surely fate that now he held it in his hands. Perhaps one day he *would* play for Pakistan. Maybe it was written. It was a thought that cheered him as he sat alone, cutting a lonely figure on the mountainside. The morning stillness was only broken by the occasional bleat of the goats as he let his thoughts bathe in the dream of one day standing alongside his sporting heroes.

It was while his thoughts were occupied with such pleasant dreams and untroubled time under the Himalayan sky allowed the wonderful images of greatness to form in his mind, that suddenly he felt the ground begin to tremble. Instantly alert, he looked around. The goats stopped eating and scattered, running headlong in all directions.

Shahbaz lowered the bat and leaned forward, clinging to the rock on which he crouched. The mountain was now shaking violently, and the boy heard the terrifying rumble and the cracking like the sound of gunfire. He was vaguely aware of the splitting of rock around him, as if the mountain itself was waking, shuddering to life as boulders began to roll from the rock faces above. The boy closed his eyes tightly and recited the *Kalima*, over and over, praying that Allah would protect him.

After what seemed an eternity the shaking stopped as suddenly as it had started. In reality only a few seconds had passed. Then there was a stillness even more terrifying.

The boy opened his eyes but remained crouched, still, hardly daring to move. As he looked around, he saw boulders strewn around him. Squinting into the valley he could no longer see the tiny buildings of the town in the distance. It was now obscured by a cloud of dust rising from where it lay.

He picked up his cricket bat and rose unsteadily to his feet, dazed and frightened by what he had experienced. He scanned the nearby slopes, but the goats were gone.

A sense of panic rose in him and his breathing became short and laboured. He turned and ran through the scrub as fast as he could to pick up the narrow path which would take him around the spur of the mountain towards his home, where his mother and younger sister would be waiting for him…

In the valley below, children were bowed in prayer as the first rumble was heard and the school building began to shudder. Prayers gave way to screams as the concrete structure started to shake violently. Madam teacher's voice was uncommonly sharp and shrill, as she instructed the girls to leave the building immediately, betraying her own mounting fear.

Some of the girls rose to their feet instantly in a bid to escape into the schoolyard. But little Rania remained on her knees, bent forward, covering her head with her hands as the concrete ceiling gave way. Then all she could remember was a darkness invaded by the sobs and cries of her injured classmates. She tried to move but was not able to. She wanted to cry out, but she could not. A great weight seemed to be pressing down on her and it was difficult for her to breathe. There was no pain. Just a numbness. And an inky blackness punctuated by the screams and murmurs of the other girls, until one by one they fell silent. She began to feel very cold. An overwhelming sense of loneliness swept through her and then sadness as she thought of her mother and father. It was the last thing she remembered before slipping into unconsciousness.

The earthquake came without warning that Saturday morning. It struck the mountains of northern Pakistan at 8.52am on October 8, 2005, during the holy month of Ramadan.

Villages were shaken from their footings, spilling into the yawning valleys below, or were buried by landslides as entire slopes dislodged and slipped from the mountainside, carrying trees and shrubbery with them on sliding slabs of earth, as if on unseen wheels. Roads were ripped from the mountainsides they hugged, and bridges collapsed into rivers and gorges. Entire townships were raised to rubble. In less than thirty seconds the fragile infrastructure of Pakistan's north-western Himalayan communities had been destroyed in the worst earthquake in living memory.

But as yet the full impact of the catastrophe was not apparent. In Islamabad, the affluent federal capital eighty miles to the south-east, reports of the disaster were just coming in as many of its wealthy inhabitants made a slow start to the weekend. Several dozen deaths were reported in the first news bulletins they awoke to. But as the morning wore on the scale of events was being felt. And strong aftershocks continued to shake the city's inhabitants from their beds.

Afsa Ali was at home with her mother when she felt the first movement which instinctively brought the women running out into the street with their neighbours, some sitting, some standing holding each other, staring uncertainly in fear and bewilderment. Just a few hundred yards from the family home, one of the two Margalla residential tower blocks crumbled and crumpled into rubble, killing scores of people instantly and trapping dozens more.

And suddenly the TV reports were a rolling kaleidoscope of chaotic scenes flashing across screens crowded by those desperate for news. The ten-storey tower had collapsed like a house of cards, burying its residents as it crashed to the ground. Many had been at home, resting following their pre-dawn meal and early prayers ahead of the long day's fast.

But no-one was sure how badly the earthquake had affected the mountain communities, where the epicentre lay. Mobile phones in the mountains were silent. Communications were down; all roads from the capital were either destroyed or blocked, making access by land impossible. Army and air force helicopters were scrambled and began to report the devastation of the stricken communities they saw from the air.

Casualty figures began to soar from dozens, to hundreds, to thousands, as Pakistan began to take in the terrible devastation the disaster had caused. Hospitals went on high alert and stood ready to receive the injured. Severe aftershocks continued throughout the day and a national emergency was declared.

At the federal hospital, Dr Shaukat Tariq returned to his office following a meeting of senior hospital staff and sat at his desk. He breathed deeply and rubbed his hands over his face, smoothing his thick moustache. He took his pipe and tobacco from his drawer, packed it and lit up, sending a plume of smoke rolling towards the ceiling. There were tears in his eyes as the images of his childhood and family home in the mountains of Kashmir ran through his mind. There was, as yet, no news from the village where he was raised and where his family home still lay, high in the Himalayan foothills.

The shrill ring of the telephone on his desk suddenly interrupted his thoughts and he lifted the receiver to his ear.

"Yes, yes… make sure the teams are ready. Full emergency support for casualties, including crush injuries, internal bleeding, laceration. Severe trauma. Yes. I'll be right there," he said in a voice that betrayed none of the emotion he was feeling. The first casualties from the earthquake were on their way by helicopter.

Heart pounding, the shepherd boy Shahbaz finally rounded the last mound that would bring him within sight of his home. The scene before him stopped him in his tracks. Twisted wooden beams protruded from the small mound of earth and stone at odd angles, where they had been forced apart as the roof collapsed, now splayed like some grotesque skeletal frame from the rubble that had been the family home. He was still not close enough to see if his mother and sister were there.

"Mama! Mama!" he cried. But there was no reply.

Then, as he slowly drew nearer, afraid of what he would discover, he saw the half-buried figure of the woman who was his mother. He saw her arm stiff with bloodied fingers as if suddenly stilled while clawing at the ground and covered in grey dust. Her face was partly veiled and turned protectively away, eyes closed, as if in sleep. A heavy beam lay across her, pinning her to the ground amid the debris.

And then he heard it. It was the faint rasping, exhausted cry of the baby. Through a blur of tears that now filled his eyes, he kneeled beside his mother. In her most desperate moment before death she had shielded the infant with her body, cradling her baby protectively with her arm beneath her shawl as the family home had collapsed.

Raising the shawl, Shahbaz leaned forward and lifted his baby sister from the arms of his mother.

The infant was distressed but seemed otherwise unharmed. The boy held his little sister to him and sat beside his dead mother, rocking slowly forwards and backwards, sobbing uncontrollably as the sun rose high above the mountain landscape…

TWO

THE GENERAL, PRESIDENT and Commander-in-Chief of the armed forces gathered his senior staff around him. Sitting behind the expansive desk in the private oak-panelled office, the uniformed man effectively wielded all power in Pakistan.

Almost dwarfed by the opulence of his trappings, including several rows of medals pinned to his buff tunic, General Pervez Musharraf's physical stature was slight, his benevolent face framed by well-groomed hair, with carefully managed greying temples and an immaculately trimmed moustache.

In a family setting, he might have presented the image of anyone's favourite uncle. And yet he was a veteran of two wars fought against India and the darling of the army before seizing power from his old political adversary Nawaz Sharif. To his credit, the carefully planned coup was bloodless. That is not to say there were not those who lived in fear of the general and his gentle smile.

For a military man, the general's voice was soft and controlled. "Gentleman," he began, addressing his faithful lieutenants, "you have seen the initial reports. We have a disaster on our doorstep. We must offer every assistance to those affected in the mountains – and quickly." The assembled four-star generals nodded, almost in unison.

"We must show purpose and determination to those in desperate need. We must unite the nation."

The top brass knew what was expected. The considerable military might of Pakistan was in process of mobilising. The general and his men also knew, though it may not have been voiced on this occasion, that the West would be watching. Help would come from the Americans.

In New York, grey-suited men of enormous international power and influence were gathering, including the lean and distinguished figure of the UN's Ghanaian Secretary-General, who took an immediate personal interest in the disaster as it was unfolding.

The strategic and political importance of Pakistan was not lost to him, nor was the importance for the international community to offer immediate assistance, should the request be received from the Pakistani government. Reports were coming in thick and fast from restricted areas within the Western embassies deep within Islamabad's high-security diplomatic area.

High commissioners of the major foreign powers within Pakistan's federal capital were pacing the corridors of their overseas missions followed by their security service chiefs and a posse of aids, holding impromptu meetings as the latest information was received from networks across the country. The information was relayed directly to their respective governments for consideration, even before Pakistan had declared an international emergency.

Additional meetings were taking place throughout the day at the UN building in New York, or by video conference link between key agency heads and international aid organisations. The machinery of the international community was in full swing, while heads of government were being briefed on the hour. By the end of the first day executive officers of Relief Action had a report on their desks to consider. The recommendation to send emergency assessment and response staff to boost its existing operation in Pakistan was set to be endorsed and actioned.

Canadian Hank Selby's name was at the top of the list of candidates to lead the organisation's supporting relief operation. Just back from assignment in neighbouring Afghanistan, his military credentials and reputation for getting things done on the ground was impressive. He could deliver in a hostile environment and was a proven leader under pressure. And he was a man of faith.

Selby took the call, rifle in hand, having just fired off a few rounds on the range, close to where his home lay in the small township of Pickle Lake, north-western Ontario, the most northerly community in the province. He liked to keep his hand in. And he liked the rugged isolation the small community offered.

His voice was clear and confident, and held a slight Canadian twang. He did not recognise the US number on the handset display. "Selby. Yeah. Sure." There was a pause while he listened. "Absolutely. I'll be home in twenty minutes and take a look. Yep. I'll come straight back." He was a man of few words. Further names for the advanced party of the emergency team were on the shortlist waiting in his inbox when Selby arrived home. He insisted on having a say on the senior staff, but in fact the executive officers were happy to have his input. Besides, he'd be running things in the earthquake zone.

Within seventy-two hours Selby was Pakistan-bound, having received a security briefing. His visa application had been fast-tracked by the Pakistani authorities, who had already received instructions to waive the usual restrictions and allow Western agencies the necessary documentation without delay.

At Selby's side on the 737 was Charlie Williams, his American security advisor. Williams was a rather serious-looking former US marine, tall and gaunt.

Like Selby, he had seen his share of military action and was a battle-weary veteran. Unlike Selby, he had his regrets and was tormented by the lives he had taken and the things he had done for the Corps. But he felt he had made his peace with God and the deal he had made was to spend the rest of his life trying to do good. He was something of a puritan. Yet he and Selby understood each other. Above all, Williams was a security expert and his job would be to assess the risks and keep the mission safe. The rest of the team was not far behind and would initially make for the office located among the comfortable residential area of Islamabad, before heading out into the mountains at the earliest opportunity.

Gail Stevenson had received the next call following Selby's. A seasoned child protection manager, she had just returned to her home in County Cork from Bangladesh. From a professional perspective, Pakistan was an irresistible challenge. She knew the vulnerable children of Pakistan would have been among the hardest hit and most at risk. It was a part of the world in which the organisation had not previously been able to have an impact. In this sense, she knew it was an opportunity.

As she gazed out of the window of her cottage from the writing desk at which she often sat to rest her eyes upon the green and pleasant Irish landscape, there was not a moment's doubt in her mind. She felt her prayers had been answered. Yet still she felt the need to take a moment's contemplation. She clasped her hands together gently and began to pray, to give thanks and seek guidance from her God. "Thank you. Thank you. Thank you," she whispered, for the chance to serve. She accepted the mission without hesitation.

Meanwhile, in nearby Afghanistan, Galina Zhevlakov was returning from a long day in the field when she received the call on the satellite phone. The Ukrainian was an expert in logistics and ensuring operational detail ran smoothly. In this instance she was returning by Land Cruiser from an assessment of aid delivery to a remote part of Herat province, gazing out at the brown, dusty landscape slipping past the vehicle's window. Her right-hand man was Farzad Ishtar, a young veteran of the Iranian Army.

Both would be on their way to join Selby's team in Pakistan before the end of the week. Her posting in Afghanistan was nearing completion – and there was nothing for her to go back to in Kiev. It would be a welcome continuation of her contract and allow her mind to be distracted from the life she had left behind. Naturally she would take Farzad with her. They were a tried and tested team and worked together well.

The young Iranian smiled at her when she told him. "If we can do Afghanistan, we can do Pakistan too, my sister," he affirmed simply in his heavy Iranian accent.

Other support would follow and additional local staff from the list of volunteers would be hired to boost required numbers. One of those was Afsa Ali from Islamabad, whose name had been submitted just six weeks before the disaster struck. Ali had recently returned from studying abroad and had wanted to help her own people since she had been a child. She felt a calling.

She was beautiful, intelligent and gifted. But she was hiding from the world. Above all, she wanted to do good and was ready to give herself to do Allah's work, wherever that might take her. The letter arrived by email. She pouted her full lips in contemplation as she read the words again. Relief Action in Islamabad had asked that she attend an interview.

Her heart seemed to skip a few beats. "Mama," she called out as she turned from the screen and went to find her mother.

It was a strange assortment of people who gathered that evening at the office, tucked away in an unassuming residential area of Islamabad for a briefing. For most it was the first time they had seen each other. Stevenson fixed her gaze on Selby, trying to gain a measure of the man who stood before her.

Aged around forty, he cut a lean figure and looked in good physical shape. He was clean-shaven, with short, greying hair and steely blue eyes. Though he was dressed casually in shirt and jeans, she noticed they were immaculately pressed. Clearly he was a man who liked to be organised, and the pose he struck, leaning forward with arms outstretched and hands upon the desk before him, suggested an air of confidence. He was someone used to taking charge. His laptop was flipped open with briefing notes he focused on, before he straightened up and stood for a moment, eyeing the group before him. He might have stepped from his regiment the week before, she mused.

She was not sure what might lie behind the faint smile on his lips or his penetrating gaze, as he prepared to address the group. She wondered idly what sort of childhood might have shaped the man who was to take charge of the relief operation. She was tired and jetlagged from the long journey.

Williams, the security man, was there, looking slightly tense, drumming lightly with his fingers on the notepad resting on his knee. It was a habit he had. The Ukrainian and Iranian logistics support had also arrived earlier that day. There were two Pakistani nationals who also sat with the group and were part of Selby's procurement team. All were watching the operations manager.

"Glad you all made it – good to see you and I am pleased to have your expertise on board," he said, addressing his team with an easiness which slightly belied his disciplined appearance. The voice was calm and clear. "We're going to need it," he added. He paused and suddenly smiled. "Got some challenges ahead before we start to roll."

The immediate priority was to establish a base in the mountains and begin moving equipment to the area, with all the required logistics to begin to reach stricken communities.

"We'll have some child protection ladies with us, but clearly the priority is to set up and get the relief operation rolling ASAP," Selby added almost dismissively. It was like a red flag to Stevenson.

"Children *are* the priority, Mr Selby." Her clipped Irish voice was clear and firm.

Selby gazed directly at her. "Of course they are. But they won't be protected unless they have food, water and shelter," he replied flatly.

Stevenson, now fully alert and feeling provoked, returned Selby's gaze and said simply, "I will be moving forward to establish safe areas for the children as my priority – that's what I am here for. And that's what the organisation stands for, Mr Selby; that's a key area of the organisation's expertise."

"Point taken, Gail," said Selby, smiling, making a tactical retreat. Lines were already being drawn, and although Stevenson was slight in stature, she was a veteran of disaster scenarios and an experienced, determined practitioner. Yet Selby had his priorities clear. And he was the man in charge.

Williams was to give a security briefing in the morning. Atif and Mohammad would help secure the required properties and liaise with the local landlords, he said, introducing the two Pakistani nationals.

Already the army had cleared and bridged some of the major routes north, and word was that the main Kashmir Highway would soon be passable. Williams had already made contacts with the respective Pakistan Army commanders on the ground and was receiving regular updates. Selby hoped to head for the disaster zone in the next couple of days with a view to securing property and start setting up operations soonest.

Stevenson was concerned. Selby made clear she was not part of the advance party. He had the overall security of the operation to consider. But she was desperate to access the disaster area. She knew too well that the children would have been among those worst affected and were the most vulnerable.

It pained her to think of their suffering. As for Selby, she felt she had her work cut out. This was going to be like the Sudan all over again.

It was late when she finally arrived at the guesthouse to bed down for the night. She carried her bags to her room and dropped them on the floor. She sat on the bed thinking for a while. Then she sank to her knees and began to pray. She was praying for the children. She had seen children suffer before and had not lost the compassion to feel their pain.

THREE

THE SCALE OF the disaster became clear with the arrival of the first patients at the government hospital. Ambulances screamed through the streets of the capital, ferrying the injured airlifted from the disaster area in a seemingly endless stream of blue lights. Injuries were severe; the crushed and broken bodies of many of the first arrivals were beyond the skills of surgeons working tirelessly to save them. As many victims were wheeled to the mortuary as were ferried to the recovery wards in those first few hours. The valiant rescue efforts of teams risking their lives to desperately locate and reach those trapped under the rubble often proved in vain.

Staff at the hospital worked around the clock, bolstered by medical students drafted from the nearby college to help boost their numbers. Many of them were themselves dazed and shocked by what they saw, moving from patient to patient during initial assessment. The numbers of children among the injured was high. The earthquake had struck at the beginning of the school day. The operating theatre was in constant use, its external red light blazing through the night. Weary surgeons worked ceaselessly, only to pause for the washing down of equipment and the next patient to be wheeled in.

During a few moments' respite in his office Dr Shaukat Tariq sat at his desk and lit a pipe. Already he had been working for twenty hours and his white coat was grubby and spattered with blood. He rubbed his fingers over tired eyes, drew a sharp intake of breath and lifted the phone to his ear.

It was Colonel Mohammad Kamran who took the call from his old friend.

"Beds. We need more beds, my friend. And blood supplies," the doctor stated wearily.

But there were no spare hospital beds to be had in Islamabad. And the blood supplies were gone. The army had already taken any surplus from the country's blood banks, whose medics were deployed in the earthquake zone. Mattresses could be commandeered. Would they do? Bandages, antibiotics and morphine the colonel could arrange.

"I have not seen such numbers before," Tariq told his friend. "And so many children."

The colonel was genuinely moved by the doctor's distress. He'd have the 200 mattresses there within the next couple of hours, with some army medics to relieve the teams working at full stretch. And the additional supplies. It was the best he could do.

"Sometimes I feel we are a cursed country," said Tariq.

"We will cope, as we always cope in testing times. It is the will of Allah," replied the colonel matter-of-factly. He paused, and when he spoke again there was genuine concern in his voice. "Get some rest when you can, my friend."

Tariq dropped the telephone receiver back into its cradle. He pulled out the bottom right-hand drawer of his desk and fished out the bottle of vodka which lay hidden there with a tumbler. He poured himself a generous measure and downed it in one. Allah would forgive him, he felt. He took a mint from the tin he kept on his desk and popped it into his mouth. Then he headed out into the corridor.

And still more patients were arriving. The flow of ambulances seemed constant and within the first day the hospital's 455 beds were full, with casualties now lying in the corridors.

The groans of acute suffering of those who now filled every corner of the hospital sounded a constant murmur of despair through the building, which seemed to be growing in intensity.

Dr Tariq was now back on the wards and in the corridors, personally directing and supporting his teams. It was clear the hospital did not have the capacity to cope. And yet he knew the city's other hospitals were also at full stretch, including the military and training hospitals in the twin city of Rawalpindi.

As he moved through the main casualty area he passed a nurse, rooted to the spot, head bent slightly forward, staring at a pool of blood, bright crimson against the white floor tiles. She seemed momentarily transfixed, unable to move.

"Nurse! Nurse Sadia!" said Tariq on his way past. Then he stopped and turned back towards her. "Nurse! Come now, move along," he repeated. The nurse gazed up and their eyes met briefly.

And a moment of understanding passed between them. Suddenly aware of her lapse, she bowed her head in apology and moved away to attend a patient.

On a table in the corridor Tariq approached a small figure covered with a brown shawl. He pulled the garment back gently to reveal an infant of no more than two years, stiff and lifeless. The little boy's tunic was blood-stained; his arm fractured and jutting at an unnatural angle. He looked at the child's face. Its eyes were closed, its face relaxed. He covered the dead child again.

"Orderly. Take this child to the mortuary," he barked. Then he sighed deeply.

He walked along the corridor, lined with injured men, women and children lying on the floor, moaning in pain, desperate for relief, some reaching out to him as he passed. He stopped at the post-surgery ward and spoke briefly to one of the nurses. Then he entered the ward. The sixty beds were all occupied by women and children.

Tariq approached the nearest bed and was joined by the nurse. The little girl on the bed was still anaesthetised. Tariq scanned the notes and frowned. The girl's name was Rania and she was nine years old. He understood she had been dug from the rubble along with the bodies of her classmates many hours after the school had collapsed. In the confusion, there were no details of her family.

The soldiers had carried the girl to the ambulance and she had been airlifted by military helicopter to the capital. She had been one of the first to arrive for emergency treatment, one of the lucky ones. But they had not been able to save her legs. Tariq laid a hand on the girl's forehead, smiled faintly and said a silent prayer. The girl was traumatised and in shock, and he did not have the heart to tell her the extent of her injuries. He turned and walked to the next bed.

The three main government hospitals in Islamabad were all receiving similar numbers of patients, as were those in Rawalpindi. Thousands of the most seriously injured had been flown to the capital within the first forty-eight hours. Others were being treated at tented military hospitals hastily set up in the mountains. And the casualty list was rising, soaring from hundreds to thousands.

In cities across Pakistan the reaction of the people was spontaneous and unified. From the port metropolis of Karachi on the Arabian Sea, to Lahore in the heart of the Punjab, and Islamabad in the north under the shadow of the mountains, there was a common will to help the stricken mountain communities.

Drop-off points for food, blankets, bedding, medical supplies and tents sprang up, seemingly on every street corner as the citizens of Pakistan gave generously for their less fortunate brothers and sisters affected by the earthquake. Those who had time and a serviceable vehicle to make the journey loaded up with supplies and headed north.

Not since Partition had the nation felt a greater sense of purpose and unity. But the roads into the mountains that were passable were few and already choked with relief convoys, and few supplies were able to reach the needy quickly.

Army engineers were still busy clearing landslides, repairing damaged roads and bridging the valleys in what was becoming a race against time. Enthusiastic would-be rescuers were politely asked to deposit their supplies at depots hastily set up by the military and turned back. Better to go back home and raise funds for relief items from there, they were told.

As the immediate relief effort continued, army and air force operations were boosted by American Chinooks brought in from bases across the Middle East and UN squadrons of helicopters from neighbouring Afghanistan. Pledges of support were coming in from governments across the globe. Pakistan was not alone in its hour of need.

Relief Action, like many international aid agencies operating in Pakistan, had already sent personnel to establish forward camps. They were ferried by helicopter into the disaster zone and focused on establishing their operations and warehouses from which to launch their relief efforts in the days ahead.

Selby and his team would be joining them as soon as a route was clear and had been negotiated with the army, making the tedious journey into the mountains by Land Cruiser. Emergency stocks of food, blankets, tents and medical supplies were already in-country.

Further appeals had been launched and additional goods would be on their way soon. Selby's own operations plan was beginning to take shape and he was keen to get on with the job and move with his core team into the mountains as soon as possible. He felt every hour at the office in Islamabad was costing lives and was increasingly aware from the reports coming in of the scale of human suffering the disaster had unleashed.

As he considered his plans in the relative comfort of his guesthouse in Islamabad, a little girl stood crying among the remnants of her village, high on the ridge of the Black Mountain in Pakistan's remote frontier region. She was hungry and tired as she clutched the fabric of her mother's loose-fitting *Shalwar Kameez*.

Her mother was picking through the rubble of her home for any household items that might still be saved.

The village of Peer Khel was no more. Built precariously among the contours of the mountain peak at more than 6,000 feet its stone and mud houses had been shaken to ruins within seconds. Nothing remained except the rubble and more than 700 men, women and children who were now without food or shelter.

Rows of fresh graves told the story of the human cost of the disaster on the village. Many had been in their homes as they had given way. Yet those who remained were left dangerously exposed. Grain stores had been swept from the mountainside by landslide, and livestock lost as homes and animal shelters had collapsed. With their houses, their livelihoods and their winter provisions gone, the villagers knew their hardship was only just beginning. The winter was coming and already snow had fallen on the higher peaks to the north, in Gilgit and Chitral where the Himalayas rose up to majestic heights against the Chinese frontier.

As the sun began to set and shadows grew long, the village elders met to discuss what should be done. A dozen or so older men sat in a circle under the sky in the hollow, sheltered by a ridge that afforded some protection from the cool wind already blowing from the north. They were dressed according to tribal custom in rough cotton *Shalwar Kameez*, with broad turbans. Some were wearing coarse woollen blankets to keep out the chill already being felt in the mountains.

They were Pathans, members of a loose network of warrior tribes that populate the mountains of north-west Pakistan and the eastern heights of neighbouring Afghanistan; a proud, independent people, whose lives have gone almost untouched by the modern world for centuries.

It was the oldest member who addressed the small group, his brown face creased by years of exposure in the mountains and his beard white with age. His name was Syed Rahman and it was said he had seen almost a hundred rainy seasons and that he still remembered the time of the British.

"No-one will come," the old man said simply. "We must go to the valley to seek help."

The others paused respectfully to consider.

"But outsiders have never helped us before," said a younger man, whose beard was still dark. "Besides," he added, "the people in the valleys do not respect our ways. The Britishers and the Americans even less." Others nodded and murmured in agreement.

The older man raised a frail hand for consideration before speaking again: "If we do nothing, our women and our children will go hungry. And the winter is coming. Our homes are gone; our food stocks destroyed," he said.

All nodded thoughtfully. And there was silence.

Finally the old man said, "We must seek counsel from the other tribes. It is not for one village to take this step alone and break the code. The *Jirga* must decide."

The others looked at him and nodded to signal their agreement. They had already received news from the other villages, which had suffered the same devastation. Across the Black Mountain, more than 130 villages had been decimated and more than 100,000 people were dangerously exposed.

A messenger would be sent and the word would go from village to village. The *Loya Jirga* – the full council of the five tribes of the Black Mountain – would have to convene. It would consider whether to seek assistance from the outside world. It would decide whether to break the region's self-imposed isolation from those beyond its tribal borders in a tradition stretching back centuries, before the time of the British and the Sikh empire before them…

FOUR

The road north was like no other Selby had ever seen. The convoy of slow-moving trucks, laden with relief supplies stretched as far as the eye could see on the Kashmir Highway, moving steadily towards the earthquake zone in the early morning sunshine. The old Bedfords were stacked high, rolling in low gears, groaning under the weight of every commodity you might imagine: sacks of grain, sugar, tents, clothing, livestock, all moving towards the mountains which rose up before them in the distance.

And yet it was the movement south which made the deeper impression, an ambling, weary surge of men, women and children on foot with their livestock, slowly lumbering southwards carrying whatever possessions they could away from the disaster which had befallen them. It seemed an endless line of human traffic trudging away from the mountains in the hope of finding relief. It was as if an entire people was on the move, literally walking out of the disaster area. And each face told the same story, with tired, haunted eyes filled with hunger and despair.

Selby's party watched silently as their Land Cruiser travelled along the highway, swinging in and out of the relief column to overtake slow-moving vehicles, speeding ahead when oncoming traffic allowed. The operations manager was accompanied in the lead vehicle by Williams and Farzad, the Iranian logistics officer. Zhevlakov and the two Pakistani nationals followed in a second vehicle. Their destination was Ghazikot township, on the edge of Mansehra town, which was to be the hub for international relief activity.

Selby's driver, Rahim, was a mountain man. The Pathan knew the roads and he knew the mountains. Better still, he knew how to drive in Pakistan and how to avoid oncoming vehicles with seconds to spare. The journey was something of a white-knuckle ride, though Selby was unphased. It was like Afghanistan. Williams, though, never seemed to ease his grip on the handrail. More unnerving for Williams was Selby's low chuckle whenever they swung back into the line of traffic to avoid a head-on collision by inches.

To Selby the journey seemed painstakingly slow. He was anxious to reach Ghazikot and start organising the operation. Progress along the highway was sluggish, as it began to snake slowly into the mountains. Though the distance was relatively small – less than eighty miles – the journey was likely to take them up to five hours, depending on the traffic, and was conditional that the road would remain clear. So he was quite happy for his driver to weave in and out of the traffic.

Williams could hardly get out of the vehicle quickly enough as they swung in to stop at one of the many tea houses which lined the highway.

"Man, can't you tell the guy to take it easy?" Williams protested.

"He is taking it easy," replied Selby, smiling.

The small flat-roofed building was set back from the main highway, crowded by heavily laden trucks parked at the front and surrounded like an island by a sea of people squatting in the dirt. Ragged family groups sat where they could find a space on the ground. Some had makeshift shelters from plastic sheeting, blankets and whatever they could forage to afford some protection, either from the chill of the night, or the heat of the sun in the afternoon.

All eyes were on Selby and Williams as they were led from their vehicle by the driver towards the open kitchen, followed by the Iranian. White faces were as yet an uncommon sight outside the capital. But not a hand was raised in plea for charity. It was curiosity which drew their unrelenting stares. These were people unaccustomed to begging. Besides, most were weary from several days on the road.

There were hundreds of families, most with young children, in what had become one of many resting points along the highway for those migrating south.

"My God," muttered Williams, almost involuntarily.

"Heartbreaking," said Selby solemnly.

As the Westerners approached the kitchen, they were immediately greeted by a young Pakistani who led them into the building to sit away from the dust, the heat, and, above all, the stench of unwashed human bodies and inadequate sanitation outside. The driver asked for jugs of water. Selby and Williams looked at each other.

"We'll stick to the bottled water in the vehicle and move out as soon as you guys have taken a few minutes to freshen up," Selby told the Iranian, who nodded and smiled. "And ask him about the road up ahead and if he knows if it is clear." The Canadian rose from his chair and walked to the doorway to gaze out and survey the people outside.

Williams fished out his phone to check for security messages and on the progress of the second vehicle, which had fallen behind. When he looked up, Selby was gone.

"Shit!" he muttered under his breath as he rose to follow Selby out of the building.

He spotted Selby almost immediately, crouching, talking to a man and a woman with a small child a short distance away. The little girl was coughing incessantly. The father was speaking in Pashto, the tribal language of the Pathans. Though he looked tired and drawn, he was animated in his conversation with Selby, who listened patiently, nodding, though he could not understand what the man was saying. It seemed, though, the family had lost everything and were hungry. It was also obvious to Selby that the little girl was most likely suffering from a chest infection and would need medication.

The Canadian smiled and rose to his feet. He casually slipped his right hand into his trouser pocket, in which he had a small wad of Pakistani rupees and held the notes unseen in his first as he dropped the arm to his side. Selby then shook the father's hand and as he did so, pressed the notes he had taken from his pocket into the man's palm, unseen by any casual observer.

"Thank you. Shukria," said Selby warmly in his Canadian twang, gazing into the Pakistani's eyes. The look of surprise turned to gratitude, as the man felt the cash against his hand.

The mother had seen it and whispered her grateful *salaams*. And so had Williams.

"C'mon," said Selby, as the two men moved away, "I think the latrine's behind those bushes."

"You gotta be careful, man," Williams replied. "If anyone had seen what you did, you'd have caused a riot. Besides," he added, "Anyone might think you're a good guy."

"Keep it to yourself, Chuck," Selby replied. And Williams chuckled. It was the first time Selby had seen him smile.

Back on the highway, the road rose steeply before them and the heavy trucks slowed to walking pace.

By the time they hit the military checkpoint at Abbottabad, the sun was already low in the sky. Two soldiers in full battle dress were armed with automatic weapons. They signalled for the vehicle to stop, waving their weapons. Initially they eyed the Westerners with suspicion. Rahim muttered something impatiently in Urdu and they were waved on to enter the garrison town.

The British influence on the architecture was immediately apparent, with its chief buildings in Georgian colonial style, rich on pillars and inflated grandeur.

The church too seemed strangely out of place, set against the surrounding mountains which formed a magnificent backdrop. Built in traditional gothic style in grey stone, with a rising steeple, it might have been plucked from any small English provincial town.

No earthquake damage seemed apparent. Not until they had left Abbottabad and were on the road to Mansehra City and the first signs of landslide could be seen. Army bulldozers were still busy clearing earth and several roadside buildings had sustained damage. But as yet, they were still to enter the earthquake zone, another hour or so by road to the north-east.

Ghazikot was a small township nestling in the valley, surrounded by the Karakorum Mountains which rose up on all sides. Its comfortable flat-roofed villas were homes for local landowners and leisure retreats for the wealthy Pakistani elite who made their money in the larger cities to the south. Due to its low-lying position in the valley, it was relatively unscathed by the earthquake. The only obvious signs of the disaster were displaced people on the move, families sitting by the roadside and the makeshift camps with their improvised shelters.

Williams was on the phone, taking directions as they drove down the hill into the township on the approach road. The checkpoint, with armed guards from the Frontier Corps, marked the turning on the left into the settlement, which was to be the international relief hub.

The Relief Action team sent ahead had already secured a team house and office accommodation. A further two warehouses had been negotiated, along with additional vehicles rented locally.

UN and aid agency vehicles seemed parked on every roadside, with teams all busy setting up their respective operational bases.

At the top of a hill on the very outskirts of the residential area they suddenly saw a young Pakistani in jeans and a T-shirt, waving frantically and smiling at them. It was Tahir, one of the advance party.

"Asalaam-u-alaikum. Welcome," he said excitedly, gazing at Selby as the vehicle drew up and came to a halt. He had seen very few Westerners, except in the movies. Selby returned the greeting and climbed out of the vehicle, gazing at the property.

He was impressed by what he saw. The extensive six-bedroomed bungalow on the hill had not been what Selby had expected. It was far grander. Once inside the walled compound in which it lay, half a dozen steps led to its columned entrance, colonial in style, from a veranda accessed from a well-kept lawn. Its outbuildings afforded further accommodation, with a dormitory below ground able to sleep a dozen and two separate rooms in a building opposite the main house. With sweeping views of the township below and the valley beyond, Selby immediately appreciated its location from a military perspective. The property could easily be protected and defended. Williams was equally impressed.

Inside the main house there was a large central dining room, with a kitchen and a further lounge. Selby took the first bedroom off from the dining room, with Williams moving into the adjoining one, while the Iranian took one of the back bedrooms. Zhevlakov would be based in the outbuilding across the yard and would be joined by Stevenson in the days ahead. Selby was mindful to maintain segregation of the sexes, strictly observed in the conservative north-west.

The men spent the next hour moving their gear in, with enough food supplies for the immediate days ahead and such essentials as an emergency first-aid kit, torches, detailed maps of the region – and fresh ground coffee. They were joined later by Zhevlakov and the Pakistani nationals for an improvised meal of canned beef soup and crusty rolls supplied by Williams, followed by piping hot coffee prepared by Selby, who had brought a battered cafetière with him.

"You make coffee like old English lady," Zhevlakov told Selby poker-faced in her heavy Eastern-European accent, looking directly at him. "Maybe you make tea in nice china cups much better?!"

"Thank you, Galina. And you have nothing to say about Chuck's soup?" he replied.

But Williams was preoccupied with the satellite phone.

"Like the dishwater," she continued drily. "Not like good Ukrainian Borscht I have as baby to make strong!"

"And put hairs on your chest," added Selby with a smile.

"You not see chest," said the Ukrainian. And they laughed, though the Pakistanis were slightly bewildered.

Williams grimaced as he looked up. "You're cooking next time," he told the Ukrainian. He took his coffee mug and headed out into the courtyard to try and raise the local Pakistan Army commander, while the others remained in candlelight around the table.

Later Selby spread the map out on the table and started marking areas of acute need from the reports he had been receiving. Meanwhile, supplies were already on the move, with the first delivery of tents, tarpaulins and blankets due to arrive at one of the warehouses in nearby Mansehra City next day.

Williams had made contact with the army commander whose division was supporting immediate relief efforts across the valley in Balakot district, close to where the earthquake had struck hardest.

Selby was keen to complete his operations plan and to determine exactly where the greatest need for emergency assistance lay. At the same time he wanted to avoid any duplication of activity with other aid agencies. No formal coordination structure had been established and the army was best placed to direct incoming international organisations. Lieutenant-Colonel Asif Khan would meet Selby for a briefing at his field office near Mansehra in the morning.

As the evening began to draw in, Selby made his way from the main house across the courtyard and climbed the steps which led to the flat roof of the outbuilding opposite. And there he stood gazing across the valley at the snow-capped mountains to the north-west as the sun began to slide beyond their peaks.

He was struck by their majesty and beauty as the sky turned a brilliant orange and the shadows suddenly fell across them like a curtain, holding them in silhouette against the glowing horizon.

He thought of the chaos and suffering which lay among the beauty he had just been gazing upon, which was where the epicentre of the earthquake had been. Images of the many desperate people he had seen along the road that day were running through his mind. And he thought of the father of the little girl he had encountered. He could still see the look of gratitude in the man's eyes as a moment of understanding had passed between them. He hoped they would make it.

FIVE

THE BRIGHT EARLY morning sun beat down on the compound with a dazzling intensity. Selby turned the ignition key and the Toyota Land Cruiser growled into life. He'd make the drive to Mansehra City himself to the local army headquarters for the briefing with the colonel, accompanied by Zhevlakov. Beside him sat Tahir, the young Pakistani who would serve as guide and interpreter.

The Ukrainian came running towards the vehicle parked in the yard, looking every inch the aid worker, wearing cargo pants, a long-sleeved shirt, a padded waistcoat and heavy boots, a rucksack slung over her shoulder. A muslin scarf covered her short, dark hair. Tall and slim, she cut an imposing figure as she approached, smiling.

"You trust no-one to drive," she said flatly, looking at Selby. It was a statement, rather than a question.

"I trust no-one, Ms Zhevlakov. Except my guide here," he replied, smiling at Tahir beside him.

"Thank you, Mr Hank," beamed the young Pakistani.

Williams emerged from the main house, phones in hand. "Selby!" he called out and approached the Land Cruiser. "You'll be needing this," he said, thrusting a satellite phone towards the Canadian.

"Every hour, please. I need to know you guys are safe," he said.

Selby took the phone and nodded.

He put the vehicle in gear and moved off, out of the enclosure, through the gate and down the hill. As he reached the main checkpoint, the Frontier Corps guards saluted in response to his acknowledgement and he turned onto the main road, smiling to himself.

Mansehra City was a sprawling town of 60,000 people. Its narrow high street with open sewers was lined with stalls and traders of every description. At its very heart, three roads converged upon a small traffic island on which a policeman stood, casually signalling to the rich assortment of traffic which flowed towards him and came to a chaotic standstill around him. There were horse-drawn carts, camels and cycles among the battered cars and heavily laden trucks.

Mansehra, the city of 'flowers in abundance', revealed its beauty only to those who knew the labyrinth of alleyways leading from its ragged main thoroughfares to hidden bazaars filled with a rainbow of exotic fabrics and fragrant perfumes.

The northern road connected the city to the busy Karakorum Highway, which tediously wound its precarious way north-easterly through treacherous mountain passes to China during the summer months, before the winter snows closed the major route to trade.

Selby took the eastern road out of the city towards the Kaghan Valley, gateway to the neighbouring Balakot district, where the disaster had struck hardest. The colonel had set up his headquarters in a spacious compound with a comfortable three-storey property overlooking Mansehra City as the road began to rise steeply towards the mountains.

The Canadian stopped the vehicle at the barrier, surrounded by coils of razor wire, and smiled at the armed soldier who approached. The white sign painted with large red letters told them it was headquarters of 479 Bridge Battalion, Engineers. Tahir spoke to the guard in Urdu, who checked their passports, then waved them through into the compound.

The jolly-faced colonel was seated behind a desk in his office as they were led in and smiled warmly. Two of his staff stood in attendance next to him. The walls of the room were covered by large operational maps, showing the worst-affected areas and troop deployments. It was exactly what Selby had been hoping for. The colonel stood and stretched out a chubby hand to Selby. He eyed Zhevlakov with slight unease and nodded courteously to the Ukrainian.

"Welcome. So very pleased to meet you," he said in perfect English. "Come, let us go, while the day is still fresh," he added abruptly, moving from behind his desk towards the office door and signalling for the foreigners to follow. Clearly he had a plan.

"Where are we going?" asked Selby.

"Into the mountains. I will show you the need," the colonel replied.

Selby glanced at Zhevlakov, who nodded in agreement, and they followed him outside to where an army Hilux now stood.

"Please," said the colonel, slipping behind the wheel. And they climbed in.

He drove out along the road towards Balakot, taking the corners at break-neck speed, it seemed, to the passengers' helpless and in increasing unease. He was a reckless driver by Western standards, but everything is relative.

This was Pakistan and he took the steep winding roads which led from Mansehra with a confident and intuitive ease, overtaking on blind hairpin bends, blowing the horn, braking hard at each corner and pushing his way past any traffic in his way.

He drove at maximum speed, dodging and swerving all the way on the twenty-mile journey towards the ruined town of Balakot.

The sights, the sounds, the smells, the craziness, set against a backdrop of snow-capped peaks and, of course, ragged, tired people lining the roadsides, assaulted the senses. They raced passed tented camps of displaced people in makeshift camps and aid distribution points, guarded by soldiers, who saluted the colonel as they tore along the road.

The jolly colonel was in charge of army engineers assigned to clearing the routes through to the earthquake zone and repairing bridges, and he was brimming with pride at their achievements. Selby was reprimanded by him twice for not showing enough admiration of his men's work along the way. They had worked wonders in the valley.

On they raced into the centre of Balakot, a sea of rubble, where sometimes they were forced to slow to walking pace, swerving around donkeys, carts, Jeeps, Bedford trucks, amid a cloud of noxious diesel fumes and smoke from cooking fires alongside the road. And there they saw desperate survivors, still digging through the rubble, or sitting dazed upon the flat concrete roofs of their collapsed houses. It seemed to Selby hardly a building was still standing.

They continued through the ruined township, then took a sharp turn onto a narrow road which climbed steeply into the mountains. Finally, after about another hour, the Hilux slid to a stop in a small tented army camp overlooking Balakot and the aid workers were asked to transfer into a waiting Land Rover. There was time enough for Selby to separate himself from the group.

He walked to the nearby ridge and gazed down into the valley from which they had come, while he held the satellite phone to his head to check in with Williams.

As he walked back, he nodded to the Ukrainian and young Pakistani. They climbed into the Land Rover, staring at each other, sharing the same thought. Were they being kidnapped?

And off they went with wheels spinning, raising dust from the narrow dirt road which wound its way ever-higher into the mountains, through ruined settlements, dodging piles of rubble, roofing timbers that protruded from broken buildings, and large concrete pillars with twisted reinforcing wire that once held up houses, shops and schools. Everywhere there were weary, haunted people along the roadside, looking numb and confused.

The Land Rover continued to lurch upwards along an impossibly narrow track that seemed to have been carved through solid rock, shaken from the cliff face by the earthquake onto the road, blocking access to the mountain villages above.

"This track took five days for my men to push through with one of your Caterpillar bulldozers – and an enormous quantity of explosives," the colonel chuckled.

Then he glanced at Selby and said, "Now you will see something no words can ever explain."

But how can one explain the devastation and the sheer misery of a people whose lives had so suddenly and catastrophically been swept away? You can't. You have to see it. You have to smell it. You have to feel it. And that is what the colonel was trying to achieve.

No Westerners had been along the track. The Land Rover, moving in low gear, turned a hairpin bend after five attempts. And then they saw it. The collapsed building with school furniture strewn down the mountainside. Too steep for people to go and collect. Among the broken desks, chairs and cupboards were scattered notebooks and exercise books which the children had been using just a few days ago.

The Land Rover drew to a gentle halt, almost in reverence, it seemed to Selby. They stepped out of the vehicle and stood taking in the scene before them for a few moments in silence.

"Six hundred girls were packed into the school when the earthquake struck," the colonel told them. What happened to them? How many died? The colonel didn't know. But he said few were dug out of the rubble alive.

Selby saw several women squatting in the piles of concrete, timber and twisted metal.

"They are the mothers of children still missing," the colonel explained in barely a whisper. "We have tried to move them on, for their own safety. But they refuse to go. Every day they come. We have stopped digging now. But still they come to cry and pray for their lost children."

They moved closer to the compressed ruins of what had been a school of more than twenty classrooms.

Selby glanced at Zhevlakov and their eyes met. No words were spoken but a silent understanding of sadness passed between them. It was a moment in which words seemed inadequate.

As they walked back to the Land Rover the colonel then told them of another issue the army had already encountered, following the disaster… human trafficking. "We intercepted trucks heading out from the Kaghan Valley days after the earthquake. Its cargo was small children, Mr Selby, mostly girls. Almost 100 of them, some aged as young as six or seven years." They were being taken for the sex trade in the cities, while others would be smuggled abroad, the colonel told them.

"These people will not be stealing any more daughters from Pakistan," he added simply.

And yet others were still trying to smuggle kidnapped girls over the mountain passes to avoid the army. These were girls whose parents and male relatives had died in the earthquake, the colonel explained.

Before they drove off, Selby put in another call to Williams, watched by the colonel, who waited patiently. Selby was not yet sure when they would be back. But it would be before nightfall, he told the American, and the colonel nodded.

On they went, up the steep ridge. Sometimes the vehicle's tyres were just inches from a sheer drop into the valley below. And they came to the remains of another school. The whole building had slipped into the valley below. Tattered remains of notebooks and textbooks were blowing gently in the cold breeze. Across from the rough track on which they were driving lay a narrow, flat piece of ground covered with rows of small fresh graves. How many? Selby couldn't quite count as the Land Rover swung around another tight, steep corner, where the vehicle slowed again.

"There are countless schools like this," said the colonel. "We could go on to higher ground and where the people are more isolated. But it is more of the same," he added. And Selby nodded solemnly.

On their return journey the devastation wrought by the earthquake was at every turn. Massive boulders had been shaken from their craggy heights and thundered downhill, crashing through houses and stables, tearing a path through the fragile buildings of mud and stone in their wake. Villages had been smashed to ruins. Landslides had engulfed entire communities.

On small parcels of stepped, flat land, there were browned stalks of maize. What had happened to the precious harvest to take the mountain communities through the bitter winter months? Were the grain stores also gone?

"The harvest was done," the colonel said. "But the grain stores are gone. The people have lost everything."

Water was also a huge issue, he told them. Springs that had run for hundreds of years suddenly stopped flowing, while new springs might suddenly appear elsewhere as a result of the earthquake, he explained.

Suddenly the Land Rover turned a corner and found its way obstructed by a bulldozer, clearing a landslide which had blocked the track they had passed through less than two hours previously.

The colonel suggested they visit a nearby settlement while they waited, and they took a trail which led from the track for about a mile.

The terrain was steep and rocky, yet Selby was surprised by the lushness of the mountains, and an abundance of grass and shrubbery which covered the lower slopes. He could also see that the mountains across the valley were densely covered by pine trees and noted that the sun was beginning to hang low over their peaks. Already it was mid-afternoon and the sun was starting to draw long shadows across the mountains.

Most of the buildings in the village they visited were severely damaged. Additional shelter had been made from corrugated iron sheets, tarpaulins covering animal shelters and tents erected for those who had lost their homes. The people smiled, thanking them for coming in their hour of need and the visitors were moved by the smiles which greeted them, despite their suffering. The villagers were sorry they could offer them no hospitality. Most had lost their homes, their possessions, their livelihoods. And their children were hungry.

When they returned to the vehicle the road was clear.

"Why don't the mountain people move down into the valleys so they can gain access to humanitarian aid?" asked Selby.

There were many reasons, the colonel said. "Firstly, there is the land," he explained. "If they leave it for any length of time, they fear they will lose their right to it. And the land is everything; it is their livelihood, their future. Many survivors also do not want to leave those loved ones behind they have so recently buried. Or, as you have seen, Mr Selby, some are still looking for those who are missing…" He paused. "And then there is their livestock. They cannot bring their animals into the camps. There is barely enough food getting through for the thousands of hungry people in the valley."

Selby nodded in understanding, while the colonel continued.

"Also, I must tell you, there is a very strong sense of community in the mountains. The people do not want to live in the camps and risk losing their identity and independence, when they think Western aid organisations will pack up and leave in six months. What happens to those living in the camps then? Tell me that, Mr Selby?"

They spent much of the remaining journey in silence, with the colonel occasionally pointing to villages across the valley, literally shaken from their mountain footings, or collapsed buildings along the wayside.

When they finally arrived back at the colonel's temporary headquarters, he highlighted the greatest areas of need on the map for Selby. And he showed the Canadian where he knew other aid agencies were already operating. What shocked and surprised Selby were the large areas across the Kaghan Valley, particularly at higher altitude, where no relief goods had yet been delivered.

As they said their farewells the jolly colonel was all smiles. He promised to provide the foreigners with dinner in his Officers' Mess back in Rawalpindi, if they would visit him when next he was there. However, he apologised that there was very little room at his temporary camp, as he had moved a group of Cuban doctors into his own accommodation and a number of tents surrounding it. They had arrived at his camp the first week of the disaster and offered to help set up a field hospital. They were doing tremendous work in the Valley.

The sun was beginning to burn orange over the mountains as Selby finally drove his Land Cruiser into Ghazikot. What he had thought might be a simple briefing with the colonel in front of a map had become an entire day in the mountains. But it had been an education and an experience he would probably never forget. In addition, he now had the information he needed to translate to his team into an effective operations plan. The Canadian did not feel it had been a day wasted.

He felt it was just the beginning of great and needy work for the organisation across the Kaghan Valley.

Later, as he gazed from his spot on the roof opposite the main house watching the sun set, the images of destruction and despair he had seen that day were running through his mind. He watched the sun slide beyond the mountain peaks and vowed to do whatever he could to help those desperate people he had seen. He knew it was a race against time before the weather would turn colder. Snow could fall on the higher ground within the next few weeks.

Zhevlakov approached and now stood beside him.

"A heavy day," he said. She nodded as they both looked across the valley.

"We need to get the rest of the team to Ghazikot," said Selby. "Can you check what supplies will be arriving in the days ahead?"

The Ukrainian nodded.

"We need to start getting help to these people in the mountains before the weather turns bad," he added. As the light began to fade they could already feel the chill of the autumn evening closing in. The two aid workers turned away from the mountains and went back into the main house.

SIX

Afsa Ali approached the heavy steel gate set back from the road in a leafy suburb of Islamabad and took a deep breath. She raised a slender, well-manicured hand and gently rapped the painted surface. A moment later the gate swung open. Her heart was racing as she was led into the Relief Action compound by the uniformed security guard. Inside the main building a receptionist smiled in greeting and invited her to sit on the comfortable sofa.

As she sat and waited to be seen she viewed the large photographs upon the white walls.

Images of smiling children beamed back at her from their frames: children splashing abundant water from a village pump; little girls with impeccable light blue school tunics and white headscarves studying from books; runny-nosed toddlers at a health clinic, receiving vaccinations.

"Madam Stevenson will see you now, Miss Ali," said the receptionist, approaching from behind her desk.

Stevenson smiled warmly as Ali was shown into the room.

The woman in her twenties wasn't quite what Stevenson had expected. She was dressed in white *Shalwar Kameez*, covered by an open flowing gown of magnificent embroidered blue fabric as an overgarment, which extended to her ankles. A white shawl covered her black hair which framed a bronze face with high, wide cheekbones and a finely chiselled nose. Her dark eyes gazed disarmingly directly into Stevenson's, and her smile was warm and full. She held herself almost defiantly, her chin tilted slightly upwards. She was beautiful. There was no doubt about it.

As the two women talked, Stevenson was impressed by the passion and commitment of the young woman before her. Her command of English was exceptional; her voice clear and composed, laced with a mixture of Pakistani and American accents. Clearly she was from a wealthy family and highly educated. But there was a determination about her which struck home.

"And what do you think you can offer people in the earthquake zone?" Stevenson asked her.

"Compassion. I want to help those less fortunate – it is what I have always felt," answered the young woman without hesitation. And Stevenson smiled.

Twenty years ago she might have given the same reply. Of the three Pakistani nationals Stevenson saw that day it was Ali who stood out. A young man named Imran Chughtai had also impressed her with his sincerity and commitment. Both Pakistanis had experience working locally for charities and seemed intelligent, passionate and desperate to help.

She offered them both a job, with an immediate start. With an existing child protection officer already in place from the Islamabad office, she felt she had the beginnings of her child protection team.

She would offer the basic protection training herself, with a view to taking them with her into the field. Her immediate priority now was to travel to the earthquake zone and begin to assess the situation. She felt time was of the essence. She'd talk to Selby that evening, so that she could make arrangements to join him in Mansehra in the days ahead. To her surprise, he was not unreceptive and agreed that Stevenson and her team could make the journey during the course of the week, subject to trainings and security clearance from Williams. And they could bring some fresh coffee.

In Mansehra things were moving swiftly. More staff had arrived in the 'quake zone, including IT support with the necessary equipment to start putting communications in place. A satellite dish was being positioned on the office roof as Selby walked out of the building with Zhevlakov and Farzad, the Iranian. The office building lay a short walk away across the scrubland which sloped away from the team house on the hill.

Selby gazed at the two men on the roof, squinting into the sun as he stood outside.

"How are things looking at the warehouse?" he asked the Ukrainian beside him.

"We have enough to start distribution," Zhevlakov replied. "Farzad is talking to the truck drivers. But the price seems high. He is negotiating," she said without emotion.

"I will make good price," added the dark-skinned Iranian. Selby nodded his approval.

Williams came out to join them. "How's the new team house looking?" Selby asked him.

"Good," replied the American. "Hired some more guards this morning. Atif seems to think they are all right," he added. "And he tells me we have a cook who can start tomorrow."

"Atif's a good man," Selby smiled. He was one of the Pakistanis Selby relied on most as a local fixer and spoke both Urdu and Pashto.

"Stevenson's bringing her team out day after," Selby continued, addressing Williams. "Can we put them in the new place?" Williams nodded.

"And security?"

"Will be in place," Williams confirmed.

"And they're bringing more fresh coffee," Selby added with a smile.

A team was also on its way from Islamabad to conduct initial emergency needs assessments across the Kaghan Valley in the days ahead. The first aid might be distributed in the mountains within the week, if everything ran to plan. It was a tall order and Selby knew it. A transport manager was en route, seconded from the South African office and an HR officer would arrive with the assessment team. Selby was pleased. He felt the operation was taking shape.

The second guesthouse able to sleep twelve had been rented along from the office. Williams would put the security arrangements in place. In addition he'd see the district Frontier Corps commander later. Major Zamir was happy to supply additional armed men to provide protection out on the street.

Two Frontier Corps men with machine guns already stood permanently on guard outside the team house on the hill. In addition, armed men were posted on every street corner across Ghazikot at the insistence of the major and the United Nations local coordinator. The Taliban were active in the mountains less than thirty miles to the west and there were concerns there might be an attack on such a concentrated hive of international activity in the area.

The UN itself had already set up operations for half a dozen agencies in the township, including the World Food Programme, UN Development Programme, UN Habitat and UNICEF, among others. And Williams was liaising closely with the people at the UN security office on the other side of the hill. The UN coordinating office would soon take over from the army and serve as the umbrella organisation to liaise directly with the government authorities while the military would take a lesser role in support of relief activity.

In nearby Mansehra City, Selby's warehouses had taken delivery of tents, tarpaulins, blankets and emergency hygiene kits. Building toolkits were also in the warehouse. Two truckloads of emergency food supplies were arriving later that day, and kerosene cookers and heaters were sitting in the port city of Karachi, ready to be transported by truck in the days ahead. Selby also had a shipment of corrugated iron sheets on its way from Dubai. The programme staff back in Islamabad were submitting proposals and courting finance from fundraising appeals which had already been launched across the organisation's global network of donor offices.

At home in Islamabad, Afsa Ali sat in the walled garden of her family home as the evening began to draw in. Inside the house her bags were packed, ready for an early start. She would travel with Stevenson's team into the mountains in the morning. The initial briefing had been invaluable, but the child protection overview Stevenson had delivered Ali had found distressing. Yet she was ready to answer the calling she felt to help those in need.

She reflected on the terrible images of suffering she had seen on the rolling TV news bulletins. She felt the pain of those in distress. And tomorrow she would be heading into the heart of it. But helping others was what she had wanted to do since she had been a small child. She felt it was her destiny, even though what she might face would not be easy. It would give her life purpose. She glanced around to ensure she was unobserved and reached for the packet of cigarettes she kept concealed in the pocket of her tunic. She took one and lit up, inhaled deeply and blew the smoke at the swarm of mosquitoes circling above her head…

The town of Balakot was gone. From the air the destruction seemed total. Rubble was spread across the valley floor as far as the eye could see. Not a single building seemed to be standing. In the distance, row upon row of white tents set up to provide emergency shelter reflected brightly in the mid-morning sunshine. The initial emotional impact was overwhelming as their UN helicopter swept in to land, sending clouds of grey dust into the air. Stevenson had seen disasters before. In Sudan. And after the South Asian tsunami. But the destruction and resulting human suffering was something she never became hardened to.

The child protection manager was first to climb out onto the makeshift airstrip, followed by the two young Pakistanis she had hired earlier that week. Saiyra Johns, the child protection officer from Islamabad, followed. A stout, jolly woman with a ready sense of humour, Ali had taken to her immediately.

A Pakistani soldier led them from the helicopter, which took off again almost immediately. They walked from the landing area and dropped their bags behind the remnants of a building and sat in the rubble, watching the flurry of activity around them. A constant stream of helicopters ferried in supplies to the landing strip. Tents, food, water and medical supplies were hastily unloaded by lines of labourers and stacked high at improvised depots guarded by soldiers, ready for immediate distribution.

They sat for a few minutes, taking in their bearings, squinting through the heat and the dust waiting for the vehicle and driver Selby had sent from Mansehra. They saw the Land Cruiser almost immediately with its distinctive blue and white livery, and moments later the vehicle drew up beside them. It was Rahim, the mountain man.

"Mr Hank sends *salaams*, Madam Sahib," he said, addressing Stevenson as he climbed out from behind the wheel to help them with their bags.

They took the dusty road strewn with rubble into the town centre.

Only the town centre was no more. Balakot's residents sat on the compressed ruins of their houses and shops along the road; hungry, ragged people, whose haunted eyes were staring vacantly with despair and disbelief, some with blood-stained bandaging. Many were clearly still in shock. Some were digging with shovels, or breaking larger pieces of concrete with sledgehammers, while others used their bare hands to move debris or pick out what valuables they could, or were still desperately seeking loved ones buried beneath the rubble.

The stench of death and decay already hung over the ruined township. No-one knew how many dead still lay beneath the mounds of concrete and earth that had just days before been a bustling market town of 30,000 people. They said only a single building remained standing – and that was the Madni Plaza concrete shopping mall in the central *markaz*.

Afsa Ali had never seen such human suffering before and fought to stop the wave of emotion welling up inside her. But she contained herself. She had to be strong. Stevenson's team was to start the process of assessing the children and their numbers, and to begin negotiating sites for safe areas, where youngsters would receive support. Their first priority was to link up with the Norwegian field team running one of the emergency camps. The Scandinavian organisation had been among the first to arrive, along with a French medical team. The man Stevenson was looking for was Jens Eriksson.

They found Eriksson in the tented encampment on the far side of the ruined central mosque. Stooped and exhausted from overwork though he was, the tall Norwegian smiled wearily when he met Stevenson and stretched out a welcoming hand. It was mayhem, he confessed. There was no real coordination. The few international aid organisations that had already set up operations were largely working in isolation, doing the best they could, he told her. The army was maintaining order, but relief trucks were being mobbed as they arrived, with supplies almost being thrown out of the trucks. People were desperate. They were hungry and they were angry that help seemed slow to arrive. In terms of emergency shelter, his team was registering hundreds of families daily. And they were still streaming into the valley from the mountains. Relief agencies were setting up tented cities to provide emergency shelter, bringing in supplies of food and water as fast as they could to sustain their growing populations.

"Everything is gone," Eriksson said wearily. "All the infrastructure. There is no water, no sanitation. There are dead bodies still under the rubble…" He paused and wiped the sweat from his face. "It's chaos," he repeated. "They can't get through the rubble quickly enough – and there's a whole army division here. The hospital is also gone. They're working out of a tent, doing surgery in the open air."

There were hundreds of children in the camp, Eriksson told them. Most were accompanied by at least one parent. Some by a grandparent, or other relative. Most had lost family members. And there were orphans too. Earlier that day a family group came in with a little boy they had found by the roadside in the mountains, he told them. And the army had brought two children a few days ago. Nobody knew what happened to their parents. The soldiers dug them out of the rubble across the other side of the town. A boy had presented himself at the gate that morning. And there was a baby too. He sighed, rubbing a hand across his unshaven face. "To be honest, we can't really cope. Most of the children are traumatised… they need special support and we don't have the resources on the ground yet. We do what we can and local charities are helping." He shrugged, almost in despair.

"Can we see the children?" Stevenson asked.

Eriksson nodded and led them through the encampment. Through the heavy smoke of cooking fires, the smell of kerosene and unwashed bodies; through lines of washing draped over guy ropes to dry in the sun, they weaved their way past families sitting on the floor outside their tents, staring at them as they went by. The Norwegian stopped outside a tent close to the camp's distribution point and turned to Stevenson.

"The boy who arrived at our gates this morning had walked for two days across the mountains. But he hasn't spoken since he first arrived," he said. "We don't know his name, or what happened to his parents. We don't even know how old he is. And there was the baby he was carrying. It survived the ordeal. He said she was his little sister." Stevenson nodded and followed him under the canvas.

The boy sat huddled protectively with his knees up in the far corner of the tent. He did not look up as they entered the tent and continued to stare vacantly at the floor. Stevenson guessed he might be nine or ten years old. Beside him sat a young Pakistani woman, one of the volunteer workers from a national charity. It was only when Stevenson approached and spoke softly to him that he looked up and she could see his tear-streaked face. She kneeled in front of him and continued to speak softly. She turned and signalled for Ali to approach.

"*Asalaam-u-alaikum, Betu,*" she said quietly, addressing the boy in Urdu. "What is your name, sweetheart?" He looked at Ali for a few moments before turning his gaze back to the floor but did not reply. Stevenson sat next to the boy for a while, watched by Eriksson and the others, but said nothing.

For a few moments she observed the youngster in silence, before gently laying a hand on his arm. And he began to sob.

Outside the tent Eriksson told them the Red Cross had set up a child-friendly space within their camp across the other side of the town. It had a child protection team in place able to offer psychosocial support and a mixture of education and play to provide a degree of normality for those children affected by the disaster. Eriksson would speak to them later about the boy.

Stevenson nodded. "Most of these kids are scared. They don't want to sleep inside. They have seen brothers, sisters and friends die in the earthquake," he added, sighing deeply. He would provide her with numbers she needed if she dropped by later.

He advised Stevenson to seek out the local army commander. "Basically, the army's running things here," he told her. "The entire local government system is gone. If you want a piece of ground to set up, go see the military. I think you'll find the major near the UNICEF field office."

When they finally found the army post, the major was out, an officious junior officer told Stevenson. They could come back tomorrow.

"We can't come back tomorrow," Stevenson told him firmly. "We'll wait."

Half an hour later the major rolled up in a Jeep and Stevenson approached him as he was about to enter his command tent. Slightly uncomfortable about the delicate matter of having to deal with a determined Western woman, Major Mohammad Nawaz was nothing but courteous.

His manner suggested he had urgent matters to attend to and a degree of impatience. But he listened to Stevenson politely.

"I beg you, Major, all we need is a piece of ground to set up a space where the children can be supported and protected. These are your children too," she insisted.

He hesitated. For a moment he seemed undecided whether to answer or retreat to the safer confines of his tent. Then he smiled. "Please come inside, Madam, and tell me exactly what you need."

Stevenson signalled for Johns to follow while her two younger team members remained outside.

When they emerged a few minutes later, Stevenson seemed pleased. "The major says we can have some land overlooking the mosque. The dear man has even promised to ensure it is cleared for us."

"I didn't think he would help us," said Ali, who had picked up on the major's initial impatience.

Stevenson smiled. "I said we'd provide some construction toolkits for the labourers he's using to help clear the rubble." And she paused. "Only Mr Selby doesn't know it yet." And she rolled her eyes skyward.

SEVEN

It was a slow news day at the *Daily Gazette*. John Cousins sat staring into his computer screen, running idly through the copy basket, glancing at the available news stories. Then he clicked open a game of solitaire and watched the cards being dealt onscreen. His colleagues had taken advantage of the unexpected autumn sunshine and headed over to the pub for lunch. And he thought he might do the same and join them, as soon as Adams returned from his break.

He glanced casually across at the in-tray on the chief sub-editor's desk and his eye caught the yellow page brief lying on top, identifying it as a colour page to design. His curiosity aroused, he minimised his game of solitaire, rose from his desk and walked across to have a closer look.

It was the double-page feature spread for tomorrow's newspaper. His first instinct was to leave it there. It was two or three hours of work. But he was intrigued by the subject of the feature article scribbled across the top: 'Pakistan earthquake'.

He could easily have walked away and Adams would have been back within the next few minutes to pick it up, releasing him to go for a beer. It was one of those moments in life. "Bugger!" he muttered, picked up the sheet of yellow paper and returned to his desk. It was an action which was to change the course of his future.

He closed down the game of solitaire, clicked open the feature story on his computer and began to read. And as he read, the enormity of what had happened 4,000 miles away began to touch him. Pakistan was a country he knew nothing about. But the graphic account of human suffering in the mountains hit home. As did the description of the desperate race by humanitarian workers to deliver essential aid before the first snows came.

The story initially came from the Relief Action communications team bidding to capture the media spotlight and was added to by the *Gazette* feature writer, who had contacted the organisation to find out more. Relief Action's UK headquarters was just down the road and that was, in effect, the local interest.

Cousins was struck by the scale of the disaster described by the organisation, which had sent a team out to launch immediate relief operations.

He was inspired by what he read about the aid workers, trying to find a way through inhospitable terrain, often working fourteen-hour days. And without food from sunrise to sunset. It was the holy month of Ramadan and most aid workers were observing local customs.

And he was strangely fascinated by the scale of the natural disaster that had impacted so many people in such a short space of time. Almost 80,000 people had been killed; 100,000 injured; and 3.5 million had lost their homes, in less than thirty seconds. Homes, schools, hospitals, roads, bridges…

everything had been swept away. He couldn't quite grasp it; it was almost beyond comprehension.

Selby's comments stood out. The operations manager in Mansehra quoted in the article was clear in his assessment: "The challenge facing us is enormous. Everything is gone and remote mountain communities are difficult to access in the harsh landscape. Those affected have lost everything. Millions are dangerously exposed and the winter is moving in. It's a race against time."

Most of the victims were children. And temperatures in the mountains would soon plummet to minus twenty or minus thirty degrees, he said.

"If we can't get aid to them before the snows set in, we may be looking at three times the existing death toll," Selby continued. And the UN was saying the same. It wasn't just the cold. There were no medicines and there was a serious risk of disease sweeping through vulnerable communities. But the operations manager was confident aid would soon be flowing to the remote mountain areas affected, despite the difficult access and the extent of destruction.

As he read on, Cousins came across the name of Balakot for the first time, an entire town that had been reduced to rubble. Now fully absorbed in the story he was drawn into, he searched for the photos accompanying the article and clicked them open. Lines of men were strung along mountain paths, being led from their broken villages into the valleys below against breathtaking Himalayan backdrops with snow-capped peaks.

Another shot showed a woman sitting in the rubble of her home, staring forlornly at the ground. A little boy was in the background, looking confused and hungry. A third picture showed an apocalyptic view of Balakot, its buildings smashed and compressed as far as the eye could see, scattered with lost, desperate people. Another showed figures bowed in prayer around their shattered mosque.

Cousins was intrigued, captivated and moved by what he had already read. He wanted to find out more and searched the internet for further reports.

Reporting within forty-eight hours of the disaster from Pakistan, *The Daily Telegraph* correspondents Nasir Malick and Peter Foster provided a harrowing online account of the chaos in Balakot, which Cousins scanned:

> *"The timing could not have been crueller,"* the report read. *"More than 1,000 boisterous children were packed into their classrooms in the town of Balakot, north-west Pakistan. It was 8.50am. Then the walls began to shake and there was no time to escape. The men were in the fields, the women were at home but the children of Balakot were crushed to death in their hundreds.*
>
> *"…Until two days ago Balakot was a small picturesque town, perched on a hillside above the River Kunar at the mouth of the Kaghan Valley, once famed as an idyllic tourist destination. Yesterday afternoon bodies lay stinking in the street, covered only with flimsy shawls, as survivors spent their energy on those still with a chance, scrabbling with crowbars and shovels to reach children entombed in layers of mangled steel and concrete."*

Cousins felt a lump in his throat but was morbidly compelled to read on.

> *"At the three main schools there were heart-rending scenes as parents listened to the agonised cries of their children. 'Save me' came the faint voice of a boy, again and again, from the ruins of a school where about 200 children were*

feared dead. 'Call my mother. Call my father.' His mother wailed: 'Bring out my child,' beating her chest as other parents and relatives pulled out the bodies of four children.

"The only means of saving lives – heavy diggers and cranes – were sitting idle on the impassable road several miles away, trapped behind a landslide that had cut off Balakot behind a small mountain of boulders and rocks.

"Helicopters thrummed overhead on their way to some place more chosen or lucky than Balakot. The people looked expectantly skywards but the relief drop did not come..."

The BBC's man on the spot had filed a similar report from the devastated township, describing dramatic scenes of hope and despair: a French rescue team working into the night had discovered five children still alive. They had survived in air pockets under concrete slabs as their school had collapsed several days previously. It was a miracle.

How many others might still be trapped beneath the rubble? It was mostly bodies being retrieved now. Gazing across the devastation of Balakot the reporter described survivors still *"desperately tearing at the rubble"* in the desperate hope of finding loved ones. It was, he concluded, *"a vision of hell..."*

Cousins had been so deeply engaged in what he read he didn't even notice Adams return to his desk. When he finished reading the reports there were tears in his eyes. As a parent himself he could relate to the pain and loss of children. Perhaps he was tired... it had been a long week.

"You nipping out, John?" asked Adams.

Cousins looked up from his screen. "Just for a smoke," he replied. "Then I'll crack on with the feature spread. I've started mapping it out," he added, then paused before adding, "It's heart-wrenching stuff."

He rose from his desk and headed for the stairs that would take him to the rear entrance of the building, where the smoking area lay. He stepped outside and leaned against the wall. He drew in the smoke deeply from his cigarette.

As he gazed up from the small yard outside he could see blue sky between the buildings. And he thought about what he had just read. How extreme and cruel life was for some, he mused. How comfortable for those in the developed world… by accident of birth.

Yet he did not feel blessed, or lucky. The truth was he felt empty. He felt his life lacked purpose. Emotionally he was hurting, following a broken marriage. He felt both an overwhelming sense of loss and guilt about what had happened. It had been his fault. He had started the affair which cost him the marriage. And for what? The resulting relationship with another woman had turned into a disaster. And when it came to an ugly end, he had lost everything. Or so it seemed.

Moving out of the family home, away from his children, had been the hardest. In addition, he felt he had lost his best friend. He may not have been in love with Sarah, but he still cared about her. They had shared happy years together when the children were young, before the distance and his sense of unhappiness developed. Now he was emotionally numb.

He returned to his desk and began editing the article on the earthquake. He mapped the pictures out and flowed the text onto the two pages. Cutting a couple of lines, he made some small adjustments. Then he pondered the headline: '*Aid challenge to reach Pakistan 'quake victims*'. He carried the picture showing the lines of people being led along the narrow track to safety large, with its snow-capped mountain backdrop. By the time he had scanned the pictures, added the strapline and captions, it was time to head home.

During the drive to the outskirts of the city where he rented a flat, he was still thinking about the Relief Action story and the devastation he had read about.

But it was after he had eaten and as he sat alone that evening that the first thought of travelling to Pakistan entered his head. He couldn't seem to shake the images of the desperate people he had read about and seen in the photographs. He felt he wanted to offer something; wanted to do something unselfish in his life. He knew he could write. He knew he could move people with words.

When he awoke the next morning he had already decided to speak to Johnson. The beady-eyed editor was old for his years and prematurely grey.

He liked Cousins and was prepared to listen to his proposition when he entered his office. Cousins had been one of the best writers the paper had ever had and there was a degree of mutual respect.

"So you want to travel into the disaster area?" he repeated, as if what Cousins told him needed clarification.

"Yes, I do. It would tie in nicely with the earthquake appeal we're running – and give readers a first-hand insight into an international story. Besides, the aim would be to link up with the Relief Action people. And that's our local angle," he added, looking directly at his editor.

Johnson frowned, leaned back in his chair and let the possibilities run through his mind, while Cousins watched him expectantly.

"All right, John," he said suddenly. "Call them up, see what they say. I'll give you the time and whatever support I can. But you'll have to pay for the flights." And he smiled, as only newspaper editors know how when they feel a good story in prospect. "And I expect a hard-hitting feature series!"

"It's a deal," said Cousins, returning the smile. He was still smiling when he strode out from Johnson's office.

"How'd it go?" asked Adams.

"I might just be on my way to Pakistan," Cousins replied. Then he went outside to have a celebratory cigarette.

Before the end of the day Cousins had spoken with the Relief Action communications team. Yes, it was possible. They were already considering a media visit. They even let Cousins have Selby's satellite phone number. If the operations manager said 'yes', they would start to put arrangements in place. Selby would expect a call tomorrow afternoon, which would be in the evening, Pakistani time.

Cousins crouched over the one telephone in the office which allowed international calls. He stared at the number written on his notepad and drew a deep breath before dialling it out carefully on the phone.

There was a click; a momentary silence. Then he heard it ringing out.

"This is Selby," answered the voice with a slight Canadian accent.

"Hello, Mr Selby, this is John Cousins from the *Gazette*… your people at HQ put me in touch. I'd like to come out and see the work you're doing…"

There was a short delay on the phone.

"Be glad to have you, John. We've got plenty of room and lots to show you," Selby said cheerfully. "Our people at HQ will point you in the right direction… look forward to seeing you soon…"

"Great," replied Cousins. "Look forward to meeting you. I'll come out to you as soon as I can. And thanks."

"No worries," said Selby and hung up.

That evening the journalist started looking for flights to Pakistan.

Whether his planned trip to the earthquake zone was an act of selfishness or inspired generosity, Cousins himself wasn't sure. In actual fact, he may have been running away. What he had no way of knowing was what he would find in the mountains of Pakistan and how it might change his life.

EIGHT

Hank Selby was a soldier. That was never in doubt. And behind the easy-going smile he was a killer. He knew it. But he felt it did not trouble him. How many men he had killed in the heat of battle he did not know. It did not matter. Afghanistan had been a bit of a 'show' and was still very raw. Too many had died and he was not sure what had been achieved.

And still it continued. The ranks of the Taliban were being replenished faster than they were being killed. Not that he lost any sleep over the turbaned 'ragheads' he and his men had dispatched. They were the enemy and could enjoy paradise with its promise of seventy-two virgins in heaven. He smiled wryly at the thought. No, it was his fallen comrades that sometimes kept him awake at night. He had done his duty. He did not kid himself it was for Queen and country, or even for the greater good of the world, or freedom, or democracy.

It was a job. And he and his men were part of a team; an exclusive club; a brotherhood which took them to extremes of human endurance and suffering together.

It was about loyalty to that cause, one's men with whom one experienced so much and trusted completely in life-and-death situations. If there was guilt, he felt it for the men he commanded who did not come home from Afghanistan, or Kosovo before that.

It was God who finally found Hank, in the shape of a young Christian bride, who sought to save him in every way a person can be saved. He had felt empty when he left the service, which had been his life since he had been no more than a boy himself. His wife Esther was on a mission to save him. Not that Selby wanted to be saved. Nevertheless, he was rescued from drowning in drink and the emptiness he felt away from the only life he had known.

But once a soldier, always a soldier. It was the thrill of danger and the challenge of a hostile environment that drew him to aid work, when the opportunity was offered through his wife's church connections. And a sense, perhaps, that he had something to give, not least of all for those friends he had lost in battle. He was an intelligent man and often wondered why. Or he puzzled over how he came to be spared. For he knew what it was to come close to death. In God, he felt he had found some answers. But to those who knew him at Relief Action he was impulsive, erratic... inspirational.

When Relief Action sought an operations manager to mobilise and oversee its relief effort in the earthquake zone, they needed someone used to working in harsh conditions. Already he had proven himself to the organisation in Afghanistan, where he had risen to the challenge, quickly establishing himself like a maverick commander in a war zone. Some saw him as a dangerous man. But he got the job done.

To his champions, Selby was seen as a necessary 'evil' in delivering essential aid in a difficult operating environment. It was the frontline which often demanded risks had to be taken to reach those in greatest need. He was a man of vision, with an ability to think outside the box. At least, beyond the restrictive parameters of a Western aid organisation operating in a conservative Muslim region. He was just the man for the job in Pakistan.

Perhaps Selby's most redeeming quality was his love for ordinary people caught up in disaster through no fault of their own. And as much as he despised the conservative, cautious purists at headquarters in their comfortable offices, he quickly developed an affection for the locals.

They were the long-suffering foot soldiers. To them, 'Mr Hank' soon became an inspiration and most followed him with unswerving, unquestioning devotion.

Selby was pleased to take the UK call from Cousins. The operation was already distributing aid supplies and he had a clear plan of how and where that need should be met. But there was something else. He had heard about the Black Mountain, an isolated tribal area on the western corner of Mansehra District. It had a reputation as a 'forbidden' area, off-limits to outsiders. He had also learned the five tribes of the Black Mountain had been devastated by the earthquake – and more than 100,000 people were in desperate need.

Yet no-one could confirm the extent of the damage. No aid agencies were prepared to enter an area with too many security risks. And the region's tribes were heavily armed, effectively their own army, police force and administration. No-one even knew how many people lived there.

No Westerners had accessed the Black Mountain in more than a century. Even the Pakistan Army was reluctant to go there. And yet, Shah, the Afghan who sought out Selby, told him the tribes needed assistance and were ready to accept outside help. To the operations manager it was an irresistible challenge. And he felt it might just be the kind of story for Cousins to report.

The journalist's first sight of Selby came in the evening following his long journey by road from Islamabad. He took one of the small battered Suzuki vans which left the bus station in the capital every half an hour, sitting shoulder-to-shoulder with ten or twelve Pakistanis in the back, sharing a seat. Not that he had any complaints. The company was amiable enough, despite the cramped conditions. But it was a 'baptism by fire' on the long, winding four-hour drive into the mountains.

Cousins had no idea where exactly he was going, nor did he speak the local language. It was already dark when the vehicle finally hit Ghazikot, unbeknown to the journalist. It was one of the Pakistani passengers who alerted him and asked the driver to stop. The young Pakistani had heard him mention Ghazikot to the driver several times earlier in the journey. By the time the Suzuki rolled to a halt they had overshot the required stop by about a mile.

Cousins never forgot what happened next. The young Pakistani insisted on getting out himself and walking the foreigner safely to the lights of Ghazikot. It was the first, but not the last, example of Pakistani hospitality he was to encounter. The young man worked at the Marriott Hotel in the capital and was travelling to assist his family in the mountains.

"It is no problem," he told Cousins. "You are visitor to our country. It is our custom and our duty to make sure you welcome and safe."

Cousins threw his backpack over his shoulder and began to follow him back along the road.

Only when they had reached the lights from the shops that lined the road into the township did the Pakistani leave the Westerner's side.

"I'll get you a taxi," said Cousins.

The young man shook his head. "I will walk, Sahib. It is not far to Mansehra." And he left Cousins standing outside the shop.

Cousins stepped inside the grocery store. It was the sort of shop which had just about everything. If only you could find it. The shopkeeper smiled helpfully at Cousins.

"*Asalaam-u-alaikum*," ventured the foreigner hopefully before breaking into English. "I am looking for the Relief Action office," he added. The man gazed at him blankly. "This is Ghazikot?"

"*Haan, haan*," the shopkeeper nodded.

Cousins was just about to fetch out his notepad with the exact address for the aid organisation when help arrived. The most enormous four-wheel drive Cousins had ever seen pulled up outside, emblazoned with the large, blue letters of the UN, and two foreigners jumped out. They nodded to Cousins as they entered the shop. And he was saved.

"I'm looking for the Relief Action office," he told them.

"Know where that is, Jack?" said the larger of the two men in an Australian accent.

The other Westerner nodded. "Over on the hill," he replied.

"Better jump in with us and we'll take you round, mate," said the first man, turning to address the shopkeeper. "Carton of Gold Leaf, please. *Shukria*."

A few moments later, Cousins climbed out of the UN vehicle and stood in front of the house on the hill. The most striking thing was its walled enclosure, strung with barbed wire, and the two armed guards outside who eyed him suspiciously. He nodded to them and approached. As he did so he heard a heavy metal bolt slide behind the main gate, which swung open to reveal the operations manager squinting at him through the darkness. Selby was impressed to see Cousins approach the compound wearing Pakistani *Shalwar Kameez*, unshaven and at a distance looking every inch a Pathan from the mountains. He was further impressed by the way in which the journalist had made his way from the capital into the mountains. He was either courageous and resourceful, or totally mad. Either was fine with Selby.

The smile with which a weary Cousins greeted the Canadian as he opened the gate cemented an instant friendship, as did the fact that the traveller had brought several packs of fresh ground coffee from the capital. And the man was not part of the Relief Action culture.

Another plus in Selby's book. In his eyes the daily prayer meetings the Christian staff attended were a drag. He was, after all, a man of action. The two men hit it off immediately.

"Good to see you made it," smiled Selby. "Wasn't quite sure when to expect you. Come on in."

"Long journey," Cousins replied and followed him into the enclosure towards the main house, whose lights shone out invitingly across the yard.

"You bring coffee?"

Cousins nodded and slapped the side pocket of his rucksack. "And sugar," said the journalist.

"Good man. You'll do well here," Selby chuckled.

Inside a group of aid workers were sitting around a large table when the two men came in. Williams was the first to rise and stretch out a hand.

"You must be the reporter guy," he said. "Come and make yourself comfortable."

Zhevlakov looked at him blankly without expression, but Farzad, the Iranian beside her, smiled warmly.

Stevenson was also there and nodded primly as she was introduced by Selby. Transport manager Brett de Villiers was also seated, and had arrived the previous day. The burly South African grinned at Cousins.

"We were taking bets earlier… on whether you would make it," he said jovially in a voice laced with Afrikaans.

"It's quite a journey," Cousins sighed.

"Sure is," chipped in Williams. "I'll brief you on security later."

Stevenson's soft Irish voice interjected. "Let the man recover." She pulled out a chair. "Come rest yourself, Mr… Mr…"

"Cousins. Thanks," and he sat beside her.

"We were just talking about the Black Mountain," said Selby. "It's a remote tribal area to the west where we understand thousands affected by the earthquake have not been reached."

"And there's a reason," said Williams pointedly.

"We've been approached by the elders of this region, who have asked us for help," continued Selby. "But it's very remote."

"It's off-limits, Hank," said Williams.

"The tribes say they will guarantee security. And they have invited us to see the damage," added Selby.

"No Westerners have been in there for more than a century," said Williams, drumming his fingers lightly on the wooden table. "And with good reason."

"Maybe so," said Selby. "But we've been through this already, Charlie."

"We have," he conceded. And with that he rose. "I'll catch you later," he said to Cousins and left the room.

"Sounds interesting," said the journalist.

The Canadian nodded, smiling. "The history of the 'mountain' is fascinating… and the tribes have lived in relative isolation for centuries. But they need help. It's an opportunity."

"It is," said Stevenson.

"It might be, Gail," Selby replied. "It just might be."

Turning to Cousins, he continued, "No Western agencies have been in there. Not since 1888, when the British and Indian Army marched from the garrison at Abbottabad to suppress the warring tribes.

"That was the last time. They stayed for three years. I found a map," added Selby.

"As part of a contemporary account. We believe it is the only map that exists of the area – and it was drawn up by British engineers in 1891. Nothing else exists," he said smiling. "There's no records. Not even with the Government of Pakistan. But we have an 'invitation' to help these people."

To Cousins it sounded like an incredible story. Like something out of a *Boys' Own* adventure.

Selby planned to make his first trip to the Black Mountain in the early hours of the morning with his guide. Cousins could hardly believe his luck. What a story. What a day. He had been bombarded by the sights, the sounds and smells of Pakistan along the road north. It was a world away from the life he knew back in England. Selby handed him a mug of hot coffee.

"Will I be able to write about it?" asked Cousins.

"As I've also said to Ms Stevenson here," said Selby, "…we will just have to see what happens. But I hope so. That's one of the reasons I wanted you out here."

Later, as Cousins stood outside on the veranda smoking a cigarette while he gazed across at the mountains, he was joined by Williams.

"He's mad, you know," said the American. "But he's a good guy."

"I'm sure," replied Cousins.

"But this is a dangerous country," Williams continued. "See that ridge in the distance?"

Cousins nodded as he gazed at the snow-capped peaks to the north-west.

"That's Taliban country… and we fire goddamn rockets over. It's not helpful." Williams was shaking his head. "And Selby still thinks he's on some kind of special mission! I've told him. I want to hear from him every hour; every goddamn hour!"

"I'm sure he'll be careful," said Cousins.

"He'd better be," said Williams. "Or I'll ground him, so help me!"

It was late when Cousins finally dragged his kit over to the dormitory across the yard from the main house to bed down. He was dead beat. He sat on the edge of his bed and smoked a final cigarette, thinking about the Black Mountain. 'Forbidden' country, tribal customs, Taliban and drones: it all seemed unreal. It was a lot to take in. They were strange thoughts to slip under the sheets with. And yet he soon fell into a deep and satisfying sleep.

It seemed no time at all before he awoke to bright sunshine streaming through the window. He swung his legs out and sat blinking in the light, taking in his surroundings. Then he pulled his clothes on and staggered over to the main house in search of that essential first cup of coffee.

He found de Villiers, the South African, still at breakfast. And hot coffee was on the stove.

But there was no sign of Selby.

He had already left for the mountains before sunrise, the South African said…

NINE

IN THE HALF-LIGHT of the early morning, a whisper of mist still veiled the mountainside as Selby reached the small plateau where the village lay. Khurram Masood had led the way along the steep, winding track from the valley below. The man from Gilgit knew the mountains like no other.

The barefooted little girl in a ragged tunic was the first to be seen and stood motionless, staring through her tangled hair at the *'gora'* slowly approaching, breathing heavily. She judged he was unmistakably a white man, despite the grey *Shalwar Kameez* he wore and the Afghan hat pulled forward low across his forehead. And there was a football wedged under his right arm.

The two men halted on seeing the girl, straightened up and stood, drawing in the clear, cool mountain air. "*Asalaam-u-alaikum,*" said the Westerner, smiling in greeting, rasping heavily following the steep climb, his breath escaping into the cold air in small white plumes. The little girl stared at him blankly with dark, unflinching eyes. She had never seen a white man before. Selby smiled again, and the girl turned and ran from them towards the ramshackle collection of dwellings whose shapes could just be distinguished through the thinning mist. It was the village of Peer Khel.

The two men looked at each other uneasily.

"For what we are about to receive…" Selby muttered between breaths, squinting into the mist towards the village, before allowing his gaze to rest on the ghostly mountain panorama, with its steep slopes dark with pine trees rising to rocky peaks.

"I am not sure what we receive," replied his companion simply. And they both smiled uncertainly at each other, unsure of whether to continue their approach, or wait a while.

Like shadows silhouetted in the grey light now breaking over the mountain, four boys, aged perhaps between ten and fourteen, could now be seen, walking out of the mist towards them. They stopped and stood awkwardly at a distance they considered safe to stare from. Selby smiled at them, but this time said nothing. The silence was total as they watched each other. The Canadian took a step forward and rolled the football towards them. They looked at him enquiringly, then at each other, before the bravest moved forward and gathered the ball up. He gazed at Selby, who nodded and smiled, gesturing towards the children with his hand that it was theirs. And now all four boys were smiling too, before running off with the ball.

More figures could now be seen walking slowly from the village towards the two men. And suddenly the visitors seemed surrounded by tribesmen, armed with an assortment of rifles, ammunition belts slung across their shoulders. Their weaponry included a variety of Kalashnikovs and even some old British Enfield rifles, Selby noted with interest.

The white man's appearance was no surprise to them. Talk of the Westerner's visit had been the topic of discussion within the village for days. He would be the first to come from the outside since the time old man Syed Rahman was a boy. And he was said to be a hundred years old. The children were excited and fearful. They heard their fathers speak of the white man and what lay beyond the mountains. And they had heard of people who did not respect their customs and beliefs.

Some of the men from the village who travelled to work in the world outside told stories of a decadent people consuming the earth. And the children, like their fathers and their fathers before them, were afraid. But, as old man Rahman would say, need breeds strange friends… and his weathered face would crease into a cackle to reveal the solitary front tooth which still stubbornly protruded from his gums.

Yet there was wisdom in the old man. Their homes were gone, their winter food supplies destroyed. There were no medicines. They were dangerously vulnerable. The bitter winds and grey skies carried the promise of snow in the days to come. And the children were cold and hungry. Many were showing signs of disease.

It had therefore been decided by the elders to send tribal representatives to seek help from the outside world they feared. This was what the great council of the five tribes, the *Loya Jirga*, had decreed. But not all the voices spoke in agreement. Some withheld their judgement. Some were afraid of what the cost might be of accepting help from beyond their mountain stronghold.

Mohammed Ali Khan held no such doubts. To him the earthquake was as if Allah Himself had spoken. The burly tribal chieftain oversaw large swathes on land with dozens of villages just like Peer Khel, as had his family since the time of the British. Khan knew what lay beyond the tribal boundary, trading with the merchants in the port city of Karachi – and he knew change was inevitable. His people's way of life held them in poverty. It had barely changed in a thousand years. And, although he enjoyed the relative comforts his status allowed, the sense of responsibility for the villagers who lived, worked and died on the lands of his forefathers was not lost to him.

For centuries the tribal warlords had resisted incursions from the outside, protected by the isolation and the inaccessibility of their mountain villages.

Yet the Black Mountain was no longer the natural fortress it once had been. The Talibs were crossing into the adjacent districts of Shangla, Buner and Swat in the north-west, while government forces were pressing from the south and east. Kala Dhaka, the Black Mountain, still held a reputation of its own. Selby knew its history. It lay in at the heart of North-West Frontier Province – the 'blazing frontier' as the Empire had known it, the rugged mountain buffer with its warring tribes which lay conveniently between British India and Afghanistan.

At the time of the earthquake, the Black Mountain retained its notoriety, in part due to its inaccessibility, partly due to the determination of its peoples to maintain an independence from what was known as Pakistan. Its status as a self-governing region stretched back to the Sikh Empire whose heart lay on the fertile plains of the Punjab and whose horse-warriors had battled for control of the Himalayan sub-ranges of the north-west, as the Moghul emperors began to lose their grip on the region. Like the British who came after, the Sikhs had found it was easier to maintain an uneasy alliance with the fiercely independent tribes in their mountain strongholds – and to let them fight among themselves.

The same applied following Indian independence from the British and Partition, with the founding of Pakistan in 1947, when the loosely connected tribes in the mountains bordering

Afghanistan were allowed to retain their autonomy.

They became Federally Administered Tribal Areas, with nominal government interference or interest. The same principle was applied to the Black Mountain tribes, who were their own army, police and judiciary. Kala Dhaka became a Provincially Administered Tribal Area, technically supported by the region's provincial government, with its seat in Peshawar close to the Khyber Pass, gateway to Afghanistan. In reality, it simply meant the region was ungovernable by other means. The real power remained with the landowning khans and the conservative mullahs.

The people of the Black Mountain were mostly desperately poor uneducated farmers, with allegiance to their local landowners, the khans. But they were allowed to lead their own lives under the feudal system which had remained unchanged for centuries. Some said it was a haven for those who needed to escape the reach of the law: bandits, robbers and murderers. It was said the Black Mountain tribal code could not deny sanctuary to those who sought refuge and protection from the outside.

And so it was that when the earthquake struck, nobody knew what impact it had on the people of Kala Dhaka. Nobody even knew how many people lived there. No official numbers had ever been recorded, because no official government machinery or its agents operated within the area.

Some said nobody cared. Certainly it was true no reliable information existed about the tribes that lived on the mountain. There wasn't even a map of the region, it was said.

That is why when the disaster shattered the fragile communities of the North-West Frontier Province, the Black Mountain was overlooked by most aid agencies. Not even the army was comfortable travelling the single road which ran along the River Indus, as it cut its lazy course southwards under the shadow of the mountain. They were not welcome, and were vulnerable to ambush by the heavily armed and unpredictable tribes. On the advice of the army, the United Nations agencies decided the security risk was too high to take a look. A UN team ventured warily by boat along the river to drop tents and emergency supplies at the foot of the mountain, and in the morning they were gone. One international aid organisation entered Kala Dhaka from the north and was fired upon by tribesmen, and were lucky to escape with their lives. They did not try it again.

"It is a lawless place, Mr Selby," the district coordinating officer said. "The home of robbers and thieves. The people are devils!"

"The people are hungry," smiled Selby.

"I advise against it," the local official repeated sternly from behind his desk. "I cannot guarantee your safety on such a mission."

He was the provincial government representative at Oghi, a small town on the edge of Mansehra District to the east which had once been home to the British administration at the fort on the hill in the days of the Raj.

"With respect, Sir, I would like to establish contact with the tribes and see what assistance may be given… with your permission, of course," Selby told the official. "My head office is aware of the risks and the assurances that must be obtained from the tribal leaders themselves. But we have to see the extent of the damage," he added.

The Pakistani official was not convinced. Finally, he told Selby, "My men can only accompany you to the border. May I suggest a meeting at the Darband, the last village in the south on the road into Kala Dhaka; it is the gateway. We have a garrison of the Frontier Corps stationed there."

Selby nodded. "Please allow me to consult with my

superiors and report back to you." He offered his thanks and he left. In his mind he knew what he had to do. The meeting had been important to confirm what he already suspected. The official would offer no real help; a police escort would be a hindrance. It might even be dangerous. The tribes did not trust the government. And neither did Selby.

Within a few days he set off from Ghazikot before the sun had risen above the mountains and took the longer, less travelled route skirting Oghi, entering the Black Mountain from Thakot in the north. He donned tribal dress and took an unmarked car into the valley.

Now he stood on top of a mountain face to face with the tribesmen he had heard and read so much about. It seemed less a welcoming committee, more a crowd curious to see the visitors. Behind the tribesmen were their children, jostling for a position to see the strangers visiting their village, younger ones peeping uncertainly from behind their fathers' loosely fitting garments. The men's approach from the valley below had been observed from a distance. The elders had received reports of his progress from the moment of Selby's first footfall onto the Black Mountain, from the men sent to wait and watch for him.

The tribal representatives had sought him out in Ghazikot; the one man who was prepared to consider action to help them. And now he was here. An invitation had been extended, with assurances, that he should come to the Black Mountain and talk further with the elders. Selby knew it was an opportunity to access an area off-limits to outsiders for centuries. The tribes told him their villages were devastated. But he had to see with his own eyes the extent of the damage. He also knew there was no other way, despite the degree of uncertainty and risk to his personal safety.

A tall, heavily built man, with a greying beard and wearing

a magnificent flowing turban, stepped forward. "Welcome to our village," said the chieftain in carefully formed English. His voice was deep but clear. Mohammed Ali Khan met the stranger's steady gaze. Then he smiled. "I am glad you are here. Come," he added gruffly, beckoning with a sweep of his arm for the visitors to follow him to the village.

"*Shukria*, thank you," Selby replied, nodding to show he understood and agreed, taking his place alongside the tribal chieftain, trailed closely by Khurram Masood and the group of villagers thronging behind them.

TEN

THE VILLAGE OF Peer Khel was gone. The mountain settlement had been reduced to a desolate, desperate landscape sprawling under the grey morning sky. Small family groups were huddled among the rocks as far as the eye could see, a patchwork of improvised shelters of plastic tarpaulins, blankets and twisted corrugated iron sheets among the craggy contours of the plateau. It was hard to know what had once been homes and what were natural piles of grey stone scattered across the slopes. And the cool breeze already held a biting chill with the promise of snow as it blew over the bleak mountainside from the north.

The devastation had been almost total. Even on the lower slopes, the flat brown buildings hugging the natural hollows for greater protection had collapsed or showed yawning cracks in their mud and stone walls where they had been split open by the violent force of the earthquake.

For the people of the mountain it was a harsh existence under normal circumstances. They lived without electricity, gas or flowing water. There was no concept of sanitation. Wood was gathered for heating and cooking; water collected daily from the natural springs. Goats provided milk and occasional meat, while cereals and small root vegetables were farmed on small, stepped strips of land on the slopes below the village. It was a basic existence, almost unchanged for centuries.

The balance of life was fragile. Suddenly it had been smashed by natural disaster. And the people were left dangerously exposed. Selby was most affected by the children he saw in ragged clothes, with matted hair and dirty faces. He noticed many had eye infections and skin irritations. Most seemed malnourished. There was no medicine and the nearest basic health unit was at least a day's walk over rugged mountain terrain. And yet he was greeted by smiles wherever Khan led him.

The tribal chieftain remained silent as they walked through the village, speaking only in reply to the questions Selby asked. When he did speak, he highlighted the desperate need of his people, who were hungry and dangerously at risk, talking in slow, carefully formed English with the guttural intonation characteristic of the Pathans. Food and shelter were the most pressing needs, and the Canadian realised that unless the people of Peer Khel received help, many would surely not survive the bitter winter approaching, when temperatures could fall to thirty degrees below zero and heavy snow would cut their access to the valleys below.

Selby liked the tribal chieftain's directness and openness. He seemed a practical realist, genuinely concerned for the desperately poor people of the village. There was also a relaxed way he had that seemed uncomplicated and unforced, which the Canadian warmed to. The significance of Khan's invitation to visit the remote village, off-limits to outsiders for centuries, was not lost on Selby.

By the time they reached the central stone building on the far side of the settlement, where they were to sit and talk, a posse of curious children were trailing them. Their mothers, though, remained unseen. The conservative areas of the north-west applied *purdah* and they were to be hidden from Western eyes.

From the outside the building looked unremarkable. Its dry-stone structure showed considerable damage, gaping cracks within its walls from the violent tremors of just a few weeks before. It stood at the base of a hollow, adjacent to the mosque which had collapsed and still lay as a mound of rubble beneath its corrugated iron roofing. Home of a prominent village elder, the stone building they approached would host the meeting of the *Jirga*, at which the Westerner was to be formally introduced. The group halted at the doorway and about a dozen elders filed in to take their place before Khan beckoned Selby to enter, while others remained outside and children crowded the windows to catch a glimpse of proceedings within.

Inside Mohammed Ali Khan cut an imposing figure as he stood before the village council in black *Shalwar Kameez* and a grey embroidered waistcoat, his magnificent turban adding to his stature in the natural light which fell upon the group from the small windows. He paused before addressing the *Jirga*, glancing at the assembled elders watching him expectantly. Selby had taken his place among them, sitting cross-legged in a circle on the magnificently carpeted floor, Khurram Masood at his side.

Khan spoke in Pashto, the language of his people. The Westerner had come from the outside to help, he told them. The white man was here at their invitation and they should show him every courtesy.

He ran a hand over his greying beard before continuing, allowing Selby's companion and guide to translate his words. There were nods of approval from the elders, as all eyes fell upon the visitor sitting among them. But there was suspicion too. In truth, most of the elders did not know what to make of the Canadian. And they were fearful of accepting any outside help. Many had never seen a white man before and his presence was a significant break from the traditions they had known.

"I know it has not been our way to bring outsiders to our villages," Khan continued, knowing so well the thoughts of the assembled *Jirga*. "But our need is great and our children are hungry. Winter is coming. Perhaps this man has been sent in answer to our prayers…" Elders nodded thoughtfully.

It was the old man, Syed Rahman, as the eldest member of the council who spoke first. "We should hear what the stranger has to say," he said.

A burly tribesman, whose intense gaze had not left Selby since he had entered the room spoke next. "The Westerner knows nothing of our ways," he said gruffly. "But we can listen to his words. It does not mean we must embrace him as a brother." It was Abdul Shahid, who had a reputation for plain speaking and carried an ugly scar over his left eye. It was said he had killed a man with his bare hands in a fight over land.

Khan nodded. "Then I will ask him to stand with me and speak," he said simply, addressing Shahid, beckoning for Selby to rise to his feet.

The Canadian stood beside the chieftain and drew a deep, uneasy breath. His mind was racing to find the right words that were simple, direct and true. Yet when he spoke his voice was calm and even.

"I am honoured to stand among you," he told the villagers. "And I thank you for the invitation to your village." He paused to allow Khurram Masood to translate.

He told them the people from his world had heard of the terrible earthquake which had destroyed the mountain villages. His job was offer help where the need was greatest.

He told them his organisation wanted to help, because it believed all people facing disaster deserved assistance in their time of need... There were further nods of approval.

It was Shahid who spoke again. "What is the price of this help? The Americans interfere in all things and have shown themselves to be the enemies of Islam."

Khan, who was still standing with Selby, raised a calming hand and uttered a sharp reprimand to his fellow tribesman. But it was Selby who answered. "We are not Americans. We are from many countries and we work with people of all nations and beliefs.

"Some of our workers are Pathans, already helping in the earthquake areas." He paused before continuing, addressing his words directly to Shahid. "The help is free. But there is a price is to be paid. That price is trust – and that your people will work alongside ours to rebuild what is lost."

Finally, he told the *Jirga*, "My people do not want to change your way of living. Our aim is to help you restore your homes and your livelihoods. That is all."

Khan nodded. "And what help can you give?" the chieftain asked Selby.

"We can bring food and medicines. And we can provide many corrugated iron sheets for new shelters. And wood. And we have toolkits. Everything you need to rebuild your villages for the winter."

"And for the mosque?" asked another voice. "You see, it is destroyed." It was Mohammed Zarman, the holy man of the village, who had been listening and watching keenly.

"We will help you rebuild the mosque," replied Selby and Khan smiled faintly. The Westerner understood. The mosque was central to everything.

But the Canadian told the *Jirga* others from the outside would need to come to make an assessment of how many families required help. The help would be given to those in greatest need. Materials for the mosque would be seen as a benefit to the entire community.

Access and security would have to be guaranteed by all five tribes. If the people of Kala Dhaka agreed, a plan could be made. But, Selby added with genuine conviction, the most important part would be mutual transparency, honesty and trust.

"We cannot speak for all the tribes today," Khan told the Canadian. "The Nusrat Khel of this area do not trust outsiders. And in the south the Madakhel mistrust even their own people. But," he added, "if it is the will of this *Jirga*, we will speak with our brothers across the mountain and call for the council of all the combined tribes to meet." He paused, looking directly at the Westerner, then towards the assembled elders. "So, I would ask those who are against this help we are offered to speak now." But there were no voices of objection.

As he made his descent from the mountain, led this time by an armed escort from the village, Selby was satisfied with the way the meeting had gone. He felt he had made a positive impression. Khan had also seemed pleased, as they shook hands and embraced. The Canadian knew there were risks. And there were many who still needed to be convinced that an intervention in such a remote area could work, not least of all the *Loya Jirga*, the combined council of the five Kala Dhaka tribes.

There was also the government of Pakistan and its local officials to consider, for whom the tribes held nothing but contempt. The army too.

And Selby still needed to assure his own management team in Islamabad – and the executive officers at global headquarters – that the need was acute, the risks were acceptable and the chances of success high.

There was no denying the opportunity which presented itself. The elders had asked for assistance. He had seen the desperate need of the people of the Black Mountain.

He was certain in his own belief that delivering aid to this remote corner of north-west Pakistan was the right thing to do. Besides, there was no-one else.

He felt the relief effort was something of a 'beauty contest' – a race for the most kudos, the best prize – and sometimes the easiest gains in the bid for recognition and international donor funding.

Many of the larger agencies were therefore focusing their efforts on Balakot and its surrounding areas, which lay at very heart of where the earthquake's epicentre had been. It was easier to receive the backing of larger donors, where the destruction had been so visible and complete. An easy win, without risks.

But for Selby, the remoteness, the mystery and the reputation of Kala Dhaka as a 'no-go' area held an irresistible draw. Certainly the people of the mountain had a fearsome reputation. But did that mean they should not be helped in their hour of need? And yes, it was a challenging area to access and operate within. There were political sensitivities too. To Selby that simply added to the appeal, not least of all due to its history and isolation.

The sun was now high and the greyness of the early mist had given way to a clear sky of brilliant blue. Though the trek down would be easier, Selby estimated it would still take them at least three hours to reach their vehicle at the foot of the mountain. The four-hour drive back to Ghazikot should see them arrive at the compound before sunset. And that would please Williams. The group paused on the mountainside to drink and rest. Selby reached for the satellite phone to report in.

Below them the mighty River Indus was a shining ribbon stretching into the distance along the valley, cutting its timeless course through the mountains southwards, dwarfed on all sides by the Himalayan landscape. And the silence was total. It was like standing on top of the world, he mused.

ELEVEN

Inside the tent children stared in wide-eyed wonder at the young woman who sat before them. Her voice was calm, even and reassuring as she read from the dog-eared storybook in her hands with more than thirty pairs of eyes resting unflinchingly upon her. The children seemed to hang upon the woman's every word, sometimes smiling as the story began to come alive for the boys and girls gathered around her, lighting their imagination, lifting their hearts with a sense of enchantment.

It was an escape from the horrors they had endured since the disaster had so suddenly shattered their young lives.

Occasionally the woman would pause, lift her beautiful face and look at the children. And she would also smile, for she loved the stories too… and she felt waves of compassion for the children of the earthquake. As she continued to read of princes and thieves, of flying carpets and powerful *djinn*[1] guarding incredible treasures, she might have been Scheherazade herself.

---

1   Genies, often described as powerful demons in South Asian stories

To the children from the mountain communities, the woman seemed just as exotic and her voice sounded like a princess as she read to them in perfect Urdu. Hers was a world unlike theirs, and she spoke the language of poets and *dastangos*[2] which, though they understood, was not native to them. It was easy for them to imagine she too might have come to them from that vaguely familiar fairy-tale world of mystery that was sometimes spoken about but existed to impoverished families only in dreams or within stories told around campfires by travellers who passed through from distant lands. Despite the cold, grey autumn day, the children felt a warmth and comfort in the book of stories Afsa Ali held in her hands, which had been part of Persian-Indo culture for generations.

This was story time at the child-friendly space at Balakot, where children were able to forget the harshness of what had befallen them for a few hours every day; a safe haven run by the child protection team of Relief Action. And it provided a breath of normality in the troubled lives of those who had been caught up in the terrible earthquake.

John Cousins was also captivated by the woman's fluty voice as he passed the tent and he gently lifted the entrance flap to gaze inside. Beyond the sea of small woolly hats, scarves and padded winter jackets, he saw the woman reading, though she did not look up from her book.

For a few moments he listened to the unfamiliar language. Though he could not understand the words, her voice was wonderfully mysterious to his ears and beautifully lyrical…

The young helper accompanying him that morning was Asim Bari. He leaned towards the Englishman and whispered, "She reads the stories of Aladdin and Ali Baba… they are well-known in our culture."

---

2   South Asian storytellers using elaborate imagery to tell traditional stories in Urdu, often romantic adventures referring to magic and sorcery.

Cousins smiled as the fantastic images of the *Arabian Nights* came into his mind from his own childhood.

"Madam Ali has a gift for the telling of such stories. She is very popular and makes the little ones forget their sadness," the young Pakistani added, and Cousins nodded.

The two men withdrew, leaving Ali and the children to their world of magic and enchantment.

The child-friendly space was a hive of lively activity. Several large tents were pitched around a cleared patch of dusty ground roughly the size of a small football field on the slopes overlooking the ruined town of Balakot. It was a place of safety for children from the stricken valley and its surrounding settlements. Many of the youngsters were from the tented encampments which had suddenly mushroomed around the ruined township. Others made their way into the valley from their mountain villages. Word of safety and of help had spread quickly through the communities decimated by disaster: it was a hope in a world of despair.

As Cousins walked accompanied by his young Pakistani companion, he would pause to watch the various activities. A small group of girls sat on a carpet laid out with drawing and colouring materials, supervised by another Relief Action worker, encouraging the children to express themselves through their pictures. In another corner children were crowded around a bucket of water as one hapless volunteer instructed the youngsters in handwashing; an ecstasy of fumbling little hands for the slippery bar of soap and splashing water. And on the far side volunteers were lining up boys and girls to take part in running races.

Asim guided Cousins to one of the smaller tents. As they approached, the young Pakistani stopped and turned to the Englishman. There was a boy inside who would not take part in activities, he explained.

"He still cries for his family," he said. "His parents are lost. We have all tried to involve him in our activities, but he likes to sit alone. And he is afraid. Like many of the children here, he fears another earthquake. Perhaps if you would see him? I think he would like to meet a British man who has travelled so far to see him…"

"Of course," Cousins replied. "But I do not speak Urdu."

"Words are not always needed. The actions speak and are understood. The boy will see you as a very important personage. And he will feel good that you visit him."

Cousins was only too pleased to oblige. He nodded and smiled in understanding, and they approached the tent.

Asim entered first, while Cousins stood outside. As he waited, he looked out across the child-friendly space. Beyond its perimeter, marked by a simple ribbon of tape, his eyes rested on row upon row of white tents – the makeshift shelters of the many families who had lost their homes. The numbers he knew were large. More than 20,000 people in Balakot alone. Thousands more were streaming into the valley from their villages in the mountains, afraid of the bitter winter in prospect. And beyond the tents, devastation along the valley as far as the eye could see.

His thoughts were interrupted by Asim emerging from the tent. Behind him was the boy, whose tear-streaked face looked up at Cousins. Asim spoke to the youngster in Urdu before addressing Cousins. "This is Shahbaz," he said. "He is very pleased to meet you." The small, hunched figure stood awkwardly before the Englishman. His face was a picture of sadness and Cousins was struck by the sorrow in the boy's eyes.

Shahbaz had never seen a white man close up. In truth he was slightly afraid. But he was curious too and gazed at the foreigner in awe. Cousins smiled warmly at the boy, whom he judged to be nine or ten years old.

"Hello, Shahbaz," he said, lowering himself to his haunches to the youngster's level. Then, turning to Asim, he asked, "How do you say 'hello' in Urdu?"

"In Pashto it is, '*Salaam. Sanga hal dhe?*'"

Cousins repeated the phrase clumsily. And the boy smiled faintly. It was the first time he had smiled since the earthquake.

"I have told him you have come far and would be very pleased to see him join the other children in the activities," said the young Pakistani.

"I would be honoured indeed," Cousins replied, and the boy smiled uncertainly as Asim translated the Englishman's response.

"Then it is done," said Asim jovially. "Soon there will be games and the challenge will be whether you can keep up with the children. They are very fast."

"I will do my very best," said Cousins, raising himself and laying a hand gently on the boy's shoulder.

"Come," said Asim. "The children are getting ready for their races. Let us go and see." The Pakistani took the boy's hand and they walked towards the games area, where boys and girls already stood in line.

Afsa Ali closed her story book and looked at the children who were still watching her intently. "*Acha*,"[3] she said simply as she rose to her feet. "It is time for games outside," she told them and there was a scramble to exit the tent, as the children streamed out into the open air.

When she emerged from the tent Ali could see the games session was about to begin.

---

3   Good, or all right, in Urdu.

For a moment her eyes rested on Cousins, who stood tall and conspicuously in line with the boys.

Shahbaz stood uncertainly at the front of one of two rows of youngsters, opposite Cousins, ready to run against him. Asim raised his hands for silence, announcing the visitor from England who was to race against Shahbaz, 'King of Falcons.' The children cheered in excitement at the novelty of a foreigner taking part in their games and crowded around in eager anticipation.

Asim raised his hands for silence again as man and boy took their starting places.

"Ready… steady…" He paused for effect. "Go!" There was a roar from the children.

Shahbaz took off like a shot, with Cousins close on his heels, as both ran across the dirt.

Ali watched the foreigner as he scampered clumsily in pursuit of the youngster the fifty yards to touch the large stone which marked the halfway point, at which both would turn and race back towards the starting line to finish. They were level as both turned and headed for home. Seeing Cousins was falling slightly behind, the boy seemed to sense the prospect of victory and ran even faster towards the finish line, the cheers of those watching ringing in his ears. Cousins was careful not to overtake his competitor.

At the same time, he did not want to be obvious in his intention to allow the boy to win. He too suddenly accelerated and overtook his young rival, only to stumble and fall over some invisible obstacle in a cloud of dust less than ten paces from the finish line…

A celebratory roar rose up from the spectators as Shahbaz crossed the line. Suddenly the hero, a sense of unexpected celebrity lit up his young face. For a few moments Cousins hung his head in exaggerated shame as he sat on the ground where he had fallen so close to victory.

"That's the reporter from England," said Saiyra Johns, who was now standing with Ali.

"He's making a bit of a fool of himself," said the younger woman absently, with apparent disinterest.

But the children were laughing at the Englishman's clumsiness as he still sat in the dust laughing with them. And Ali smiled too.

It was Asim who stepped towards Cousins to help him to his feet.

"Thank you, Mr John, Sahib," he said while Cousins dusted himself down. "Shahbaz is very happy to have won the race."

"A pleasure," the Englishman replied. He glanced over to the children, where Shahbaz was surrounded by several boys enjoying their apparent admiration, while groups of little girls still stood watching the white man, giggling at his demise. He took the hand Asim offered to him and raised himself to his feet.

"What does Shahbaz mean?" he asked as he dusted himself down. He had been told that all Muslim names held meaning.

And Asim smiled at the Englishman. "It was as I said, Mr John. Shahbaz means 'King of Falcons.'"

"He certainly flew," Cousins replied and Asim nodded.

"He did, Sir."

And suddenly the next boys' race was underway, to renewed cheering… and the 'gora's' novelty had passed. He collected his shoulder bag and camera from where he had left them, and stood watching the children, where Asim was directing activities. In the context of the devastation he witnessed all around, he found their joy profoundly moving.

Standing outside her tent, the beautiful storyteller was still watching the children too.

She had covered her head with her shawl and stood motionless, her gaze fixed on the excitement of the races, taking in the happy scene of children playing.

Cousins walked to the perimeter, then ducked under the tape which marked the boundary of the play area to head for higher ground, where he wanted to photograph the child-friendly space against the backdrop of the destruction in which it lay, framed by the mountains beyond.

He walked across the rocky terrain and picked his spot at the base of the mountain, where the ground suddenly rose sharply. And there he sat, among the boulders surveying the scene which was laid out before him across the valley.

Somehow it seemed unreal. Here he was in the mountains of Pakistan, so far from everything he knew, gazing across the disaster area. The town was gone. He could not see a single building which still stood.

Surrounding the ruined city were fields of tents, a patchwork of white canvas. In the distance, across the river which flowed through the valley, he could see the central mosque. Its circular walls had fallen outwards and its unsupported dome had caved in. Still the people came to bow and sink to their knees to give thanks to their God as the sun began to set. Many had lost everything in the earthquake. Yet their faith remained. Unshakeable.

He took the camera from its case and raised it to frame his shots, focused, then clicked away on auto. Then he stopped. He could hear the sound of the children singing, their voices soaring over the devastation from the child-friendly space. He lowered his camera. It was a cheering sound of normal life, of hope for the future among the scenes of destruction strewn all around…

And it was thanks to the tireless child play specialists at Relief Action. Cousins took a deep breath and sighed. Then he headed back to the child-friendly space to pick up his driver.

When he arrived at Mansehra, Selby was already back at the team house, drinking coffee.

He looked up as Cousins approached. "How was your day?" he smiled in greeting.

Cousins nodded and pulled up a chair alongside the Canadian.

"Good. Been to the child-friendly space at Balakot."

"Excellent."

"Those guys do good work with the children. Very moving," he told Selby. "How was the Black Mountain?"

"Interesting," the Canadian smiled. "Very interesting. Saw the destruction up there in one of the villages. And along the Indus Valley. I'd guess damage ranges between twenty to about ninety per cent. The village of Peer Khel, up on the ridge was almost completely flattened—"

"And you say they've had no help?" asked Cousins.

"No-one's interested. Access is difficult. Security is an issue. And there's no information about the area," Selby replied. "But I met with the village *Jirga* and the elders want help. Need it. The people are dangerously exposed – and they know it. They will put the word around. I also met with the tribal chieftain. I think we can work with him and he will arrange security. Name's Mohammed Ali Khan. Seems to command a good deal of respect. I just have to convince Williams," added Selby with a wry smile. Then he looked directly at Cousins. "I'm going to need some help and advice. I'd like you to come to the Black Mountain with me…"

TWELVE

It was true the city was like no other in Pakistan. Built in the 1960s on the plains below the first folds of the Himalayas on what had been jungle and scrubland, the federal capital was regarded as a modern marvel of urban design. Islamabad was something of an El Dorado; a shining city of plenty and a magnet to the poorest of the poor who came from their villages in search of better fortunes and to eat the crumbs which might fall from those occupying the top tables of Pakistani society.

Usually that meant domestic employment within a wealthy household. The opulent villas might hire half a dozen servants, if they were modest about their means. Less than a stone's throw from the comfortable residential areas, ragged children would beg in the streets. The lucky ones might be taken in, perhaps offered by their relatives to wealthy families as playmates and carers for their children, or to work from sunrise to sunset on household chores. The less lucky would call for waste which could be recycled or scavenge the rubbish dumps for anything discarded which might still hold value – and survive by any means possible.

Islamabad was and remains a city for the elite, the rich and the powerful – and those who worked the machinery of government and high office. And yet there was another distinct group of privileged individuals: a ragtag mixture of expatriates known as aid workers whose international humanitarian organisations had their offices in the capital. The city was a secure haven in the event of tensions, within the strict security cordon which surrounded its centre, to which aid workers would flee for safety and comfort when evacuation from the 'field' was necessary.

Selby travelled back to the city infrequently. Usually it was by necessity, to attend briefings at the Relief Action office. He preferred Mansehra, set within the majesty and remoteness of the mountains. For him the uninspired concrete buildings of Islamabad, with their flat roofs and lack of architectural flair, were dull. The city mimicked all that was to his mind bad about affluent Western society and he found no comfort in the upmarket shopping, or the ordered traffic which flowed smoothly under the watchful eye of the Islamabad Traffic Police along highways bordered by pretty flowers. To Selby it was all false; it was a city without character and no soul. It was a pretence.

Its extreme wealth sickened him in a country where millions were kept poor and struggled daily to survive.

For him personally the modern infrastructure and abundance available to him was no consolation. Quite the contrary. He disliked the capital and all it represented. It was a bastion of corruption, power and greed. It was a city where money and privilege allowed its residents to focus on their selfish indulgences – and look the other way. Even if it was sometimes under the gaze of poor children stunted by malnutrition. Islamabad seemed to stand against everything that had brought him to Pakistan.

The main plaza of Jinnah Super Market was one of the major shopping areas in the heart of the city's central F-7 sector. The sector was popular with international aid agencies. Part of the reason lay in its proximity to government buildings and the additional security checkpoints in place. It was also close to the diplomatic enclave, a walled area topped with razor wire reserved for the missions of the major Western powers represented in Pakistan, including the US and British embassies and, it was said, their intelligence networks.

On a visit back to the capital Selby decided one Saturday morning to explore the narrow alleyways leading from the main shopping areas to the smaller plazas, less trodden by its wealthier inhabitants. It was one of his few indulgences. Second-hand books. And Islamabad boasted many stalls, shops and dealers in a country where the printed word was still prized above all else and its children were as hungry for knowledge as they sometimes were for food. And English was still the official language of business and government.

The shopping centre was quiet when the Land Cruiser swept into the empty parking lot and the Canadian climbed out. He told his driver not to wait. Selby would call him when he was ready to be picked up. The air was clear and cool in the early morning sunshine and as yet the beggars which laid siege to shoppers were not yet in evidence. Shopkeepers were still making final preparations before opening their doors for business. Two children sat on the pavement with their boxes of shoe brushes, cloths and polish, but Selby was too nimble for them to approach. His ethics would not allow children to shine his boots, though he would often give them money, or call in at the bakery to buy them biscuits.

He did not linger in the main plaza. Instead he headed across the square for one of the alleys which led away to the far side, which he knew were lined with smaller shops, which included dealers in second-hand books.

Selby discovered the map entirely by accident. He was looking for anything he could lay his hands on which might describe the history and culture of the north-west frontier region, where the earthquake had struck hardest. The book by Colonel Harold Carmichael Wylly was an unexpected find.

The Canadian enjoyed browsing from shop to shop and the interaction with the shopkeepers, who were impeccably polite and attentive. And there was always someone who spoke English if he at first failed to make himself understood, if not in the shop next door, then the next one along. Communication was somehow always possible. And always there were smiles. Often he would be offered a cup of chai and sometimes he would accept, savouring the sweet milky brew and enjoying the informal company of the people he had come to love. Williams would have had a fit. Even walking through the capital unaccompanied was against security protocol.

The ancient volume was found in the history section in one of the tiny shops, stacked high with old books of every description, leaving barely enough room to squeeze passed the shelving lining every available inch of space, floor to ceiling. It was one of half a dozen books the shopkeeper brought hopefully to the Canadian following his enquiry.

But there it was. *From the Black Mountain to Waziristan*. It drew on first-hand accounts and military reports of the day detailing the activities of the regiments which had in 1888 marched from the mountain garrison at Abbottabad to suppress the tribes of Kala Dhaka. Selby could not believe his luck. As he began to turn the pages a thrill of boyish excitement ran through him. He almost laughed out loud.

In addition to the description of the military expedition, the book included explanations of the tribal structures which existed across North-West Frontier Province in British India at the time, and their allegiances. It was a crusty colonial work of an old soldier born and raised in British India, with something of a passion for its peoples. The colonel himself had served in north-west Pakistan and clearly knew the region.

In later years, following a distinguished and decorated career in the British Army, Wylly retired to a sleepy village in the English countryside, living out his days writing about the military campaigns mounted across the far reaches of the empire in distant lands, including his beloved India, the Middle East and North Africa.

The dusty book Selby now held in his hands was an original early edition, printed in 1912 and authored by the seasoned British officer who knew the remote area which was now a focus for Selby and the Relief Action aid effort. Wylly's narrative was workmanlike and matter-of-fact, but detailed. It described the incident in which two British officers were attacked and killed while patrolling the edge of the Black Mountain and their small escort harried back to Oghi Fort by the Hassanzai tribe.

The response from the British Raj was swift and strong. Some 10,000 men, including mountain artillery batteries, were mobilised and set out from the garrison at Abbottabad, some fifty miles to the south-east. The battles that followed as the force split into four columns and approached the Black Mountain to face the hostile tribesmen of roughly equal numbers were described as fierce. The Pathan warriors were proud, brave and seasoned mountain fighters. Yet they were hopelessly outgunned. Their long-barrelled *jezzails*[4] or

---

4   A simple and often handmade muzzle-loading long barrelled flintlock, commonly used in South Asia.

muskets, swords, shields and knives were no match for the highly trained British force equipped with the latest Martini-Henry breech loading rifles.

The outcome was never in doubt. Though the tribes fought bravely, they were beaten back. Villages were raised and a new, uneasy peace was agreed with the respective *Jirgas*. At least for the time being.

Wylly, ever-thorough, even carried the casualty lists which showed as many troops died from disease during the long march across the mountains as through combat.

More remarkable still to Selby was the map of the Black Mountain, tucked within the book's fly-leaf.

"It is the only map of the area that exists," the operations manager told Cousins as he related the story with enthusiasm. "There's nothing else. I've searched, believe me," he added, gazing at the Englishman as if he scarcely believed it himself.

"After the British suppressed the tribes, their engineers stayed and completed a detailed survey of the area. The map they produced is accurate to the yard. And it's more than a hundred years old," he continued. The intention was to construct roads allowing British Indian forces to skirt the Black Mountain more easily on future expeditions. Yet the tribes did not want easy access to their territory. Trouble flared again in 1891 but was easily quelled as the British and Indian soldiers returned.

The roads, though, were never built.

When the army finally left later that year there was nothing. "No foreigners or outside intervention of any kind has been recorded since. That's also confirmed by the *Loya Jirga*, which has to give its permission for outsiders to enter," the Canadian explained. And that made Selby the first white man to visit the Black Mountain in over a century. The two men stared at each other.

"That's one hell of a story," Cousins said finally, his mind racing.

"It's one of the reasons you are here," said the Canadian with one of his disarming smiles. "And it is why I would like you to consider coming back when you have finished your assignment for the paper," he added. "These people are remote and hard to access.

"They've had no help since the earthquake. No-one even knows how many people are there or how far the arc of earthquake damage extends into the area. But we're going to get help to them. And I'd like you to tell the story…"

He told the journalist about Mohammed Ali Khan and about the visit he had made that day. What he had seen had confirmed what the elders who came to Mansehra had told him. Kala Dhaka, the Black Mountain, had suffered extensive damage. Its people were desperate.

As an ex-military man, the area fired Selby's imagination. He felt it was more than coincidence. Perhaps it was fate. Certainly it was an opportunity. It was an adventure which set the adrenaline pumping, not least of all due to its reputation as a forbidden, forgotten and neglected region, barely changed in centuries.

Cousins was captivated. It was an incredible story. Its history, its reputation and its remoteness. Khan had told Selby that more than 100,000 people on the mountain were facing exposure, starvation and disease. They had not been reached by any aid organisation since the disaster. And it was now January.

Later that night as Cousins lay in his bed, thoughts raced through his mind. He could hardly believe the story Selby had related to him, or that within forty-eight hours he was set to visit the Black Mountain itself… and that he was being invited to support the relief operation and document the aid distribution.

That same evening Gail Stevenson sat hunched at the table in her room, scanning reports from her field team on the laptop, a Marmite sandwich in hand, a cup of coffee within easy reach.

The figures were good. Hundreds of children were attending the two child-friendly spaces already set up. The first had been in Balakot. A second had just been established at Kaghan, higher up the valley. More were planned.

Yet she knew many thousands of children needed additional support. They had lost family members, homes, possessions and an entire way of life. Of course the first concerns were food, shelter and clothing. Those who came into the camps received basic support. Yet life in the tented settlements brought its own traumas. And many families had remained in the mountains, reluctant to leave their ruined villages. She knew too that Relief Action would have to reach out to those communities. Children were at risk. She took a bite from her sandwich, enjoying the strength of the Marmite she had applied. It was one of the few comforts she brought with her whenever she travelled overseas.

Her team was growing, bolstered by enthusiastic volunteers. She would meet with Selby again to discuss where the areas of priority lay within the region. After all, he was the operations manager and emergency relief was now being delivered to villages across Mansehra and Balakot districts.

Further areas were also undergoing rapid needs assessments with a view to expand distributions of essential non-food items, including CGI[5] sheets, tarpaulins, toolkits, tents, sleeping bags and winter clothing. It would make

---

5 Corrugated Galvanised Iron sheets, commonly used in lightweight construction, often as roofing.

sense to build on relationships already being forged with communities receiving aid and the relevant authorities to extend child protection activities.

She had also heard about Selby's interest in the tribes of the Black Mountain. She knew the region had never been assessed. She could only guess at the hardships facing its children. A chance to visit the area for the first time seemed an irresistible child protection draw. No data had ever been recorded there. She felt she was duty-bound to push for access. She'd speak with Selby in the morning. She took another bite of her sandwich.

Suddenly her chair began to shudder. The cup on the table was shaking, sending ripples across the surface of the coffee it contained. Stevenson instinctively rose and crossed the floor which was now moving beneath her feet. Moments later she emerged into the cool evening air and breathed a sigh of relief as the ground was suddenly still.

Afsa Ali was already sitting on the grass in front of her, smoking a cigarette as Stevenson stepped from the building. The two women stared at each other for a moment. They had just experienced one of the many aftershocks from the earthquake, which would run to several hundred in the months ahead.

"You all right?" Stevenson enquired of the young Pakistani woman.

Ali nodded. "I'm getting used to it," she smiled and blew a puff of smoke into the air. Seeing a woman dressed in *Shalwar Kameez* with a hijab covering her head and calmly smoking seemed a strange sight to Stevenson.

"I didn't realise you smoked," she said.

"Sometimes," Ali replied. "In moments of stress." Then she paused. "But my mother doesn't know."

"Then I won't tell her," Stevenson said simply, as she

approached and sat on the grass beside her. "As long as you let me have one of your cigarettes!" And both women smiled. Stevenson took one of the cigarettes offered and squatted beside the young Pakistani.

Cousins also stood outside, on the far end of the building which provided access to the dormitory in which he slept. It was the first time he had felt an aftershock and he was a little shaken by the experience. He saw the two women sitting on the grass in the light which shone from the main house but did not approach. Instead he crossed the lawn to the bungalow where Selby, Williams and de Villiers stood on the terrace.

"This is the fourth one this week," said Selby.

"Everyone OK your side?" Williams asked, gazing at Cousins as he approached.

The Englishman nodded. "Think so."

"As if we didn't have enough going on," muttered the American, screwing his face up. "Maniacs!"

"Why, what else is going on?" Cousins asked.

Williams looked at Selby and seemed to hesitate before he spoke again. "More drones were fired into the Federally Administered Tribal Areas today... and that's just over that mountain range there," he said, pointing across to the north-west.

"That's a danger to all of us," added Selby. "Raises tensions. Makes us potential targets. Bloody Yanks!"

Williams raised an eyebrow but did not comment.

Selby also knew there might be protests following Friday prayers, when anti-Western feeling might be incited by religious leaders at the mosques.

"We've seen it before," Williams commented wearily. "Crowds build, roads are blocked. Sometimes effigies are burned. Even here in Mansehra. Last time there was a threat by protesters to march on the agencies here in Ghazikot."

Selby looked concerned. "And that might mean an evac back to the capital. But let's see what happens in the days ahead…"

When finally Cousins returned to his bed he lay awake for some time. Outside on the balcony which overlooked the valley he could hear the guards armed with machine guns pacing up and down. It was a stark reminder, if ever one was needed, that he was a long way from home as he drifted into a restless sleep…

THIRTEEN

She heard the distant throb of rotor blades and instinctively gazed skywards.

From the ruined village, Shahida Bibi watched the three small silhouettes grow larger as they drew near and the helicopters then pass overhead in a roar of noise. And just as quickly, they receded across the peaks from sight. The aircraft laden with supplies were travelling further north to mountain settlements reachable by no other means.

Yet the effect was devastating. To Shahida it seemed she and her villagers had been forsaken; that help for them would never come. They had been forgotten. And they would go hungry and cold for another day. She felt like crying, yet no tears would come. They had already been shed for the little girl she had lost in the landslide below the village. And she had two other children to keep alive in the days ahead.

"Allah punishes us for our sins," the woman beside her wailed in despair. Yet Shahida said nothing. She did not believe that. God was merciful. Allah was everything. There had to be a reason for what had happened for the greater good. She believed that. She had to believe, for life to go on.

The village of Dandar lay high above Balakot town in the Saraash Valley. It was a collection of loosely connected hamlets on the mountainside of almost 4,000 men, women and children. Its people were simple farmers, squeezing a living from the limited land which had been cut and stepped into the steep slopes on which they lived. It had been farmed this way for generations and it was almost as if time had stood still in the remote mountains that were barely touched by the slow march of time.

But like the town in the valley below, Dandar had been destroyed in the earthquake, as had countless other villages scattered over the mountains. They were desperate hours immediately after the disaster. Homes had collapsed, burying entire families. People clawed at the rubble with their bare hands to rescue loved ones. Then they would bury their family members with what ceremony they were able, laying the dead in the ground of which they seemed a part and had now been returned. After that, the shock of what had happened began to sink in.

Dazed and numbed people began scavenging to save what scant possessions they could from the piles of earth and rubble that remained of their homes.

Others simply sat among the destruction, desolate, bewildered by what had overtaken their community so suddenly, unable to take in the harsh reality which now confronted them. Life had changed; everything they had known was gone.

The loss of life went hand in hand with the loss of land, livestock, food supplies, water sources and livelihoods. In short, everything had been destroyed. Yet the biggest threat was the loss of hope itself. And so the people clung to the only hope they had: their religion. It was what enabled them to accept such crushing hardship. It is what allowed them to go on.

In the days that followed, the rain came. Sheets of cold, hard rain from leaden skies. It seemed to penetrate everything and turned the ruined villages to mud. There were flash floods too.

Torrents of water which swept from the higher ground, gushing through the stricken settlements, adding to the misery of a people teetering on the very edge of survival.

The villagers sheltered among the debris, huddled against the elements on the mountain in their misery, praying for relief. Everything they valued had been smashed. Even the mosque, so central to their lives, had fallen, its twisted corrugated iron roof resting on the stone and earth debris that had been its walls. Still they came to pray among the rubble.

The army had been first to reach the village on the third day. The major told the villagers who crowded around him his men had not been able to clear the roads any quicker. He was sorry for their sorrow and their pain. The soldiers brought food and tents and blankets. It was chaos, as hungry, desperate people scrambled for supplies. Some villagers had barely eaten since the disaster. But then the army moved on. They had other villages to reach on higher ground and would have to clear roads ahead and breach valleys where the bridges had collapsed.

To Shahida it all seemed unreal. It was almost impossible to grasp that from one day to another all could be lost. Life before the earthquake had been simple and secure. She was barely more than a girl when she was married according to her family's wishes to a man old enough to be her father.

Mohammed Rasheed was a humble farmer, making a meagre living from the small patch of land which lay below the village, growing rice and vegetables.

He was, according to local custom, a good husband, who did not beat her. The couple had a small flat-roofed home of mud and stone on the edge of the village, and enough to eat, even when the harvests were poor. There was no kitchen or latrine. Shahida prepared her meals over an open fire inside, or sometimes outside, the home. The toilet was a hole in the ground away from the dwelling. Water was available from the nearby spring, half an hour away across winding mountain paths.

There was no gas or electricity except for those who could afford it, in cylinders or by generator. And yet they had all they needed. A roof over their heads, the land to farm and enough food to eat.

She was afraid when her first child came. She was still only fifteen years old. The old woman told her there was nothing to bringing a child. It was the most natural thing in the world. God would see her through. Yet nothing had prepared her for the searing pain of childbirth which tore through her in the long hours of her labour. But the old woman was there, cooling her forehead with water, telling her when to push and when to rest. And there was such relief and a rush of joy when her baby came and was held to her. It was a beautiful little boy. Allah had blessed her.

And more children followed in quick succession. But just a few years into the marriage, Rasheed fell ill, and after years of sickness and struggle out in the fields, he finally succumbed to tuberculosis. For weeks he languished in bed, coughing out his last days as the disease destroyed his lungs, and she became a widow. Still in her early twenties, Shahida was left with four young children to raise on her own. And there was no other man in the village who would take her in. Not with four children. Prematurely aged by overwork and the harshness of her life, Shahida began to farm the land herself, working dawn to dusk on the small strip of land.

The women of the village helped watch over her children, but often she would return to her mud house weary with fatigue. And life went on; the seasons turned. Somehow she coped.

In time Shahida became accomplished in the fields. She took advice from the men and help from the women of the village when it was offered. She grew vegetables and cereal. And she was lucky in the years that followed.

The harvests were good, so that as time passed she was able to buy three chickens and a goat. And her son and two eldest daughters grew to an age when they were able to gather wood and fetch the water. Life became easier.

She was able to supplement her meagre income by selling surplus fresh vegetables, eggs and goat's milk at the local *markaz*. Sometimes Shahida was able to earn additional money through sewing for other households. It was enough for the basic family food requirements and a regular diet of roti and rice, or lentils and occasional vegetables. The family was not able to afford meat, or fruit, although there were wild cherries in the summer. Yet Shahida was thankful for every day that passed.

Then one evening shortly before the rains came that year her youngest daughter Zebeda caught the fever and her condition worsened in the days ahead.

The mother watched helplessly as the toddler crumpled and screamed out from the searing abdominal pain. The child would not eat. But still she would vomit until nothing more would come. The mother watched helplessly as she grew thinner and weaker with each passing day. The simple medicine that might have saved her was not available in the village and there was no doctor within a day's walk. The little girl cried and cried. Her cries became weaker. Then one night she became quiet and died in Shahida's arms. The little girl was not yet three and Shahida buried her daughter with her own hands under the shade of the solitary *Chinar* tree on the land close to the home.

Her future hopes rested on her son, Tariq. The boy was her joy, and she was determined that he should receive an education and one day go to college. Shahida had not been able to attend school as a girl herself and was illiterate. She had been saving from her small income for the boy's school uniform so that he could start his education in the year ahead. Life before the earthquake had been hard. Now even that was gone, along with another of her children, and she prayed for a miracle.

The aid workers from Mansehra came one grey autumn morning, a small convoy of Jeeps and Land Cruisers. They brought with them emergency supplies. But they also made promises of regular food, clothing and building materials as soon as they could gauge the needs of the village and put in place a means to ferry the aid from the valley below. Above all, the arrival of the white men who led the mission brought hope.

Selby looked every inch the man in charge, as he trudged purposefully through the mud, directing his teams. He was shocked by what he saw. The village looked as if it lay at the centre of a war zone. Many homes had been destroyed completely and not a single building seemed to have escaped damage. Everything seemed laid to waste in a sea of mud. But the people had improvised, finding shelter among the ruined landscape with anything which might afford some protection. It was a desolate scene.

Almost immediately following their arrival, the aid workers were surrounded by crowds of villagers, desperate for help. It was no easy task calming the throngs of hungry, exhausted people. Households had to be visited to establish what was needed most before anything could be distributed. And then there was the question of where the distribution of emergency supplies should take place. But with the help of the imam and the village elders, the frenzy subsided and the villagers understood there was a process. Reassurance was given that all in need would receive assistance.

Shahida watched Selby from a distance. She had not seen a *'gora'* before. She assumed he was American and had heard about a faraway land in the west, which had a different religion and different customs. Some said its people were devils. But he did not look like a bad man. The other white man seemed to be his assistant. And she noticed there were women in the group of aid workers too. Some were also white, but dressed according to Islam, covering their heads. Others were clearly Pakistani.

Later she was visited in her shelter by a young woman from Islamabad who wanted to know her circumstances. So she told her about her life and what was gone. She told of her hardship and the aid worker was kind and understanding. So she told her about her dreams too. The woman wrote down on paper the details of Shahida's life. It was Afsa Ali, who was also gathering information for Stevenson's child protection team. Ali told the mother there would be help. She also wanted to know about Shahida's children. And the mother's heart lifted. Allah be praised!

She blessed the young woman from Islamabad, who became tearful as she smiled and nodded in acknowledgement before she left. Later that day a ticket was delivered to Shahida. It was to be exchanged for a tent, blankets and emergency food rations for the family if she would come to the distribution point close to the mosque and make her mark with the print from her index finger.

Selby's mission that day was to visit three villages to distribute emergency aid and rapidly assess the needs of the communities, essential to shape the Relief Action plans, which needed to be put in place before the weather grew worse with the coming winter.

As it was, access following the disaster was a major issue. Roads were narrow and precarious, still subject to landslides on a daily basis. And the rains did not help. They had to work with the army, following the engineers as they cleared the way through the mountains. Waiting for routes to be passable was frustrating and the weather seemed to be turning against them. Soon the rain would turn to snow.

Selby took up a position on higher ground to gaze down upon the village of Dandar. He was assessing structural needs, plotting the best access points and how the road might be improved. Two engineers were already on their way to Mansehra to join his team. He was trying to obtain a sense of what practical help he and his team could deliver in the weeks and months ahead.

But where to begin? Homes were destroyed. Schools needed rebuilding; land needed to be reclaimed along with lost livelihoods. Water supplies had also been disrupted and would have to be restored. Some springs had entirely disappeared. There were no medicines either. And then there was the condition of the roads.

Aid agencies would work together in partnership. And Selby was clear local NGOs could support and better access the remote mountain areas. They could also put large numbers of local volunteers on the ground. But in truth, longer-term plans did not yet exist. Partnerships and joint working would need to be established and draw on specialist expertise offered by respective agencies. Relief Action's experience lay in child protection and education. It also had expertise in construction, particularly of schools. But for now, each international aid organisation was focused on emergency distributions of food, shelter, hygiene kits and other essential non-food items to keep people alive.

Selby had access to heavy trucks, which could move large amounts of supplies to the foot of the mountain. But getting the stuff from the valley up to remote villages accessed by dirt tracks cut into the mountain was a challenge. It would require a fleet of four-wheel drive vehicles. And they were hard to come by and expensive to hire. The thought of using porters, perhaps men from the village in a 'cash-for-work' scheme to literally carry the aid up from the valley was an option.

From the road below it was a two-hour trek to the first village. But it was possible.

Then he smiled. Mules. Pack mules. Maybe that was the answer. He'd seen it in the mountains of Afghanistan. The thought of Zhevlakov haggling for mules in the markets came into his mind and suddenly he laughed out loud. He was sure the Ukrainian would negotiate a tough deal.

He was still smiling as Williams scrambled up the small rocky outcrop to join him.

"My God! How are these people surviving?" he muttered as he stood beside Selby.

"I don't know," replied the Canadian vacantly.

"It's the children," Williams continued.

"Yep. Some of them look in a poor way."

Williams nodded. And the two men fell silent as they gazed out across the scene below them.

When Williams spoke again there was an urgency in his voice. "We have to move," he said, gesturing at the sky. Dark clouds were rearing up over the mountains, threatening more heavy rain.

But Selby was still thinking about the logistical challenge. "Pack mules!" he said out loud.

Williams looked at him quizzically.

"Bloody donkeys!" Selby exclaimed, gazing at his American colleague. "To transport the supplies up from the valley. Why not?!"

"Donkeys," Williams uttered flatly. "You can explain on the way back to Mansehra. We have to move while we still can," he insisted. Selby nodded and the two men headed back into the village to round up the others.

Selby was quiet on the return journey. His mind was racing. He was considering how to shape the relief programme and just what kind of support would be most effective to help the villages he had seen. He now had a fair idea of their situation and their needs. He knew what he had available: food, clothing, tents, tools, building materials… but how best to get the supplies to them? And there was the possibility of other support. Perhaps the roads could be improved before the winter. Funding across international donor offices was in full swing.

What he didn't yet know was whether those affected by the earthquake would be likely to remain where they were, or whether they would have to migrate from their ruined villages into the valleys to sit out the winter in tented camps, more easily supplied. The Government of Pakistan's plan for the stricken people of the North-West Frontier Province had not yet been shared.

Nor could he know how Relief Action might be required to support any official strategy.

For now he was taking the lead from the army and staying close to the jolly colonel. And he was determined to get the emergency aid to the people just as fast as he could.

Certainly there was plenty to think about. The days ahead would be fraught with difficulties. But what may have daunted, or even overwhelmed, another man was an exciting challenge to the Canadian. It fired him up. It gave him a buzz.

Besides, he'd faced worse situations under fire in Afghanistan. And he had always won through.

In the village of Dandar, Shahida Bibi prepared to pray in the ruins of her home. As the sun began to set over the mountains, she took a small plastic bottle of water. First she rinsed her feet. Then she washed her hands and face, ears, neck, eyes, and lastly her mouth using small amounts of water. As the shadows began to fall, she stood to face the west, cupped her ears with her hands and recited the *Kalima*, before sinking to her knees and bending forward, as if to kiss the ground before her. *Allahu Akbar!* God is great!

She thanked God and prayed for the aid workers who had come to her village that day. She prayed for Allah to bless the white men she saw and especially the young woman from Islamabad who was kind. Now she was able to cry again. She cried for the daughter she had lost in the earthquake, now resting beneath the *Chinar* tree. But they were also tears of gratitude as the heavy drops of rain began to patter on the plastic sheeting of her makeshift shelter.

FOURTEEN

THE BOY WAS traumatised and close to exhaustion when Eriksson first saw him. It was his eyes that struck the Norwegian to the core, deep pools of despair gazing right at him from the muddied face, framed by tangled hair which fell across his brow. His beige *Shalwar Kameez* was stained dark with dirt and torn, and Eriksson noticed the boy's feet were chapped and bleeding within plastic sandals.

"My mother is dead and my father is gone," he repeated to Eriksson, who had been asked to come quickly the gates of the camp. There was a new arrival; an orphaned boy and he had hurried to the gatehouse. The boy had walked from the mountain on the far side of the valley carrying the ragged bundle in his arms. He said he had not eaten for two days. And there he stood at the entrance to the tented camp, pleading for help, his face a picture of misery as he held out the package to the guards, imploring them to lift it from him.

The uniformed guard immediately realised it contained a child as he took the bundle in his hands and looked apprehensively at his two colleagues before drawing the ragged fabric back to reveal the baby's tiny face. "Fetch Mr Eriksson Sahib... and Fatima Bibi. Quickly!" he said with urgency, and one of the guards hurried off towards the tented camp. A blanket was thrown over the boy's shoulders and he was guided to a chair. Cold, hungry and tired, he could scarcely speak to tell his story. "Everything is gone," he kept repeating, telling them he had walked a long way. He thought he would die. In his arms he had carried the baby, lying with a small cricket bat and wrapped in blankets. It was his little sister, he said.

Fatima Bibi and the women had already arrived to tend the infant when Eriksson entered the gatehouse. The self-appointed matriarch and grandmother was revered and respected by the younger women of the camp community whom she supported with the assuredness of her age and experience. The baby was weak and cold. But she had survived her ordeal. And she was hungry too, sucking steadily, gratefully on the breast offered by a young mother as the other women looked on, shielding them from the gaze of the men and supervised by Fatima Bibi. There was no shortage of women who stood ready to care for the baby. Many of them had lost children of their own.

And this was a story of hope, which spread joyously through the tented camp. They said it was a miracle. Allah be praised!

Biscuits were brought for the boy and Eriksson kneeled beside him as he crammed them hungrily, desperately into his mouth and drank the water that was offered.

The aid worker asked him what had happened. Shahbaz spoke in broken Urdu, overwhelmed by emotion, relayed by the guard who had taken the child from him.

His mother was dead. He had sat beside her on the mountainside holding his sister to him, rocking to and fro, numbed by the enormity of what had happened. It seemed he had sat there a long time, dazed and confused, uncertain what to do. Finally, he had covered his mother with blankets and left the ruined family home to find help, taking his baby sister with him.

But at the nearby village there was no help. The houses were collapsed and among the devastation, there was a frenzy of digging and despair. It was the same in all the villages the boy came to. All had been devastated. Everywhere was grief and tragedy and shock. "Go down to the valley below, *Beta*," the villagers told him. "There will surely be help for you there." And some had given milk for the baby.

During the days he walked for hours until it seemed he was driven by sheer will alone and his steps became automatic, in defiance of the elements as he was carried by one thought alone: to find refuge for himself and his baby sister. At night the boy sought shelter among the rocks, scrub and the contours of the mountain to shield himself from the weather. This he had learned as a shepherd. And he had cradled his sister close to his body for warmth.

Finally he had come into the valley. But the town was gone. Not a single building still stood.

Soldiers were helping to dig for survivors, or to retrieve bodies from the rubble, or were directing people to hasty aid distributions set up along the roadside from trucks. For many, the enormity of what had happened was too much. They simply sat, staring into space, their eyes filled with grief, numb with shock. It seemed to Shahbaz he was wandering in a nightmare from which there was no waking. Finally he approached a soldier, who directed him to the Norwegian mission near the fallen mosque, where he was sure there was help.

The boy was one of many orphaned and lost children in the camp. Most had arrived with extended family members, or had travelled within groups of villagers who came down from their mountain communities for help. There was an area for unaccompanied children in the centre of the camp, consisting of two large tents, close to an area for families with children. It was closely supervised by staff, with help from Fatima Bibi and the women, who supported cooking and food distribution. There was also an area set aside for children's activities and a medical tent. Eriksson's own tent was close to this area, as was the administration centre.

Hundreds of tents provided an instant canvas village for those who came. And there was water and food. Enough to keep people alive in the immediate aftermath of the disaster. But within a few days it was almost full. And more camps were hastily set up by the army and by those international aid agencies that were able to reach the stricken town.

Unlike most of the other children, Shahbaz had no uncles or aunts; no extended family Eriksson could establish. After his initial arrival, the boy seemed unable to speak.

He was in deep shock and would sit for hours, staring into space. Sometimes he would cry. And in his sleep he cradled his cricket bat. And he would talk in that restless sleep, or suddenly cry out as he found himself back on the mountain, huddled as the boulders fell around him in a deafening sound as the ground shook violently beneath his body. Sometimes he would dream of his father. Or he would find himself tending his goats on the mountainside under the clear blue Himalayan sky without a care in the world.

Eriksson and his staff were frustrated in their efforts to gain any further information from the boy. He had simply stopped speaking. Aside from the fact that his mother and father were dead and he had no uncles locally, the Norwegian had little to go on. And he wasn't sure what was to be done. He had facilities in the camp providing shelter, food and water.

But he did not have a mandate to care for and support lost or orphaned children. It is why he called on Relief Action, an organisation he knew had expertise in child protection and were already on the ground.

It was a day or two later that Stevenson and her team arrived and met with Eriksson, and they assessed the children in the camp. The child-friendly space in Balakot had been established, following the agreement made with the major, and the youngsters and their mothers were urged to attend. Shahbaz did not initially want to go. He was still distressed. And yet he was comforted by the presence of other children and reluctantly he agreed to go. But he was also in awe of the beautiful lady who had spoken so kindly to him. It was one of the reasons he finally agreed to go with the others to the child-friendly space near the shattered mosque.

He was one of those who had heard Afsa Ali read and had for a few moments been able to escape his sadness. After that, he became a regular to attend the Relief Action activities, which included an opportunity to attend lessons for the first time in his young life. Yet still he would not speak or smile.

That had taken time and the 'gora' who had raced with him that day and fallen to the ground.

Shahbaz smiled faintly as he recalled his triumph over the clumsy Englishman. Most of all, he liked the Westerner and the way he had laughed at his own misfortune. He hoped the Britisher would visit again.

Shahbaz was curious to know all about him and the world he came from.

FIFTEEN

John Cousins felt himself shaken out of a deep sleep. He'd been dreaming of a life 4,000 miles away. But it was a life that had long since gone. Different place; different time. It was now a distant shadow of things that once had been. In the dream his wife Sarah had been smiling kindly. The children were playing at home. And he was laughing with them. It was an idyllic family scene, from which he did not wish to wake. Again he felt a hand upon his shoulder, gently shaking him from sleep.

"Mr John!" rasped the insistent voice in a loud whisper.

Now instantly alert, Cousins sat up in his bed, staring into the darkness.

"Mr Hank say we must be ready!" It was Khurram Masood, the mountain guide.

As he rubbed his eyes he could just make out Masood's outline through the darkness, whom Selby had sent to rouse him.

"Mr Hank say we leave before the sun," said the man from the north, and left Cousins sitting in the dark to make ready.

This was the day. Selby was heading back into Kala Dhaka to talk again with the tribal chieftain and his counterparts across the mountain. Things were moving at pace. Besides, time was limited. The bitter Himalayan winter was set to move in and the rain would give way to snow any day now, which threatened to isolate the mountain communities, cutting off access. Agreement with the five tribes needed to be reached to guarantee the success of any distribution of aid. And each tribe had to agree access, but also its share of aid, which had to be seen as fair and equal, according to the needs of its villages. Just as importantly, the respective tribal elders and the mullahs had to be convinced that outside intervention would not threaten the region's long-established autonomy.

Selby was only too aware of the sensitivities and happy to work with the tribes. He knew the risks. The tribes had a history of rivalries and disputes, sometimes stretching back centuries. They often centred on land or political differences, even alliances once made during the time of the British or the Sikhs before them. Mohammed Ali Khan was a key ally, respected across the tribal divides. Already the chieftain had spoken at other *Jirgas* and word had travelled across the Black Mountain.

Yet Selby had two other major factors in his favour to bring aid to the region, which he hoped would unite the tribes in accepting outside help for the first time in their history: need and the coming winter.

Acceptance and agreement by the *Loya Jirga*, the council of all five Kala Dhaka tribes, was essential. Only then would Selby's planned distribution be guaranteed the security by each tribe necessary. The last thing he wanted to spark was tribal conflict or violence.

He wanted Cousins to understand. There was an opportunity to assist more than 100,000 desperate people who had not been reached since the earthquake had struck. Yet there were dangers. What he didn't reinforce to the journalist was the high risk of violence. Each tribe was heavily armed. The relationship between the factions was sometimes delicate and the people of the mountain notoriously volatile. The peace was fragile.

Nevertheless, Selby was not a man to shy away from risk in reaching objectives. Besides, he knew that once each tribe had given its word to allow access, then security within the immediate area was guaranteed. Pathans had a code. Once their word was given, then it would be so. It was a question of honour. Some might say honour among thieves. For the area's reputation was not good and the Black Mountain said to harbour bandits.

But the Hassanzai, where Mohammed Ali Khan held his lands, was one of the largest tribes, dominating the centre of the mountain and controlling access along the road which followed the River Indus. And therefore the other tribes, which included the Basikhel, Akazai and Madakhel, were likely to fall into line. All but the Nusrat Khel, which held central parts of Kala Dhaka and were said to be unpredictable. The Madakhel too, centred largely across the west bank of the Indus, were said to harbour age-old feuds with the tribes across the river. Such was the balance that day, which was relatively unchanged since the days of the British Raj.

"It's going to be an adventure," Selby had said, smiling. "One for the grandkids."

By the same token, the Canadian was determined to keep the mission safe. Yet he was driven to reach those desperate people that no-one seemed willing or able to assist following the earthquake. And he liked a challenge. He thrived on it. It was his strength and weakness.

He was pleased Cousins had agreed to be part of the small team working on the Kala Dhaka distribution. The journalist seemed to have a natural way with the local people and an enthusiasm which was contagious. In truth the reporter was shielded to a degree by a naïvety and his lack of knowledge about a region that was in fact highly dangerous.

Cousins threw the sheets back. He fumbled for his lighter and lit a candle, then climbed into his clothes in its flickering glow, shivering in the bitter cold. Outside the temperature was still sub-zero. The last few days had brought the first chill of the winter with an icy blast from the northern areas which had already seen deep snow.

And there he sat for a few moments, gathering himself for the day ahead. Beneath his *Shalwar Kameez* he had the thermal underwear he'd slept in. Now he had an additional two layers under his loose-fitting coarse cotton tunic. Selby insisted they dress according to local custom. It was not just about a sense of respecting the culture. On their way they would attract less attention as they travelled the main highway north passed Oghi before sweeping north-west towards Thakot.

He lit up a cigarette and blew the smoke towards the ceiling. He figured he didn't have time to fumble with the gas fire. With icy fingers he pulled on his boots and laced them up in the light of the single candle. Then he wrapped his scarf around his neck, threw on his ski jacket and stood blowing into his hands.

He'd already packed his bag the night before, but quickly checked its contents. He took an additional notepad from the chest of drawers beside his bed, slid it into a side pocket and tossed the small rucksack over his shoulder. Cousins reached for the round, flat Afghan hat Selby had passed to him the night before and pulled it onto his head. He blew the candle out and headed for the door.

Stepping out into the cool morning air, he gazed across the yard towards the lights shining from the main house. He shivered as he strode over the hard, cold ground towards the building.

Inside he found Selby, Williams and Khurram Masood around the table, supping coffee, and they all looked up at him as he entered.

Selby smiled. "Morning, John. Or should I say *Asalaam-u-Alaikum*. You look the part! Grab yourself a coffee. Then we'll need to move." Cousins smiled and helped himself from the pot on the stove. A map was spread on the table and the three seated men had been studying the route into Kala Dhaka as Cousins joined them.

"I'm not happy about this," said Williams. "Not happy at all."

"We've been through this, Chuck," Selby replied. "It's the best way in. And we'll be back by nightfall."

"You'd better be," said the American.

Selby smiled. "No worries. And we'll call in as soon as we get to Thakot."

"You ready?" Selby gazed at Cousins. The journalist grimaced and nodded, before downing the rest of his coffee.

"Just remember, no camera this time," the Canadian added.

Again, Cousins nodded in understanding. "No camera," he repeated. He was to be an observer and introduced to the elders of Kala Dhaka as an adviser. The meeting, Selby had told him, was crucial in establishing whether the aid distribution would be able to go ahead. The Canadian would be addressing the *Jirga* with senior representatives from each tribe. Its decision was likely to be final.

The enormity of what lay before them was beginning to sober Cousins from the drowsiness of those first waking minutes and he began to wonder just what he was to be a part of.

"Don't worry, John," said Selby cheerily. "It will be all right. As long as you follow what I say and not what I do." And then he looked at Williams. "Remember," he added, "one to tell the grandkids!" And he paused. "Besides, I'll be doing the talking. You just need to observe."

Again, Cousin's nodded.

"Just remember, keep me posted," added Williams. "On the hour, every hour."

Selby nodded, taking the satellite phone from the American. "And back before nightfall," said the latter.

"Before nightfall," repeated the Canadian, before finishing his coffee and rising from his chair.

"OK, let's move," he announced, and he led the journalist and Khurram Masood out into the darkness, leaving Williams sitting at the table.

"Good luck," he called out after them.

Selby fired up the Land Cruiser and pulled off slowly across the yard. He waited as the guard slid back the heavy bolts and pulled the metal gateway open, saluting as the vehicle swung out onto the road and down the hill towards the nearby town, through dark and silent streets. Not a single light was to be seen and it was as yet too early even for the call to prayer summoning the faithful from their sleep.

They headed out of Mansehra towards the Karakorum Highway, which would take them northwards to Battagram. Each of the men was preoccupied by his own thoughts. Selby knew the route. He had travelled it before. Masood was contemplating the trek on foot, while Cousins gazed out of the window, watching the passing landscape. By the time they passed the turn for Oghi the first silver sliver of light could be seen shimmering behind the mountain peaks to the east. A few miles ahead they turned away from the light and towards the inky blackness which still blanketed the mountains ahead towards Thakot.

Yet it was still dark when they reached the small collection of flat-roofed concrete houses which was the last major settlement before turning south and taking the narrow road into the Indus valley towards the Black Mountain.

The road became narrow, winding through the lower slopes of the less populated areas beyond the small town as it took them along the river towards Kala Dhaka. Having left the main highway, the road was now strewn with boulders. It seemed clear the route was not maintained and was damaged from the earthquake, forcing their vehicle to sometimes slow to a walking pace and engage its four-wheel-drive.

After almost two hours on the road they pulled over. It would be the last stop before they were to meet Khan's men. It was an opportunity for Selby to check their position on the map and for Khurram Masood to report to Williams on the phone, while Cousins stepped from the vehicle to light up a cigarette.

"Careful, John," warned Selby. "Please stay close to the vehicle. You never know who might be watching from the hills. And all the tribesmen are heavily armed," he added.

Cousins did as he was told and kept a keen eye on the mountains, still dark in the half-light of the early morning, while puffing on his cigarette. Moments later he climbed back into the Land Cruiser.

"Our good friend Mohammed Ali Khan, who will be awaiting us here, at the village of Judbah," said Selby, indicating a point circled on the map in red. "That's still Basikhel territory."

"We will then be escorted deeper into Kala Dhaka to the appointed place. Khan assures me it lies on the edge of his lands at a location representatives of the other four tribes are comfortable to meet and can easily access." The Canadian paused. "Any questions?"

Cousins had a few but remained silent.

"Remember," said Selby, "we have been invited by the tribal elders and will be offered every courtesy as their guests. I have no doubt we will be 100 per cent safe. Just let me do the talking. Khurram, you will please translate very, very carefully everything I say."

"Yes, Mr Hank, Sahib."

"And John," added Selby, "just smile, watch and listen. It's going to be an adventure." And with that he grinned, slid the Land Cruiser back into gear and they resumed their journey...

The gunmen were waiting as the Westerners approached. Their battered Hilux blocked the road and the solitary tribesman who stood on the rear of vehicle watching for them suddenly cried out.

From his position he could see the Land Cruiser's lights piercing the darkness in the distance as it wound its way slowly towards them.

The group of warriors crouching over a fire of pinecones at the side of the road rose to their feet as soon as the vehicle had been sighted. Most had loose-hanging blankets draped over their shoulders, wrapped against the cold, concealing gun belts and a variety of weaponry. They wore the Afghan hats of the region and had scarves pulled up over their faces to reveal only their eyes. By any standard, they appeared a formidable force and might have been bandits, or Taliban foot soldiers. But they were Khan's men.

As the Land Cruiser turned the final corner and came into full view a few hundred metres on the road ahead, the tribesmen stood, grouped around their vehicle, rifles now in hand. The Land Cruiser drew near, slowed and came to a halt a few metres from the men blocking the road. Selby cut the engine and climbed out, as did Cousins and Khurram Masood. And for a moment the two groups eyed each other.

"Who is Selby, Sahib?" asked one of the gunmen gruffly.

"I'm Selby," replied the Canadian, stepping forward.

The tribesman bowed slightly in respect. "Khan has sent us to escort you to the village," he explained in Pashto, as Khurram Masood translated. Selby was to follow them with the Land Cruiser deeper into Kala Dhaka. It was not far. Then they would leave their vehicles and walk from the valley into the mountains to a village where the elders of the five tribes would meet with them.

Selby nodded in agreement and moments later the two vehicles were travelling together along the road which followed the river valley deeper into the heart of the Black Mountain as the sun began to rise. Less than half an hour later they stood at the foot of the mountain where a path would lead them up to the village.

SIXTEEN

A LL EYES WERE on the Westerners as they climbed the rocky incline which rose up as they made their final approach to the mountain village of Tilli, where some twenty or thirty armed tribesmen waited on the ridge above, eager to catch their first sight of Selby and his companions. The hike had been long, the winding mountain trail steep.

It had seemed strange company on their trek from the valley below. The gunmen had been largely silent, occasionally exchanging glances, moving swiftly along the narrow track, rifles slung over their shoulders. Few words were exchanged during the hours of their steady ascent to the village in the early chill as the shadows of the mountains receded and the sun rose higher in the clear blue sky. Occasionally they would signal a halt to allow the Westerners to rest, as they struggled to keep up with the tribesmen under the exertion of the climb and the thinning of the air as they steadily rose higher above the River Indus.

Among those waiting on the ridge was the distinguished figure of Mohammed Ali Khan, who stood with Salim Shah, the Afghan. But there were other notables too waiting for their arrival, including the village mullah, with a full beard and a black-and-white scarf covering his head. The khan and the holy man were the only unarmed members of the group. The cleric eyed the outsiders with suspicion as they approached. But he saw an opportunity too. He, like many of the village, saw the priority to rebuild its shattered mosque, which lay at the centre of all spiritual life within the stricken community. It was a key symbol of hope for the future. Its reconstruction would please Allah.

Also part of the group were two new members joining negotiations who had learned with interest the possibility of outside aid to the area. Though they were originally from the tribal area, they operated primarily beyond its borders, running a small educational charity in the city of Peshawar, which lay across the mountains towards the south-west, close to the Khyber Pass, gateway to Afghanistan. And they supported a school in Karachi, whose slums were swollen with large numbers of migrant Pathans from the north-west. But they knew the mountain well and had close links with the Basikhel and Madakhel tribes.

Suur Gul Rafiq and his associate Atul Karim gazed upon the approaching Westerners for the first time. The two men saw a chance to further their own work. Suur Gul was a passionate advocate of education to break the cycle of poverty in the poorest areas within his country and particularly across the Black Mountain, where his family roots lay. He understood Kala Dhaka well, including its power structure.

His partner, Karim, shared the same passions for his people. But for now they would observe at the invitation of Khan. They were not sure about the Afghan. He was a Pathan and was therefore familiar with their tribal system and had experience across the border. But they didn't fully trust him.

He was not from the mountain. Besides, he had links to the local politicians. And they were not trusted either.

Khan stepped forward and embraced Selby. "*Asalaam-u-alaikum*. Welcome." He offered the same greeting to Cousins, who felt the burly chieftain's firm embrace. Then they shook hands.

"This is my colleague John Cousins, from England," Selby explained. "He will be working with me and with our friend Salim on the Black Mountain. And I trust him completely."

It was all the explanation required.

It was not the first time Cousins had seen the Afghan. Salim Shah had come to the house on the hill for meetings with Selby and the two men had been introduced. The Afghan had been all smiles. He was clean-shaven but wore traditional *Shalwar Kameez* and an Afghan hat. He seemed sincere enough. And his team was experienced in working with the tribal structure. He could deliver the aid in partnership with the Western organisation as its implementing partner on the ground. More importantly, he knew how to secure the necessary agreements with the tribes.

The group followed Khan to a small stone house in the centre of the village, clearly showing signs of damage from the earthquake. The following entourage were bristling with arms. Cousins had never seen anything like it. Yet he did not feel unsafe. Quite the contrary. He'd never felt safer. And at every turn curious children peeped from behind the blankets draping doorways or from the safety of an open window.

Selby took a keen interest in the weaponry, talking with one of the armed tribesmen as they walked, who offered up his weapon for the Canadian to examine. He tried to explain he was a fellow warrior. The rifle was an old Enfield .303 that must have been sixty years old. Yet it was still a weapon prized by the tribesmen for its outstanding range and accuracy. It had probably come into the possession of the tribesmen from the British.

At the doorway they paused, and Khan invited the visitors to enter. Inside there were rugs and cushions on the floor, and they were asked to sit and join those already seated within a circle to talk. They were the elders of the tribe.

Khan and the mullah followed the outsiders in, trailed by other senior members of the village. The Afghan would translate. Khan explained the people of the mountain lived their own lives, as they had done for centuries. He confirmed no outside intervention had been known since the time the British came marching into the area to suppress its people. And they had shunned outside intervention since then.

It was clear from the outset the people would welcome aid if their customs were observed. Already there was trust. And Khan said his people realised their need was great. It was why they had reached out beyond their borders. It was the worst disaster in living memory. It was not only the scale of the earthquake, which had caused so much devastation. It was the timing: just after harvest. Their winter provisions had perished also. He also talked of the trust that had developed between the Westerner, whom he described as a warrior and a brother. His determination to meet and listen had gained respect, when others had turned their backs on the people of Kala Dhaka.

Selby seemed genuinely moved by the tributes that were paid to him. Yet to him, helping the people of the mountain was the obvious thing to do. He was also fascinated by the region's history. It was an honour to be invited to the Black Mountain which he had heard so much about, he told the elders. He would respect their customs and give them the tools to rebuild their communities. His organisation was not interested in the region's politics or changing the lives as they had lived them for centuries. That was all.

The village elders listened and watched intently. Selby told them he already had what they needed in his warehouses. He suggested a priority distribution could take place for those in most desperate need. The Afghan's team had already identified 2,000 people among the Hassanzai tribe from its assessments in the area who needed urgent aid. Kotkhay, which lay on the road running along the valley in the south, was suggested as a distribution point. It was easily accessible for the trucks which would be required. It could serve as a test. But security would need to be guaranteed by all the tribes of Kala Dhaka. The other tribes would be required to allow the aid convoy to pass through their lands in the knowledge that they themselves would have to wait.

The assembled elders nodded. They felt it was possible, though there were still concerns across the mountain. They would need a personal guarantee from Selby that all the tribes would eventually receive an appropriate share, according to need. And that included the Madakhel tribe, whose people lay across the River Indus on the west bank. A troublesome, restless people, Khan had said. As were the Nusrat Khel. And yet he felt an agreement could be reached. There was just one more thing. The support of the mullahs was required.

The mullah with the full beard and headdress rose to address the group. Not a sound could be heard within the stone house as he stood and drew breath, his brow knitted in thought. He had listened to the discussions. He could not explain why his people had been overcome by catastrophe. Who could question that which is written, the holy man said, which was Allah's will? But he felt there was purpose to the coming of the Westerners in their hour of need. He saw there was goodness and sincerity in those who had come from outside. Allah be praised. But he told the elders the mosques were destroyed. They had to be rebuilt.

Selby listened and nodded as the Afghan translated his words. Others nodded too. Therefore the mullah felt, as others did, that a priority had to be given to reconstructing the mountain's places of worship. Additional CGI sheets and other materials would be required for this purpose. Such was the condition for access to Kala Dhaka, which would allow acceptance by the people with God's blessing.

It was no surprise to Selby. The Afghan had forewarned him and he had already considered. He felt it was possible to build in an additional quota of materials to ensure the backing of the mullahs who were such a key element within the region's power structure. And he knew the importance faith held in the lives of those across the mountain. Religion lay at the centre of their lives. Therefore he nodded as the mullah's words were relayed to him. Yet he was reluctant to give a firm commitment.

When he spoke, he assured the elders he had listened. He understood their reservations and their conditions. He was supportive of the reconstruction of the mosques, which he knew provided a central community resource in every village and was important to their faith. He would have to confer and seek approval from his chiefs. Yet he felt this could be obtained and he would provide an answer in the immediate days ahead. But he would require assurances that the people would accept aid and a distribution to the most needy, as the Afghan's assessments had identified. And he would need a concrete assurance of safety and security from every tribe. In addition, he told them it was a requirement that the distribution be recorded by the Afghan's men, who would work alongside Pathans embedded from Relief Action. And finally, he asked for permission to tell the outside world that his people and the people of the mountain would work as one.

It was Khan who stood again to address the group. He thanked Selby and his people. There was support across the mountain for help at this dark time, if it was Allah's will. He felt a first distribution to the neediest would serve to support the urgency of those who had been hardest hit and to test the will of the other tribes. He would personally speak in support of the outside intervention with other chieftains. The tribes would confer and the *Loya Jirga* give its answer. Then he thanked the visitors for attending the meeting. They would take refreshment.

And with that chai was served, with an assortment of finger foods, which included chicken, rice and daal, and other local pastries neither Selby or Cousins were familiar with.

The Englishman had sat and observed proceedings. He was a little in awe of the occasion. Overwhelmed. He couldn't quite believe he sat in a remote mountain village in the Himalayas in the company of tribal elders. Armed gunmen were outside. His senses had been bombarded by new experiences as he had sat, watched and listened. He was fascinated by their local dress. Never had he seen such a varied collection of headgear. And when they spoke their alien language flowed over him. Its tones sounded harsh and unfamiliar. He had not been able to catch much of the translation by the Afghan. But from the body language he observed he felt the meeting had been a success. His immediate focus now was on the food which he had been presented with. And he remembered what Selby had told him. He was to eat with his right hand only, or risk insulting their hosts.

After they had eaten the mullah prepared to pray. The elders held their open hands out in front of them as the holy man recited his prayers to Allah, offering his blessings for the coming of the visitors and their safe trek back into the valley below. Following the *'Ameen'* Selby stood and offered his thanks for the hospitality of the village and signalled to Cousins the meeting was over. Outside they were embraced by Khan. The Afghan would stay to discuss further details about a possible first distribution with the tribal chieftain.

When Suur Gul emerged from the stone house he stood at a distance and watched the visitors as the small group escorted by the gunmen disappeared over the ridge and out of sight. He felt the visit was highly significant, and that he himself and Karim might yet play a part in events that were still to unfold. He felt he could work with Selby and the Englishman, and that the prayers for his people had been answered. He had a strong sense their destinies were entwined.

As they began their descent Selby told his English companion he felt the meeting had been highly positive. He had been expecting a request for materials to help rebuild the mosques. It was a condition that had to be met to pacify the mullahs who were so influential within the region. The village of Tilli lay at the heart of Kala Dhaka and was home to the Black Mountain Syeds, he explained, a small sub-clan said to be direct descendants of the Holy Prophet Mohammed.

Its elders would carry considerable influence with the people of Kala Dhaka. It was the first time Selby felt sure the full distribution would now go ahead.

SEVENTEEN

Keith Bailey sat at his desk and read through the report. Bailey was the senior man in Islamabad for the UK's Department for International Development. He leaned back in his chair, rubbed a hand over the stubble on his chin and grimaced as the rain spattered against his office window. In the courtyard below large brown puddles were forming, dimpled by the persistent downpour.

He closed the buff folder on his desk and sighed. It was a good day, despite the miserable weather outside. Not least of all because he had managed to obtain the pork sausages he had been craving from the High Commission canteen staff. And his driver was on his way to pick them up. The British government was briefed on the situation in Kala Dhaka. The small tribal area had been the subject of concern for some time. A line had to be drawn against the advancing militancy edging ever closer to the capital. The earthquake therefore presented an opportunity for intervention.

Although the British powers in Pakistan felt unable to offer direct support on the ground, they were keen to stabilise the region by other means. And that's where Bailey came in. He was aware of the activity in Kala Dhaka and the challenge it posed; he had heard the area had been severely affected by the disaster and about the NGO which had drawn fire on its attempt to enter. News had also reached him of an unprecedented approach by tribal elders for assistance from Relief Action. And Selby was a known name to the British.

Bailey was aware the Americans were watching too and had their informants on the ground. Both governments had an interest to keep the Taliban out. Yet they had to maintain an 'understanding of cooperation' with the Government of Pakistan. It was a delicate balance, which sometimes impacted aid and development decisions. It came with the territory. That was the nature of the region's politics.

Yet Bailey knew just the man to approach. Jim Maddison had more than five years in Pakistan. Before that he had worked with agencies in Bangladesh and Sub-Saharan Africa. He had his own network of contacts in-country of those with power and influence, which extended to the upper echelons of the Pakistani government. Maddison was the head of Relief Action in Pakistan.

Ultimately the final decision would need to be endorsed by the Foreign Office. There were 'wheels within wheels', which Bailey knew were already turning. He was a veteran of overseas aid and development. And Pakistan was a hive of intrigue.

The cell phone on his desk sounded with a shrill ring and he lifted it to his ear. A Pakistani voice informed him an urgent package had just been delivered by his driver. Would he like it sent up to his office? The sausages had arrived.

"Splendid. Yes, if you would, please." His voice was clear and betrayed a hint of the privileged education he had received in a respectable public school somewhere in the home counties. "*Shukria,*" he added in the same, clipped English accent. Then he dialled out Maddison's number on the phone…

Meanwhile, somewhere within the machinery of US government – a department tediously named the Bureau for International Narcotics and Law Enforcement Affairs, otherwise known as the INL – Kala Dhaka had been identified by those with an interest in Pakistan as a key area for action. The points of focus on the mountain were not unlike those of the British. The Pakistani government's agenda was less clear, although the policy it presented to the Americans was one of cooperation. After all, it was fighting militancy too. And there were potentially millions of dollars which might be made available.

The big concern for the Bureau was the opium poppy. It was no secret that Pakistan was a major player in the trafficking of opium, heroin and morphine, which yielded millions of dollars to the syndicates operating within the country, from the tribal areas of the north-west to the sprawling port metropolis of Karachi on the Arabian Sea.

The north-west was an integral part of the region known in the trade as the 'Golden Crescent' which embraced the mountainous areas of Afghanistan, Iran and Pakistan. Afghanistan lay undisputed at the Crescent's centre as the world's largest producer of opium, while the lawless 1,000-mile Pakistani border with its neighbour provided many unmonitored routes across a line on the map which divided the two nations. It was, in truth, no more than that. Also of concern were suspicions that increasing acres of farmland were coming under opium poppy cultivation within the tribal areas of Pakistan. The crop was easy to grow, even in poor soil. It yielded lucrative rewards for all involved, not least the desperately poor farmers in the mountains. And Kala Dhaka had its poppy fields too.

There were two things about the Black Mountain which particularly disturbed the Bureau. The first was its proximity to Islamabad. It lay just eighty miles from the federal capital. It was closer still to the Pakistani garrison town of Abbottabad, with its army officer training centre, the Pakistan Military Academy.

The second were reported incursions into the area by militants driven from the neighbouring areas of Swat and Buner to the north and to the west.

The decisive factor for the Americans, however, was the growing body of intelligence that suggested the opium trade was being controlled by militants and was now funding the Taliban and al-Qaeda. The US government's approach to Kala Dhaka, therefore, was through its international drugs and narcotics agency, which in turn was aligned to its 'War on Terror' policy.

The idea was to 'invest' millions of dollars to help develop the Black Mountain area, offering incentives to its tribes through infrastructure improvement and direct cash compensation for its farmers to forsake the opium poppy. Tribal chieftains would be 'encouraged' to repel incursions by radical elements. The plan came to be known as the Kala Dhaka Area Development Project, officially a cooperation between the US government, the Government of Pakistan and the regional government of North-West Frontier Province. The earthquake would allow an acceleration of the strategy.

Faceless bureaucrats in Washington worked with agents from the INL and CIA attached to the US mission which lay within the embassy deep inside Islamabad's fortified diplomatic enclave. They in turn ran a network of local operatives and informants across Pakistan. The Bureau also had its 'eyes and ears' on the ground in Kala Dhaka. Their man on the mountain would be above suspicion or reproach. He was an established landowner, or khan who like his father and his father before him was part of the ruling elite.

Known only as 'Z', he reported directly to the Americans in return for regular cash deposits made to 'untraceable' overseas bank accounts which lay beyond the reach of the Pakistani authorities. As a Pathan he held no loyalty to Pakistan, which generally considered his people inferior degenerates, living a lawless existence in the frontier region.

He had nothing but contempt for the federal government in Islamabad, who viewed them as untrustworthy bandits and thieves. And he despised the army, the real power in Pakistan and all its apparatus, including its formidable secret service, the Inter-Services Intelligence agency. To him it all seemed covertly corrupt. Hypocritical. Like so much in Pakistan.

And he liked to quote verses from Holy Qur'an, dropping them almost absently into conversation. Often they would exalt Allah, the all-seeing, all-knowing. As a child he had excelled in religious studies and had been able to recite entire Surahs by heart. Beautifully. In reality he felt forsaken by his family, his country and his religion. 'Z' was gay. 'He knows all that you keep secret as well as all that you bring into the open: for God has full knowledge of what lies in the hearts (of men)', drawing an obligatory *Ameen*'. The irony was not lost on him. And he would smile to himself, his eyes hidden beneath the dark sunglasses for which he had a fondness.

It was another reason he was attracted to the Western way which allowed the open pursuit of personal indulgence which had to be so carefully concealed within his own country. Including his own sexuality. His religion, therefore, one might say, was essentially one of self-interest and yet he liked to think of himself as an enlightened individual, cleverer than most. It gave him pleasure to know things that others did not. Including the aspects of his own life he kept hidden. It gave him a sense of superiority. Of control. Of satisfaction. And he would smile.

He therefore enjoyed leading the double life and all the rewards it brought. In short, it seemed the best of both worlds. On the one hand, he was a privileged local khan who followed the Pathan traditions of the north-west; a respected custodian of the lands and traditions of his people. On the other, he was a man of unprecedented means, particularly whenever he travelled overseas, able to fully act out the lifestyle he wished. Besides, he liked the idea of being an agent. A spy. It was a charade, as much of his life was, which allowed him to play out his fantasies. What he didn't know was that Pakistani intelligence also had its sights on Kala Dhaka.

In Islamabad, Jim Maddison had a reputation as an informed, relaxed and competent 'pair of hands'. He was not a man to put himself under stress. He liked to pace himself and had a taste for the finer things in life, evident from an expanded waistline. They included good food and drink, a young wife from Eritrea, and a wide circle of friends. His home, in a fashionable part of the capital, was a three-storey villa with extensive gardens. It came with the job. And there were servants too. It was a life far removed from rural Virginia where he had been raised.

Work in Pakistan had been steady, almost tranquil when first he'd taken up his post. Certainly compared to Afghanistan. He did what was necessary to be considered effective. In truth, he felt contented. His post in Pakistan was undemanding. Fulfilling, even, in that he was able to implement long-term development programmes that sought to promote education opportunities almost at leisure.

Others focused on health and hygiene issues, and child nutrition. He had no children of his own. It was perhaps the one great sadness in his life.

Balding, greying and middle-aged, he was seen as an easy-going veteran of the international aid and development community. A quiet American. And he was. He held no desire to attract attention.

The former art historian had travelled and seen life. He held no strong notions of patriotism. He was, in a sense, stateless. International. He had lived in Pakistan long enough to feel comfortable. And he embraced the local culture. It was true, aspects of Pakistani life were restrictive. But his privileged position brought freedoms too. Which is why he had stayed in Pakistan. Yet suddenly things had changed. The earthquake had seen his operation effectively double, swept into an emergency response.

There was now an unrelenting sense of urgency with which he was not entirely comfortable. He was therefore pleased to have Selby onboard to head the emergency side of the operation up in Mansehra and direct from his office in the capital. Besides, there were longstanding educational programmes in the Punjab which had to be maintained.

As the grey skies slipped into dusk almost unnoticed, Maddison sat in his drawing room with a cup of coffee, gazing absently at the artworks which decorated its walls, reflecting on the earlier phone call he had received. It had taken him by surprise. He knew Bailey was part of the British government's aid programme in Pakistan. They had met several times casually. Foreign aid and development workers in Islamabad were part of a small community. International agencies working in Pakistan pre-earthquake had been relatively low in number. Sooner or later everyone was likely to meet at the usual haunts: trendy art galleries, the clubs within the diplomatic enclave, the upmarket restaurants. Or perhaps at the UN club on Kohsar Road.

Would he like to meet for lunch, the Englishman asked? There was a matter he would like to discuss. No, not at the British Club in the enclave. Did he know Kuch Khaas? Maddison knew the place, just off the Margalla Road facing the hills. Within the security of its walled enclosure the café had become a magnet for international staff to meet for coffee and a bite to eat within its gardens, untroubled by the hustle and bustle of everyday Pakistani life beyond its boundaries. The meeting was set for 1pm the next day. Maddison was intrigued. A strange rush of excitement ran through him. He had a sense the meeting would be significant. Besides, he knew enough about the business to know the subject of their meeting was likely to be of some importance.

It was not every day the head of a major government development agency extended an invitation for lunch. But there had been no mention of Kala Dhaka. Yet Bailey had a clear agenda. He would outline the reports his people had of the destruction to the area.

He would suggest, unofficially, of course, that if Relief Action held an interest in assisting the people of Kala Dhaka a proposal for funding might be considered. The department and the Hong Kong government had cash to contribute to the emergency response. That was as much as he was able to say. The rest would depend on Maddison. Bailey wasn't sure how the American might respond, but he hoped he would embrace the initiative. It was, in effect, an invitation from the British government to submit a proposal for cash to fund a multi-million-dollar aid programme within the isolated tribal area. But these were strange times in Pakistan…

EIGHTEEN

Severe blizzards swept down from the Northern Areas that second week in January, covering the stricken settlement of Manda Gucha in three feet of snow in as many days. The high-altitude community had been one of the first to receive emergency aid from Selby's team. Resting at the base of the Musa ka Musala mountain, which rises dramatically above the Siran and Kaghan valleys to 13,300 feet, it was also the most remote. Now the ramshackle collection of broken buildings, shacks and tents lay under a thick blanket of snow, isolated once more and exposed to the severity of the Himalayan winter, cut off from the world beyond. Its only lifeline would now be supplies flown into the mountains by helicopter, if the snowfall relented.

Operating under the umbrella of the World Food Programme, twenty-four helicopters flew a constant stream of missions into the earthquake zone, daylight hours and weather permitting, in what was to become the UN's largest-ever humanitarian air operation. The United Nations Humanitarian

Air Service had agreed to fly four metric tonnes of aid into the remote area if the skies remained clear, and Cousins had made his way from Mansehra the previous evening back to the federal capital to pick up the flight at Selby's suggestion. The Canadian was keen for him to accompany his team on the aerial mission so that he could report first-hand from the extreme limits of the emergency operation which was still ongoing.

Cousins arrived at the airstrip to find Farzad, the Iranian, and two Pakistani monitors from the team checking off the boxes of items as they were being loaded.

They would accompany the mission to ensure the distribution on the ground was monitored and recorded, and that the families identified from the surrounding hamlets would receive the items to help keep them alive.

"Weather is good," smiled the Iranian, pausing to draw heavily from the cool morning air as Cousins approached. "We move soon before snow. Should be OK, *insh'Allah*," he added. And he gestured for the journalist to climb aboard.

As soon as they were fully loaded the twin turbines hummed into life, rising to a whine. The whirring of the rotor blades accelerated and the Mi8 transport lifted slowly from the tarmac, turning sharply to head due north. Moments later it had cleared the Margalla Hills, cutting a path through the grey sky over snow-capped peaks which lay like a crumpled white blanket below, its epic folds rising from the landscape as far as the eye could see.

Less than forty minutes later the helicopter was dropping into the Siran Valley to make its final approach to Manda Gucha on the slopes immediately ahead. It hovered briefly over the makeshift landing strip before the machine sank to touch down, sending a flurry of snow on the ground in all directions towards the villagers already gathered below in desperate anticipation.

The assortment of crates, boxes and sacks were hastily unloaded and stacked, aided by the helicopter's pilot, co-pilot and flight engineer, watched by those who waited in the biting cold to pick up what might keep their families warm in the sub-zero temperature holding the valley in its icy grip. As dark clouds gathered on the horizon, no-one knew when more snow might fall, and the team worked with a sense of urgency.

Cousins too lent a hand, noting among the consignment of food kits sacks of children's winter jackets from Korea and other padded clothing from Australia, including hats and gloves. But there were boxes of tarpaulins too. Many families were living in canvas tents that were not winterised and the tarpaulins would allow the snow to slide from them and prevent the canopies from collapsing under the weight, the Iranian explained.

As the distribution began, the throng of villagers had to be strictly, sometimes forcibly, held back as each man offered up his thumbprint in exchange for his family's entitlement. The women kept largely out of sight, as was their custom in the presence of outsiders.

Cousins watched and took a selection of photographs, then walked across the snow to approach a group of young men wrapped within their blankets against the cold, standing among the nearby tents. He was from England, he explained.

"A Britisher!" they established, smiling, and one of the men was sent to fetch a relative who spoke the language. There was always someone.

The man, when he arrived, introduced himself as Sharafat and embraced Cousins as a brother. He was very fond of the British and had worked for them many years ago as a driver in the days when he lived in Lahore. "Very, very good peoples," he said.

The mountain communities had suffered considerable devastation, he explained, leading the journalist through the snow-bound settlement, passing families huddled among the ruins of their homes over open fires, or stoves to keep warm.

And he would catch a glimpse of a bangled wrist extending from an all-encompassing shawl wrapped around a mother, or attract the gaze from the curious dark eyes of a child through an open tent flap as he passed. The air was heavy with the pungent reek of kerosene and the sickly odour of unwashed bodies. Some shared their dwellings with their animals, and Cousins wondered how families coped with basic hygiene.

Three tiny, snow-covered mounds on the edge of the village were a poignant reminder of the scale of loss suffered in the earthquake. Here lay the children of one family. There had been no warning that October morning. The violent shuddering of the earth was accompanied by a loud crash as the family home was shaken to destruction and the roof fell in. The mother and father dug their children from the rubble with bleeding hands and laid them to rest according to their custom the same day, close to where they had lived out their short lives. It was one of many similar stories, whose terrible echo was heard in hundreds of villages just like Manda Gucha scattered across the mountain ranges of the north-west.

Sharafat, a father of six, had also lost a child. "Some of my childrens were at school; some in home, spreading grain to dry when earthquake came. Our one-year-old son, Hamza, died when house was destroyed." The tragedy was told simply.

Then a look of despair filled his eyes as he recalled that terrible moment, the creases in his dark, weather-beaten skin deepened as he grimaced in sadness. Also lost in the earthquake were his livestock, crushed as the cattle shed caved in.

"We have lost everything," he said. "There is nothing for our livelihood, our home is gone and these are very hard times." Cousins felt his pain and instinctively put a hand on the burley villager's shoulder.

For days following the disaster the village stood isolated and alone before the first assistance came. The ferocity of the earthquake had shaken bridges and sections of the road into the valleys below. Other parts were blocked by landslide.

The Pakistan Army worked day and night to clear and repair the single track which hugs the valley under the shadow of the ragged mountains, winding its way towards the remote communities among the towering landscape of brutal beauty.

One of the first international aid organisations into the area was Selby's team from Relief Action, establishing a distribution point at Manda Gucha for 500 families within a ten-mile radius with the help of the Pakistan Army. Food and non-food items were distributed three or four times a week by trucks and Jeeps, weather permitting, at nine sites across the area.

Items included food, bedding, corrugated metal sheets and wood received with grateful hands to reinforce temporary shelters against the harsh winter in prospect. The villagers were not accustomed to charity. But they needed the means to survive and the tools to rebuild their community. Later Selby told Cousins the organisation had provided more than 2,000 families across the earthquake zone with winterised tents, cooking sets, blankets and tarpaulins. The cold was being tackled by 5,500 kerosene heaters in the tented camps and 42,500 people had been supplied with food. And yet more was needed.

Sharafat's family lived in a single room of what remained of their home on the mountainside overlooking the road, about a mile from Manda Gucha, shored up with wood and corrugated metal sheeting. Temperatures plummeted below zero at night. There was no electricity, water or heating except for the kerosene stove provided.

"We wrap ourselves in quilts and blankets and keep each other warm," he said. The food rations were not sufficient, but enough on which to survive, he added.

Three months on from the disaster the community was clearly still grieving. And yet a new danger threatened with the arrival of the extreme cold and heavy snowfall, adding to the misery of the families whose lives had been shattered by the earthquake. Further snow might come at any time until March to isolate the stricken mountain communities, severing access by road for weeks, or even months at a time.

Sharafat told Cousins the bitter winter the previous year had seen a snowfall of twenty feet in the region and temperatures regularly fall below minus twenty degrees Celsius.

This time an entire people were exposed; the earthquake had left more than three million without adequate shelter, taken away their grain supplies and livestock, and left them teetering on the very edge of survival. It was almost impossible to grasp.

When Cousins returned to the distribution point, he had drawn a small posse of curious villagers following in his wake. He watched the last families receive their aid items and carry them off to their homes. The flight crew was growing impatient with the darkening of the skies. As they boarded the helicopter and prepared to lift off, it seemed the whole village assembled to wish them well. Invitations to join families for chai had been extended, but there was no time. Most villagers had never seen a white face, the Iranian explained, and were excited he had visited.

It seemed to Cousins being British was a passport to instant warmth and acceptance here. To the people of Manda

Gucha it was a sign that the outside world was aware of their plight and cared.

"We are so happy you have come to see what is happening here. So very grateful to the English peoples and we are feeling that the world cares about our childrens. *Shukria!* Thank you, thank you," Sharafat had told Cousins, embracing him.

The humility and simplicity of the people was moving. And Cousins felt a deep sadness. While he was able to return to the comfort of Islamabad, little more than half an hour's flying time to the south, he felt it was a world away from the hardship he had witnessed.

After the helicopter touched down in the capital, he declined the offer to go into the city to eat with the distribution team. Instead he asked to be dropped at the Relief Action office which lay in the affluent suburb close to the diplomatic area. He felt he needed some time to process the trip by helicopter into the mountains. Besides, he wanted to begin his report for the newspaper before the scheduled drive back to Mansehra later that afternoon. His time in Pakistan was coming to an end.

When his driver arrived and he climbed into the Land Cruiser, he was tired. Another three or four hours back into the earthquake zone along a road choked with traffic was in prospect. He threw his bag into the vehicle and slumped onto the back seat. He would try to sleep the time away. Besides, perhaps better not to see the hair-raising risks in overtaking the slow-moving trucks rumbling north on impossible roads winding their way into the mountains which were an inevitable part of the journey. He let the regular beeping of horns and cursing of the driver flow over him.

When finally the vehicle rolled up at the team house on the hill in Mansehra it was already dark.

Williams and Selby were sitting in the lounge, watching a DVD on the television. Box sets could be cheaply obtained from the capital for just a few hundred rupees and were a welcome distraction during the long evenings so often confined inside. The two men were halfway through three seasons of *Star Trek*.

"How was it?" asked the Canadian.

"It's a lot to take in," Cousins replied.

"Come and join us," Williams offered. "Or there's coffee on the stove," he added.

"Coffee sounds good," and with that he headed to the kitchen area.

Selby came to join him as he sat at the table reading through his notes. "You all right? Get what you needed?"

Cousins nodded. "It's quite overwhelming, though," said the journalist.

"It is," the Canadian agreed. "But the people of Manda Gucha are the lucky ones. Some mountain communities still haven't been reached. It's a logistical nightmare. Already some areas have four or five feet of snow," he explained.

"It's a new experience for me," conceded Cousins. "But I admire the people. I find their courage..." he struggled to find the right words, "...their resilience, their warmth inspiring."

"Me too. Sometimes it's bloody tough to see," Selby replied. "But I think it's probably the most rewarding work I've ever done."

"Hair-raising, too," said Cousins. "That driver of yours. Bloody mad!"

"Rahim, the mountain man? He's a good guy."

"Crazy driving! Kept yelling '*Ghada ka bacha*', or something."

"Crazy helps here!" Selby replied as a matter of fact. "*Ghada ka bacha*," he stated flatly. Then he laughed adding, "I wouldn't repeat that in the mountains. Means 'son of a donkey'. They'd fucking shoot you!"

He drew a deep breath before continuing, "John… I'm bloody glad you're here. I really am. And I like the way you work." Then he paused. "Look, I've been thinking… we need someone out here; you know, a comms guy."

Then, gazing directly at Cousins, he added "Would you come back… to work with me? If I offered you a contract. We have a story to tell here. The Black Mountain, I mean."

The offer took the Englishman by surprise. And yet there was no doubt in his mind. He had to return. His reply, therefore, was almost immediate. "Yes, yes, I would. Thank you!"

"Bloody brilliant!" grinned Selby. "I'll work out a contract."

And the two men smiled at each other.

The Canadian rose from his chair. "See you in the morning, John. Best get some rest. You look dead beat."

And he left Cousins to his thoughts.

The journalist could scarcely believe the offer he had just received.

What he had seen and experienced in the mountains had affected him deeply. It put his own problems back home in perspective. He felt moved and inspired. And he felt a return to Pakistan would add a sense of purpose to his life. It was an opportunity do some good. It was an adventure; a dream. And he had not known those feelings for a long time.

Later, as he sat on the edge of his bed in candlelight gazing into the orange glow from the gas fire, Cousins reflected on the people he had seen that day and the harshness of their lives. It was extreme. He thought about Sharafat. He would be sleeping within the ruins of his home on the rocky outcrop above the road in sub-zero temperatures, huddled with the members of his family for warmth against the cold, hoping all of them would wake to see another day dawn. As Cousins slipped beneath the sheets and sank into the relative comfort of his mattress, in Manda Gucha the snow began to fall once more upon the tiny graves on the edge of the village.

NINETEEN

It was with a strange mixture of sadness and relief that Cousins arrived for the early flight back to London. He embraced the driver, Rahim, and promised he would return. The mountain man gazed directly into his eyes and smiled warmly. Then they shook hands and he watched the Englishman disappear into the throng of people gathered around the departure building. Cousins was happy to be on his way home and yet he had seen things that had made a profound impact on him. Thousands of desperately poor people in the earthquake zone still faced severe hardship. He had seen with his own eyes the harshness of their lives. He had felt their pain. Now he was leaving. Later that day he would be landing at Heathrow.

Check-in was a bustle of frustrated activity.

Islamabad had a reputation as one of the worst airports in the world, where lines of overladen passengers with excess baggage snaked through the terminal all the way back to the entrance. Never had he seen so much additional luggage. Families with taped cardboard boxes stacked precariously on trolleys, sometimes with small children riding on top. Some were forced to unpack their cargo at security by officials who would discretely offer to forego the inconvenience for a cash payment. For others there was panic and confusion after being pulled from the line by an official to fill out last-minute documentation. It was organised chaos.

He was one of a handful of white passengers conspicuously apparent in a sea of brown faces. And he had waited patiently, growing increasingly agitated by the number of people trying to push ahead at every opportunity. There seemed no concept of waiting in line. It was every man, woman and child for themselves. A smartly dressed European woman clutching a UN pass had strolled confidently to the front of the line, with an air of authority. It was the last straw.

"There's a queue here, lady," Cousins called out.

"Grow up," she had replied dismissively, barely glancing behind her. And she carried on regardless, held up her ID card to an official and disappeared through passport control.

When finally he was aboard the aircraft he breathed a heavy sigh. He lifted his hand luggage and slid it into the overhead locker, then sank into his seat. Of course he was looking forward to seeing his family. His mother; his children. And his friends.

The gleaming white Boeing 777, with a ribbon of red and blue livery, taxied out onto the runway, then paused before accelerating and lifting off into the clear January sky.

A long, dreary flight lay ahead. Cousins was grateful he had the aisle to himself, as the aircraft hummed along on its steady course, cruising north-west at 34,000 feet towards the life he had left behind less than two weeks ago. He kicked off his shoes and leaned back into the seat, his head filled with images of Pakistan as he drifted in and out of sleep. It would be early afternoon local time before they would land.

After almost eight hours in the air, which included a breakfast, a lunch and several beverages, the aircraft began its slow descent towards London, and a sense of excitement rose within him as it dropped beneath the clouds and he caught his first glimpse of the sprawling capital below. The wing flaps lifted to slow the aircraft as it juddered, then swept towards its final approach. He closed his eyes and whispered a silent prayer. Minutes later he felt the comforting jolt of the aircraft as the wheels hit the runway and sighed.

He gazed out at the flat buildings still rushing past the window under a grey sky. But he was smiling, relieved to be back on British soil.

Queuing at passport control, the UK border official raised an eyebrow as he flicked through Cousins' passport and came to the Pakistani visa. But he said nothing.

He handed the document back. "Welcome home, Sir."

"Thank you," smiled Cousins. "It's good to be back."

He made his way to baggage reclaim with only one thought. He was desperate for a smoke. Inside the baggage hall he headed for the toilets, entered a cubicle and lit up. He was past caring whether he would be discovered. After a few puffs he flushed the butt down the toilet and went to the basins to freshen up. He caught sight of himself in the mirror. He looked tired and dishevelled, his face carrying three days of beard growth. There were dark rings beneath his eyes and his hair was a mess. And yet he felt he had good reason to feel jaded; there was a justification in his scruffiness. They had been long, tiring days in Pakistan, physically and emotionally draining, his senses bombarded by new experience. The long flight hadn't helped. He'd only been able to grab snatches of restless sleep. While he waited for his bag he reached for his mobile phone and dialled out his mother's number.

"Yeah, landed safely. Just waiting for my bag, Mum."

Expressions of relief were uttered on the other end of the line.

His mother was a worrier with an inclination for drama. But she was assured he was back safely.

He'd still have to take the Tube into the capital and then buy a rail ticket for the train back to the Midlands. He should be home early evening. The luggage carousel jolted into motion, sparking a surge forward in those hoping to spot their bags and make their getaway, and moments later the random assortment of baggage flowed into view. He held no high expectation of an early escape. His always seemed to be one of the last bags to emerge.

It was at St Pancras station that he finally decided to have his first cup of coffee. And that's when it really hit him. Christ! The cost of a cappuccino was more than most people earned for a day's hard labour in Pakistan. Still, it was good coffee. A line had to be drawn. He felt able to relax for the first time since leaving the UK. He sat watching idly the hundreds of people passing by. He was struck by their diversity. All nationalities, races, religions. It was so very different in Pakistan.

He was looking forward to seeing his children. He'd thought about them often while he had been away, and particularly whenever he had encountered children. He wanted to tell them about Pakistan.

But he didn't relish the thought of explaining he would be flying back again in a matter of days. In fact, he wasn't sure what to say to them. The boys would understand more. Yet

Holli was still so very young. And she was very close to her father. He was saddened that he only saw them every other weekend.

By the time the train rolled into Leicester station it was getting dark. And still there was a bus to catch. He finally arrived at his flat exhausted but was glad to be in familiar surroundings. It felt good to be home. He'd left the place tidier than he remembered.

He made himself a cup of coffee and sat smoking at the kitchen table, taking in the comforting feeling of being back. Then he sent several text messages on his mobile phone. He'd be seeing everyone on the days ahead, including his mother…

"But what are you going to tell the children?" The elderly woman looked at him enquiringly. Anxiously. "There's poverty and need here," she continued. "Why on earth do you have to travel back to Pakistan, of all places?"

Cousins looked away from his mother and stared at his hands. "It's something I have to do," he stated simply.

"But why?" she insisted.

"I suppose I feel I can make a difference," he said, looking up.

It would be futile to explain further. He'd tried. And she knew her son well enough to know that he wasn't going to change his mind. But she was worried about him. Was always worried about him.

"I don't know why you can't just stay with your job at the newspaper. It's steady, isn't it?"

He nodded. "Yes, it's steady." And he paused. "But I have seen things out there, Mum. It's heartbreaking…"

"I just hope you know what you're doing," she interrupted. She didn't seem to hear. Perhaps she didn't want to. He had felt empty, unfulfilled, since the breakdown of his marriage. And he was hurting. It was as though he had a huge need to fill. Besides, how could she understand how he had been affected by what he had seen in Pakistan? It was a different world which had to be experienced to be understood. But she loved him, even though she sometimes considered him reckless. It was the same with the marriage to Sarah. She didn't really understand. Yet she would always be there for him. And that was enough.

"Are you ready for your soup now?" she asked.

He nodded. "Thanks, Mum."

He had not yet seen his children since returning. It had been arranged for tomorrow. He'd missed them terribly. He held his little girl and felt her arms tighten around him as he hugged her to him.

"I love you. So much," he told her.

"I love you too, Daddy." Then he felt her body shaking with emotion as she began to sob. And he too was overcome with emotion.

Holli was his youngest child, just turned eleven. She had always been Daddy's little girl. She did not understand why he had left her mother. It was something terrible, her mother had said. But she didn't believe it. He had been her inspiration for as long as she could remember; had always been there for her. Now he wasn't. Worse still, he was going back to Pakistan.

"It's OK," he assured her. "I'll be coming back every few weeks." He paused, searching for the right words. "It is something I have to do," he told her. Already he regretted mentioning he would be returning.

"But I don't want you to go away again," she repeated, tears rolling down her face.

"I know, sweetheart. But I have been offered this work to help very poor people."

"Mummy says we're poor now!" She looked at her father, tears slowly rolling down her face, a picture of misery.

"Listen," he said. "I'll be back every few weeks. It is just for a short time."

She pulled back to look at him. It was a face she trusted. She had always loved him. There must also be a reason Mummy and Daddy did not love each other anymore. In truth, she felt it was her mother's fault. Yet it was in a sense irrelevant to her. All she knew was that she still loved and missed her father desperately. And now he was going back to a country halfway across the world.

"You do trust me, don't you?" he asked her. Again she looked at him while she considered.

"Do you?" he repeated. And she slowly nodded.

"Come on," he said, lifting her from his lap. "Let's go shopping. I'll buy you something nice before I take you back to Mummy. OK?"

There was so much he wanted to tell her. It was the same with his boys. Aiden was eighteen, practically an adult. He seemed to understand. Besides, he already had a steady girlfriend and was planning to move into his own place soon. He had his own life now. His brother Tristan was three years younger. He was still angry with his father that he had moved out from the family home. Dad had failed them. It had hit them all hard. Family life had been good and Cousins had played an active part.

But what could he say? They were all too young to understand; were still hurt and confused and trying to make sense of the absence of their father at home. In short, their world had been shattered. He knew it but had seemed powerless to prevent it. The marriage was over several years previously. He and Sarah had both tried to make it work, until finally he could no longer go on.

Now his children had to contend with their father working overseas in a country they had barely heard of. There had been an earthquake. The boys grasped that much and could understand that people were in desperate need. But why did he have to go; why their dad? It wasn't just the work. He wanted to tell them his life was empty without them; that he missed them terribly. The emotional pain was almost impossible to bear. He wanted to say so many things.

He was no longer part of their everyday lives, marginalised by the fact that he simply wasn't at home anymore. That's what pained him most of all: he'd had to leave the family home. Sarah had insisted.

And it was that emptiness that was driving him to the extremes of humanitarian aid work. It was a distraction; a compensation to try to fill the huge emotional void he was feeling. Living so close to them and yet not being able to see the children who had been the centre of his universe.

Sure, he felt responsible for leaving the marriage; felt guilty, not least of all for becoming involved with another woman. But it did not mean he loved the children any less, or that he had not enjoyed family life. He wanted to tell them he was sorry for the way things had turned out. But he never did. Perhaps he was simply running away. And yet he felt he had to. It was a way to cope with the heartbreak and would offer a chance to heal.

He wasn't yet sure how he would handle his job at the newspaper. His immediate priority was to deliver the feature series he had promised. He felt he had some powerful photography and strong personal stories of hardship from families caught up in the disaster that would bring their tragedy alive in the minds of the newspaper's readers. Johnson would be pleased. But he didn't know how his editor would react to his imminent departure. He'd have to wait for the terms of his contract to be finalised by Selby in the days ahead. Perhaps it would all come to nothing.

TWENTY

THE PAIN OF hunger was etched onto the contorted, tear-streaked face of a child crying for food in an isolated village more than 6,000 feet up in the Himalayan foothills. The little girl's misery seemed to cut through the boundaries of language, culture and ancient taboos. It was the cry of acute human suffering which sounded with resonance across the world from her remote mountain settlement. It was a cry for help. Her village lay in the heart of Kala Dhaka, its borders barred to outsiders for centuries and almost untouched by modern life.

Here at the mountaintop community of Peer Khel, more than 700 men, women and children faced a desperate daily battle for survival. They had received no help since the earthquake in October shook their houses to destruction. Their homes gone, families huddled in the ruins of their village and in makeshift shelters against temperatures which fell to minus five degrees Celsius when the sun dipped below the surrounding peaks.

Their winter provisions destroyed and depleted, hunger was a companion to despair. There was no medicine to combat the ever-present threat of disease. It was one of hundreds of villages dotted at altitude across the Black Mountain, whose people had been overcome by the catastrophe that autumn morning. An estimated 1,000 died when the disaster struck. Yet nobody really knew how many had been lost, how many were injured or had since died on the mountain. No help had come. Nor had it been expected. Yet the people were now desperate with the onset of winter.

Haunted dark eyes gazed from smeared faces through tangled hair as children gathered to watch with curiosity the small group of outsiders who had trekked across the mountain passes to reach their village. The visitors included Cousins, the Iranian and the Afghan, who had crossed into their lands from Mansehra, less than forty miles to the south-east. Yet they might have been from another planet. It was a different world which lay within the tribal boundary.

Following months of delicate negotiations with village elders for access to this forbidden land of brutal beauty, a gateway from the outside had been opened on the promise of aid entering the region. They had agreed a further visit, this time including the Englishman. Independent, proud and deeply suspicious of outsiders, it had been decided the visitors would be given safe passage to come and see the level of destruction the people had suffered deeper and higher onto the mountain. An invitation had been extended and with it came a guarantee of security. And the tribes were honour-bound to keep their word.

On the small plateau near the top of the mountain, each member of the weary group which had climbed two hours from the Indus Valley below was warmly embraced by the village elders, even the Westerner sweating profusely and gasping for breath in the cool, thin air of the Himalayan heights.

There was an invitation to talk and take chai in the open air, framed against the surrounding mountain peaks, where the elders were willing to tell their story to the Westerner. To Cousins it seemed like sitting on top of the world...

Village elder Rehmat Said sat with a young boy huddled at his side, who stared at Cousins in wide-eyed wonder. The full-bearded tribesman wearing a flowing dark turban described the devastation the earthquake had on his home. He told Cousins his youngest grandson was killed when the family home collapsed. "Everything is destroyed or is buried under the ground. You can see and look at our situation. We have nothing, not even cups to drink water and have not received anything to help us."

And it was true. The area was a wasteland. Not a building stood unscathed. An assortment of materials served as makeshift cover within the rubble and broken stone walls as far as the eye could see.

"Most of the men walk for many hours to find work in the valley or beyond in some of the larger towns and are sending money to their families. But it is not enough and life is hard," Rehman Ezaar, another senior elder, told him, staring intently into the Westerner's eyes. "If we do not have help, more people will die." His gaze held the look of loss and despair which was prevalent in the people who clung to life on the mountain. He said the most desperate need was for shelter. But medicines were also needed for basic treatments to fight infection and flu which might easily lead to loss of life in those weakened by malnutrition and exposure. Tuberculosis was common within the community and leprosy was not unknown.

If Cousins had held any doubts, his trek from the valley below had vindicated his decision to return. Of that there was no doubt, as he sat under the grey sky with the elders, sipping the sweet chai. The climb had been steep and hard. The air was thin and his body ached as he had risen ever higher from the valley, carrying on his back a pack laden with an assortment of random supplies which had been hastily, desperately received by the group of villagers who had greeted them. The community needed help.

It was also clear the villagers would accept assistance from outside. What was also increasingly obvious to him was that the needs of the people he met were no different to those of human beings anywhere: shelter, food and the means to support loved ones.

They simply wanted assurances that their way of life and their customs would be respected; that access to their world would not be abused. They were not accustomed to intervention from beyond their immediate borders and were suspicious. But they were desperate too.

After the meeting Cousins stood for a few moments alone in contemplation, while the Afghan spoke with the elders. He would tell them aid would come in the days ahead. The Englishman gazed across the mountains which rose up to meet the horizon in all directions and adjusted the cotton scarf around his neck as the chilly breeze blew against his cheek. Far below he could see the Indus like a small shining ribbon cutting its course through the mountains. Soon they would be on their way back down into the valley.

Two days later, in the low morning sun, seven trucks laden with aid rolled slowly along the rocky road which followed the course of the river under the shadow of the mountain. The arrival of quilts, blankets, jackets, work tools, tarpaulins and building materials at the village of Kotkhay was celebrated by tribesmen with jubilant gunfire, cracking across the mountain peaks and echoing through the valleys. And yet the exuberance of the gunmen was in stark contrast to the scenes up in the mountains, where no aid had yet penetrated.

At Mansehra base camp Selby had scanned the map with furrowed brow, making final preparations in plotting the first, low-scale delivery of aid. He was reasonably confident his calculations were accurate. But he couldn't be fully certain. It was a chance he was willing to take. He'd travelled the road; had seen the village when he had met elders from the immediate villages for chai at the foot of the mountain. And when he had first visited the village of Peer Khel to see for himself the level of destruction across the high-altitude settlements.

But he had come in from the north that day by Land Cruiser before the first light had broken over the peaks of Kala Dhaka. And he could not be certain the route from the opposite direction was clear, or exactly how far Kotkhay lay from the south. He would have to rely on the hand-drawn map from 1891 which had accompanied Wylly's account of the Black Mountain military campaigns. Would the heavy trucks be able to negotiate the damaged road, strewn with potholes and boulders? And would the other tribes keep their word and allow the small convoy to pass through their territory? His intelligence on which to base his route for the first aid distribution was therefore limited. He had to trust the Afghan.

Driving through the thin red line Selby had marked onto the map was like crossing a time zone to a land almost untouched for centuries, as the mountain rose up before them and the road swept downwards towards the river. His vehicle rolled steadily along the winding, narrow road which led into the valley, which rose in stretches above the Indus, sheer rock rearing up on the driver's side, tyres sometimes inches from a steep drop into the river below.

A crowd of several hundred villagers had already gathered at Kotkhay, set on the banks overlooking the water. The small settlement lay within the region populated by the Hassanzai tribe. It had been one of the villages raised by the British some hundred years previously. The trucks had arrived escorted by the Afghan and his team an hour, or so beforehand. When Selby and Cousins rolled up, tailed by a second vehicle with Relief Action monitors, boxes of aid were already stacked at the roadside, guarded by the Afghan's men, who stood solemnly, rifles slung over their shoulders, waiting, watching.

The priority distribution to more than 2,000 people deemed to be in greatest need was set to begin. In effect, though, it was a trial; a test run. The success and guaranteed security of the operation would signal the start of a rolling programme of aid to tens of thousands of people from the mountain still in desperate need, including those in more remote villages at higher altitudes, like the small community at Peer Khel further north the Westerners had both seen. Selby knew other agencies would be watching too, waiting to gauge the outcome of this first Western foray into Kala Dhaka. And that might encourage additional support from a range of larger international actors in the weeks and months ahead.

But as yet, outside intervention was a delicate matter. Tensions were running high. Negotiations with the tribal leaders had been sensitive and had already taken more than six weeks. But the people were now increasingly desperate and willing to consider outside help. It was the first time the combined tribal councils, the *Loya Jirga*, had issued an invitation for Westerners to enter their lands in living memory.

The Afghan's men had identified 13,000 households across the mountain dangerously exposed and in need of immediate aid. With an average family numbering eight, that meant more than 100,000 beneficiaries, if Relief Action's programme went ahead. Selby had been surprised by the numbers. But that was largely because official records simply did not exist for the area; the people were literally not on the map.

So while Relief Action knew they were there and that they had been affected, nobody was certain how many, or how badly, the earthquake had impacted the people across the mountain, Selby had explained. The assessments from the Afghan's team were the first indication Relief Action had been able to obtain.

The arc of the earthquake damage had swept across the tribal boundary, but no-one knew how far it extended, or how extensive the damage had been. In some areas it was worse than anyone had imagined.

But why had no full-scale relief reached these people almost four months on from the disaster? It was an obvious question from a journalist. Cousins didn't understand.

International aid agencies had been trying to enter the area. But without the agreement and invitation of the tribal leaders, they faced the prospect of armed attack. The people would have preferred to carry on without help and maintained their independence. For most of the bigger international agencies the danger was too great; the security issues too complex.

"It's been frustrating, taking time, patience and diplomacy," Selby told Cousins, sighing deeply.

But he was also sceptical. "The aid business is like a bloody beauty contest," he said. The town of Balakot, which lay close to the earthquake's epicentre, was more visible, easier and less risky to reach, yielding immediate, high-impact results. And that was good for the donors, he explained.

But now there was also an opportunity for Relief Action to achieve a creditable first – and it was prepared to offer its full support with trucks and commodities to meet the need on the mountain, once security was guaranteed. A donor had emerged almost immediately. And Selby had the backing of Maddison, who in turn had secured the support from his US-based global headquarters. The condition was to work with a 'local' implementing partner. Officially Relief Action would not be working directly within the tribal area.

Instead it would operate through the Afghan with a staff largely drawn from Pathans, who understood the tribal culture and would be more easily accepted by the communities on the mountain. That would appease the political powers in the region. Relief Action would discretely second its own Pathan staff to the Afghan's team and monitor activities to ensure that the distribution was corruption-free and could be properly recorded. That was the plan. And Maddison had been able to secure the political backing of the Government of Pakistan.

At Kotkhay the distribution seemed to run smoothly as families identified themselves, checked by the Relief Action monitors and under the watchful eye of the Afghan's gunmen. And steadily the boxes of aid disappeared. Solemn faces gave way to smiles. Selby was relieved and embraced the Afghan. No issues had been reported. It was time to climb back into their vehicles and take the painstaking journey back to Mansehra, which they should make well before nightfall.

"We'll be the first Western agency ever to deliver significant aid into the Black Mountain area – the biggest outside intervention since the British and Indian Army marched into the region more than 100 years ago," Selby reminded Cousins. "And that's an incredible story to tell," he added, smiling like an excited schoolboy. "But it will only be possible in partnership with the Afghan and the trust of the five tribes."

Cousins was smiling too. He'd prepare a media release that evening for Selby's approval and submission to Relief Action's headquarters. The story would be fielded by its media people and was likely to go global. And more was set to follow, once the full programme began to roll. He thought about the people he had met on the mountain. The image of the little girl crying with hunger in Peer Khel ran through his mind. He felt happy she and her people would soon be receiving aid too.

TWENTY-ONE

Afsa Ali stood on the terrace of the guesthouse smoking a cigarette. She blew the smoke idly into the cool afternoon air and gazed towards the mountains. For the past few weeks she had been working in Islamabad on child protection policies with Stevenson's staff in the capital. And now she was back as part of the Mansehra operations team.

She'd be visiting child-friendly spaces in the days ahead and was looking forward to working in the 'field' once more with the children, which she enjoyed. It was what brought her greatest fulfilment and a sense of purpose. And there were plans to establish several additional safe areas for children in the mountains.

From her position she saw the Land Cruisers approach and pull up at a house a few hundred yards along the road unobserved. It was one of several guesthouses like her own, now being used by Relief Action staff in Ghazikot, which lay in the hollow across an expanse of waste ground from the house on the hill. She watched the Englishman as he climbed out of the vehicle, then reach back into the Land Cruiser to grab his coat and bag. Selby also eased himself from the vehicle and the two men embraced in the road. Both were dressed in loose *Shalwar Kameez*. The trousers and tunic Cousins wore were black, not uncommon in the tribal areas, which suited the Englishman well, she mused. The colour complemented his dark features and from a distance he could even have been mistaken for a Pathan. But the field boots were the obvious giveaway. And there was a camera hung across his shoulder. He might have been considered ruggedly handsome.

Ali took several steps back so that she would not be seen and watched as Cousins turned. He pulled the grey Afghan hat low across his forehead, threw his bag over his shoulder and strode towards the house. He was tired from the journey but keen to write the story. First, though, he would make himself a lemon tea, something he had acquired a taste for following his own return to Pakistan.

Shadows were growing long and the winter sun was beginning to set. Ali finished her cigarette. She shivered in the late afternoon chill. Then she too turned and stepped into her guesthouse. Her room was ample and there was a small kitchen area on the ground floor where staff could store food and make snacks. Most, however, usually ate at the house on the hill, which employed two cooks. And an invitation had been extended for Ali, Stevenson and Johns to join the others at the main house. She wondered if the Englishman would be there. The women had spoken about his role in the Black Mountain distribution. Stevenson was keen for her team to access the area for assessment. And Ali was the natural candidate.

It was already dark when Cousins stepped out into the early evening and took the path across the wasteland towards the house on the hill. In his hand, a folder with the story of the Kotkhay distribution for Selby. Already he knew Relief

Action's team in Germany, a major fundraising hub for the organisation, wanted to speak to him. Several key media were interested in the story of the distribution to the 'forgotten' people of Kala Dhaka and the idea of the 'lost tribes' on the mountain reached by the organisation against all odds. They liked too the angle of the old army map Selby had to work from – and, of course, the fact that it was the first recorded contact with the remote area since 1891. It had all the elements. Relief Action's media people in the UK thought the BBC might be interested too. But Cousins would also file a story for his local paper. He felt he owed Johnson that.

Selby was already seated at the table when Cousins walked in.

"Here's your story," he said, handing it to the Canadian. "Have a look and let me know if you're happy. I can make any amendments and then send it to head office," the journalist said.

Selby took the story and began reading it immediately, while the Englishman helped himself to coffee. It was always an uncomfortable moment, waiting for someone to read your story, and Cousins looked decidedly awkward.

Selby looked up. "Bloody brilliant!" he exclaimed, gazing at the Englishman. "Send it, John. No changes."

"And Islamabad?" Cousins wasn't sure where Maddison fitted in.

"He'll be OK with it. Says we can handle it from this side. And he trusts our media people. But copy him in."

Cousins nodded. "That's good. I'll send it over later. Mind if I grab a bite to eat first?"

"No worries. They'll still be at breakfast in the States," Selby smiled.

"The Germans are interested. And maybe the BBC too," the journalist added.

"Great! Think you'll be busy. That's exactly why I brought you back!"

They were joined by Zhevlakov and the Iranian.

"Distribution was good," said the Ukrainian.

And Selby nodded. "We also have the funding and the backing to go ahead, once we have confirmed that all five tribes are happy. Galina, where are we with the CGI sheets?"

"Should all arrive in warehouse next week," she replied. "If there are no delays."

Selby and Williams were to hold meetings with the Afghan on the timing and scale of the next wave of distributions. They would be larger and embrace families from four tribes: the Basikhel, Hassanzai, Nusrat Khel and Akazai. The fifth tribe, the Madakhel, would be more problematic. Its people lay primarily across the Indus River on its west bank, requiring boats. Selby and his team were also still to consider how to distribute at higher points across Kala Dhaka. Whether it was possible by Jeep, or if it was more feasible to use pack animals, or even porters, had not yet been decided.

But these were logistical questions that were surmountable. The operations manager knew it was the questions over security and the region's politics which were the greatest challenges. And they seemed to be resolved. Even the Government of Pakistan had signalled its endorsement to Maddison in Islamabad, a major factor in allowing the story to be told. So Selby felt satisfied all was going to plan. The next step would be the full approval of the wider distribution by the *Loya Jirga*.

"By the way, what's for dinner?" asked Selby as Williams approached.

"Chicken curry and daal, I believe. Again. And chapati," Williams said flatly.

"I hear all went well today," he added.

"It did. No tensions," said Selby.

"Islamabad is very twitchy about this. Not to mention global HQ. If anything goes wrong…"

But the conversation was ended by the arrival of the food from the kitchen, as bowls of piping curry, daal and rice were ferried in, followed by the steaming chapati.

"I know, Chuck," said Selby, gazing at his security chief. "We've already been through this."

And they ate.

Cousins was just leaving when the group was joined by Stevenson and Ali, and he nodded to both women. He had seen the young Pakistani woman before. It was the storyteller from the child-friendly space. For a moment their eyes met. Her mouth was lightly poised between a smile and silence. He hesitated. For an instant he seemed rooted to the spot, transfixed, still gazing into her dark eyes. Then she smiled. And he smiled too. He wanted to say something but seemed unable to speak. Instead, he smiled again and excused himself.

"Catch you all later," he said as normally as he was able, addressing the group and left.

He had to send the story over to head office.

On his way back to his guesthouse he was thinking about the storyteller. Something had happened; something unspoken had passed between them. She was beautiful. Of that there was no doubt. But by the time he was back in his room he had dismissed her from his mind. He was being foolish. He was much older than she was. He was white and she was a Pakistani Muslim. Besides, he felt he was in the mountains to focus on people in desperate need. He sighed and opened his laptop.

―∞―

Ali too was troubled by the brief encounter with the Englishman, which had gone unnoticed among those staff present, except for Stevenson.

"I think he likes you," she told her young colleague with a hint of mischief.

"Who?" replied Ali, who could already feel the heat of a blush coming to her face.

"You know very well," said Stevenson in a motherly tone. "The journalist guy."

"I don't think so," said Ali dismissively.

And the two women fell into silence.

"Well, Gail, how's the child protection team?" Selby asked.

"Good," replied Stevenson. "Three safe areas for the children and more to come." Then she paused.

"I hear it went well today." Another pause. "When are you going to allow us access to Kala Dhaka?"

The Canadian smiled. "You know as well as I do, they operate strict Purdah... besides, negotiations for any access have been very sensitive."

"Could you please at least consider raising it with the tribes, Mr Selby? Sir," she added playfully, returning his smile.

"You're a persistent woman!"

"Persistent is my middle name," she responded.

And they sat smiling at each other.

"All right. I will consider it. But when the time is right," Selby told her.

"Thank you!" The child protection manager felt she had gained a major concession.

"But it is unlikely the tribes will allow Western women," he added.

"Very dangerous," commented Zhevlakov, who had been listening in.

"We just want to assess the children," Stevenson insisted.

"I know, Gail," Selby replied. "Let's see." And he pushed his chair back and rose from the dining table. "We'll see," he repeated, before leaving the room.

"He's right, you know," said Williams. "Besides, Kala Dhaka's a big security risk."

"I know, Charles. But I have to try," she told him and he nodded. Then he too left with Zhevlakov and the Iranian. The two women found themselves sitting alone at the table.

"Perhaps you could talk to the Englishman," Stevenson said. "He seems very close to this Black Mountain adventure." Again, the young Pakistani blushed a little.

Later when Cousins returned to the house on the hill he saw Ali sitting on the ground with Johns, smoking on the terrace outside which overlooked the valley. He smiled and nodded as he passed them and entered the team house. But on finding no-one in the dining room, he returned.

"Mind if I join you?" he asked the two women.

"Please," said Johns, gesturing that he should sit with them. "We were just talking about Kala Dhaka," she added.

"It was a good day," Cousins said, kneeling and taking his place on the ground beside them. He too lit up a cigarette and blew the smoke away from the women into the evening air towards the valley. "The people are desperate."

"What is the situation with the children?" asked Ali, studying him fully for the first time. He liked to hear her voice; its tone; its pitch and the accent with which she spoke.

He cast his eyes to the ground. "Lots of infections. Malnutrition, I'd say. No food. No medicines. And very little shelter." And he felt the emotion rise into his throat, as he thought of the ragged children he'd seen. For a moment they fell silent.

"We'd like to assess the children," said Johns. "Do you think that will be possible?"

"It's a dangerous place," Cousins replied. "And the women are kept from sight—"

"We understand that. We are Pakistani," Johns added.

"And we would be willing to follow local custom and work with the women of Kala Dhaka," Ali ventured. "I have my hijab with me... and I speak the language. I would be prepared to take the risk. What would they do to me?" she added.

Cousins hesitated.

He looked into her dark eyes. She had a point. He too was concerned for the children on the mountain.

"We can talk to the Afghan," he suggested. "I'll mention it again to Hank, see what he thinks."

"Thank you," said Johns. "We just want to assess the children and see how we might support them."

Cousins nodded.

"We can go veiled and work according to their custom to build a relationship with the community," added Ali.

"I'll see what I can do."

"*Meherbani.*"

Cousins raised his eyebrows.

"It means 'thank you very kindly,'" Ali explained. "With blessings." And she smiled.

"No 'thank you' required," Cousins replied, returning the smile.

"By the way, how is the orphan boy from the child-friendly space? Shahbaz."

"I've spoken to Gail about him," said Ali. "And we are going to see if we can make him part of our child sponsorship programme to help support him. It will also pay for his education," she added.

"That's good."

"Yes. He's starting to join in with things…" And she paused. "Incidentally, I'm Afsa Ali; this is my colleague Saiyra Johns." She handed him a business card.

"Nice to meet you both. Name's John Cousins."

Again, they gazed out across the valley towards the mountains. The night was cool and clear and the moon was high, casting a silvery glow upon the landscape stretching out before them.

Cousins sighed. He was tired.

"I have to go," he announced, suddenly feeling a little awkward. "Full day with the media tomorrow." And with that he rose to his feet and bade the women goodnight.

"Good luck," Johns called after him.

"*Shukria!*" And he headed across the courtyard to the gate.

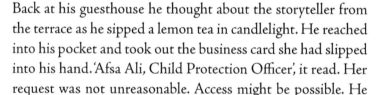

Back at his guesthouse he thought about the storyteller from the terrace as he sipped a lemon tea in candlelight. He reached into his pocket and took out the business card she had slipped into his hand. 'Afsa Ali, Child Protection Officer', it read. Her request was not unreasonable. Access might be possible. He smiled as he pictured her face and the way she held herself. She had made an impression.

He would speak to Selby in the morning. He was exhausted. But he felt fulfilled. Another full day was in prospect tomorrow, speaking to the Relief Action media team in Germany. Its people in the UK wanted to talk to him too. And he was set to visit another village first thing in the morning. He took another sip of tea.

Still the image of the young Pakistani woman would not leave him. He reached for his phone and tapped out a message to her. It had been lovely to meet her. And yes, he would ask about Kala Dhaka. He'd see what could be done. And did she realise how beautiful she looked in moonlight?

Should he send it? He hesitated. Somehow he felt it was a key moment. Was it appropriate? Probably not. He was aware he was a member of the international expat team. She was part of the national staff, a local girl. Yet he felt compelled to action. She was one of the most beautiful women he had ever seen. He was a long way from home and lonely. He hit the 'send' button and smiled.

TWENTY-TWO

THE PING OF the text message heralded a sense of panic within the girl. It was from an 'unknown' sender, but as she picked up her mobile phone she could see from the first line it was from the Englishman, even before she opened it. And her heart leapt into her throat. Her eyes widened as she read the full message. What was he thinking? And yet there rose within her a sense of excitement.

It was not what she had expected. Nor was it welcome. She felt a blush rise to her neck and into her cheeks.

"It's the Englishman," she said, without betraying the sense of panic that she felt within her. "Says he will ask about Kala Dhaka."

But she did not share with Johns the full content of the message, who still sat beside her at the house on the hill.

"That's good," replied her companion, throwing her a searching look.

"We'll see," said Ali.

"Did he say anything else?"

"He's going to speak to Mr Selby."

"That's really good. I think he likes you," Johns added.

"Mr Selby?"

"The Englishman," Johns said smiling.

"I don't think so," she replied, conscious that it was the second time she had said so that evening. Her mind was racing. She didn't understand. It was not why she had travelled to Mansehra. She was clear there was no room for men in her personal life. She had resigned herself to a single life. And she wanted to devote herself to God's work. Wasn't that why Allah had saved her? She had left the man she loved in New Zealand. At least it felt like love. In essence she had run away.

But the relationship had been destructive for her. And she had returned to Pakistan to embrace her religion. Her relationships with the men she had cared for had been disastrous and she had vowed to live her life alone. Clearly she was not meant for a life of personal happiness with another man. Of that she was certain. God had saved her from men and from herself. She would devote herself to His work. Her religion was now everything to her. Therefore she did not respond to the message she had received from Cousins. Instead she would pray about it. That was where she now found her guidance and comfort. It was where she sought her answers. When finally she returned to her own guesthouse she spent a restless night. His message had disturbed her. Not least because part of her was curious about the mysterious Englishman and what had brought him to Pakistan. She might even have been attracted to him.

Cousins had slept well. He had thought about Ali, but he had fallen swiftly into a deep and comforting sleep. He therefore awoke refreshed to face the new morning of brilliant, crisp sunshine. There had been no response on the phone to his message from the girl. But perhaps that was for the best. He threw the sheets off and padded out barefoot to the kitchen. His cook and housekeeper were not due for another half an hour. Each guesthouse had domestic support and Irfan the cook would float between several guesthouses to provide a basic breakfast. For Cousins it was usually egg and toast. Sometimes there was processed cheese, or even turkey bacon. The Englishman opened the door to the balcony and stepped out into the early morning sunshine, resting his eyes on the distant mountains which now carried a light dusting of snow.

He had to be at the office early to meet with Tahir. The young Pathan would accompany him to a distribution in the Kaghan Valley that morning. Later he would speak to the Germans, who wanted his first-hand account from Kala Dhaka. He stepped back into the kitchen and lit the stove. He emptied a bottle of water into the kettle and placed it onto the gas ring. Coffee was required. Then he sat at the table, opened his laptop and connected to the internet. There was a mail from the German office confirming the time of the telephone interview later that day, but nothing from England. Neither had the newspaper confirmed receipt of his story. But it was still early. Pakistan was five hours ahead. He disappeared into the bedroom and began to dress.

Tahir greeted him at the office with the broadest smile. He was twenty minutes late but the cheerfulness of the Pathan was enough to forgive him the slight delay. Besides, the Englishman had learned that in Pakistan there was a different perception of time. Appointments and tasks were followed by an inevitable *insh'Allah*. If God willed it. Tahir was attached to the monitoring team, but he also held an interest in child protection. Sometimes he assisted in the child-friendly spaces to support Stevenson's staff.

He came from a wealthy Pathan family in Abbottabad and had recently graduated from Peshawar University. But when the earthquake struck, he had applied to Relief Action and now he held ambitions to make a career in the aid and development sector.

The village lay at the foot of the mountains in the valley close to Balakot, the town completely destroyed in the disaster. And yet it was relatively easy to access from the road which had been cleared of landslides and ran along the valley. When Cousins arrived the distribution was already underway, as villagers offered up their thumbprints for their essential supplies. Today it was for food and winter clothing for the children. He took a series of photographs and spoke to several villagers, accompanied by Tahir. The distributions were still a lifeline to hundreds of communities reliant on help, particularly during the hard winter months in prospect.

The young Pakistani was curious about England. What was it like, he asked Cousins?

"It's very green. The weather is very changeable. But we get lots of rain," the Englishman replied.

"And is everyone rich?"

"No, not everyone. Many people are poor." Cousins hesitated. Already he had come to realise that few in his home country could even imagine the desperate poverty he had already seen in Pakistan.

"Are you rich?" Cousins shook his head. "But I am fortunate." He smiled at the Pathan.

Was he married, the young man ventured further? It was an inevitable question asked so frequently within the first few moments of meeting.

He had been married. And he had older children. And no, he wasn't looking to marry again, although he had observed Pakistani women were very beautiful. And yes, he liked the country and its people. Particularly Pathans. And Tahir had seemed very pleased. But it was true. He found their directness appealing. And he found them to be open and loyal. He also liked their code of honour.

The relief effort was continuing and was likely to do so in the weeks ahead until the advent of spring. The mountain was far from the only focus for Selby's operation. The main priority was still to supply the many thousands in the mountains with essential aid and shelter to see them through the bitter days to come. Protecting children was a large part of Relief Action's work too and there were plans to expand activities and to help rebuild some of the many schools across the mountains which had been destroyed. An education manager had arrived earlier that week.

An engineer was on his way from Eastern Europe and already two local building specialists had joined the team to look at several reconstruction projects that might focus on water supply issues. Road repair and construction was also on the agenda. An agricultural specialist from East Africa was also on his way to support livelihoods. The team was growing and beginning to shape itself in readiness for the subsequent recovery phase.

For Selby the Black Mountain remained something of a personal quest. He was fascinated by the area's history, its isolation and its culture. It was a challenge he was unable to resist, and he took a keen personal interest in understanding the power structure and its people. Its military history added to the appeal. But he also had a natural inclination to support the underdog – and he felt the five tribes of Kala Dhaka had been neglected, even shunned, for generations. It therefore remained a forgotten backwater and was one of the poorest pockets of Pakistan in a land renowned for its poverty.

Of course, he saw an opportunity to achieve a prestigious first for Relief Action. Which is why he had been so keen to bring Cousins back to tell the story. It was an exciting tale to tell and had all the elements to attract widescale media attention. And that would help retain the public spotlight on the disaster with a media which all too quickly lost interest and moved its attention elsewhere. The Canadian was, therefore, delighted by the initial interest within Europe, not least of all because both the UK and German offices provided valuable funding for the relief effort which was still ongoing. The operations manager was pleased to have Cousins on his team. He recognised the importance of telling the story to a wider audience and its role in supporting public appeals.

Now the Englishman was back at the office, dialling a German number on his mobile phone. He felt he might offer a few phrases in the language he'd studied at college to embellish the interview and steer the story. But what was the word for tribe? *Stamm*, he recalled. And aid items? He was thankful for the internet. Yet he needn't have worried. The German communications officer spoke perfect English and had clearly understood his media release.

But what had it been like to be the first Westerners to set foot on the Black Mountain for more than 100 years? That was easy.

"Like stepping back in time," he had replied. "A different world!"

And suddenly he found he was in full flow.

"The people are completely self-governing. Isolated. They are their own army, police force and judiciary. But the earthquake destroyed their simple way of life – and the people are hungry and facing disease."

Thousands had lost their homes and their livelihoods in the disaster and the winter was setting in. The mountains had already seen snow. But the people had not been reached, such was their isolation.

And the map? There were no maps. The only map which existed was drawn up when the British and Indian Army surveyed the area back in 1891. And that was discovered by accident…

No other outside interventions had taken place since. Cousins followed his script perfectly and sensed the growing excitement in the German on the other end of the line, who felt sure there would be considerable interest across the media. He liked the idea that a gateway to a forbidden land was now open. Would Cousins be available for interview in the days ahead? The German would be in touch.

When the call had ended Cousins was exhausted. He felt it was time for a lemon tea at his guesthouse. He noticed there was a message on his phone. It was from Afsa Ali. Cousins opened it with a sense of apprehension. Already he had regretted his line about the moonlight. And yet it was true. Ali thanked him for his message. Also for his agreement to ask about access to the Black Mountain. She apologised for the delay in her response. But she said she had been surprised by his reference to her appearance in moonlight. She would welcome further discussions with him about Kala Dhaka, which she was very interested in. It was impeccably polite.

Cousins smiled. He felt he had managed to get away with it. And he was excited by the prospect of seeing her again. He would consider before responding. Besides, he still had to write the story of the latest aid drop for Relief Action's website. After he'd written his media release he had felt unusually tired and had slumped onto his bed.

When he awoke the sun was already beginning to set over the mountains. He'd slept for more than two hours. He decided to spend the evening at his guesthouse. Selby was away for meetings in Islamabad and he felt he needed some time alone. He would forego the house on the hill and raid the fridge instead. Besides, he had no real appetite for a full evening meal.

Later, as he stood on the balcony gazing out across the valley, he was joined by the two local engineers, who came out to smoke. Salman was from Islamabad, while his colleague, Zamir had studied at Abbottabad. What was England like? Why had he come? And was he married? Inevitably they exchanged stories of how they came to be in Mansehra. Salman spoke of the girl he loved in the capital, whose family would never approve of their union. Zamir too told the Englishman he volunteered with Relief Action to forget about his love for a woman who had married someone else. And it struck Cousins all three of them seemed to have travelled to the earthquake zone to forget the heartaches they carried with them in life.

And as the men stood on the balcony overlooking the valley framed by the timeless mountains and the moon shone down upon them, each thought about their lost loves. It was like a lonely-hearts club. Broken hearts. There was nothing new in that. Nor was it exclusive to any race, or culture. It was part of the human condition, Cousins reflected. He blew the smoke from his cigarette into the cool evening air and smiled wistfully to himself…

TWENTY-THREE

They had come down from their mountain villages in their thousands and now lived in tented camps across the valley floors. And there they languished, waiting for the winter to pass. Conditions were adequate. Enough to keep a person alive. There was food, water and shelter. And there was access to medicines too. Yet for many, hope was ebbing away. The people had left behind everything they had known, without any certainty they would ever return. And if they did, what would there be to return to? No-one was certain. First came the rains. Then the bitter cold. And as the first snows covered the tented camps, for many hope gave way to despair. They felt displaced and forsaken. Traumatised by their loss. But for now there was no alternative. They would have to sit out the winter. And survive.

Education for many of the children meant gathering at a large UNICEF tent. But school materials and, more importantly, teachers, were in short supply. Others attended child-friendly spaces set up by a variety of agencies, including

Relief Action. Hundreds of humanitarian organisations were now operating across Pakistan's north-west. Yet it was still not enough.

The army was pulling back. The international force from NATO was also set to depart with the coming of the spring. Coordination of the increasing number of aid agencies became the responsibility of the United Nations in tandem with the Government of Pakistan's newly formed Earthquake Reconstruction and Rehabilitation Authority. Yet it was a cumbersome, slow-moving beast, vulnerable to corruption. The country had not been prepared for a disaster of the scale which overcame it. Much of the government infrastructure across the stricken region had also been damaged or destroyed and was in a state of paralysis.

For those who opted to remain in their mountain villages, conditions were precarious. Most were reliant on aid distributions. But supplies were distributed irregularly and when they came it was often not enough. Some stayed for fear of losing their land or their livestock.

Others were fearful of life in the valleys, away from everything they knew. Others still could not bring themselves to leave the loved ones they had so recently buried on the mountainsides.

The Black Mountain was one of the few pockets that had not received any aid. It remained a forgotten, neglected backwater, as it had been for centuries. The Government of Pakistan knew of its situation, which was almost unique. And yet the government felt assured the area's provision was finally in hand. Which was convenient. Otherwise there might not have been any assistance for the peoples of Kala Dhaka at all.

The British were also following developments on the mountain and were satisfied immediate needs would now be met. Its international development agency had stepped forward to fund the Relief Action initiative. And the Americans who also held an interest in the small tribal area would now wait until the spring to push forward their long-term initiatives through the Kala Dhaka Area Development Project.

In the meantime, their man was watching the Relief Action programme and had reported that the first aid drop had taken place at the village of Kotkhay. It was very much to their purpose and for now they were content to watch and wait. But a worrying development was an approach to the local politicians. Their agent reported stories of bribery and potential corruption in return for political support. They were aware of the Afghan and rumours that promises were being made.

But the stories had not reached the ears of Selby or Maddison in Islamabad. Nor were the British aware. They understood the regional politicians were largely ineffective, insignificant and mistrusted. It was the landowners and the mullahs who held the power in Kala Dhaka. And that was largely true. Yet there were members of the landowning khans whose influence could be bought and who sought to profit from the promises made. Access through their lands would come at a price.

In Mansehra, Selby was planning the next wave of distributions with his team. The Afghan gave no indication of any trouble ahead. The warehouses were full and the trucks had been commissioned. There was a tentative date, depending on the weather. Initially the plan would be to distribute along the road which followed the river. The people could come down from the mountain and carry away their supplies. But Selby was still considering distribution points further onto the mountain and closer to high altitude communities like Peer Khel.

He was concerned aid might not reach the intended recipients, or that those in desperate need might not be able to come down from their villages into the valley. Access was the issue. As far as Selby was aware, the single road in Kala Dhaka ran along the valley floor, running north to south. There were only steep and rocky mountain trails to dozens of villages in need of aid. De Villiers, the South African, was establishing whether pack animals were available and viable. He was waiting to hear. There would be a final meeting with the Afghan. A decision would have to be made. What Selby and his team didn't know was that Shah was already making separate agreements with several tribal chieftains which might threaten the entire operation...

"What's the latest on the mules?" asked Selby.

The South African shook his head. "Expensive. Suddenly. And not easy to get hold of," he added.

Then there were the logistics. The animals would need to be transported into the tribal area, fed and watered. And afterwards they would have to be ferried out again. Unless they left them there. It would also require additional time to load them up and lead them into the mountains, adding to the security risk. In the event, Selby decided against the idea. And Williams was relieved. Zhevlakov was of the same opinion. Each tribe, each village was to be responsible for collecting and transporting its own aid items.

It was not ideal. But it seemed the only solution to deliver the aid, meet the most immediate needs and minimise the risks. A balance had to be struck. The rest would be the responsibility of the tribes.

Cousins stood on the terrace at the team house on the hill. He'd been pacing, breathing deeply, clutching his notebook. In a few minutes he was due to take a call from the BBC for an interview.

The Black Mountain story had generated excitement across the Relief Action network of offices. Its media team in the UK had secured a first broadcast interview and he was about to talk to veteran broadcaster John Humphrys on BBC Radio 4's *Today* programme. He took another look at his notes and the opening phrase he had written out.

His phone rang. He took a deep breath and gazed out at the snow-capped mountains bathed in mid-morning sunshine for inspiration. Heart pounding, he answered the call. The producer on the other end of the line told him to relax. Mr Humphrys would be asking him about the significance of the Black Mountain distribution and to relate to listeners what he had seen. They would come to him in a moment. Could he hold the line? He could hear the broadcaster framing the story. Then he heard his name and suddenly he was talking live. The rest was pretty much a blur; instinctive. And before he knew it, the call was over. He hadn't looked at his notes once. Yet he knew there were things he should have mentioned.

But he was experienced enough to know there is never enough time to mention everything. Two or three key points was all that could be hoped for.

He hoped he had sounded all right. Now he was able to relax. He felt he deserved a coffee and turned towards the main house, relieved.

A beautifully carved wooden plaque hung over the doorway, its intricate Arabic calligraphy combining its swirling letters as one. It was the most important prayer of all, Tahir had told him, the declaration of Islamic faith. To read it and to understand its words was to believe, the young Pathan had told him. It was the first *Kalima*. 'There is no God but Allah and Mohammed is His messenger.' He stood contemplating the beauty of its script. And he thought about Ali. Then he entered the house.

The truth was he felt inspired by what he had seen and felt in the mountains. The resilience and warmth of those affected by tragedy; the sheer scale of devastation, even three months on; and the tireless efforts of the aid operation which still saw staff working fourteen-hour days in the harshest of environments. But it was the beauty of the land, its people and their culture which had moved him. How many desperate people had he sat with in the rubble of their homes; how many fresh graves had he seen on the mountainsides? Yet still the people were thankful to their God and offered up smiles and cups of chai. They wanted to know about England, about his life. And they were grateful he had travelled so far to see them. He was moved by their strength. Kala Dhaka was just one element of his experience which added to his sense of awe and a deep fulfilment in being part of something remarkable.

He finished his coffee on the terrace, looking out at the mountains as he so often had. Then he headed down the hill to the office. He wanted to see if Selby was there and tell him how the BBC interview had been. He also wanted to ask about the Black Mountain distribution. And he had promised the child protection team to explore whether there might be scope for them to access the area. He wondered when he might see Ali again.

It happens when you least expect it. He walked into the office and there she was with Stevenson.

He smiled and said hello as they looked up.

"How are you today, Mr Cousins?" asked Stevenson cheerfully.

"Good, thank you."

Like Ali, Stevenson was dressed in *Shalwar Kameez* and a loosely wrapped headscarf. They were heading into the field to visit a community where they hoped to establish a new child-friendly space.

Did he want to come?

He declined and explained he was on a mission to find Selby. And he told them he would speak to him about the children of Kala Dhaka.

"Bless you, Mr Cousins," smiled Stevenson. Ali was smiling too. And he left them to head upstairs to Selby's office. The operations manager was on his mobile phone as the Englishman stood at the door of his office. The Canadian waved him in. He finished the call and smiled at Cousins. "Our UK people say you were bloody brilliant on the radio!"

"Thanks. I'm not sure that's true."

"It was perfect, John. Well done."

"How's it looking for the distribution?"

Selby raised his eyebrows and grimaced. "We should know in the next day, or two for sure, when we meet with Shah. The date's set for next week. I understand the tribes are ready. We're all set to go. Eighty trucks," he added.

Cousins nodded. "I was talking to the child protection people—"

But Selby cut him short. "I know," he grinned. "That bloody woman… driving me crazy. I've told her. She has to wait until the main distribution is done."

"I said I would ask when I spoke to her team."

"Afsa Ali?" And he looked at Cousins knowingly. "Be careful, John. I know she's nice to look at, but she's just as bad. Won't take no for an answer."

Cousins said nothing.

"It's all right," the Canadian added. "But they know they need to come through me…" And he paused. "I do understand where they're coming from. Really, I do. And they will get their access. When it's safe."

The Englishman nodded and moved towards the window to look outside.

"Jeez, John!" Selby suddenly rose from his desk and pulled Cousins out of the light. "There could be snipers in the hills. Can't be too careful."

The journalist was taken aback by the sudden action. "Sure," he said uncertainly.

Selby's mood seemed to change just as quickly. "Can't be too careful," he repeated absently as he gazed cautiously out of the office window towards the hills. Then he smiled and sat behind his desk. And the tension was gone from his face. "There's a trip out to Abbottabad tomorrow morning," he told Cousins. "A chance to do some shopping, have a bite to eat. Will do us all good to get out, take a breather."

"Sure. That would be good," the Englishman replied.

"Minibus leaves at 10am."

"I'll be there." And he left the operations manager staring absently out of the window. He wanted to check for messages on his email. He was still waiting to hear from the Germans.

Later, when Cousins arrived for dinner at the team house, Selby seemed his usual self.

They were joined by de Villiers. Zhevlakov and the Iranian also sat with them. And there were several national staff from the monitoring team. But neither Stevenson nor Ali were there. They were still on their way back from the mountains. Williams too was conspicuously absent. He never seemed to miss a meal.

"He's stressed out," said Selby. "He's troubled by Kala Dhaka. And ghosts…"

"Ghosts?"

"When you've served and seen some shit. Seen death. Those ghosts can haunt you." Then he fell silent.

When Cousins stepped from the house on the hill, a full moon had already risen above the mountains. He stood for a moment, gazing at the beauty of the valley framed by the dark, distant peaks silhouetted against the night sky. He saw Imran and Tahir approach on the road and offered his *salaams*, as he was about to strike out down the hill and across the waste ground towards his guesthouse.

"Where are you guys coming from?" Cousins asked.

"From the guesthouse, Mr John," Tahir replied.

"But that's this way," said the Englishman, pointing across scrub and grass-covered slope. "It's quicker to cut across," he insisted, pointing again into the darkness.

"In daylight, yes," said Imran. "But now is dark."

"What do you mean? I always cut across."

"At night-time there are snakes. We take the road."

Cousins nodded. "*Shukria*. I think I'll take the road, then..."

Back at his guesthouse he sat out on the terrace with a lemon tea and smoked a final cigarette before turning in. He was pleased that the BBC interview had gone well. Then he thought about ghosts and snakes. And the next day in prospect, which marked the beginning of the weekend. He was looking forward to the trip to Abbottabad in the morning. He wondered whether Ali would be there.

TWENTY-FOUR

IT MIGHT HAVE seemed an odd collection of people who gathered in the vehicle compound at Relief Action that morning, waiting for the minibus which would take them to the nearby city of Abbottabad. Strangers drawn together from different corners of the world to work in foreign fields. Mercenaries, missionaries and misfits, standing alongside local staff with one common goal: to assist those impacted by disaster. And now, in a rare moment of respite, they were going shopping.

When Cousins arrived, de Villiers was already waving the vehicle out from a row of Land Cruisers lined up outside the office. Selby and Zhevlakov were there with Farzad, the Iranian. The Ukrainian wore a headscarf, as did other female members of the group. They included Stevenson, Johns and Ali, all dressed traditionally. Several young Pakistani men Cousins recognised from the distribution team were there, as was the newly arrived engineer from Bosnia whom he had not yet met. Somebody said he had served as a tank commander in the civil war. But he looked friendly enough and was talking to Stevenson as Cousins approached. His name was Daris Petrović. The Englishman nodded a good morning. The group was finally joined by Tahir, the young Pathan, who came running from the office to join them.

They were about to board the bus when Williams appeared, strutting out across the compound. As he stood before them he looked gaunt, dishevelled and tired.

"Morning, people," he said, addressing the group. "Just a few words on safety before you leave…" He sounded weary. "You'll be glad to know the army reports no security issues today. But stay together. Don't go wandering off. Keep your personal items safe and zipped up. Try to avoid any crowds. Make sure you have each other's mobile numbers. And don't get lost and miss the bus back," he said as if cautioning children about to embark on a school trip. The bus was set to leave Abbottabad by 1500, sharp, he added. They should stay close to Selby. They could call him at the office if there were any security worries.

"And have a good time," he said finally.

Cousins sat close to Selby near the front of the bus. The Englishman felt he should keep his distance from Stevenson's team, not least because he felt an attraction for Ali. She held similar thoughts as she chatted to Stevenson and the bus pulled out from Ghazikot onto the main highway towards Abbottabad, some thirty minutes away.

"I thought Williams looked tired," said the Englishman, leaning across towards Selby and swaying slightly with the motion of the bus as it travelled along the uneven road.

"I'm worried about him," he replied. "Spends most of his time in his room. And that's not healthy."

"I've hardly seen him over the last few days," Cousins said.

"He's increasingly concerned about security. There are ongoing tensions in the tribal areas up towards the Afghan border. Bloody Americans are still firing drones into the area.

"And he worries about the safety of Kala Dhaka. Got some personal stuff going on too," added Selby. "Father's dying of cancer."

"Shit!"

"It's tough enough out here without personal issues," the Canadian continued. "Doesn't do him any favours, though, hiding away. But he's due for a trip home. Been here since October."

And they fell silent as the bus rolled along the main road towards the garrison town.

"Should be there in a bit. Just remember, though," Selby added with a smile, "always keep moving. Look confident as you walk, as if you have a purpose. Nobody will bother you."

They were soon entering the outskirts of the city, which looked remarkably British, with colonial-style buildings in extensive grounds, their grand pillars and neatly trimmed privet hedges echoing a bygone era. The roads were well maintained, with newly painted white lines and central reservations bursting with greenery. And there were Victorian stone churches set back from the road with pointed steeples as if transplanted straight from the shires of rural England. All set against the imposing backdrop of the distant, snow-capped mountains.

It had been a military town in the days of the Raj and a major outpost from which to stage expeditions to quell the 'Blazing Frontier'. And it was from here that the force of 10,000 men of the British and Indian Army had marched out towards Kala Dhaka to bring the tribes of the Black Mountain into submission back in 1888, Selby told him.

After Partition, the Pakistan Army took over the city from the British and maintained its military status, now serving as headquarters for the Frontier Force Regiment, the Baloch Regiment and Pakistan Army Medical Corps. Its elite Kakul Military Academy also lay within its boundaries, Selby explained. And yet the town's appearance might have suggested the British had left the previous week. But the group's interest today lay in its bustling trade provided by a vibrant assortment of shops, markets and bazaars.

As their vehicle approached the main shopping area and slowed to a walking pace in the traffic, Selby suddenly rose from his seat.

"Right, I'm off," he announced, ordering the driver to stop and let him out. "I'll see you guys later. Make sure you don't get lost!" And with that, he stepped from the bus before it had even rolled to a halt and disappeared, striding confidently into the teeming crowds…

The bus continued into the city centre and finally pulled up in a busy side street. Cousins stepped from the bus and stood to one side, taking in the hustle and bustle of Pakistani life thronging along its thoroughfares. He turned and suddenly there she was, standing right beside him.

"Hello, Ms Ali."

"Hello," she replied, glancing over her shoulder to see where her colleagues were.

"Fancy meeting you here," he said smiling. "Do you come here often?"

But the humour was lost and she took his words literally. "It's my first time," she told him, blushing slightly.

"Mine too," he admitted.

And then Stevenson arrived to the rescue. Or so he thought. "Ah, Mr Cousins… will you be joining us?"

Cousins and Ali looked at each other, sharing the same thought. And suddenly they both smiled.

"My pleasure," said the Englishman.

Ali's colleague Saiyra Johns joined them, along with Petrović, the Bosnian engineer whom Stevenson had taken under her wing. The women were interested in clothing, Cousins was looking for something traditional to take back to the UK and the Bosnian was happy just to tag along to obtain his first view of Pakistani life up close. Zhevlakov and the others were more interested in food. And so the two parties decided to strike out in different directions.

Cousins and the Bosnian fell behind, chatting as they strolled along, while the women led, heading towards the main *markaz*. And he was able to observe Ali's frame as they walked. She was slim and of medium height. Impeccably dressed in her immaculately pressed *Shalwar Kameez*, draped in a long outer robe which stretched almost to her ankles. And as the time passed, the small group became more relaxed as they darted in and out of shops, or lingered at stalls, chatting and laughing as they made their way along. Cousins had stopped at a stall with an assortment of garments, including hats, scarves and blankets.

He'd promised to bring back an Afghan hat for Mike. They had known each other since school days and were still close. He was also looking for a cotton scarf for himself. The one he picked out was black and white. How much, asked the Englishman clumsily in Urdu? The stallholder said it would be 600 rupees. "Special price."

"Just a moment," Stevenson urged, swooping to his assistance. "Offer him half!"

Ali and Johns now also stood beside him.

Ali spoke to the trader in Urdu. She told Cousins he would take 400 rupees.

Following a further interjection by Ali it became 300. "Special, special price, for friend of Pakistani sister," the trader added with a smile.

Cousins reached into his pocket and fished out the required notes, handing them to the man.

"*Shukria!*" said the Englishman.

"And thank you," he said, turning to Ali.

"You're welcome."

He looked into her smiling eyes. Her headscarf had now slipped back to her shoulders, revealing her dark hair which had fallen partly across her face.

"You speak Urdu words well," she added.

"Thank you. I try. People seem to respond. I think it's important," he replied.

"But you are not good at haggling," she said. "You should never offer the asking price. Especially if you are a foreigner."

"I'll try to remember," he said.

"The traders like to bargain. It's part of the culture. They enjoy it," she explained.

"I find the culture fascinating," he told her. "The country, the people and their religion. And I'd like to know more."

"You've made a start," she told him.

"Your faith seems central to everything."

"Islam is what saved me from myself," she said simply.

"I lost my faith as a child," he replied. And it was true. The belief had been lost following the death of his baby brother. "But there's something special here. I'd like to know more."

She hesitated. Then she said, "I'll help you if you would like me to."

The offer took him entirely by surprise as much as it did her.

The others had already moved along to the next stall, where Stevenson expressed an interest in a colourful new *Shalwar Kameez* and was taking advice from Johns, while Petrović stood, looking mildly detached and bored.

"I'd better rescue the new guy," Cousins said, nodding towards the hapless Bosnian. And they went to join them. For the next few hours they wove in an out of the crowds, drifting along the busy streets, taking in the sights and sounds, buying when they found something of interest. He felt an intimate exchange had taken place with Ali. But they spent the rest of their time as part of the group enjoying the simplicity of a shopping trip away from the pain and suffering they had seen in the mountains to the north. It was a welcome distraction…

On the outskirts of the city a white SUV pulled up outside an imposing walled enclosure. A stocky man in local dress with a turban climbed out. He glanced anxiously around him before he rapped on the sturdy metal gates. He returned to the vehicle as they swung open and he drove inside the compound. The extensive three-storey building which lay inside was home to two families, which included several wives and a multitude of children. On the upper floor a bearded man in *Shalwar Kameez* looked out across Abbottabad through the slats of a shuttered window. He longed to leave the enclosure and walk among the people. But the risk of detection was too great. An AK47 rested in the corner of the darkened, sparsely furnished room. A table lay near the window, with papers stacked and surrounded by several metal filing cabinets.

And there was a mattress on the floor against the far wall. Flickering images from a muted television added a sense of detachment and ambivalence to the outside world, a vague reminder that life went on beyond the confines of the shuttered room. The man at the window turned towards the closed door behind him at the sound of approaching footsteps and narrowed his eyes.

The door opened and the man in the turban entered the room, offering his *Salaams*. In his hands was a padded envelope, which he passed to the man at the window as he smiled and stepped forward. They embraced and spoke in Arabic. The recipient of the envelope asked a series of questions. He had a kindly face and one might have thought there was compassion in the Saudi Arabian's eyes. He opened the package and squinted in the half-light as he scanned the documents it contained. He was the terrorist most wanted by the Western world and carried a $25 million price on his head. The man was Osama bin Laden and he had been hiding in Abbottabad since the end of 2005.

TWENTY-FIVE

THE BOY HAD drawn his family in heavy crayon on the scrap of paper as he lay upon the floor. A man and a woman stood on top of a mountain and the sun was shining. The figures were crude representations of the people he loved. His mother was cradling a baby and he had placed himself beside them. He added a smile to the image of himself in the picture. But in reality he was not smiling and his heart was still heavy whenever he thought about his parents. In fact, he still smiled infrequently. His drawing showed a life that was gone. It now seemed a distant dream. And yet the longing for it had not diminished with the passing of time. He pushed the crayons away and rested his chin on his hands, staring absently at the inside of the tent.

It was now nearly five months since that fateful day on the mountainside when the ground beneath him had started to shake. He, like many of the children who came from the tented camps to the child-friendly space, was still facing an uncertain future.

"*Acha!*" said the woman in *Shalwar Kameez*, who kneeled down beside him as she gazed upon his drawing. The children had been asked to create a picture of their favourite things and she knew what the boy was expressing. It was a representation of grief.

Relief Action's child protection team had worked hard to support the boy and his baby sister. Both were still under the care of Eriksson at the camp in the ruined city of Balakot. Exhaustive enquiries to locate extended family had been made, without success. Official records were sparse and much of the documentation that had existed was gone. The machinery of government within the earthquake zone was still paralysed, its infrastructure destroyed, many of its staff themselves displaced. And the boy himself did not know where his uncle and aunts were, whether they still lived, or even if they wanted him.

But one morning a man had arrived at the camp. He had been searching for his brother's family and had travelled from beyond the valley. He was the children's uncle and he would provide for them in his village near Jhelum. It lay below the Kashmiri border in the shadow of the mountains to the south-east and had been relatively untouched by the disaster. Shahbaz had been overcome by emotion when he saw his uncle, and the two had embraced. It had been agreed to hand the children over to his care. But the aim was to secure support for the boy through Relief Action's child sponsorship programme, which would help finance his education. As yet, though, the scheme was still to be implemented in Pakistan. But Stevenson's team were lobbying hard.

The English visitor to the child-friendly space brought a smile to the boy's face as he entered the tent and approached. He remembered the Westerner. And he knew the woman who was on her knees beside him on the mat. Cousins stepped forward as the boy raised himself from the ground. The foreigner reached out to shake his hand.

"It's good to see you," he said, and Ali translated. "I understand you will be going to live with your family. That's good," he added.

The boy shrugged his shoulders.

"I came to say 'goodbye.'"

Shahbaz looked at Cousins but said nothing.

"I wanted to give you something and wish you well," Cousins told him.

And he took the scarf from around his neck and laid it over the boy's shoulders. It was the scarf he had purchased in Abbottabad. For protection, he told him. Against the cold. To keep the dust from his face, the mosquitoes from his neck and the sun from his head. The boy understood and smiled awkwardly. There was also something the white man wanted him to have from his country. And he produced a coin from his pocket.

"It has the British queen's head on it," he explained, pointing to the monarch's head. "If you carry it with you it will bring you luck on your travels." The Englishman placed the coin in the boy's palm. Then he laid a fatherly hand on his shoulder. "Good luck," he repeated.

The boy looked into the Englishman's eyes and a moment of understanding passed between them. "*Shukria*," he responded, adding that he hoped God would smile upon the man.

Cousins was moved by the boy's words. He smiled, then turned away. He did not want the boy to see the emotion he felt. He had to return to the office. The uncle was set to collect his nephew and niece in the days ahead. He hoped the boy would find happiness once more. It was the last time he would ever see the young Pathan…

As Cousins walked slowly across the child-friendly space with Ali, he felt a mixture of sadness and hope for the boy.

"Do you think he will be all right?" he asked the young Pakistani beside him.

"We'll keep in touch with the uncle," she replied. "We will try to find a sponsor for him."

"Can I help? I would be happy to sponsor him," said Cousins.

They halted as they approached the Land Cruiser that was waiting to drive him back to the office. Ali looked at the Englishman and smiled before she spoke. "That's very kind. But it needs to go through our team in Islamabad," she told him. "I will let you know."

"Thank you," he said. "Will I see you later, at the team house?"

"Perhaps," she replied.

And she watched him as he climbed into the vehicle and it moved off. She would spend the afternoon with the children and head back to Mansehra with the rest of the team after they had finished for the day.

She wasn't sure how to feel about the Englishman. He seemed kind. And she was curious about his life and why he had come to Pakistan.

He wasn't like the other Westerners, whose Christian faith was part of the reason they worked for Relief Action. But she also wondered about his interest in Islam and was drawn by what he had told her about being inspired to regain his faith. She could relate to that. She knew what it was to lose faith; had felt unhappiness and confusion without it. Now that she had reaffirmed her belief in Allah, everything suddenly made sense. She felt cleansed. She also knew guiding others towards her faith was not only her duty but potentially brought blessings from her God. She felt her mother would approve.

Perhaps there was a reason she felt drawn to the Westerner. At the same time she felt a sense of danger. He was a man she was attracted to. She enjoyed his company. Therefore, she felt conflicted and a little afraid. She would pray for guidance.

Back at the office Cousins was set for further media interviews. The German TV network ZDF had received the footage and photography from his recent visit to Peer Khel on the mountain. They wanted to talk to him. At the same time BBC TV and the American CNN network also wanted the story. In addition, Johnson had run his piece in the local newspaper, which particularly pleased him. And there was interest from national print media. Things were moving at pace and he was set for a busy few days. The story of the Black Mountain was going global. Yet he took it all in his stride. He felt driven by his own passion for the people and their circumstances he had witnessed with his own eyes. He felt his life was being directed by events beyond his control. That he was being swept along. Almost as if things were being coordinated by a higher force. And he had not had that feeling for a very long time.

He too was curious about Ali. Though she was clear about the strength of her faith, she wasn't like other national staff. He knew she had studied overseas and was in this sense very Western. He liked the way in which she spoke so precisely, so articulately with her sing-song Pakistani accent, laced by a tinge of American. She was well-educated and well-travelled. He had been surprised to see her smoking.

Clearly she was willing to go against convention. And she had hinted at a troubled past that had almost destroyed her. Perhaps she too was running away from an unhappy life. He felt he wanted to know more. Not just because she was young and beautiful, or that he was lonely and a long way from home. Or that he was experiencing a new and exotic culture that she seemed part of.

He arrived early that evening at the house on the hill. He'd been looking for Selby to update him on his media work. The interview with the German broadcaster had run smoothly. The BBC had already broadcast a TV piece from the media package they had received from Relief Action's UK communications team and there was talk of him being interviewed in London when next he was due to return. But that was now likely to be after the next distribution across the mountain, when he was due to travel to England at the end of his current contract. Selby had already told him he had negotiated an extension of his work with Maddison, but his Pakistani visa was due to expire anyway. He'd have to visit the High Commission in London to obtain another one.

The authorities were under instructions to grant the necessary permissions, yet journalists were restricted to stays no longer than eight weeks. And an interview with the commission's media section was inevitable. That meant hours of form-filling, copies of documents, the precious letter of invitation from Relief Action and the long delays in crowded corridors to be seen by an endless stream of officials.

The operations manager was in a buoyant mood, free from the tensions that had seemed to weigh so heavily upon him in the last few days. He was pleased with Cousins' work. In addition, everything was ready for the wider distribution across Kala Dhaka. In Islamabad, Maddison was fully behind the operation. He had requested some briefing notes on the Black Mountain for the Government of Pakistan. The president was to be informed.

"We need to carry the Pakistani government along with us on this one," Selby explained. "Can you put something together to keep them up to speed?"

Cousins was taken aback. His mind was racing. "No problem," he told Selby in a voice which sounded alien to him.

It seemed incredible that just a few months previously he had been sitting in his newspaper office and had first read the story of the earthquake. Now he was in the mountains of Pakistan and part of the small team supporting the first outside intervention within the isolated tribal area in more than a century. The story had drawn international interest. And he was to provide a briefing for the president of Pakistan! It all seemed unreal. He told Selby he'd prepare some notes for Maddison that evening.

"And the Afghan is ready to meet," added the Canadian with the broadest grin. "Looks like the distribution is on."

TWENTY-SIX

The days that followed were a flurry of activity. Cousins was busy with media work, punctuated by visits into the field to document ongoing distributions to mountain villages. A further story had been identified for him to cover and he was set to visit a settlement high above the Saraash Valley with one of the local engineers working with Petrović. Now that the snows had passed, the people within the tented camps were being urged by their government to return to their villages in the weeks ahead to rebuild their lives. But in the village of Dandar the water supply was gone and more than 2,000 people were hoping to return with the onset of the spring. A visit was planned for the days ahead to see what could be done. Meanwhile details had been finalised for the Black Mountain distribution. Selby was just waiting for the Afghan to come in to agree the final route and distribution points.

Cousins had not seen Ali for several days. Then suddenly, he received a text message. She had been thinking about him and his questions about her faith. And she had prayed for him.

She had some material with her he might find helpful in his quest to regain his faith. Would he like to meet over a cup of chai? He was touched by her note, not least of all because he couldn't remember the last time anyone had prayed for him. Like the blessings he had received from villagers he had met in the mountains, it was something in the culture he found endearing.

She was nervous as she approached his guesthouse that evening, clutching the small volume printed in English which described the five pillars of Islam. The weather had turned milder and so they had decided to meet on his terrace. Besides, it would not have been appropriate for her to spend time with him alone in his room. As she sat outside, he approached, carrying a cup of hot chocolate in each hand. She had gained a taste for it during her student days, she explained. And there they sat as the moon rose above the mountains and, like the accomplished storyteller he'd seen in the child-friendly space when first he had observed her, she began to explain the foundations of her faith. Like the children, he was captivated.

After she had left him that evening, he flicked idly through the pages of the book she had brought for him.

It outlined the fundamental basis of her religion: faith, prayer, charity, fasting and Hajj, the pilgrimage to Mecca every Muslim is required to undertake during their lifetime. She also explained the process of prayer and detailed the practice of washing beforehand with water, starting with the hands and forearms, and finishing by washing the feet. It was known as *Wulu*.

It was an act of purifying oneself before prayer, which included the eyes, the nose, the ears, the neck and the mouth, she explained, pointing to each. And of course, he would need a prayer mat. But she did not believe all five daily prayers were necessary to be a good Muslim. She herself had tried and was simply unable to rise in the morning before the sun, she admitted.

Besides, she believed it was not quantity but the quality of the prayer. It was the sincerity that mattered and the purity of thought. Perhaps he should regard prayer as a meditation, rather than a direct communication with God, as she sometimes did herself. A time to reflect on God's blessings, the people and the things that were important to a good life that would please Allah. He smiled as he reflected on the passion and sincerity of her belief.

After she had left him, he wandered into the kitchen and glanced at the two white cups from which they had drunk the hot chocolate. One of them carried the heavy imprint of bright lipstick, a reminder of where her lips had rested against its rim. He was reluctant to rinse the cup. He could still see her face, her brown eyes heavily outlined with kohl, gazing at him over the vessel as she had raised it to her lips. He sighed. He stepped out from the balcony to smoke a last cigarette before heading to his room.

But he did not sleep immediately. As he lay in bed, his mind was filled by the images of what he had seen and felt since his arrival in Pakistan. The experience was intense, almost overwhelming.

And he thought about Ali. He wondered what she made of him. He was flattered by her attention and touched by her kindness. He also admired her passion and courage. She had been one of the first aid workers to reach the devastated town of Balakot in the immediate aftermath of the disaster. She was also determined to access the Black Mountain to assess the children, despite the challenges and potential dangers. And that was a very real prospect as the wider distribution across the tribal area drew closer. A big day was in prospect. The Afghan was expected in the morning…

A battered, grey pick-up drove into the Relief Action vehicle compound and came to a halt, raising a cloud of dust that blew out across the valley in the early morning sun. The Afghan climbed out, then leaned back into the Hilux to mutter something to his driver.

Three Pathans in tribal dress sat in the back of the vehicle. He told them to wait and strode towards the office. Upstairs Selby, Williams and Zhevlakov sat around a large conference table upon which a map of Mansehra District was laid out. They were joined by Cousins, who stepped from an adjoining office to sit with them at the table. All eyes were on the Afghan as he entered the room.

Selby rose from his seat and the two men greeted each other warmly.

"Good to see you, brother. Welcome," said the Canadian.

But the Afghan looked troubled. He did not sit at the table and remained standing. "There is problem," he told them. You could have heard a pin drop.

"What do you mean?" the Canadian asked him. "What kind of problem?"

Shah hesitated. "We cannot make distribution." And he paused, before he continued. "Khans in the south say we cannot pass through their lands. There is no agreement with this tribe," he added awkwardly.

"But we have the backing of the *Loya Jirga*," said Selby.

The Afghan shook his head. "This khan put branch in road and says no-one pass. And if khan puts stick in road it means we cannot pass stick," he told them.

"But everything is ready. And there's no other route for the trucks," the Canadian said.

"Khan says we must do what he asks. But we can make agreement," Shah replied.

"What exactly does he want?" Williams asked.

"He ask for more CGI sheets and other NFIs for his people who have suffered greatly in earthquake," the Afghan responded.

"You mean we have to bribe him," said the American. And he looked across to Selby.

The operations manager fixed his gaze upon the Afghan. "Will he allow the distribution if we give him what he wants?"

The Afghan shrugged. "Maybe he take stick from road. I can arrange."

"And raise tensions with the other tribes," said Williams flatly. "We don't want to start a war!"

"I can talk with the khan," said the Afghan.

An anger rose within Cousins, as he thought about the people of Peer Khel still exposed on the mountain.

"This is bullshit," he said, suddenly rising from his seat with such a force that his chair flew from behind him and toppled over.

"Easy, John," Selby said, urging a sense of calm before he addressed the Afghan.

"You said everything was agreed. Now you say it isn't, unless we pay this chieftain to let us through…"

Shah explained the sub-clan which controlled the stretch of road to the south had demanded additional materials above its agreed allocation. What could he do?

Two things seemed apparent to the Canadian. Firstly, any departure on the aid already agreed would create tribal tensions and potential conflict. Secondly, he now felt sure the Afghan had betrayed them. Ali Khan had been right to express his doubts. It was highly likely the Afghan would also benefit from the deal with the rogue chieftain and that aid items would appear on the black market at the bazaar in Darband. But Shah was adamant. That would be the additional cost for the distribution to go ahead as planned. Selby told him Relief Action would need to consider.

After the Afghan had left the four Relief Action workers sat to determine their options.

"I don't trust him," Cousins said.

"I don't like it at all," Williams added.

"He is like snake," said the Ukrainian.

"But in one thing the Afghan is right," Selby told them. "We now have a big problem…"

And it was true. Following further meetings with Williams and a phone call to Maddison in Islamabad, the Canadian felt he had no option except to put the Black Mountain distribution on hold. Shah's costs for the initial distribution in Kotkhay also came in higher than expected. But it was decided to pay the Afghan anyway. Yet his association with Relief Action was finished. They were now without an implementing partner on which the operation had depended. Meetings with Mohammed Ali Khan also failed to yield an immediate solution. And the tribes were becoming impatient, increasingly desperate for the aid that would relieve their suffering.

And then the rain came. Dark storm clouds rolled in across the mountains and the heavens opened in persistent downpours over several days. The coming of the storms coincided with the early winter thaw, turning roads to rivers and washing tides of mud from the mountainsides. Flash floods flowed through entire villages already devastated by earthquake, compounding the misery of those hoping for an early spring respite. With the severe turn in the weather came the threat of landslides to further hamper access across the ill-fated north-west. And there were days when aid distribution simply wasn't possible.

The mood was increasingly sombre with each passing day at the house on the hill. Yet there was nothing for it. Aid operations would have to wait until the rain subsided.

The frustrations over the delayed distribution to thousands across the Black Mountain who had still not received aid was growing. No solution seemed in sight, not even when finally the rain passed. And still the warehouses remained full with their quotas of CGI sheeting, mattresses and building kits earmarked for the people of Kala Dhaka standing idle. The British were concerned. Maddison assured them distributions would still take place as soon as a new implementing partner could be found. He was already in discussion with several local NGOs.

But time was marching on and the peoples on the mountain saw no alternative but to slowly start to rebuild their villages with what scant materials they had. No-one wanted tribal conflict. Not over aid from outside, which some said would never come. The people were resigned to their fate and focused on survival. Ultimately it was in Allah's hands. And the Americans watched and waited. Their man on the mountain was keeping them informed. They decided to see what might develop with the coming of the spring.

TWENTY-SEVEN

Under darkened skies they made their way from the office across the grass and scrubland, up towards the house on the hill. As the clouds rolled in from the north and reared angrily above the mountains, Ali and Cousins glanced anxiously skyward. A storm was coming.

"I don't know what's going to happen," he replied in answer to her question about the Black Mountain as they walked.

"It will happen as it is meant to, as it is written," she said.

"You believe that?"

"That is what I believe," she affirmed. And they fell silent.

But they were on a mission of a different kind this morning, as they quickened their pace under the threat of the approaching storm. Selby was concerned about Williams, who had become increasingly withdrawn and he had asked them to keep an eye on the American while he was away in Islamabad for meetings.

As they approached the house, Cousins stood for a moment in awe under the prayer carved so intricately over the main entrance. "It's amazing," he said.

"It is the first prayer in the Holy Qur'an," she told him.

"Can you read it?" he asked.

"Yes, I can. It's Arabic," she said. "It is the first Surah we are taught."

And she recited it to him as he listened intently, taking in the exotic sound of her voice.

"Beautiful," he commented, smiling at her. Then they stepped inside.

The dining room was deserted, with breakfast pots discarded upon the main table. In the kitchen they heard the clatter of activity and then saw Jawed emerge. He was one of the team's cooks and smiled as he saw them.

"*Asalaam-u-alaikum,*" Cousins said in greeting.

"*Walaikum Salaam!*"

"Have you seen Mr Williams?" the Englishman asked.

"Mr Williams in room," replied the Pakistani. "No breakfast," he added.

"*Shukria!*" And they headed into the adjacent hallway towards the American's room.

As they stood outside the solid wooden door, they looked at each other apprehensively, hesitating, before finally Cousins knocked. At first there was no reply from within. He knocked again.

"Yeah…" came the American's reluctant response.

"It's John. And Miss Ali's here with me."

"Just a minute," came the muffled reply.

A few moments later they heard the click of the lock and

the door opened wide enough to see the American squinting through the narrow gap at them with tired eyes.

"We've come to see if you're OK," explained Cousins. He didn't know what else to say.

"I'm all right," Williams replied. "Thank you."

"Hank's worried about you," Cousins told him. "He's sent us to rescue you," he added with a smile.

The American's first inclination was to shut the door.

"Coffee?" ventured the Englishman. "We've walked all the way up the hill to see you…"

Williams seemed to consider all options. Then he grinned, almost in resignation, rubbing a hand across his greying blonde hair.

"All right. Just give me a minute." And he closed the door.

When he emerged, he found Ali and Cousins in the dining room. For a moment he stood watching them unseen, before he slowly walked across, stooping slightly like an old man on his way to sit with them. His face was creased with worry and there were dark rings under his eyes. It looked as though he hadn't slept for days and he was unshaven. He looked broken. And yet he was glad they had come to see him.

As they sat over coffee, he told them his father was dying; his mother wasn't coping. But it was more than that. He'd had a troubled childhood. Had never felt close to his father, who had expected greater things from him, particularly as he had excelled at high school, especially in music, for which he held a passion.

They'd hoped he would become a classical pianist. A music teacher, perhaps. And suddenly Williams laughed. Imagine that, he told them. He'd always felt the disappointment of his parents, who were deeply religious. He'd felt unloved. It's why he joined the marines. Just to get away. He hadn't seen his father for years. Now he felt he needed to make his peace. And there were tears in his eyes as he thought about his elderly parents.

"Then you must go," Ali told him.

Williams sat in contemplation, a picture of sadness. "But I have a responsibility here," he said.

"You have a responsibility to yourself and your family," the Englishman responded.

"First rule of aid work," he added. "Look after yourself, or you're no bloody good to anybody." It was what the American had told him when he had arrived. And Williams nodded slowly, as if conceding the inevitable in hearing his own words quoted back to him.

He was feeling the emotional pressure, it was true. He'd travelled to Pakistan with Selby immediately after the earthquake and had not been back to the States since, not even at Christmas. Instead he had taken a few days off in the 'plastic paradise' that was Dubai and all it had to offer. But it wasn't the same as heading back to Seattle, where he'd been born and raised. He was due extended leave anyway. He needed to see his parents. And yes, he would speak to Selby.

After Cousins and Ali left, he sat outside on the terrace, gazing across at the beauty of the distant mountains whose peaks were being enveloped by the dark and dramatic storm clouds. It was a country of contrasts, he mused. Such beauty; such pain and suffering for its people. And the ever-present threat of violence which went hand in hand with the daily battle for survival. More than that, he knew the country lay at the centre of a power struggle across the region, which would continue regardless of earthquakes, floods and famines. And the aid workers could only seek to do their best. They were merely pawns in a greater game. Like a sticking plaster. The underlying, long-term issues would persist and fester in a country that held no real interest in changing the status quo. At least not for the countless millions who lived out their lives in acute poverty.

Yet as he sat there thinking about Pakistan, he suddenly felt as if a great weight had been lifted. He could take a break from it all. He didn't know either of his visitors well, but somehow that had in itself been helpful. He liked them both. And he thought they looked good together. In fact, he liked people even though he sometimes struggled to connect and came across as socially awkward. He knew they were right and was grateful for their concern. Besides, he realised that months of intense pressure as part of the relentless emergency relief operation had taken its toll on his mental and physical health. He decided to return to his room to freshen up. Afterwards he would head down the hill to the office. And he would speak to Selby.

On the way back to the office Cousins and Ali passed a group of children playing cricket on the waste ground. They were from the small encampment of tents and makeshift shelters which had steadily grown over several weeks next to the house on the hill. Although not part of the official emergency aid effort, they were offered tents and surplus items that sometimes clogged Selby's warehouses. And the child protection team was working with the mothers and children.

A pile of bricks served as a makeshift wicket protected by a young batsman clasping a small wooden plank awaiting an incoming tennis ball. Cousins was known to the children as a familiar face on his way to and from the house on the hill and stepped up to bowl a couple of balls, much to the children's delight, while Ali smiled as she looked on. Cricket was not really his game and the children were far more accomplished, even though some of them could not have been older than nine or ten. But he took enjoyment in having his delivery hit for 'six' or the infectious joy in being bowled out by boys who barely came up to his waist. And he would laugh with them. The game was the national obsession. Young and old could be found on any strip of ground playing the sport with makeshift equipment, even up in the remotest mountain villages. Cousins made a mental note to purchase a couple of cricket bats for the youngsters next time he was in Mansehra as they left the children and headed for the office.

After collecting his laptop, he retreated to his guesthouse just as the wind began to blow, whipping up the dust before the impending storm. Sometimes it was easier for him to work without the distractions of staff coming in and out of the office. The first heavy drops of rain began to fall as he entered his guesthouse. He was glad they had spoken to Williams. But he realised he too was tired. The heavy rain began to lash down and he thought about the people up in the mountains. He often wondered what became of the people he met. Some had a profound impact on him, images of their lives playing through his mind.

Like the old man with the reddened beard at a village high above the valley who had sat motionless at the graveside, clutching his prayer beads and crying silently for his wife, the mound of earth beside him covered in gold and silver ribbons. He had not looked up, although he had been aware of their approach. Instead his head remained bowed in grief, staring vacantly at the ground. Yes, they could sit a while with him, as he lamented the passing of the woman with whom had shared his life. She had died from injuries sustained in the earthquake, he told them. But not immediately. And though he had prayed for her shattered legs to heal, in the end Allah had taken her to him as infection had ravished her body and she had slowly grown weaker. And one night, as she lay burning with fever, the breath went out of her. He had lost his companion in life.

But now her agonies were over. She was at peace. Allah was indeed merciful. Yet the old man missed her. She had been a good woman and they had raised a family together. Now she was gone, like so much that had been lost in the disaster. His home was destroyed and his livestock gone. And most painful of all, now he had lost his wife. He came to sit with her every day. It brought him comfort. They had nurtured their sons and watched them grow strong. They now lived and worked in Karachi, and he had not seen his sons for many months. But he was happy that they now had wives and families of their own. And he smiled wistfully. Life, he said, was a journey mapped by an all-powerful, unseen hand. Allah did not burden his people with that which they could not bear. There was a purpose in everything. He had known joy for many years. And for that he was grateful. Somehow, life would go on. The old man thanked the Englishman for his kindness. He hoped he would be blessed with happiness, he said, clutching his prayer beads. Then they had left the old man to his grief.

And there was the distraught young mother who had sought out Cousins on the mountainside. Her baby had died of dysentery just a few days before. Because there was no doctor within walking distance of her village. Would he please come and see her baby's grave? Would he tell the world the story of her lost child? The baby girl's death was not due to the earthquake. It was due to the sickness that claimed so many infants that were falling ill. Due to poverty, ignorance and the lack of basic medicine. For want of a few pills. The grief-stricken mother's imploring eyes were so full of sorrow and pain he couldn't get the young woman out of his mind.

And he could still see the tiny mound of earth he had gazed upon under which her dead baby rested. It was tragic. But there were thousands of stories like hers.

Later he read that one in ten children in Pakistan were not expected to reach their fifth birthday. The UNICEF report made for grim reading. And he came to realise the terrible suffering he encountered in the mountains was not the result of the earthquake.

The disaster had simply compounded the problems of millions who lived out their lives in acute poverty whose daily struggle was to have enough food to eat and maintain a roof over their heads. And as the rain continued pour relentlessly onto the mountains, he realised how privileged he was. Simply by accident of birth...

TWENTY-EIGHT

THE TINY KITTEN died as he cradled it in the palm of his hand. It had been several days since Cousins had discovered the small scrap of life abandoned by its mother outside on the muddy road, drowning in the cold and persistent rain. He was tired. And suddenly he began to cry. Perhaps if he had discovered it sooner… acted more quickly. He remembered delaying, unsure of whether to intervene or allow nature to take its course and let the kitten die where it lay.

As it was, the battle was over. Its life had slipped helplessly from his grasp as he sat alone on the veranda watching the sun rise on a new day above the mountain peaks. The kitten had no longer taken the milk. Not since the day before. And yet, even as it had been moments from death and he had stroked the tiny animal gently with his thumb, it began to purr. Then it was still. He felt his eyes blur and tears begin to roll down his cheeks. He had slept only intermittently during the night. Several times he had tried to feed the kitten. And each time it had seemed weaker.

It wasn't just its loss that affected him. It wasn't the wasted effort either. The small failure struck a chord in a country where so much effort seemed futile. He had simply seen too much suffering: too much hunger and poverty. And he was angry with a world that allowed such things to continue. It was a simple as that. He wasn't really crying for the kitten. He was crying for humanity. His reaction was against cruelty, injustice and, worse still, the indifference towards the suffering he had witnessed.

"What the fuck am I doing here?" he whispered. "What the fuck…"

What was he doing in Pakistan, this vast and alien country, 4,000 miles from home?

He thought about his ex-wife… and the times when they had been happy. Life had seemed less complicated. Happier. Simpler. And he missed his children, now approaching adulthood without him. He wondered if they realised how much he loved them, how much he missed them. Would they ever understand why he had felt compelled to travel to Pakistan and try to do something good for others? Perhaps he felt the need for redemption, following a failed marriage. He felt lost. He felt lonely. And he felt beaten.

Why was he here? He wasn't sure he knew. Something about giving a voice to those who are seldom heard? Maybe. To do some good by highlighting the desperate need of vulnerable people. Perhaps. To escape, to heal… it is what they said of aid workers. Mercenaries, missionaries and misfits. Perhaps he had been a little of all three in Pakistan over the last few months.

But had he really changed anything? Had he *really* helped?

And why was he crying? He had seen death before, when he had reported on the first Gulf War. And in Pakistan since his arrival. He hadn't been able to save anyone. It was the suffering of children that affected him most. But he had not cried. Now, suddenly, the tears were flowing... for the kitten, for the suffering, for the children of Pakistan.

He opened his hand and gazed at the animal. The life had gone from its tiny body. Just like that. Like the children. And the 80,000 lives suddenly ended by the earthquake. In just a few seconds. It was almost unfathomable. And he was tired of the terrible stories of loss he encountered in every village, every town he visited. So many families were still grieving and struggled on a daily basis for the most basic needs. Food, shelter, medicine. The entire region remained in crisis. People were still living under canvas or within the rubble of their homes. And he was deeply affected by the ragged, dirty-faced children he encountered, so often racked with infection and malnutrition.

He had lost count of mothers grieving for their children, sometimes because there was simply no doctor within walking distance. And he felt powerless. Helpless. Sometimes the scale of suffering was simply overwhelming. Cousins gazed at the clouds above the distant hills, their orange glow promising a break from the relentless rain that had lashed the north-west for the last few days. He rose from his seat on the veranda, still cradling the kitten in his hand and went back inside the guesthouse. He placed the animal carefully in the shoebox that had been its home for the last two days and went back to bed. He would ask the housekeeper to bury it out in the yard later. He needed some rest.

As he lay under the covers staring at the ceiling, he thought about the communities he had visited on the Black Mountain. Their suffering was acute. Still they had received no help following the earthquake. And it was nearly spring. The Afghan had proven treacherous, with an agenda of his own. He alone seemed to stand in the way of much-need relief for thousands of families struggling to survive on the mountain.

Selby had been right to suspend the operation. And yet they had only been able to reach a small number of families. There had to be a way.

The Canadian was increasingly away from the office for meetings in Islamabad or with agencies, large and small, to explore working in partnership within Kala Dhaka. But many were not willing to operate within the remote area, where security could not be guaranteed through usual means. Others simply did not have the expertise or the capacity. Ali had also returned to the capital for training and to work on policy documents with her team in Islamabad. Cousins wasn't sure when she was due to return. But he missed their meetings. In the meantime he continued to report on the ongoing distributions and other stories. And in the evenings he would sometimes see Stevenson or Zhevlakov and the Iranian. And he liked Petrović, the Bosnian engineer.

But he knew he too needed some time back home. And it was coming. Eight weeks following his return to the earthquake zone and a trip to England was now in prospect. He wasn't entirely sure whether he would return to Pakistan after that. Selby had said he wanted him back to support the Black Mountain operation. But when, or even if, the distribution would go ahead remained unclear. That was dependent on finding a way to gain safe access and a local implementing partner on which they could rely. As yet, neither Selby, Relief Action nor Mohammed Ali Khan could see a way forward.

Therefore, the thought of returning to England for respite was like a beacon of light that shone out to him: come home. Rest. Recuperate. And return? He wasn't sure how to feel. But he knew he needed a breather. He required some normality. Familiar surroundings. And a chance to evaluate. The following week he had packed his bags and was heading for the airport.

He had no thoughts about the immediate future except to get home and to be among the sights and sounds he knew; to see loved ones and friends. In addition to seeing his parents and his children, he wanted to spend some time visiting Mike in the south-west. They'd always been close and went way back to school days. His friend was one of the few he felt really understood why he had returned to Pakistan. He knew how devastated Cousins had been following the breakdown of his marriage and leaving the family home…

It was good to be back in England, Cousins reflected, as he drove towards the south-west. It was a long drive. But it was a straight, fast run on the motorway.

He had rediscovered the joy of driving on smooth, well-maintained roads, so orderly by comparison to Pakistan. And as he passed into Somerset his heart began to lift as he drove through its rural, rolling landscape, with fields of green either side. Less than an hour later he was enjoying the leafy, winding roads of South Devon as the sun broke through the clouds, heading for the picture-postcard town of Totnes.

But it was more than that. The ancient town was like a haven, a sanctuary set apart from the hustle and bustle of modern life, with a strong alternative community that drew artists, writers and musicians in droves. They lived alongside the town's wealthier, more conservative inhabitants and somehow the combination worked. He smiled as he made the final winding approach down the hill and he saw the ancient Norman fort perched above the town alongside the red stone tower of St Mary's Church in the distance, rising above the small white houses built around the castle mound all the way down to the River Dart at its base. It was, without doubt, a beautiful old town, set within the rural Devon countryside that was in stark contrast to the arid climate of north-west Pakistan, with its rocky mountain peaks, where daytime temperatures were already climbing towards thirty degrees with the advent of spring.

He parked his car in a side road off the High Street and moments later was climbing with his rucksack over his shoulder back up the steep hill under the shadow of the ancient stone castle. They were familiar surroundings to him. He had visited his old friend often, in good times and bad.

Moments later he stood at Mike's front door. The two friends hugged. It had been too long, they agreed. A cup of tea beckoned. His friend wanted to know all about his travels. Then they would eat. And later, a beer at the old Bay Horse Inn.

"I've met someone!" Cousins announced.

"What do you mean?" Mike smiled and took a sip of beer. But he knew his friend's tendency to act on impulse. "I thought you'd given up on women," he added.

And Cousins told him about the beautiful storyteller he had met.

"For a moment, I thought you were serious," said Mike, still smiling.

"I am," Cousins told his friend. "I think I have met the woman I'm going to marry."

For a moment Mike simply stared at him uncertainly. "In your dreams, right?" he said.

"Perhaps." It was wishful thinking. But as Cousins reflected, he suddenly realised the impact Ali had made on him. Then he laughed. "I'm sure she's not interested in me." It was a statement which underplayed the challenges any potential union between them would pose. After all, she was Pakistani. And she was Muslim.

He was white and Christian. Besides, he'd travelled halfway across the world to a conservative muslim region, into a disaster area, where meeting a woman had been the last thing on his mind. At least that's what he told himself.

"For a moment I thought you'd bagged a woman over there..." Mike said, and they downed their beer before heading back to his place to smoke some weed.

Cousins was smiling broadly by the time he negotiated the stairs to the spare room. His legs were heavy, his mind blurred by the cannabis he'd smoked. Aspects of life which had been troubling him now seemed slightly absurd. He felt at peace. Sitting on the side of the bed he made a concentrated effort to pull his clothes off and slumped onto the mattress into a satisfying sleep.

When he awoke, Mike had already left for work. On the table he found a note from his friend and a variety of cereals on the breakfast bar. He was to help himself. Cousins would travel back to the midlands later that morning. It had been a flying visit. But he had wanted to see his friend. Yet he would take time to stroll along the town's High Street, down to the church. And before he hit the road for the midlands he wanted to visit the nearby Dartington Estate, which lay just beyond the confines of the town, with its ancient hall set within its beautiful grounds. It was a place of peace and beauty in which he had often taken solace.

As he sat at a table in the bright sunshine of a March afternoon outside the estate's White Hart restaurant, his mind soared beyond the sweeping lawns and landscaped gardens that delighted his eye. Suddenly his thoughts were back in the mountains of Pakistan. In his mind he saw the brown faces of the people he had come to care for. He pictured their ready smiles and the dark eyes of the children gazing at him through matted hair, barefooted and runny-nosed. And knew there was no question: he would have to return.

He had to go back to the grandeur of the mountains rising from the first folds of the Himalayas; had to see once more the scorched earth of the plains which lay below them, with their lush pockets of greenery. Above all he wanted to see again the smiling people of the villages and hamlets of Pakistan's northwest frontier regions. He would tell their story. And he looked forward to seeing Afsa Ali again. He smiled as he pictured her face.

The shadow of Dartington Hall grew long across its neatly clipped lawns in the afternoon sun. He still had a long drive ahead of him. He drank the last of the coffee from the delicate china cup and rested it gently in its saucer. Then he left, still smiling...

TWENTY-NINE

HE STOOD ON the rocky outcrop at the base of the valley in the shadow of the mountain and gazed at the expectant faces gathered to hear him speak. At his side was Khurram Masood, who would translate his words. The elders from across the Black Mountain had come from far and wide following a plea to all five tribes by Mohammed Ali Khan to hear what the Westerner had to say. Many had made the trek from their villages for many hours. And as they waited expectantly under the glare of the morning sun, they wanted to know if aid would come.

Cousins had returned from England to find Selby on leave. A sealed envelope had been waiting in his room at the guesthouse. The handwritten note inside was from the Canadian. He would be back in Mansehra next week. But an important meeting had been arranged to address what was effectively a gathering of the *Loya Jirga*. And he asked the Englishman to attend in his absence. He was sorry he couldn't make it.

But the visit to the tribal area was to be a matter strictly between those directly involved in the project. A block on all travel to Kala Dhaka had been imposed by Relief Action at the insistence of Williams, due to concerns that tribal tensions might flare following the delay to the aid distribution. Williams was therefore not to be informed. Mohammed Ali Khan would guarantee security. Masood, the man from Gilgit, would assist. However, Maddison in Islamabad was aware of the meeting set to take place. Cousins was to call for unity, for guarantees of security across the five tribes and for their assistance in working towards bringing the aid to those who needed it. The Canadian was still hopeful an implementing partner would be found. He would explain everything on his return. Cousins was to destroy the letter after he had read it.

The Englishman wasn't quite sure how to feel. He was stunned by the letter from Selby. It wasn't the return to Mansehra he had imagined. And for the first time since he had arrived in Pakistan he felt uncertain and uneasy. He sat on the edge of the bed, still clutching Selby's note. He trusted Selby. At the same time, he wasn't really sure what was going on. Yet he felt passionate about the people of Kala Dhaka. He therefore decided he would follow the Canadian's instructions. He would attend the meeting. He was under no illusion there was an element of risk. And he would need to keep the visit from Williams. In the letter Selby said he would take responsibility. He picked up his cell phone and keyed out Khurram Masood's number…

They sat or stood in small groups among the grey rocks and the low scrub scattered on the light brown earth at the foot of the mountain. All wore shades of loose-fitting *Shalwar*

Kameez in grey or beige, black or white. Some faces were framed with traditional flowing turbans, others wore Afghan hats popular with Pathans, while some came in prayer caps. Many of them were armed or were accompanied by their own gunmen. As Cousins stood before the assembled elders it all suddenly seemed a little dangerous.

He felt out on a limb, among a people who were a law unto themselves. It occurred to him he was a long way from everything he knew. He asked Masood to translate word for word what he was about to tell the elders and all eyes turned towards him. Then he drew a deep breath.

First he welcomed those who had travelled so far to hear what he had to say. He was speaking for Selby, his chief, who would return next week. Relief Action was committed to delivering aid to the Black Mountain. But they were still trying to find a way. Agreement across the five tribes would have to be unanimous, including those in the south. There had to be unity. For the sake of all those in need; for the sake of the women and children of Kala Dhaka. The aid would help them to rebuild their communities. And Relief Action would secure a new partner to work with.

But why had the aid only been delivered to a handful of families? What was the delay in delivering the promised materials to all who needed them? So he told them the Afghan had not delivered his promises; that he had made separate deals with the politicians. And that was something Relief Action could not work with. And he told them about barred access from the south. There was a murmur as Khan came to stand beside the Englishman. He confirmed what the Westerner had said. And he pledged he would work to ensure the agreement across the mountain and that those assembled should do the same. The tribes had to set aside their differences if they wanted the aid for the good of all of Kala Dhaka.

Among those who listened were Suur Gul Rafiq and his associate Atul Karim. They had seen the Englishman before, and they recognised in him a sincerity and passion to try to overcome the issues that faced bringing the aid to the area. And they felt sure they could work with the Westerners. It seemed the opportunity they had waited for to link with outside funding to bring aid into Kala Dhaka. They had their own organisation and a network of locals they could draw on.

They knew the area well and had links to the chieftains of the Basikhel and Madakhel tribes. They also had access to the troublesome khan to the south. In addition, they had the ear of the mullahs.

In short, they would be able to work with the various tribal factions at grassroots level. And they had the capacity to put trusted men on the ground. The two men therefore decided that an approach would be made to the Englishman. But they would first speak to Ali Khan.

Cousins decided to take the road south along the River Indus towards Darband on their return to check the route was clear. Ali Khan would accompany them to ensure their safe passage. His Hilux led the way along the dusty, rock-strewn road, with four gunmen in the back of the vehicle. This was the route the trucks bringing the aid were set to take and it led directly into the lands of the tribal chief who had sought a deal with the Afghan. The men knew there was an element of risk. But Khan was confident he would be able to negotiate with the troublesome local chieftain. And he felt the presence of the Englishman might be helpful. It was a risk they were prepared to take.

The sun already hung low in the sky as they drove southwards and into the area which carried the risk of encounter with the local chieftain's men. Up ahead they could see a flat-roofed building by the roadside with several vehicles parked outside. As they drew closer they could make out a group of armed tribesmen. They approached slowly and drew to a halt. Ali Khan was out of his vehicle almost before it had come to a stop and hailed a grey-haired chieftain who stood flanked by gunmen. Cousins also climbed from his Land Cruiser, followed closely by Masood. Khan's own men waited in the back of the pick-up, rifles resting on their laps. And there, standing face to face before the Englishman, was Zaram Khan, the local chieftain, who gazed directly into his eyes.

"*Asalaam-u-alaikum*," said the Englishman. He had heard much about the local khan, he added. And without a moment's hesitation he stepped forward and embraced the chieftain firmly. "*Shukria, shukria*," he said, pulling back as the two men eyed each other. It was a rare moment when the khan had been taken entirely by surprise. But the Englishman seemed oblivious to any tensions which were reflected in the khan's men as they watched uneasily to see what would happen next.

"It is good to meet," said Cousins, smiling. "We will bring the aid to your people with your permission. Many trucks. With your agreement."

Ali Khan translated. But he added all the other tribes had met and agreed it would be so. And the local chieftain should raise no objection. Zaram Khan betrayed no emotion. His heavily kohled eyes remained fixed on the Englishman, then narrowed. He told Ali Khan his only concern was that the needs of his people would be met. But if the other tribes had agreed, he too would allow the distribution.

Then he grinned, revealing brown and broken teeth. He knew resistance would risk conflict. The presence of Mohammed Ali Khan, who claimed to speak for the *Loya Jirga*, was in itself a significant message.

"Very honoured to meet you," Cousins repeated, and then offered his respects once more before climbing back into his vehicle. Ali Khan was relieved and smiled inwardly. And they continued their journey. The foreigner was either very brave or very naïve. Ali Khan wasn't sure which. What he didn't doubt was the Englishman's sincerity. And he was impressed by his determination. He felt an important result had been achieved. In essence, the entire peoples of the Black Mountain were now in agreement.

Khan's vehicle led the final few miles to Darband, the small town of flat-roofed buildings strung out along the road just outside the tribal area's southern boundary, where they pulled over. The chieftain told Cousins he was pleased. He felt security for the aid distribution could now be guaranteed. The rest would be up to Relief Action. And as the Englishman's Land Cruiser drove off, he stood and watched it disappear into the distance, rubbing a thoughtful hand over his greying beard. He felt certain an arrangement could now be made for the aid to come. Besides, he had a plan.

Darkness was falling as Cousins and Masood turned from the main highway and pulled up at the guard post at the entrance to the aid hub in Ghazikot. He waved to the Frontier Corps men and they drove through the checkpoint, into the streets lined with villas that were now offices for international aid agencies supporting the relief effort. The Land Cruiser pulled into the Relief Action vehicle compound and the two men climbed out. The Englishman's immediate priority was to avoid Williams.

It was de Villiers who strode out towards them from the office. "Williams is looking for you," he said. "He's been worried."

"He always worries. We were delayed up near Battagram," Cousins told him.

"He's been trying to get hold of you!" the South African replied.

"No signal up there." And that much was true of many of the remote villages further north.

'Officially' they had been in Battagram, which lay beyond the reach of the regular cell phone network. And it was from there they crossed the border into the tribal area. And no-one needed to know otherwise.

But for now Cousins would go to ground. He'd put a call in to let Williams know he had returned safely to base and would see the security chief in the morning.

"Sure," Williams said on the phone. "But be certain to drop by the office in the morning," the American added. He didn't believe a word Cousins had said about Battagram. He was almost sure the journalist had been into the tribal area. He didn't trust Selby or the Englishman. But he needed to be certain.

That evening, as Cousins sat on the veranda smoking a cigarette and reflecting on the day's events, a text message was sent from a house in the old quarter of Peshawar. The Englishman reached for his mobile phone. It was from an unknown sender; someone called Atul Karim. He had heard Cousins speak earlier that day under the shadow of the mountain. He knew Kala Dhaka and helped to run a local NGO. He would like to arrange a meeting.

As the Englishman sat gazing at the message on his phone, his mind was racing. He didn't know who Atul Karim was or how he had obtained his mobile number. But it was an exciting development and might be just the breakthrough they had been looking for. He would have to respond. He thanked Karim for his message and said he and Selby would be very pleased to meet in Mansehra in the days ahead. He would confirm location, date and time. He could hardly wait to tell Selby what had happened. What a remarkable day it had been.

THIRTY

THERE WAS NO celebration to mark the return of Qazi-ur Rahman and his family to the village of Dandar, high above the Saraash Valley in the mountains of the north-west. It was a silent, sombre affair, following a dangerous journey by an overloaded Jeep on the winding track cut into the mountainside. Expectations among the children before the precarious ride from the valley below had been high. Perhaps some of them had expected more; had forgotten the total devastation they had left behind after the earthquake had shattered their world.

The family left the tented village in Upper Narha, Balakot that day to gaze upon the rubble of their homes for the first time since they had been evacuated to receive aid in the valley below. Little had changed since those first, frightening dark hours. Only the weather was kinder; spring sunshine bathing the green mountain slopes with a gentle warmth to bring a hint of hope. For months they had languished in the camp at the foot of the mountains where they received shelter and food during the winter months, waiting for the warmer weather which might allow a return to their village. They had been long days in unfamiliar surroundings, away from everything they knew.

Still the Englishman and the engineer who accompanied him were greeted by smiles as they sat high in the Himalayan foothills, surrounded by majestic snow-capped peaks and were offered refreshing green tea in the shade of the solitary *Chinar* tree. The reminders during their two-hour hike to reach the village of those lost in these remote mountain areas lay at every turn; graveyards with row upon row of tiny mounds marking the scale of tragedy in human lives. In the distance the township of Balakot still lay strewn across the valley floor, like a toy town of tiny bricks swept aside to total destruction by an angry child.

They had needed to rest frequently. What started at a brisk pace became a mechanical trudge. Small, regular steps. A slow and steady pace. It was what Cousins had already learned from his treks across the mountain. But his Pakistani companion was young and keen to impress, moving off at speed and attacking the mountainside like a local. Many times they were forced to halt. And twice the young engineer had been sick. He was from Islamabad and unused to the altitude.

Qazi-ur Rahman was taking a break from clearing the wreckage of his home to tell his story. The village suffered complete devastation; every house destroyed, crops and livestock lost. The debris of a shattered community lay all around them. He was initially joined by Cousins, who rolled his sleeves up and stood bent shoulder to shoulder with the Pakistani, sweating in the hot sun digging the small plot of land upon which the family home had stood. A canvas tent was pitched on the edge of the small area of land, the family's only shelter.

Salman, the engineer, watched in fascination. He had never seen a Westerner engaged in rigorous manual work, least of all alongside a poor villager. As they stood for a moment's respite to draw breath from their labours, Rahman was smiling, moved by the Englishman's gesture. For Cousins it had been an opportunity to signal solidarity and gain a sense of the physical challenge of those returning from the valleys to their points of origin. It was hard, back-breaking work, likely to take many weeks. The young engineer seized the opportunity to take a photograph to capture the moment as the two men stood side by side. He had also taken several pictures while the Englishman had been digging and helping Rahman remove some of the heavier boulders which had been buried in the earth which had covered the land.

A little girl also watched, peeping from the safety of the nearby tent which currently served as shelter for the family. Her name was Fatima and she was in awe of the white visitor who had been working with her father. She had never seen a '*gora*' before and stared in wide-eyed wonder at the strange visitor. Finally, she plucked up enough courage to venture from the confines of the tent, shadowed by her mother, who was veiled and stood at a distance from the men, as was the custom of her village.

As they sat in the dappled shade of the *Chinar* tree sipping their tea, Rahman told the Englishman the return had been hard for his family.

"We have so many problems that we hardly know where to begin," he told Cousins. "It will take up to thirty days to clear the rubble before we can even start to rebuild our homes," he added.

Each family had received eight sheets of corrugated iron and that was enough to construct one small room only, he explained. The land on which he grew his crops, the essence of their livelihood, would also need to be cleared and prepared. Without crops or livestock, the family had no income, except by drawing on the first payment of government compensation for reconstruction: 25,000 Pakistani rupees, which Cousins calculated to be around 400 dollars. Food was available, the villagers told him, but only by hiring a Jeep at a cost of 1,000 rupees to drive into the Saraash Valley once a week to collect needed provisions.

Qazi-ur Rahman's story was typical of those many thousands who were now returning to their point of origin with the advent of spring to face a fresh battle – how to rebuild their shattered lives from scratch. At Dandar, 400 families had made the trek back to their village in line with government directives for them to go home to begin rebuilding their communities, their lives. Yet their homes were still rubble, their livelihoods lost. The despair could be seen etched into the faces of those responsible for the wellbeing of their families.

Before the earthquake, life had been good for Qazi-ur Rahman, his wife and nine children, leading a simple rural existence high in the Himalayan foothills, scratching a living from farming a few acres of land, supplemented by milk from their goats and eggs provided by a handful of chickens. Even now, he said, it was hard to believe everything had been swept away. His father was killed in the earthquake. He also lost a daughter, nephew and niece. The land and livestock on which he and his family depended were gone.

"We are respecting the directives to return to our village, but we are not happy," he told Cousins. "We do not have adequate homes, no water, the road is not good and no electricity."

The nearest water point for the 4,000 people who had returned to Dandar was a two-kilometre trek across the mountains. The pipework from a nearby spring had been destroyed; the water source itself, now dry, disrupted by a shift in the rock. But there was water higher in the mountains, he explained, which might be harnessed. It was something Salman was to explore in the days ahead.

Dandar was one of eleven villages above the valley being assessed and monitored by specialist Relief Action teams in developing its support programming to help communities rebuild their lives. An immediate priority was to create child-friendly spaces to ensure children would continue to have a safe area in which to play and learn. Two had already been established in the valley, with another three planned at higher altitude, Stevenson had explained to Cousins.

Education would also play a major part of long-term planning, working in partnership with local authorities. And there was talk of school reconstruction. Relief Action had also appointed community mobilisers – members of the local communities able to help identify where assistance was needed and act as a link with the aid organisation.

"The immediate relief effort might be over, but the rehabilitation phase is no less daunting and will be a long haul to enable communities to rebuild a basic level of living standards," Stevenson told Cousins, adding in her clipped Irish accent, "As you have seen, the suffering is still large-scale and the way ahead fraught with dangers and difficult challenges."

Other initiatives being considered focused on livelihood development, education and health, with Selby's teams set to work closely in partnership with local communities, national and international agencies. The emergency aid phase was coming to a close. Already the Pakistan Army had largely withdrawn from its role and the international support from NATO had come to an end. The helicopters had stopped flying their aid missions. The early recovery phase was set to begin.

With the mass return of villagers, water was in many instances an issue. Many springs and supply systems had been disrupted or destroyed in the earthquake, and Selby had given

Petrović a mandate to explore what might be done. Salman had been tasked with an initial assessment of the needs of the village, and he left Cousins with Rahman to map out and explore the immediate area, as well as to speak to other households who had recently made their return. An old man in the village offered to show him where a spring lay which could supply the village. But the trek was long and would require a separate visit.

When the engineer returned it was time for the visitors to say farewell and begin their descent.

"I am happy you are coming and you can see we still need help. *Shukria*," said Rahman. "Thanks to God that we are safe but I do not know what future there is for our children and I am very sad when I compare the picture of our life before the earthquake with the picture of life now," he added with a look of despair.

But before the visitors left, Rahman led them to a narrow strip of ground cleared and prepared for planting during the three days since his return, along the perimeter of his land. He pointed to a newly planted pine sapling and smiled. It was new growth. Cousins followed the line of his finger and saw it was one of a dozen or so, which would afford protection as they grew. It was a small start, but he wanted the Englishman to know it was a beginning. It was a new hope…

The next morning when Cousins strolled into the Relief Action office, the photographs Salman had taken the previous day had been printed out and posted onto the noticeboard in the reception area. They showed the Englishman digging in the rubble, lifting boulders and smiling as he stood beside Rahman, the villager whom they had met. In one of the photographs the little girl could be seen standing, watching her father with the *gora*. Beneath the pictures Salman had written a caption: "Mr John digs Dandar village." A smiley face had been added.

"I see you are a man of many talents, Mr Cousins," said Stevenson, who had approached unseen behind him. Ali was with her.

"Thank you," the Englishman replied, turning towards the women and feeling a flush come to his face. "The villagers up there have returned to nothing," he added.

"We have much work to do still," the child protection manager said. "It's good that you have seen it and can write about it."

She told him her team was working with the village and plans for a child-friendly space in the area were well advanced. They also hoped to secure funding to rebuild dozens of schools, which was to be discussed on Selby's return in the days ahead.

"That's good," he replied. And he nodded politely and excused himself.

He wanted to speak to Ali but couldn't think of anything to say. Besides, he felt a little awkward, not least of all in the presence of Stevenson. He thought Ali looked beautiful in her *Shalwar Kameez*, her bronze face framed by a loose-hanging headscarf and her full lips slightly parted. He didn't mention the Black Mountain. He wasn't sure how significant the approach from Karim was, or whether it would lead to any progress. Besides, it was a matter for Selby.

"See you later," he said and mustered his best smile before escaping into his office.

That evening he received a text message from Ali. Was he coming to the house on the hill later? And she liked the pictures of him working in Dandar village...

THIRTY-ONE

The two men made their way by battered Hilux on the road from Peshawar without escort, aside from their trusted driver. Instead they carried with them papers which documented the work they had carried out educating boys and girls from the poorest parts of Pakistan. But they brought something else of immense value to the meeting in Mansehra. It was a detailed knowledge of the Black Mountain.

They seemed very different from the Afghan. They did not come with promises. Instead they wanted to show what they had already achieved in their work through Sitara Education Foundation. Selby was impressed by the men who sat before him. Suur Gul Rafiq was clean-shaven, with a light complexion for a Pakistani, often a feature only to be found in those from the northern areas or Kashmir. His eyes were also a lighter shade of brown and seemed to hold a warmth and sincerity; and his speech was gentle and courteous. He seemed a modest man.

His companion had eyes that seemed to shine and twinkle. When he smiled, which was often, the corners of the moustache lifted his close-cropped beard, which leant him a contagious sense of mischief. He let his colleague do most of the talking but would contribute to enforce a point with enthusiasm. They seemed an accomplished double act who knew each other well from years of working together. And they shared a passion for their people.

The Canadian warmed to them immediately. Cousins too liked their professionalism and matter-of-fact approach. Their credentials were impressive, as was their passion. And Selby felt instinctively he could do business with them. Their proposition was simple. They were aware of the bid by Relief Action to assist the stricken communities of Kala Dhaka. They knew of Selby and had heard Cousins speak at the foot of the mountain. And they could put experienced men on the ground in numbers. They felt they were ideally placed to work with the international aid organisation.

They told Selby they held close links to the tribes of the Black Mountain; the stricken communities were essentially their people and they knew that for generations the area had been neglected. Kala Dhaka was, therefore, as Suur Gul described, "...one of the most backwards of places in Pakistan. But the peoples are good."

He knew them well and could forgive them their shortcomings, which were largely borne through ignorance and poverty. The two men understood Selby needed a reliable implementing partner. They had an organisation in place and could draw on a network of trained people to assist.

In addition, they could move quickly to confirm the extent of need across the mountain and would be willing and able to complete their own rapid assessment to confirm the Afghan's numbers.

They knew the tribes needed help, would accept outside aid and were now willing to allow access to their lands. The mullahs would also support outside intervention if additional materials were provided to assist the reconstruction of their mosques. The local politicians were of little consequence. But time was of the essence. They believed they could work swiftly and effectively with Relief Action and would be pleased to embed additional expertise by placing local staff from the international organisation among their teams. They understood immediately the requirement for accurate monitoring and reporting.

But the men had a further ace to play. Local knowledge. There was another route into the very heart of the Black Mountain unknown to outsiders. It was a road which wound its way from Oghi in the east and rose onto the mountain, up to the high plateau which lay hidden at altitude among the ragged peaks of Kala Dhaka. It was a fertile area cradled by the encompassing mountain range, which featured lush farmland and wild cherry trees, and fields of opium poppy could be found swaying in the gentle breeze like a restless ocean of pink and purple. It was the route into the heart of a forbidden territory the Afghan had kept from them.

Cousins and Selby stared at each other as Suur Gul traced an invisible line with his forefinger on the map which they had spread before them. From Oghi he showed the unmarked track up into the centre of the mountain, resting his finger where it ended. Was it passable by truck? The two men believed it might be possible. Certainly by Jeep, and that would allow access to high-altitude communities across the mountain. The Madakhel tribe, across the mighty Indus river, was a different proposition. But they were Karim's people and he held no doubt a distribution by boat was possible.

Selby felt he had found the implementing partner he needed to move the distribution forward and it was agreed Suur Gul and Karim should begin mobilising their teams for rapid assessment across the mountain in the days ahead. The Canadian would formalise the contract. And he would identify members of his own staff to assist and begin working under secondment with the two Pathans.

He would take care of things his side. That meant approval from Islamabad and, of course, briefing his own senior team to begin working on the Black Mountain distribution, which would include Zhevlakov, Farzad, de Villiers and Williams. They would aim to be ready to move at a moment's notice, subject to confirmation of the numbers of families in need.

In addition, Selby would, with the permission of the tribes, scout out the suitability of the route from Oghi up into the mountain accompanied by Suur Gul's men. That aside, they would retain the essential elements of the original distribution plan along the valley to the four tribes on the east bank of the Indus. The Madakhel would receive their aid separately by boat. Suur Gul and Karim felt this could be achieved.

It was therefore agreed and they shook hands. After the two men had left the Mansehra office Selby sat smiling at Cousins.

"Can you believe it?" he said. "Looks like we can get the aid to these people after all."

It seemed a significant moment, which Cousins was still trying to digest. But the Englishman was smiling too. De Villiers would be pleased he wouldn't have to worry about mules or porters. They would establish a distribution point on the plateau and ferry aid by Jeep.

Williams was far less enthusiastic. For the American the Black Mountain distribution carried a high degree of risk. Would the tribes keep their word during the operation? Would the Madakhel watch and wait while the rival tribes received their aid before them? What if they came under attack? The Relief Action team would be out on a limb, without protection.

He had the welfare of all staff to consider. He was against it. But Selby was adamant. He felt certain if the tribes had guaranteed security, it would be so. Maddison was to have the final say.

And yet when word came through from Islamabad, Selby was to go ahead. The Pakistani government was also aware and endorsed the distribution. In theory, support would be available from the Frontier Corps stationed in Darband in the event of any serious trouble. And on that basis, Maddison had secured the backing from Relief Action's American head office. What settled any doubt was a request from UNICEF for Relief Action to distribute sanitation kits to the people of Kala Dhaka.

The days that followed saw a series of meetings with Mohammed Ali Khan and the two men from Sitara Education. Rapid assessments took place in scores of remote villages as teams moved across the mountain and met with elders. The numbers of those in need were broadly confirmed: more than 100,000 people were still in desperate need. But at least Suur Gul and Karim had verified figures of their own.

The final date and time was set; a final briefing took place. Selby would move with the main column of trucks along the road which followed the valley, while Cousins was to accompany the Jeeps taking the road from Oghi into the villages which lay at altitude on the plateau.

The operation would see eighty trucks laden with aid set off from warehouses in Mansehra roll into the tribal area, while more than a dozen Jeeps would establish a distribution point at the heart of the mountain for those hardest-to-reach villages.

On the evening before the distribution, the sense of expectation was almost tangible. As they sat at the house on the hill over dinner, Selby was in buoyant mood, which was contagious. He felt the day ahead would be an adventure. More than that, though, he was relieved that finally the operation was to go ahead after so many months of sensitive negotiation.

And he was happy that a neglected people would receive their aid, against all the odds. Williams was more subdued. Yet he was resigned to the risk that the distribution would bring. His contacts with the Pakistani military reported no additional threats in the area and the weather forecast was good.

The child protection team was also excited. Stevenson knew a successful distribution brought the prospect of her team entering the Black Mountain closer. Ali and Johns joined her at the table with the others. Cousins was aware of Ali throughout and tried to keep his gaze from her, but they did not speak over dinner. Conversation was dominated by the forthcoming distribution.

"…and John's going to have one hell of a story to write home about," Selby boomed jovially.

And all eyes turned to the Englishman. "It's a great story to tell," he said, slightly embarrassed, feeling Ali's gaze upon him.

Later, as they began to disperse after the meal and Cousins rose to leave for his guesthouse with Petrović, Ali had made her way towards them.

"I just wanted to wish you every blessing for tomorrow," she said, standing beside the Englishman. "Best of British, as they say." And she smiled right at him.

"Thank you," he replied, gazing into her deep brown eyes. The moment seemed to last an eternity, though in reality only an instant passed before she turned and re-joined Stevenson and Johns, leaving the two men standing.

"She's beautiful," Petrović commented.

"She is," Cousins said absently and sighed deeply.

"I approve," the Bosnian added, smiling knowingly.

"I wish," the Englishman replied with a chuckle.

"Seven o'clock, John. Sharp!" called Selby after them as the two men made their way from the dining table. Cousins raised a hand in acknowledgement as they opened the door and stepped into the darkness. 'Blessings and good luck', she had said. His heart was dancing...

News reached the Americans that the intervention to help secure the Black Mountain was moving forward. The British effort could only help their own plan for development within the tribal area. Their agent would monitor events as they unfolded. He too believed his people would honour their word and was pleased they would receive the much-needed aid. He knew the politicians had been out-manoeuvred and there was little they could do. It was, therefore, with a sense of satisfaction that he travelled from Islamabad up to the mountains to his ancestral lands in the northern corner of Kala Dhaka. He could hardly wait to shed his Western clothing and throw on a more comfortable *Shalwar Kameez*.

He looked forward to spending time in the mountains he had loved since he was a boy. He told himself his collusion with the Americans was for the greater good of his people. And he felt that the Relief Action distribution would be a meaningful step towards keeping the radicals from the region. Maddison had told the British the distribution was ready to roll. At an office within the British High Commission in Islamabad, Keith Bailey was able to report the good news. His faith had not been misplaced. His superiors were pleased. He smiled to himself. Even he was pleasantly surprised a deal had been reached with the troublesome tribes of the Black Mountain. He felt Selby must be a remarkably determined and resourceful man. Either that, or he was plain crazy. Bailey might have been right on all counts...

THIRTY-TWO

THE TRIBAL CHIEFTAIN narrowed his eyes and gazed into the early morning sun. From the mountaintop the distant column of trucks could be clearly seen across the river, snaking along the road which hugged the valley, churning up a cloud of dust as it moved slowly, unmistakably towards them.

The khan and his most trusted men watched from the ridge in silence as the line of heavily laden vehicles stretched as far as the eye could see and was visible all the way back to Darband, rolling steadily onwards. It was a wondrous sight to behold. He raised his rifle and squinted along the barrel at the lead vehicle focused in his sights. He could easily have squeezed the trigger and hit the target with certainty, even at that distance. Instead he grinned and a moment later lowered the weapon. He would not interfere with the distribution. He had given his word.

The Madakhel chieftain felt a sense of relief for his people. He saw the promises were finally being fulfilled. It was surely only a matter of days before his own villages would receive the materials they needed to speed the reconstruction of their homes and livelihoods.

Besides, the Madakhel were a patient people. They had waited and watched, never expecting help from the outside. A few more days would not matter. And he knew the commissioning of boats needed to ferry supplies across the river to his people was already underway.

"*Zu!*" he said abruptly, and the men dispersed immediately, retreating from their position to their vehicle on the track below.

At the head of the convoy rumbling steadily along the ribbon of road in the distance was Selby's Land Cruiser. He was trailed by the Hilux carrying Suur Gul Rafiq and Mohammed Ali Khan, with a contingent of gunmen sitting in the back. And yet the party was remarkably relaxed as they travelled along the road under the early-morning sun in the shadow of the mountain. Selby could hardly keep the smile from his face. He himself was driving, hunched over the wheel in local dress, a loose cotton scarf around his neck. He kept the vehicle in low gear, in four-wheel-drive to allow him to negotiate the rocky road. He was also concerned for the trucks strung out behind him, mostly old Bedfords stacked high with aid. He hoped their axles would hold out. He cackled with delight as the adrenaline flowed through him, much to the bemusement of the young Pathan who sat beside him.

Several miles ahead lay the first distribution point awaiting delivery, where a crowd of villagers several hundred strong had gathered in anticipation of the long-awaited goods. A monitoring team was already in place and had set up wooden tables in readiness. And there the group waited in silence for the coming of the first trucks. Armed sentries stood back from the area, occasionally glancing up at the mountain for any sign of ambush. Yet they need not have worried. Word had gone out across the region a truce was to be observed. And it carried the authority of the *Loya Jirga*.

At the same time a string of Jeeps entered the Black Mountain from the east, climbing up along the winding road from Oghi which led to the hidden plateau. Leading the way was the Land Cruiser driven by Rahim, the mountain man, flanked by the Englishman on the front passenger seat. Atul Karim sat immediately behind Cousins and occasionally pointed out various landmarks or confirmed which way to go when they hit a fork in the dirt track. They were accompanied by Farzad, the Iranian, charged with overseeing the monitoring.

The route was very different from the road which followed the river in the valley below. The track was less rocky and wound its way through a landscape covered in thick pine which rose before them.

But there were pockets of flowering fruit trees too in the hollows and hamlets which lay scattered on land cultivated for maize, wheat and even small irrigated strips of rice paddy. It was a different, hidden side to Kala Dhaka.

Along the dusty track bathed in brilliant sunshine they saw villagers carrying firewood, foliage or water pots balanced elegantly on the heads of young girls, one hand on hip, one raised to steady the vessel. Or they would pass women crouched in the fields tending their crops, who would turn coyly from them as they roared along. And there were children by the roadside too, who would smile and run excitedly alongside the vehicles as they passed. And over the brow of a hill Cousins observed a group of little girls in colourful *Shalwar Kameez* and headscarves strung out along the road, each carrying three or four clay bricks precariously on their heads, holding them in place with both hands. And they smiled and stared as the vehicles approached. Then their eyes would grow wide as they spotted the Englishman. For they had not seen a white man before.

When finally they reached the distribution point, Karim's men were ready and waited with a group of villagers sitting on the ground by the roadside. Any casual observer would have noted the Englishman as soon as he stepped from his vehicle even before the dust had settled. He stood out immediately to the curious eyes fixed upon him of all those gathered, despite his dark complexion, his local dress and the heavy stubble on his face. He had a camera hanging from his neck and wore boots rather than sandals. Yet even the way in which he carried himself marked him as an outsider.

A small group of elders stepped forward from the shade of a stunted Juniper tree and greeted him with smiles to endorse the arrival of the Westerner. Therefore it was plainly understood by all who watched that he came with their approval. And it allowed him to move freely among the people.

Goods were hastily unloaded from the Jeeps by many hands working at speed, directed by the Iranian under Karim's watchful eye as the line of villagers formed in readiness to collect their allotted aid. Many were accompanied by brothers, uncles, cousins, even children to collect their CGI sheets, toolkits, mattresses and hygiene kits. And for the following hour the distribution point was a frenzy of activity as the goods were carried away across the mountain.

"The elders are very grateful. And the mullahs too give their blessings," Karim told the Englishman as they watched. "Many thought this day would never come," he added.

And the old men smiled as Cousins nodded in understanding. "We are very pleased to help your people rebuild their lives," he told them.

A clean-shaven young khan stepped forward and addressed Cousins directly in perfect English, distinguished by his dark sunglasses and bleached-white *Shalwar Kameez*. "My people are very happy to receive the aid. Thank you."

The journalist smiled. "Very welcome."

He didn't catch the name. Cousins was taken by the arm to meet some of the villagers and take some photographs. And when he looked for the man in white, he had gone...

The young khan was pleased to have met the Englishman he had observed at distance for so long. The American agent slipped away and climbed into the Hilux waiting to take him back to the capital, and smiled to himself.

Cousins himself felt relaxed. Despite the presence of gunmen, despite the underlying tension and the remoteness of the area, there were smiles. And with those smiles came a deep sense of fulfilment within him as the last of the NFIs were finally received. It was a sense of satisfaction mirrored in Karim, who stood before him, as the distribution team gathered around them, relieved that all had gone smoothly.

"*Zabardast,*" said the Pathan, smiling. It was an expression of excellence. No other words seemed necessary as the two men grinned at each other and watched the last of the villagers carrying away their aid items.

Down in the valley the operation seemed to run like clockwork. As the trucks advanced, several would pull into a distribution point to unload while the remaining convoy pressed on until reaching the next destination, with Selby leading the way. Ali Khan and Suur Gul would stop at each distribution to ensure all was well, before continuing northwards to oversee how things were progressing at the next. Each had its separate team fielded by the local NGO, with Pathan monitors from Relief Action.

It wasn't until Selby reached the final location almost twenty miles into the tribal area that he pulled the Land

Cruiser over and stepped out of the vehicle, blinking in the bright sunlight to gaze at the scene before him. He was now on the border of the lands held by the Basikhel set for the largest of the four distributions along the route, involving the last nineteen trucks of aid for 20,000 people. Hundreds of villagers had already gathered. In the excitement that followed, tribesmen fired into the air as the vehicles pulled over and dozens of men came forward ready to unload the precious cargo.

The Canadian had never seen anything like it.

For a few moments he simply stood staring, taking in the incredible scenes: the efficiency of the distribution teams unloading the trucks and stacking the goods; the heat, the dust; the gunfire; and the swelling numbers of those who had walked across the mountain to collect their aid. But it was more. There was a sense of relief and jubilation. All set against the breathtaking panorama of the majestic peaks under the spring sunshine. It was a moment he felt he would never forget.

"Bloody marvellous," he exclaimed before turning to his Pathan companion, adding, "It's one to tell the grandchildren, for sure." Then he smiled, took a deep breath and headed over to the elders who had come to see their people finally receive the aid they needed. For the people of the mountain it was also a day that would live long in their memory. Selby's name would not be forgotten for many years to come. And there were blessings extended to the Canadian, the Englishman and all those who had come to Kala Dhaka to assist its people.

As the distribution of goods finally began, Selby took out the satellite phone and called in to Williams. Cousins had already reported in and was on his way back to Mansehra. All was well. Williams sounded relieved. Selby himself would remain until Ali Khan and Suur Gul arrived. The first of those trucks already unloaded at the earlier distribution points were back on the road and set to pass the Canadian's position shortly. They would continue northwards to Thakot, where they would leave the tribal area and join the Karakorum Highway to loop southwards, back to Mansehra.

When Ali Khan and Suur Gul finally joined Selby, the sun was already at its highest point above the mountain. But they were excited to report all distributions were progressing to schedule. The goal was to have all Relief Action drivers and staff back in Mansehra before nightfall. Williams had insisted. Selby put in a final call to the security chief. He told him he would be on his way shortly. Before he left, he stood with Ali Khan and Suur Gul.

"The people will want to give thanks," said the tribal chieftain. "Now they can build their homes."

"Seeing this is all the thanks I need," Selby replied, gazing at the distribution in progress.

"For my people it is like blessing from Allah. And from a white man," said the chieftain with a wry smile. Suur Gul was smiling too. "It will be remembered in Kala Dhaka," added Khan. And the men shook hands.

"We will meet again soon to discuss the distribution across the river. That's a challenge for another day." And with that Selby headed back to his Land Cruiser and pulled onto the road towards Thakot.

When finally he arrived at the house on the hill, there was a buzz of excitement. Cousins rose from the dinner table, as ever, coffee in hand, smiling as the Canadian entered. And the two men embraced.

"We did it," Selby said, grinning at the Englishman, before turning to speak to those who had lingered after their meal in anticipation of his return. All the expat staff members were there. So were most of the senior monitors from the distribution teams. And so too was Afsa Ali, with Stevenson.

"Bloody brilliant work today," the Canadian said, addressing his staff. "Absolutely brilliant," he repeated. "Thank you to all of you. It is an amazing achievement. What a great team!" And he paused, smiling, seemingly out of words. He was exhausted. "Tell you what, though, I could sure use a cup of coffee!"

It was de Villiers who rose from his seat. "To Kala Dhaka and a successful distribution," he said, lifting his teacup. "To Hank and the team! One of the craziest men I ever knew!" And a toast was raised to Selby with an assortment of beverages.

"I'll drink to that," the Canadian replied jovially. "If only I had a drink…"

"Get the man a drink!" de Villiers shouted across towards those closest to the kitchen, and a moment later a cool bottle of cola was thrust into the operation manager's hand.

"This water in my glass I dream is vodka," Zhevlakov cried. "And I say *Na Zdorovie!*"

"*Na Zdorovie*," came the response in unison from all those gathered as a second toast.

The sense of relief that the operation had been a success was written in smiles across the faces of the Relief Action team as they resumed their seats and an excited chatter filled the room. The tension of the intense planning over the last few days had lifted. It had, indeed, been a team effort. Only Williams stood solemnly, thoughtfully, watching the Canadian who stood with de Villiers and Petrović. He caught Selby's gaze and the security chief approached, leaning forward to mutter something into the Canadian's ear. Selby nodded. The smile dropped from his face and the two men left the room.

"So you did it," she said.

Cousins turned towards Afsa Ali and smiled. "Yes, we did it!"

"I'm glad it went well. It's a big achievement."

"Thank you," said the Englishman. "It was a good day for the people of Kala Dhaka."

"We're hoping it might open a door. For the children—"

"You don't give up, you people, do you?" he said, giving her a sideways look.

"No, we don't..." she said. But she was smiling too.

"Let's step into the garden, where we can talk better," he suggested. "I think I need some air." And she followed him outside into the coolness of the early evening as the sun began to slip below the mountain peaks.

In the cocktail lounge at the British Club deep inside Islamabad's diplomatic enclave, Keith Bailey was handed an envelope by the white-gloved steward.

"Excuse me, gentlemen," he said courteously, stepping aside from the small group of officials in evening dress. The news it contained was good. "They've pulled it off," he mused, almost out loud.

He returned to the group of embassy officials and Foreign Office staff and suddenly exclaimed, "Gentlemen, the drinks are on me!"

THIRTY-THREE

No-one could have foreseen the accident. The man lived locally and was familiar with the mountain roads. He was an experienced driver. Whether he swerved to avoid the large boulder, or whether he misjudged the edge of the road was not known. Perhaps he was careless following the aid drop in heading out of Kala Dhaka to return to Mansehra with the empty wagon as speedily as possible. Or maybe he was simply tired and momentarily lost concentration. The driver immediately behind the ill-fated vehicle said the truck ahead seemed to suddenly career from the road and into the chasm below for no apparent reason, just outside the tribal boundary. They had already passed Thakot and were heading towards the Karakorum Highway. No other vehicle was involved. When the mangled truck was finally reached, the diver was found to be dead.

Williams delivered the news stony-faced. The colour seemed to drain from Selby. There would have to be an investigation and the authorities informed. The organisation would be expected to visit the man's family, whom Williams understood lived locally on the edge of Mansehra. Compensation could be paid as an act of goodwill.

Yet it had been an accident on roads that were known to be treacherous and was, in a sense, an occupational hazard. The accident had also occurred outside the tribal area after the distribution had been completed. The man and the truck had been contracted through an outside agency.

He was not a member of staff. There was no reason to expect any further repercussions, Williams stated simply. It was always a worry.

"And we should attend the funeral," said the American. "That's likely to be tomorrow, or as soon as things can be arranged by the family. We need to be seen showing every support," he added, and Selby nodded in agreement.

"I'll go with de Villiers and a couple of the local staff," the Canadian said.

"Amjad can assist with the local authorities," Williams suggested. The former Pakistan Army man was the security chief's deputy and had good connections. The organisation must be seen to have taken all precautions to minimise risk. And it should present itself as compassionate and supportive beyond any legal or moral requirement. It was simply an accident.

"You know these things have the potential to blow up into an issue," Williams continued.

"They do," Selby replied thoughtfully. "But that's the business we're in."

Yet it was a bitter blow and cast a shadow over the entire operation, which had otherwise been an unprecedented success. Yes, Selby knew there had been an element of risk. Hazards always existed in delivering aid in what was considered a hostile environment. But it had affected him.

The question he asked himself was whether a man's life was a price worth paying to help alleviate the suffering of many thousands. His conclusion did not make him feel any better.

News of the driver's death was not officially announced across the organisation. Cousins was briefed in confidence by Williams and Selby in case anything was likely to appear in the local media and was asked to prepare a statement in readiness. Yet the news was common knowledge among staff within twenty-four hours. And there was a subdued mood across the organisation which dampened the initial exuberance following the Black Mountain distribution.

At the burial, de Villiers, Williams and Selby stood respectfully, head bowed, flanked by local Relief Action staff. The body was carried into the cemetery from the mosque draped in white cloth to wails from family members. The imam recited verses from the Qur'an as the assembled congregation held their hands before them in prayer and the dead man was lowered into the ground, facing west towards Mecca. And as family members threw handfuls of dust into the grave, Selby noticed Williams was trembling. He glanced at the American's face and saw that he was crying…

Cousins was not required to attend. Instead he spent the morning scanning the local newspapers and reviewing the statement he had written. He wondered how the dead man's family would cope.

He had left a widow and three young children, with no means of support. He didn't know what compensation they would receive. But he hoped Relief Action would be generous. As a humanitarian organisation it would seem only right. He sighed deeply and took a sip of his lemon tea.

Then he viewed the pictures he had taken during the distribution and earmarked half a dozen to submit. He would write his report in the afternoon, ready for Selby's approval on his return. It had been an incredible experience, he reflected; it had been an adventure. Interest across the media was still strong, as it was within the international aid communities. And he was pleased he had been able to play a part in bringing the earthquake back into the international media spotlight. Supporting the distribution to thousands of neglected people within the small tribal area had been an unexpected and fulfilling bonus. He was considering how to begin his feature-length account when the ping on his mobile phone alerted him to a message. It was from Afsa Ali.

She was on her way to Islamabad to help deliver a training on child protection for staff at the Relief Action office and would spend the subsequent weekend with her family. If he was due to visit the city perhaps they could meet. Would he like to visit the Faisal Mosque for prayers?

Normally he stayed in Mansehra, which he preferred. Like Selby, he was unimpressed by the capital's modernity, its lack of character and its obscene wealth. It only seemed to amplify the poverty of the mountain communities he had seen. But this was a very different prospect. He was due a weekend in the city. Most of the international staff went regularly for respite from the pressures of their work. And he felt an excitement rise in him at the prospect of meeting Ali. He replied almost immediately.

Yes, he could be in Islamabad and would be delighted to visit the mosque one evening over the weekend. If she could please let him know what day and time would suit, and where they could meet. He would look forward to seeing her and thanked her for her message. And he had a small gift for her, a collection of lyrical poems by famed Bengali writer Tagore.

Then he smiled as he pictured her face and took another sip of his tea. He decided to make a start on his report, so that he could submit it to Selby before his departure to the capital in the morning...

The Murree Road sweeps down from the rolling hills into Islamabad from the north-east, where the greenery of the mountain slopes give way to grey suburban carriageways flowing with heavy traffic. Joining the busy Kashmir Highway took them to the southern edge of the city, before they were able to turn onto Ataturk Avenue, back towards the Margalla Hills.

The city's wide avenues and boulevards were choked with traffic in the Friday rush before afternoon prayers. Along the way they passed the colossal Marriott Hotel which stands like a fortress as they skirted the heart of the city to reach the Margalla Road on which his guesthouse lay. The Jacaranda 'family' guesthouse was one of the quieter city hostelries. It was set back from the road within a walled garden of palm and banana trees which afforded welcome shade from the heat of the day. And there was a Jacaranda tree in full bloom of blue and purple blossom set at the side of the main house. It was a welcoming sight after the long drive from the mountains as Cousins stepped wearily from the Land Cruiser.

He asked the driver to pick him up the next day at noon. Then he checked in at the front desk and went up to his room. Suddenly he realised how tired he was. He was thankful he had the rest of the day to relax and flopped onto the bed. As he lay there on his back staring up at the whirring ceiling fan he fell into a deep and satisfying sleep.

The next day he rose to a morning of brilliant sunshine and a view of the Margalla Hills from his window. To feel the spray of a decent shower was a reminder of a simple pleasure he had been denied in Mansehra and left him feeling refreshed and energised. Perhaps he should visit the city more often. It was a chance to clear the mind and process. He had spent the evening at the guesthouse in his room, surfacing only to feast on chicken and fries from the kitchens downstairs in the small dining area. He had been the solitary diner. Then he had returned to his room and sent several text messages to his family. And to Mike, to tell him he was set to meet the young woman he had told him about. He thought about his children and wondered what they were doing. Then picked up a book and read until he felt overtaken by fatigue once more.

He breakfasted light with egg and toast and then sat in the garden to savour his coffee under the trees. With him was the copy of Tagore's *Gitanjali* for Ali. He had purchased the volume during one of his many visits to Dartington Hall. The Indian artist, poet and philosopher had visited the estate many times and the collection of Bengali verse had won him the Nobel prize for literature in the early part of the last century. And as he flicked through its pages, Cousins was moved by the power of the imagery, which seemed to resonate with him. He thought Ali would appreciate the spiritual emphasis to the prose.

They were to meet in the evening at six, when she would pick him up from outside the Relief Action office. Gillian Taylor, one of the organisation's senior child protection leads from head office, was also in town and had expressed an interest in praying at the mosque. She would be escorted by Stevenson and Johns. Imran would be there to guide Cousins, whom he knew as one of the distribution monitors in Mansehra. The Pakistani would show him the protocol to follow for prayer.

Strict segregation was enforced, with men and women required to worship separately. It would be an experience.

In the meantime, he decided to head into the city. Jinnah Supermarket would be a good place to start. Selby had introduced him to the shopping complex, and he knew it boasted one of the biggest and best bookstores in Pakistan. The discovery of a row of traditional craft shops on its far side had been a highlight. Best of all, he had found a jar of Marmite in one of the local supermarkets. He would deliver it to Stevenson next time her saw her.

Later, as he waited for his vehicle to take him to meet Ali, he was uncertain what to expect from the evening ahead. He was nervous at the prospect of seeing her. He had come to view her as more than a colleague. He was also unsure how it would work out with the other members of the child protection team who would accompany them to the mosque. He would have preferred to have met her on her own, although he realised it would be culturally inappropriate. In the event Ali was waiting for him alone. The others had already gone ahead. She looked stunning in her traditional dress, draped by a long, flowing outer garment and she raised her shawl from her shoulders to cover her head as his vehicle drew near.

In truth, she was nervous herself. Perhaps even a little confused. According to her culture, she should not have met him without a chaperone. But she had been brought up in a liberal family and was spirited. After all, he was a work colleague, she told herself. It was a friendship. Yet she knew it was becoming more than that. She was curious about him and felt an undeniable attraction. The fact that she knew meeting him was against convention made it even more difficult to resist. For there was a rebelliousness to her nature. Therefore, as his Land Cruiser pulled up and he stepped out towards her in his *Shalwar Kameez*, she felt a thrill of excitement.

"It's great to see you," he smiled.

"You too," she replied simply. He could tell she was nervous.

"The others will meet us there," she explained. "So I'm your driver for this evening." But now she was smiling too.

"More glamorous than the last one," he said. And she glanced at him uncertainly.

"That's my car," she said, gesturing towards the black Toyota Corolla parked immediately outside the office. He followed her over to the vehicle and they climbed in, then watched her slide the key into the ignition and start the engine. It was the first time he had noticed her hands.

They were beautiful hands, with long, elegant fingers. He could sense she felt awkward under his gaze, so he turned to look from the window.

"Have you been driving long?" he asked.

"I learned when I was fourteen," she told him.

"Crikey! That's young." And he casually lifted his arm to grab the handrail.

"It's not unusual here," she said. And she put the car into gear and pulled off.

Though self-conscious in his company, she was a competent diver. What were his impressions of Islamabad, she asked? He hadn't seen much of the city, he replied tactfully, not wishing to offend. It was very modern, she conceded, which she considered both good and bad. The viewing platform in the hills was, she felt, the place to view the city. From a distance! And he wasn't sure if she intended the joke but smiled. Lahore was very different, she told him, with fine traditional architecture, a sense of history and a vibrant arts scene. He had heard that, he said. And they fell silent as they approached their destination, which suddenly came into view.

There was nothing understated about the Faisal Mosque. Its magnificence rose up in brilliant white stone at the end of its long approach from the main road, framed against the Margalla Hills. It was the perfect fusion of modern architecture combined with the cultural traditions of Islam, its four pointed minarets standing like sentinels to protect its angular central prayer hall. It was a breathtaking structure on an epic scale that did not disappoint the eye as its surface reflected the last rays of the setting sun and the call the prayer rang out. A tide of people streamed along the walkways towards the mosque as she pulled into a parking space. But the two white women were easy spotted, standing with their Pakistani companions outside the main entrance.

"Mr Cousins," exclaimed Stevenson with a hint of mischief.

"Gail, Miss Johns," Cousins nodded courteously in greeting.

"This is Gillian Taylor, visiting us from the States for a few days," Stevenson added, introducing a tall American. "This is Mr Cousins, our communications officer. Imran I think you know."

Again he nodded as the American woman smiled at him. And he shook hands with Imran.

"We'll have to leave you now," said Ali.

"That's right," Stevenson added. "We women have to pray in the ladies' gallery. We'll catch you later."

"Imran will stay with you," Ali told Cousins. And he watched as the women disappeared into the thronging crowd.

Imran lead him up the marble steps towards the main prayer hall, where the Pakistani told him he would have to remove his boots and socks. Then he showed him the row of basins where people were washing their faces, hands and feet under running water, the required purification before prayer. As Cousins took his place at a basin, he watched and followed the actions of the man beside him. Imran waited for him and there they stood, barefoot, ready to enter the *Masjid* hall. Inside hundreds already stood in rows on the sweeping communal prayer mat. The Englishman took a deep breath and followed Imran inside.

THIRTY-FOUR

Afsa Ali stood motionless on the marble walkway framed by the grandeur of the white mosque, set against its dramatic mountain backdrop. Her face was turned towards the cool air blowing from the north in contemplation, and the flowing fabric of her gown fluttered in the soothing breeze like a delicate flame. Conspicuous by her lack of movement, she was like a fixed point in a kaleidoscope of motion as people leaving the mosque passed by, seemingly oblivious to all around her.

A flush of crimson light still outlined the dark peaks on which her eyes rested, and she felt the wind caress her face as she watched the last remnants of the day slip away. She seemed at peace.

Cousins was captivated by the beauty of the scene he observed at distance, reluctant to approach and thereby cause the moment to pass.

After evening prayers he had become separated from Imran in the crowd as it had surged from the central hall towards the exit to escape into the open air and had taken up his position outside against a stone pillar in the hope he would spot one of his companions. That's when he saw her as the last of the worshippers began to disperse. He had been content to watch her in unguarded reflection for several moments unobserved. It was while he contemplated his next move that a familiar voice rang out behind him.

"Ah… Mr Cousins. There you are." It was Stevenson who came to stand beside him. "We thought we had lost you, and Miss Ali came to look for you," she added as they both gazed across to the young woman who had not yet spotted them.

"She's waiting for you. You should go to her." And as he turned towards Stevenson he saw she was smiling.

"Have a nice evening," she added. "No doubt we shall see you both in Mansehra Monday morning." And then she was gone.

He walked barefoot across the cool marble concourse to her, boots in hand, and she turned her face towards him, smiling in recognition as he approached. For a moment they stood facing each other, uncertain what to say. And for an instant, it seemed, the world stood still. It was a moment of recognition.

It was Cousins who spoke first. "Glad I found you!"

"I was worried about you when Imran told me he had lost you," she said.

"We became separated in the rush," he explained. "So I decided to wait outside."

"I think the others have already gone," she said and he nodded.

"It's a beautiful setting," he said. "Thank you!"

"I'm glad you enjoyed it," she replied, then hesitated. "Perhaps you would like to go for coffee," she ventured, surprised and thrilled by her own boldness.

"Coffee would be lovely. If that is OK," he said, his heart on fire.

"There's a place just a few minutes away," she told him. "But you will have to put your boots back on," she smiled. And as they both gazed down at his feet, he felt slightly self-conscious.

Then he too smiled. "Good idea!" And he chuckled at himself.

The American-themed café she had chosen was a popular hotspot for coffees, cakes and ice cream, surrounded by a small garden with outdoor tables set among the flowering shrubbery. It was teeming with Islamabad's trendy young elite, hungry to feed their appetite for a Western liberalism that was easy for the privileged to pursue. It lay within an area known for its well-frequented eateries, Shisha bars and ice cream parlours just off the Kohsar Road in the city's fashionable F-7 district.

They took a table in a corner of the garden largely shielded by vegetation. The coffee and the cakes were famed across the capital, she told him, as he picked up a menu from the table.

"Thank you again," he said.

"For…?"

"For meeting me. For showing me the Faisal Mosque. And for bringing me for coffee," he replied. "I hope you won't get into trouble."

"I am your guide," she told him simply. "It is my duty." Though even as she spoke she knew it wasn't really true. She had wanted to meet him; wanted to know more about him. And she knew that her parents would not have approved had they known she was alone with a man she barely knew. Especially a foreigner. But she trusted her own instincts and was happy to be in his company. Her privileged status, her own confidence and the fact that Islamabad was a liberal, Westernised city gave her assurance.

"How did the prayers feel for you?" she asked.

The experience had been quite overwhelming, he admitted. He had never stood with several hundred people praying as one. And the mosque was impressive.

Though he did not understand Arabic, he had followed the pauses in the Imam's address, inviting the responses from those gathered before him, copying the actions of those around him as they rose, knelt and prostrated. The prayers themselves had felt comforting, cleansing, allowing a purity of thought as if in meditation. He found it calming.

"That is how I feel," she said, contemplating what prayer meant for her. "It gives me comfort. For me it is direct communication with my God. But sometimes I use it to consider, to think how I might be a better person, or to offer blessings for other people. It does make me feel humble and grateful; closer to God. And that's reassuring. Allah is central to everything."

She told him she had lost her faith in her teens and had felt empty. She described it like a bereavement which had almost destroyed her. She had felt lost. So she had searched for inner fulfilment, exploring many faiths. And yet that sense of inner peace eluded her. She became sad and depressed. Forsaken. And her life had crumbled with the failure of successive relationships. Until she woke up one morning and felt the need to pray to Allah. And it had felt like coming home. So she had returned to the faith and her family in Islamabad. And slowly, with prayer and faith, she began to recover.

"It felt like a redemption; a second chance. As if I had been saved," she concluded.

The sincerity and conviction with which she spoke of her inner turmoil did not leave him unmoved. And he could only guess at the personal trauma she had experienced as a young Muslim woman studying overseas who had lost her way in a world very different to her own.

"That's when I realised nothing in my life was more important than Allah and that I wanted to do His work. And that I would probably spend the rest of my life alone."

Their drinks arrived and they both leaned back as the waiter placed them on the table.

"That would be sad," he said as the waiter discretely withdrew.

"Why would that be so sad?"

"Because you are much too beautiful," he said unashamedly. She wasn't sure how she should respond.

And she felt herself blush.

"Sorry," he said instinctively. Then he remembered the book.

"I have something for you," he said, fishing out the volume of poetry from his pocket and presenting it to her. Tagore she knew. Who in South Asia didn't? And she was thrilled.

"Thank you. That's very kind," she said, flicking open the book and fluttering through its pages.

"He was an amazing guy. May I?" he ventured, reaching out his hand. And she handed the book back to him.

He looked for his favourite poem within its pages, composed himself and began reading to her:

"'It is the pang of separation that spreads throughout the world and gives birth to shapes innumerable in the infinite sky.'

"That's a beautiful line, isn't it?" he commented, before reading the remaining two verses.

He smiled as he closed the book and handed it back to her.

"That's lovely," she said. "Thank you."

Instinctively he reached across the table and took her hand in his. It was the first time there had been physical contact between them. It was a powerful moment of intimacy which felt entirely natural. As if they belonged together. Suddenly it felt as if everything had changed. And they sat looking at each other, a little overcome by their feelings. She smiled and squeezed his hand gently before releasing it.

"Perhaps we'd better go," he said huskily. "I'll pay for these," he added, regaining his composure. He rose from his seat and walked towards the café as calmly as he could to settle the bill. But his heart was racing. When he returned she was already standing.

"What would your family say if they knew we were together alone?" he asked.

"They don't need to know," she replied. "But probably they would disapprove."

"So why did you meet me?"

"Because I like you," she replied simply. And they left the garden to walk to the car.

When they arrived back at his guesthouse he felt an overwhelming desire to kiss her goodnight. But he didn't. Instead he thanked her again for a wonderful evening. As he opened the door to get out she put a hand lightly on his shoulder and he turned towards her.

"Will you pray about us, please?" she asked him. "As hard as you can. And ask Allah what he wants from us?" It might have seemed a strange request. But he knew it was important to her and her faith, which he respected. So he assured her he would do so and said goodnight. He smiled as he closed the door and watched her drive off into the night.

When she arrived back at the family home her mother was already sleeping. But she could see the light still burned in her father's study. She popped her head in and said goodnight.

Had she had a good evening, he asked her in Urdu, looking up from his reading? And she nodded. Her colleagues had enjoyed the Faisal Mosque. She sensed he wanted to talk but she was keen to escape to her room.

"Goodnight, Papa." And she planted a kiss on his cheek.

In the confines of her room she sat on the bed and thought about the Englishman and the attraction she felt for him. She couldn't understand how it had happened. It was not what she had sought. But now that she had met him, she couldn't seem to fight the feelings the were developing for him. She pulled out the book of poetry from her bag and found the passage he had read to her. And as she read it again she could still hear his voice. It was a beautiful BBC voice, she mused. And she smiled. She wondered if it was wrong to seek happiness in another human being in the eyes of her God? After all, he was a Westerner and a Christian. But he seemed open to Islam. Perhaps Allah had a purpose in bringing him into her life. She would pray about it.

Across the city Cousins also sat thinking about the evening at the mosque. What an extraordinary night. Clearly something special was developing with Ali in a way he would not have dreamed possible. Had they really held hands at the café afterwards? Yet his entire experience in Pakistan had been incredible and he felt as if he was being swept along by events beyond his control, as if directed by a higher power. And he felt grateful.

He had been moved by what he had seen in the mountains and the resilience of the people in the face of heartbreaking loss. And yet their faith remained intact. He had encountered nothing but kindness in Pakistan and was humbled by their hospitality, and their willingness to share what little they had. Even offering to share their emergency biscuit rations in the rubble of their homes over a cup of chai. With ready smiles. He was inspired too by the tireless enthusiasm of the aid workers he had met. He had been offered a chance of happiness and personal satisfaction which he had never expected to know again. He couldn't quite make sense of it all.

He sank to his knees and began to pray. He prayed in thanks for the last few months in the earthquake zone. He prayed for the people in the mountains he had come to know and respect. And he prayed to keep a promise to the woman he was falling in love with. When he rose to his feet there were tears in his eyes. He wasn't sure what he had done to deserve the fulfilment he had found 4,000 miles from home…

THIRTY-FIVE

They sat on the hill overlooking the township as the sun set over the mountains.

His shoulder leaned gently against hers and they held hands under the folds of her shawl as they watched the sky turn orange. Since returning to Mansehra they had seen each other at every opportunity, often after long days in the 'field'. And they would sit outside on the terrace of his guesthouse, which lay just inside its walled enclosure, sipping refreshing green tea, sharing their hopes, their dreams and their beliefs as they teetered on the brink of a passion. There seemed a new and exciting purpose to life. It was a drive as old as creation.

"Is what we are doing wrong?" she asked him.

"It doesn't feel wrong," he answered.

"Do you think people know? About us."

"I'm sure they suspect…" And he paused. "It's the smiles I get. Especially whenever you are mentioned."

"We should be careful," she said. "This is the north-west." And he nodded.

But their interest in each other had not gone unnoticed. It was in fact an open secret among Relief Action staff that they were seeing each other and that their friendship seemed to be developing into something deeper and more intimate. Yet they were discreet. Both knew a liaison was essentially forbidden according to the conservative practices of the north-west. But they were popular with their colleagues and their situation somehow touched a romanticism in those around them, and stirred a gentle smile whenever they were seen together. Even in the locals, whose popular culture had long echoed the bittersweet pangs of forbidden love.

Yet she was more concerned about keeping favour with God. She believed Allah could see into the hearts of all. Surely then He knew. And if He disapproved, He would make it known. She believed that. It was from her God that she sought guidance and not from the conventions dictated by the society in which she lived. But it held her back as she agonised over her feelings towards him and the physical intimacy she craved, and how it would sit within her faith.

"Did you pray for us that night after the mosque?" She hadn't asked him directly before.

"I did," he told her. "And an image did come into my mind."

"What did you see?" she asked, turning towards him, almost afraid of what he would say, because she believed in such things.

"I saw we were together." He hesitated. "And that there would be children…" He smiled at the thought. "I saw the vivid image of a beautiful little boy," he continued. "And behind him, less clearly defined, two little girls."

"Why didn't you tell me?"

"I wasn't sure," he said, looking for the right words. "It wasn't a dream. But it was more than a thought. More like a vision. I didn't want to freak you out. Especially as you said you felt you would never have children."

It was true. She had said it. But as she considered, she realised that her perspective had changed. The idea of having a child no longer filled her with fear.

"*Would* you marry me?" she asked.

"I would," he replied simply, without hesitation. "Is that a proposition, Miss Ali?" he asked, smiling.

And she laughed. "What makes you think I'd have you?" she said playfully.

"Because you know I be good to you." And with that he rose, pulling her up to her feet, as the last sliver of orange slowly slipped below the mountain peaks on the distant horizon.

"We should be getting back," he said, and they took the trail down towards the guesthouses in the hollow.

"Would you really marry me?" she asked him as they walked. "A Pakistani Muslim."

"Course I would."

"You'd have to convert to Islam."

"I'd have no hesitation in converting," he told her. And it was true.

It was a pleasant thought. Not least because she believed him. And it set her thinking.

The call from Selby sounded urgent. Could he come to the house on the hill? There was something he needed to discuss with Cousins. He wolfed down the last of his Marmite toast and was out of the door, taking the path across the waste ground in the early-morning sunshine up towards the main house, where the Canadian awaited his arrival. The operations manager was troubled by the latest reports that had been relayed to him. He needed to speak to the Englishman. When Cousins arrived the Canadian looked agitated and signalled for the journalist to follow him into the adjoining lounge.

"John, there's been a development… several, actually," Selby said, drawing a deep breath.

"What's happened?" Cousins asked with a degree of apprehension.

"There's been some tension between the tribes. In Kala Dhaka. Some shooting. We think sparked by the delay in delivering the aid across the river. We don't know the full details. Amjad's trying to find out more." And he paused. "We'll have to move as soon as we can."

In addition, the Government of Pakistan was calling for a report from Maddison of activities to date. Could he help with the government briefing by adding to the narrative? He'd make sure all the stats were provided.

It might even find its way onto the president's desk.

Cousins raised his eyebrows. "Of course," he told Selby.

So this wasn't about Ali. He breathed an inward sigh of relief.

"And I've decided to press ahead in Kala Dhaka, unless we hear otherwise," the Canadian added. "I'd like you to report on the distribution across the Indus." He'd already briefed Galina and de Villiers, and they were moving in readiness with Suur Gul and Karim.

What did Williams make of the situation, Cousins asked?

"That's the other thing," said Selby. "He left yesterday—"

"Bloody hell!"

"His father died. He needed to be with his family. But I am not sure he will be back."

"I'm so sorry to hear," said the Englishman.

"It wasn't wholly unexpected. But it hit him hard. In the meantime I've asked Amjad to take charge of security and he's been keeping the army and Frontier Corps onside. But I do need those words for Maddison. If you would."

Cousins nodded. "Sure, I'll start working on it. When do you need something?"

"Yesterday," he smiled. "Oh, and there's a meeting with the guys from Sitara Education in the morning. Can you be there?"

"Sure," he replied, and turned to leave.

"One more thing," said Selby.

Cousins paused at the door.

"I hear you've got a thing going with Miss Ali…"

Cousins felt the colour rise to his cheeks.

"Just be careful, John. She is national staff."

"I will, Hank." And he left.

After he'd gone Selby sat deep in thought. His first concern was to complete the last distribution on the mountain. It had to happen, or he feared there would be bloodshed.

The loss of Williams was just one of those things. He felt for the American. But perhaps it was for the best. As for Cousins? He thought he and Ali made an attractive couple and hoped things would work out for them. He hoped they would be discreet. A staff problem was the last thing he needed. He headed towards the kitchen in search of coffee.

That evening Ali arrived at Cousins' guesthouse with a gift of her own. It was something she had bought for him in Islamabad. But she had been waiting for the right moment.

"I'd like you to sit down," she said as he opened the gate to let her into the walled enclosure. "I have something very special for you." He lowered himself onto the steps that led into the main house as she took a package from her carrier bag and handed it to him.

It was carefully wrapped in a traditional patterned scarf in shades of orange and purple.

"I'd like you to have it. I think it is time," she said and sat down beside him.

She watched him carefully unwrap the item. It was heavy. Perhaps a book of some kind.

"Feels like the complete works of Tagore," he smiled.

But as he folded back the last of the fabric he saw it was his own beautifully bound copy of the Holy Qur'an.

"It has an accompanying English text," she explained.

He was initially lost for words, for he knew its significance. According to her faith, it was the greatest gift of all. And inside the cover she had written:

> *I received the Qur'an as a present once and it changed my life – I hope it does the same for you... and then it will become truly, the greatest gift. Read it with a desire to know the truth, read it with humility and love of God in your heart; and don't be afraid to ask questions.*
>
> *I hope and pray your spiritual quest ends in the fulfilment of your deepest desires...*
>
> *Go with God*
>
> *Afsa*

"Thank you," he said. "I think it's the most beautiful gift I've ever received."

And he told her he felt truly honoured. Smiling she reached out and placed her forefinger to his lips to silence him.

"Read it with an open heart," she said simply. "And whatever happens between us, treasure it forever."

"I will," he promised.

She told him she would help him; that questions were a normal part of the search for spiritual truth, but that answers would come, as they had for her. Faith was a journey. And sometimes the journey was long.

"Thank you," he repeated, reaching out to take her hand in his. It was then that he noticed the deep scarring on her wrist for the first time. And a pang of sadness ran through him. He looked questioningly into her eyes.

"There was a time I no longer wanted to live," she told him without expression. And he leaned forward to kiss her scars tenderly to show that he understood and somehow make it better.

"It's all right now," she said. "Really it is. I was in a bad place. It is no secret. It was the Qur'an that helped me to find peace again."

She asked him about his life. So he told her about his work as a journalist and how he had come to be in Pakistan. He also told her about his failed marriage and his children. And the regrets he had of no longer being a meaningful part of their life. He also told her about the guilt he felt. And that he was thankful to have an opportunity to do some good. Perhaps that was why his work in the earthquake zone had felt so fulfilling.

"Feels like a new beginning."

"For me too," she said.

Yet he wanted to achieve so much more.

"That's the thing I've come to realise about aid work," he said. "The more you do, the more you realise it is never enough. It's like a tiny drop in an ocean of need."

"We can only do the best we can," she said thoughtfully. "But I think whatever you do, even if just one person's life is changed for the better, then it is all worthwhile. That's a success."

And they fell silent.

"Do you think we really make a difference?" he asked.

She seemed to consider carefully before she replied. "In the short term, yes. Look at all the people that have been helped after the earthquake. And in Kala Dhaka," she said. "And that is many thousands of people. But in the long term, Pakistan won't change. The poverty, the ignorance and the suffering will continue."

The country did not really want change, she believed. At least not the ruling classes. And they held the power. It was in their interest to maintain the status quo. It would take a social revolution.

And Pakistan was not ready, willing, or able to even contemplate such a change. It was not like India, she said, where people were empowered to aspire to better lives through education.

"In Pakistan if you are poor, you are very poor. And if you are rich, you are super rich. There is no middle ground," she told him. In fact, she could think of nothing at all to be proud of in Pakistan.

He told her he felt that was sad. And that he did not agree; that he had seen great resilience in the poor. He told her he admired the strength of faith he had witnessed in the mountains and the warmth in the hospitality that had been extended to him at every turn. He loved the landscape, the sights, the sounds, the smells of exotic spices and vibrant flowing fabrics. To him, Pakistan was a rich land of exotic diversity and mystery.

"Perhaps you are right," she conceded. "But it may be easier for you to see coming to Pakistan from the outside. You have not lived a life in Pakistan and come as a Westerner with privilege."

"Don't you come from a privileged background?" he asked.

"I do. But it didn't bring me happiness or contentment. I've come to realise material wealth means nothing. Nothing," she added for emphasis. "The peace I found comes from my faith. And if you pursue that faith with all your heart, I believe God will provide." And she smiled at him.

In some ways she felt he was younger than her. Sometimes he had a boyish, almost naïve quality she found endearing. She finished her green tea and lowered the china cup gently onto the step before raising her eyes to his. She had to go, she said. Not that she wanted to leave him. But she still had her report to write for Stevenson. She'd had a busy day at the child-friendly space.

As they rose from the steps they turned to face each other, both a little awkward in what might follow next. He smiled and led her across the terrace to a corner which lay in shadow, away from the yellow light burning in the street outside. And they embraced for the first time. Then she tilted her face towards his and they kissed…

THIRTY-SIX

T*HE DARK-SKINNED PILOT* stood proudly astern in magnificent, flowing cotton garments and loosely bound tribal headwrap fluttering in the light breeze as he set the ferry on course for the opposite bank. He guided the small craft into the strong current towards the group of villagers awaiting his arrival across the wide expanse of water. The boat lay low in the river, laden with aid supplies. A young gunman in black sat at the bow, the sunlight reflecting from the gun metal of his AK47. In the craggy mountains directly ahead, framed against the clear blue sky, lay the quake-stricken villages of the Madakhel tribe, the last of the region's five peoples to receive essential aid following the disaster.

An expansive floodplain swept from the river to the road, where a line of trucks was strung out along the base of the mountain which provided a stark and rocky backdrop. The scene was a hive of activity, as supplies were unloaded hastily from the vehicles under the watchful eye of Khan's armed men, who paced uneasily as they watched over the distribution. An undeniable tension hung over the flurry of hands through which items were being passed by human chain towards the river and were being stacked, ready to be loaded onto the small fleet of boats waiting at the water's edge.

Selby stood with Karim and Suur Gul, partly shielded by the grasses which grew tall in patches on the sandy earth near the river and gently swayed in the heat of the late spring sunshine. The news was that the peace might be fragile; that they should drop the aid as rapidly as possible and leave Kala Dhaka before any tensions spilled over into violence.

"The Madakhel say they will hold the peace. The same from the other tribes. But we are being closely watched," Suur Gul told the Canadian, his eyes betraying his concern. "We should not stay beyond our welcome."

Selby nodded thoughtfully in agreement. But his worry was for the team on the opposite bank distributing the items for the families which came down into the valley from their mountain villages in their hundreds. The team needed the time. The required monitoring had to take place. Each family had to present the appropriate token in exchange for the goods they received, which needed to be recorded. More than 1,500 Madakhel families were due to receive aid and for the first hour the two lines at the distribution point thronged with several hundred people and never seemed to diminish.

"How much time does the team across the river still need?" the Canadian asked.

"We should be ready in perhaps one more hour, *insh'Allah*," Karim replied. "I think it will be OK," he assured him. Selby was not convinced. "Let's hope so."

The small boat laden with CGI sheets and mattresses glided towards the bank and Cousins stepped ashore into Madakhel territory, followed by Khurram Masood. He scrambled up the steep and rocky slope, protecting the camera which hung from his neck in his right hand. The tribal leader who stood before him was none other than the khan who had watched from the mountaintop and observed the distribution to the other four tribes across the river several days earlier. Ismail Mohammed Khan gazed at the white man who had come ashore stony-faced, looking directly into the Westerner's eyes, as if trying to gauge his character. His beard was flaming red with henna and his unflinching eyes heavily outlined with kohl as he stood tall in magnificent white robes and turban before the Englishman. He was everything one might have expected a tribal warrior chieftain to be. Unusually, he was not armed, aside from the unseen pistol lodged in the waistband under his tunic within the small of his back. But he was flanked by several trusted tribesmen brandishing weapons.

Unfazed, Cousins greeted him with the Muslim *Asalaam-u-alaikum* and the chieftain nodded, maintaining the same steely gaze. Then he smiled unexpectedly, showing the creases in his dark, weather-beaten skin. He told Cousins he was welcome. It was a good day for his people and that he had not believed he would see help come to Kala Dhaka from the outside. Many families had been affected by the earthquake and the assistance would speed their recovery. And Masood translated.

The Englishman pointed to his camera and asked if he could take a photograph. The chieftain nodded and struck up a formal pose, gazing directly into the lens as the journalist raised his camera. Cousins offered his thanks and gestured across to the ongoing distribution, signalling that he would like to take more pictures. Again the khan nodded his permission and the journalist approached the villagers standing in line to collect their aid items, shooting from various angles on auto. He knew he had limited time. He then lowered his camera and stood watching the stream of aid-bearing villagers stretching into the far distance, carrying away their goods along the winding mountain tracks, like tiny ants, before disappearing over the crests and peaks.

"Come Mr John." It was Masood. "Mr Hank say we return very soon." Cousins nodded and followed the man from Gilgit back to the boats, where aid was still being brought ashore. The two men climbed aboard the next empty boat heading across the water. Back on the opposite bank tensions were mounting.

Selby was with the trucks, whose drivers he had told to move off as soon as they had been emptied and take the road back to Mansehra.

"How are things looking?" the Englishman asked as he approached.

"Last truckload," replied the Canadian, waving another vehicle off. "Roll it!" he roared, and the truck pulled out onto the road in a plume of blue diesel smoke and dust.

"As soon as the last of the aid is in the boats we should leave," he said. "Suur Gul and Karim will handle the rest and allow us to get our people out safely. Job done!"

He was smiling at the Englishman. "People said aid intervention here couldn't be done. It was a pocket of unknown mountainous territory of some 100 square kilometres – a forbidden zone whose people were literally not on the map and had a fearsome reputation for treachery and violence. But we've done it…" He turned from Cousins towards the truck still standing. "Right, that's it. Move it!" he shouted and as it began rolling, he turned back to the Englishman.

Selby was right. And the significance of the delivery of aid across the river was not lost on the journalist. Its success would mark the conclusion of a historic intervention to an area off-limits for centuries. Of course there had been challenges. Physical access to the remote area was difficult, the few narrow roads cut into the mountainside damaged, at risk of landslide or simply impassable. Security was always a worry.

Building trust and obtaining guarantees on security had been essential hurdles to negotiate, meeting with religious leaders and tribal councils to allow access for detailed assessments by outside agencies for the first time. It could not have been achieved without months of sensitive negotiations to develop the necessary understanding between the tribes with complete transparency. And then only through a local implementing partner like Sitara. But the tribal rivalries still held the threat of violence at the very moment of triumph. Yet they were so close. Selby could feel the flow of adrenaline driving him forward. Failure at this point was in his mind inconceivable.

"Let's take a look down at the water," he said, and Cousins followed him to the river, where they found Suur Gul. The situation was deteriorating. The Hassanzai elders had been angered to see Madakhel tribesmen crossing the water into their territory to assist with the unloading. Years of tribal rivalry, blood feuds and mistrust stretching back centuries would have to be contained. It could still end badly and he had sent Karim across the river to speak with the Madakhel chieftains. Their people should wait for the aid to come ashore. His men would see that it would be so. And assurances had been relayed to the Hassanzai too. The presence of outsiders was another factor adding to the sense of unease. Selby felt it too.

Could Suur Gul's people handle the delivery of the remaining aid across the river and to those who needed it? The Pathan said they could. They were his people. He would see to it, with Ali Khan's support on the Hassanzai side. Selby made his decision. He sent Masood back to the road above the floodplain. Then he walked over to Cousins, who was still taking photographs as the last aid items were being carried to the riverbank.

"Best put that away, John," he said with a sense of urgency. "Time for us to leave. Now," and the Englishman followed as they headed at pace back to their vehicle at the roadside, where Khurram Masood waited. Before Cousins climbed in, he took a last look across the Indus. He had a strong sense it might be the last time he would ever set foot in Kala Dhaka.

"Now, John," barked Selby, and Cousins lowered himself into the passenger seat as the Canadian put the Land Cruiser into gear and pulled onto the road to head south. They should be across the tribal boundary within thirty minutes. Their mission would be complete. A second vehicle pulled out to follow a few moments later with several gunmen tasked with seeing the Westerners safely across the border.

Mohammed Ali Khan stood with his men and watched the vehicles disappear into the distance.

He was confident he could maintain the peace. He knew his people. And he knew the Madakhel. Besides, this was destined to be a glorious day. He put his faith in Allah that it would be so. A major step in building trust would have been achieved; a bridge between the outside world and the people of Kala Dhaka established. He never thought he would live to see that day. That was the miracle from Allah (Almighty) he felt he was witnessing. Yet he knew the challenges for his people to rebuild their shattered lives in the months and years ahead would be immense. But it was a beginning. Then he smiled wistfully. He felt sure he would see the Westerners again.

"I can't believe we've actually done it," said Selby, turning to the Englishman as they approached the tribal boundary.

"It's been an incredible experience," the Englishman replied. "An amazing achievement."

"Amazing? You've no idea the blood, sweat and tears that went into this. But yeah, it's been an adventure, all the way," he smiled. "Got everything you need for the story?"

"Just need a quote from you."

"Been quite a journey," Selby added, as if voicing his thoughts out loud. "But it's been fucking brilliant!"

"Can I quote you on that?"

And the Canadian laughed. It was as much an expression of relief as it was a response to Cousins. Moments later they were driving passed the flat concrete buildings that marked the beginning of Darband and the vehicle that had been tailing them since they had left the distribution had disappeared.

Within twenty-four hours a call had been made to the British government's Department for International Development in Islamabad. Keith Bailey was told the final phase of the aid operation in Kala Dhaka had been a success and was now concluded. Full monitoring had taken place and a comprehensive donor report would follow in the days ahead. Some items would undoubtedly find their way onto the black market at Darband and elsewhere. It was to be expected. But essential aid had been delivered to the people of the Black Mountain against all expectations. Further, a gateway had been established that might allow further development and stabilisation of the area to take place. Bailey was satisfied.

Meanwhile the Americans received similar news from their man on the mountain. In a flowery report brimming with enthusiasm, 'Z' reported all the tribes had received significant aid. There had been some tensions between the tribes following a delay to the final distribution across the river, but no bloodshed. Nothing unusual for Kala Dhaka. But the peace had held. All five tribes had essentially cooperated. And that was 'most definitely a small miracle'. Thanks be to Allah.

It was among the regional politicians that there was most dissent, he had learned. They effectively felt bypassed by the national government, which had given its backing to a Western agency to operate in an area which had been off-limits for centuries. The area was under the jurisdiction of the Regional Assembly, not the federal government.

But what irked some 'very much indeed' was that they had been denied an opportunity to exert any power, control or to gain financially from the outside intervention. Selby and the men from Sitara had dealt directly with the power base within Kala Dhaka. That was not how the politics were usually conducted. And 'Z' had smiled to himself. Like the British, the American agencies were alerted by their man that further investment in the area was likely to be welcomed and could help secure it against 'undesirable' agents, he concluded.

Meanwhile, the Pakistani government's spy network, the army's Inter-Services Intelligence agency was also following developments on the Black Mountain.

And Hank Selby had been on its radar for some time. What particularly interested them was the Canadian's military background. His details lay alongside those of the Sitara Education Foundation and the links its founders had to Kala Dhaka. Handwritten notes in the margins said they were champions of education for the poor. A commendable goal. Yet they were also said to have connections with other Western donors which should be further examined.

But a new subject for investigation had been added to the ISI file on Kala Dhaka. An Englishman had arrived in Pakistan on a journalist visa and had been working with Selby. His name was Jonathan Edward Cousins. No other details were known.

THIRTY-SEVEN

THE INVITATION ARRIVED a few days after the distribution across the river. It was delivered to the Relief Action office in Mansehra by the men from Sitara Education Foundation. The message was from Mohammed Ali Khan. Selby and Cousins were invited to return to the Black Mountain. Khan and his people wished to offer their thanks to the Westerners. Suur Gul and Karim would escort them for a meeting close to the village of Tilli on the slopes occupied by the Syeds, said to represent the spiritual heart of the mountain, direct descendants of the Holy Prophet himself (Peace be upon Him). They wished to extend their blessings. It came as a surprise to Selby. He would take the Iranian with him, who had helped coordinate the distribution on the ground and Masood to translate. For the Englishman it was an unexpected opportunity to see Kala Dhaka one last time.

The mountain seemed to have a different feel as the mid-morning sun shone upon its wooded slopes and the rays that penetrated its lofty pine trees dappled the road in patches of golden light. Perhaps it was because they knew their mission had been completed: the aid had been delivered. This time they were invited to celebrate its success in the knowledge they had helped those who would not otherwise have been reached. The tension had lifted. All five tribes were satisfied they had received their share of aid items for those families who needed them most. And the religious leaders too had gained from the Western intervention by receiving materials for the rebuilding of their mosques.

The battered Sitara Hilux led the way along the lesser-known track into the tribal area, winding its course up into Hassanzai territory where the Syed village lay within a hollow on the mountain's south-western flank, overlooking a small plateau of cultivated land. They drew to a halt in the village centre, just off the main track and a committee of bearded elders assembled to welcome them as they stepped from their vehicles. It was the familiar figure of the Hassanzai chieftain, Mohammed Ali Khan, who smiled and stepped forward to greet them.

Selby spoke for the Relief Action team, telling Khan he and his colleagues were honoured to receive his invitation. And the two men embraced before the party moved towards the mud and stone building which overlooked the village square. Cousins noted there were several armed men posted around its walls, who looked on casually. It was perhaps the only reminder that they were once more within Kala Dhaka. That and a nearby field of purple opium poppies swaying in the gentle breeze that blew down from the mountain.

Inside, the darkened room was penetrated only by the bright shaft of light which shone through the window from outside and fell upon the carpeted flooring. Selby and his companions sat cross-legged in a row, flanked by Khan, with the village elders and the mullahs taking their places in a semi-circle before them. The tribal chieftain told the visitors the elders were representatives of the Syeds, who were revered by the five tribes on the mountain. The outsiders were to be honoured with a banquet. But first they were to receive blessings.

Cousins watched as a grey-bearded mullah closed his eyes and began reciting verses in Arabic, his open palms held before him in prayer. And the visitors duly dropped their gaze and stretched out their hands too. After the final *Ameen* there was a flurry of activity as food and drink was delivered and placed in the centre of the room on the ground before the visitors. First came the steel water jugs and cups, followed by plates of goat and chicken, rice and daal. And there was freshwater fish too from the Indus and steaming naan breads.

"*Shukria,*" Selby exclaimed cheerfully as each dish, seemingly more exotic, was placed before him.

"This is wonderful, thank you." And Masood translated his words. Cousins too was in awe.

"Is great honour, Mr John," said Masood, leaning towards the Englishman, as he surveyed the rich assortment of food being served.

Eating according to local custom had initially presented something of a challenge to the journalist on his arrival in Pakistan. He had, with practise, become proficient breaking off small pieces of chapati, or naan bread, pinching them into small pouches between finger and thumb, and scooping up food from hand to mouth. But he had learned left-handed, much to Selby's horror, who had told him that it was effectively an insult. He might be shot in the tribal area.

All good things had to be performed right-handed. To do otherwise was *haram*. And so, he had painstakingly learned the art with the use of his other, unnatural hand.

But, after many months in Pakistan, they now sat and ate as natives. And the food was like no other they had tasted. There was nothing artificial or preserved. Everything was freshly cooked, or baked, in the way that it had been for centuries, seasoned with a rich variety of herbs and spices that exploded onto the palate. It was one of the best meals the Englishman had ever tasted. And he said so, much to the delight of their hosts.

After they had eaten, Khan stood to address the gathering. He had not had dealings with a Westerner before, he said. He hadn't been sure what to expect. But he had seen in Selby's eyes that he was a man who could be trusted. And it was so and would always be so. They had met as strangers from different cultures and had undergone a journey together. And now they were parting as friends. And the Westerner's friends were his friends, as they were to the people of Kala Dhaka. Not only through words, but actions. And that friendship had transcended religious and cultural boundaries. He thanked his brothers from Sitara for their part in helping to bring the aid. And the elders nodded their agreement.

Selby and his companions were moved by Khan's speech. The Canadian was not a man of words himself. He acknowledged the great part trust had played in the relationship with the people of Kala Dhaka, adding that it had to be built on honesty. He said he felt honoured he and his team had been able to work with the people of the Black Mountain and learn about their culture. He felt a bridge of trust had been built. Khan invited him to stand. And the two men embraced. Then he asked Cousins, Farzad and Masood to rise also and the burley chieftain hugged them too.

"We have gift before leaving," he said gruffly in English. "So that you remember the people of Kala Dhaka and know you are welcome as brothers." And the visitors were presented with garlands of flowers and finally, last of all, the Westerners each received a magnificent turban headdress from the tribal leader, which he placed ceremoniously upon their heads.

"Now you are honorary members of Hassanzai tribe." And he laughed.

Selby and Cousins were taken aback. Smiling, they looked at each other and nodded their thanks in appreciation to Khan and the assembled elders.

"We shall never forget and are honoured to be your brothers," Selby told them, and they were led outside, blinking in the brilliant sunshine.

"One more thing," Khan told Selby. "You must shoot in sky." And a tribesman stepped forward and handed him a rifle. The Canadian brought the Enfield to his shoulder, raised the barrel skyward and squeezed the trigger. The shot cracked and echoed across the mountain. Cousins was then handed the weapon and fired off his round to the cheers of the tribesmen.

"It is done," said the chieftain, smiling, and nodded for two gunmen to step forward brandishing AK47s. They too pointed their weapons out across the mountain and emptied their magazines in a stutter of machine-gun fire into the clear blue sky as the Westerners watched.

Khan insisted on escorting the visitors back to the tribal boundary and they followed his Hilux out of the village watched by the assembled elders.

"How does it feel to be a member of the Hassanzai tribe?" Selby smiled, as they followed Khan's vehicle along the track around the ridge of the mountain.

"Amazing," replied the Englishman. There was no other word.

Suddenly, Khan's vehicle slowed as they approached the crest of a hill and his arm extended from the vehicle window, signalling that they should draw to a halt.

As they climbed out of their Land Cruiser, Suur Gul explained there was something the khan wanted them to see.

"Come," said the chieftain and they followed him from the dirt track into the trees towards what appeared to be a ruined settlement, with broken-down walls and piles of stones long since overgrown with grasses and moss. It was the site of the old British encampment, where the soldiers had based themselves following their expedition to suppress the Black Mountain tribes back in 1888.

It was from here the army engineers had surveyed the mountain. This was the point from which they had first mapped the area all those years ago. Selby was overwhelmed. In a sense this was where it all began; where the map he himself had discovered was first drawn up.

"Can you believe it?" he uttered, smiling at Cousins.

And yet what was to come was even more unexpected.

Mohammed Ali Khan told Cousins he understood he had no home of his own. And the thought disturbed the chieftain. Therefore it had been decided to gift the Englishman a piece of land. The site of the old garrison was there for Cousins to use; it was his whenever he wanted it. He would always be welcome in Kala Dhaka.

The journalist was totally unprepared by the khan's offer. He couldn't quite take it in.

"It is yours," the chieftain said.

Selby and Cousins looked at each other uncertainly.

Suur Gul confirmed to the Westerners the offer of land was sincere. And he reminded the Englishman of the dream he had voiced one day to return to the Black Mountain and to build a resource centre, where the people could come for livelihood training and medicines. He recalled he had said so. During their conversations Cousins had spoken about his life back in England and mentioned that he did not have a house of his own. And that was true in that he lived in a small, rented flat.

Perhaps elements of the Englishman's situation were lost in translation. What the Pathans understood was that he had no home of his own. And it distressed them. Especially when they considered he had travelled to Pakistan to help the people of Kala Dhaka in their hour of need. Therefore, they felt a gesture was required and had considered what they believed to be an ideal solution.

"I don't know what to say…" Cousins began, overwhelmed by the offer. "Thank you."

"Land we have," said the chieftain, smiling. "And we will pray for the day you return to Kala Dhaka."

"I hope we will see each other again," the Englishman told the khan.

"Then we will watch for you, *insh'Allah*. Know that you take with you our blessings." And they said their farewells. Khan watched as the vehicles moved off down the hill along the winding track and disappeared from into the distance.

"So now you're a landowner in Kala Dhaka," said Selby after they had pulled away.

"Unbelievable," Cousins replied.

"It's not such a bad idea," the Canadian continued. "The resource centre. The guys from Sitara would be interested. Who knows, perhaps Relief Action will support additional development."

And Cousins smiled, as he imagined a centre standing on the site of the old British encampment. "Maybe it will happen one day," he mused.

When they arrived at the house on the hill, they were still wearing the garlands around their necks and carried their magnificent headpieces with them as they stepped inside. Zhevlakov, de Villiers and Petrović were sitting at the dining room table when they entered.

"My God, they have returned," said the Ukrainian. "Tribal warriors are back from adventure."

"Impressive gear," de Villiers added. "But the fancy-dress party's down the road at the UN house," he quipped, gesturing with his thumb over his shoulder.

But Petrović said nothing. Instead he took the tribal headdress Cousins handed to him to examine. And he nodded his approval.

"You are looking at honorary members of the Hassanzai tribe," Selby informed them cheerfully. "And our friends on the mountain have offered John some land. If he'll go back and build a resource centre on it," he said, heading to the kitchen to fetch a couple of cold colas.

"And you know what?" Cousins smiled, as the Canadian returned, clutching bottles in both hands. "I might just do that."

"I'll drink to that," the Canadian said handing out the ice-cold bottles. "And to our friends on the mountain!"

Ali had missed their triumphant return from Kala Dhaka. She had spent the last few days in Islamabad. But later Cousins called her and shared the news of his day.

"I can imagine you looked very distinguished," she told him.

"*Very*," he replied. And she laughed.

She was excited for him and could hardly wait to see him again on her imminent return to Mansehra. She told him she felt she had been searching for him all her life. She was praying for them with all her might.

"Think about me and I am with you, always," she told him. And he felt it was true.

As they said 'goodnight', she paused.

"I love you," she whispered. It was the first time she had said it. And he felt a rush of emotion as he told her that he loved her too.

After the call, he sat on the balcony staring at his phone, smiling stupidly. Then he gazed up at the moonlit night. The brilliance of a million stars seemed to shine down upon him and he sighed. If ever he held any doubts they seemed to dissipate into the night sky. He felt blessed. And it seemed to him as if God and the forces of the universe were conspiring to set him on a course he could never have foreseen. And as he pictured Ali's face, he wondered whether it really could be true what she believed: that their destinies were already written.

THIRTY-EIGHT

SHE CAME TO him under the cover of darkness when the intoxicating scent of jasmine hung heavy in the air and the sweet sweat of the early summer lingered on the brow. He had been waiting for her, he whispered as she stepped inside. He took her in his arms and they held each other in the unrelenting heat of the night which seemed all-encompassing, smothering each other hungrily in sensual kisses.

How she had yearned for his touch, she thought, as he guided his fingers over the smooth contours of her skin and they sank onto his bed as their breathing grew deep and heavy in their excitement. There was an ecstasy of fumbling as clothing was stripped away and they lay against each other naked, burning with desire. And in a frenzy of passion they melted together as one.

Their sighs gradually subsided and gave way to a sense of physical and spiritual fulfilment as they both lay contented, panting, bathed in sweat following the physical exertion of their sexual union. He lay on his back, breathing deeply, and she snuggled against his body, feeling the rise and fall of his chest against her as he cradled her with his arm. All was quiet now, save for the steady whirring of the ceiling fan.

"That was wonderful," he told her.

"Heaven," she replied. "I don't believe anything so beautiful can be wrong," she added.

"It isn't," he assured her, then pausing for a moment. "Afsa…"

"Yes, my angel."

"I love you!"

"And I love you. Madly." And as her lips pressed against his skin to kiss his shoulder, he felt she was smiling. Then she turned onto her back and lay gazing into the darkness.

When she spoke next it was with a sense of sadness. "What's going to become of us when you leave?" she asked.

She knew he was leaving Pakistan soon to return to England. Now that the distribution in Kala Dhaka had been completed, his work was coming to an end. And she couldn't imagine life without him. Their last few days had been idyllic… dreamlike. Intense and passionate.

They had been driven by an intensity to be with each other that seemed beyond their understanding, beyond question, beyond reason. And yet they had to hide their passion for each other and their intimate liaisons. But he took reckless risks in scaling the obstacles that stood between their need to be with each other. He would visit her in the early hours, when the moon was high over the mountains and the heat of the day finally gave way to the cool air that came from the north, scaling the rear perimeter wall of her guesthouse. It allowed him to avoid the guard at the gate and slip into the house unseen as the other women slept, and tiptoe to her room where she waited to embrace him.

Often they spent the night together and would hold each other until the eastern sky turned orange, when he would leave her to return to his own guesthouse.

Or sometimes he would stay until the other ladies of the house had left or were at breakfast in the dining room before descending the stairs unseen and coolly striding out into the morning air. Once he had returned to his own guesthouse in the early hours as the sun began to rise, lowering himself down from the wall, only to realise that his jacket had caught on the metal spikes that topped the enclosure. And his jacket had been torn from top to bottom. As he entered the house and reached the upper floor, he had encountered the security guard, who started at his sudden appearance at the top of the stairs. Neither should have been there. He voiced a confident, "Good morning," and walked passed the hapless Pakistani. And nothing was ever said.

Another time following a nocturnal liaison with Ali, he had found himself balancing precariously on the top of the wall which divided her guesthouse from the office of the Salvation Army. He crouched down, then lowered himself slowly to the ground outside, only to turn and find himself facing a pack of wild dogs, which slowly began advancing upon him. As he stood motionless, contemplating his next action, a young security guard suddenly stepped out of the shadows. The Pakistani picked up a half-brick and threw it with precision at the lead animal, and the dogs turned and ran into the night. Then the guard stepped back out of sight. The encounter remained their secret. Possibly because Cousins had always treated the young guard kindly, with a friendly smile. Or perhaps the young man was touched by the sense of romanticism of the Englishman's secret liaisons. And that may have been true of others who suspected or knew of the couple's relationship.

Sometimes Ali would recite from Holy Qur'an to him as they sat together in the evenings. He loved to hear her read in Arabic, even though he could not understand the words and allowed the exotic sound of her soothing voice to flow over him. She taught him about the practices of Islam she had known from childhood and explained her beliefs. And she taught him how to pray and what phrases he should use to reflect the appropriate verses. Though he had learned the *Kalima*, the Muslim declaration of faith, other words and phrases could be uttered in English. Allah would understand. And often they would pray together, side by side on the mat, seeking guidance, asking for understanding and searching for answers.

She told herself her faith was based on the principles of Sufism; that she could strive to find her own individual connection with God from within, beyond the confines of convention she found so restrictive. After all, mainstream Islam would condemn them for their relationship. Yet her own happiness added to strengthen her own faith. She believed Allah had heard her prayers over the last few years for personal fulfilment.

For his part, he was intoxicated by her love, by the intensity of experience in an unknown land and by the exploration of his own spirituality, for which she was a focus and a guide. And he was grateful to a higher power he recognised as God.

But soon he would be leaving and the reality of their situation came ever closer to crashing into their world with the passing of each day. And she became ever more desperate by the thought that soon he would be gone. He told her he would speak to Selby to see if his contract could be extended. But he was doubtful. The Canadian had been clear he had been hired for a reason. And that had been to support the Kala Dhaka distribution and field the story. Even so, it was worth a try.

Selby was in his office, standing at the wall map of Mansehra District featuring the blue and red markers highlighting the location of the distributions that had taken place or were still underway. But more recently other colours featured on its landscape, with the launch of new projects in education and livelihood support initiatives.

He smiled as Cousins entered. "Good job on Kala Dhaka. The story read like poetry," he told the journalist. "Head office have been raving about it."

"Thanks," the Englishman replied. "In a way it's what I wanted to talk to you about…"

Was there any possibility of further work for him in Pakistan?

Selby had been expecting the question. And he had already asked Maddison in Islamabad. He genuinely liked the Englishman and felt they made a good team.

The distribution had laid the foundation for further initiatives. But there was no budget for an international consultant. And head office had decided to appoint someone from their existing team to the media and communications role, with a view to develop a national member of staff to take over in the months ahead. That would build local capacity and was only right. Besides, the Mansehra operation was set to be scaled down, now that the emergency and immediate relief effort was over, with a new emphasis on long-term development. He himself might be leaving soon.

"I'm sorry, John. I'll be sad to see you leave. But we've had a good run," he added. However, he did know the UK communications people were keen to set up media interviews with him on his return. Beyond that, he couldn't say. Cousins should approach other organisations, he advised. He'd certainly recommend him for any similar post. Perhaps there would be scope to work with Sitara. Then he took a deep breath. "What are you going to do about Miss Ali?" he asked.

"We feel we have a future…"

Selby looked at Cousins and sighed. "She's a very determined and headstrong young lady…" The Canadian wasn't sure how to frame what he wanted to say next. "She's a Pakistani national. That means she has a different culture and a different religion. Are you sure you understand everything that means? What about her family, John? It's not going to be like Bollywood, all singing and dancing," he added.

The Englishman said nothing.

"I know Afsa comes from a wealthy, educated family in Islamabad, which might be a different world. But here in the north-west, people are still stoned for going against conventions we in the West wouldn't turn a hair over. That's Pakistan. You know what I'm saying?"

"I do, Hank."

"I've not said anything before," the Canadian continued. "Not least of all because you're a bloody romantic and wear your heart on your sleeve. That's why you're a good writer. And because I like you. But be sure you know what you are taking on." Then he paused, containing his exasperation.

"We love each other. We'll find a way," the Englishman said.

Selby looked at his friend and smiled. "Just be careful, all right. I know you're both over twenty-one. I wish you both well."

"I know. And thanks for everything."

"It's been quite a journey, hasn't it?" the Canadian said. And the two men grinned at each other.

After Cousins left, Selby picked up his cell phone to call Stevenson. He was concerned and wanted to know what her thoughts were. Cousins appreciated Selby's frankness and concern. He'd liked him from the moment they had met at the house on the hill that first evening. And he was grateful for the opportunity he had engineered for him in Pakistan. But now his time was done.

Ali remained philosophical. Things would happen as they were meant to. If he couldn't get a job back in Pakistan, she'd simply come and see him in England, she told him. Despite the objections her parents would undoubtedly raise. She would find a way. She'd visited London once as a child with her parents for a holiday. Now she'd like to visit again. She was sure she would be able to arrange it. And she had the financial means. At least it would allow them to be together again soon. Ali was no stranger to the liberalism and diversity of Western culture. As an overseas student, she had spent nearly four years in the States and then New Zealand. It wasn't as if she hadn't spent time in the West. Truth be told, in her heart of hearts she wasn't even certain her long-term destiny lay in Pakistan. So she relished the idea of a trip to see him and learn more about his life in England. What would his children make of her, she wondered? They would love her as he did, he assured her. And the more she thought about it, the more she liked the idea, as a new optimism took root.

Stevenson was supportive too. She had been surprised to take a call from Selby on such a delicate staff matter. He was truly concerned for the couple in a way that seemed to show a sensitive, softer side to his nature she had previously missed. She assured him she was aware of the situation and that she and Ali had talked at length on several occasions. She believed Ali was a woman of exceptional talent and maturity. She was highly educated and Westernised. And she liked Cousins too. She felt the pair were a good match and made a handsome couple. Therefore she was not overly concerned for their future. Like Selby, she wished the couple well and felt they had as much a chance of happiness as anyone else. She had known her young team member for many months and had never before seen her so blissfully happy. The rest was a matter for providence, she felt. Besides, she knew the young woman had her faith, which remained strong.

And so, as the date of his return drew near, their passion reached a new level of intensity. But whatever doubts Ali held, she felt there would be an answer. If they were destined to be together, then Allah would make the path easy for them, she reasoned. If it was written, then it would be so. And she believed it.

"We'll find a way," Cousins assured her.

"Allah will show us the way," she replied.

The Englishman's departure from Mansehra was a low-key affair. Besides, Selby was not one for sentimental goodbyes. As the two men stood facing each other, smiling, a look of understanding passed between them. It did not need to be voiced. They had experienced something remarkable together. Something they would always share. But it was over now.

"Safe journey," said the Canadian, as they shook hands, watched by Petrović, de Villiers and Farzad, who had also gathered to say farewell. Stevenson and her team had already left for Islamabad earlier, and Ali had arranged to meet Cousins in the evening. She would drive him to the airport the following morning.

"Thanks for everything, Hank."

"No, thank *you*. Won't be the same without you."

"I'll miss the mountains. And the people most of all. It's been awesome," said the Englishman.

And they embraced.

He shook hands with the others. Then he picked up his bags and stepped towards the waiting vehicle.

The small group waved and watched as the Land Cruiser moved off. Then they turned away and walked back into the office. Selby hoped he would see Cousins in Pakistan again. He had the feeling he would.

As finally they stood at Islamabad airport, she felt a part of her was leaving. She wanted to hold him but knew she could not. Muslim convention would not allow it. So much to say. And yet they didn't have the words. At least they had been able to have one final evening together, which neither had wanted to end.

"I love you, Afsa Ali," Cousins told her softly, gazing into her brown eyes.

"I love you too," she replied.

He smiled at her and she saw there were tears in his eyes as he struggled to contain his feelings.

"Bye, my love," he whispered, then hoisted his rucksack over his shoulder and turned to walk into the thronging crowd. She longed to call out to him. But she was only able to stand helplessly and watch him walk away. She smiled as he turned to glance at her one last time before he disappeared from view. Then he was gone. For a few moments she remained where she was. And she realised she was crying.

Cousins passed through security and found himself staring at the departure area teeming with people. Yet he did not really see. He was numb, choked by emotion. He was on his way back to England; he was on his way home. What was home? And yet already he knew. Even as he had left her. Pakistan had changed him. He had felt a fulfilment in the mountains and a new purpose in life which brought a sense of deep contentment. Then he smiled. He realised he would have to return. He had found the woman he loved...

EPILOGUE

IN A SMALL apartment in Rawalpindi, a young Pakistani packed his kitbag. Many years had passed since the earthquake had shaken the mountains of north-west Pakistan. He remembered it well; had never forgotten the day his life had changed forever. In just a few seconds. He could still feel himself crouching on the hillside in fear as his goats scattered and the mountain had shuddered and trembled as if heaving itself into life. It was the day he lost his mother and father forever.

Shahbaz stood tall and lean, no longer a boy, but a man. There was an assurance about him; a calmness reflected by a confidence which flowed from achievement. He was an educated young man with a determination in his eyes. But he had not forgotten. The trauma of grief and the loneliness of his trek down into the valley following the disaster had haunted him for many years. And the sadness of his childhood loss still sometimes cast its shadow over his life. Nor had he forgotten the kindness of strangers.

He smoothed his fingers over a neatly trimmed beard in thought, watching the images on the TV screen showing the scale of destruction wrought by the cyclone that had hit the rim of Africa, sweeping its way through three countries; saw the terrible scenes of human suffering. And he knew he was taking the right course. Soon he would be deep in the heart of the emergency.

No, he had never forgotten. His sponsored education through Relief Action had been a reminder as he had grown older and had given him a sense of hope. And he wanted to use his education to do good. It gave him a purpose in life and he was determined to succeed. He wondered idly what had become of the Englishman who had come to Pakistan, as he often had. And he smiled. He took the small, well-worn coin from his pocket and stared at it. It had indeed brought him luck. He'd fulfilled the promise of an education and was now part of the humanitarian response team being sent out to Mozambique. And he thought about the young storyteller who had been so kind to him and others too. He had often wondered what drove such people to travel to foreign fields to help others. But now he felt he understood.

On the kitchen table his bag was almost packed. He crossed to the bedroom, knelt down to retrieve something from under his mattress and pulled out an item wrapped within a plastic carrier bag. He opened it and took out a child's cricket bat. He stared at it as he held it in his hands, then rubbed his brown fingers along its length and for a moment, just a moment, he was back on the mountainside as a young boy under the Himalayan sky.

He stepped out of his bedroom and over to the kitchen table, sliding the bat into the bag. He walked to the TV and switched it off. Then he collected his kitbag from the table and threw it over his shoulder. On his way out he whispered the

Kalima, closed the door behind him and stepped towards the waiting taxi that would take him to the airport…

―∞―

Gail Stevenson had lobbied hard for the child sponsorship scheme to be implemented by Relief Action in Pakistan. And she had succeeded. One of the first children to benefit was Shahbaz, whose education was supported in the years that followed Cousins' departure. And his little sister Zabiha was supported too, cared for by the boy's extended family which farmed on the fertile plains of the Northern Punjab, which lay in the shadow of the Himalayas near Jhelum.

Hank Selby left Pakistan soon after the Englishman. Some said it was a rapid departure. It was rumoured the army's ISI wanted to interview him. It was thought he returned to Canada and became a ranger in the far north. As far as anyone knew, he never worked within the aid and development sector again. And it wasn't long before the team in Mansehra was dispersed, some finding their way to the next humanitarian emergency. Maddison had also left Pakistan before the end of the year and the last anyone ever heard from the quiet American was that he was working for a development organisation in Myanmar.

On a moonless night in May 2011, almost five years after Cousins had left Kala Dhaka for the last time, a small group of helicopters flew low over the mountains into Pakistani airspace from Afghanistan undetected. Onboard two modified Black Hawks hugging the Kabul River valley was a contingent US Navy SEALs. They were followed by two back-up Chinook helicopters. They were on a daring covert mission to capture or kill America's most wanted terrorist. Intelligence suggested Osama bin Laden was in hiding with his immediate family within a large, walled property identified on the outskirts of Abbottabad. Within the hour the al-Qaeda chief was dead.

The next day the US government announced it had carried out the raid and that Osama bin Laden had been killed during its operation to capture him. John Cousins saw the news detailing the mission. It had been launched without the knowledge of the Pakistani government, or cooperation with its armed forces. He was stunned to hear the assault had taken place at a compound on the outskirts of the garrison town of Abbottabad – and that bin Laden had most likely been based there since the end of 2005. As he watched, almost disbelieving, he was joined by a South Asian woman in her early thirties who came to sit beside him. She had just put their little boy to bed and came to watch the news with her husband.

It was Afsa Ali. Both were stunned, not least by the likelihood that bin Laden had been based just a short drive from their aid operation in Mansehra.

What the report did not say was that before the final assault on Abbottabad at least one American helicopter had set down on farmland in the remote mountain region of Kala Dhaka, where the US military presence had remained 'undetected' for a full forty minutes while the raid was in progress, just a few minutes' flying time to the south-east. Yet there were some to whom the helicopters' arrival in Kala Dhaka had not been entirely a surprise. When the American agent on the Black Mountain heard the news, it triggered no particular emotion.

'Z' held no sympathy for the Taliban or al-Qaeda. Nor was he disturbed that American forces had violated Pakistani sovereignty by launching its secret raid. He didn't blame the Americans, for he knew the double game played out by the Pakistani government. He was now living in Islamabad spending his time travelling between the capital and the northwest, writing poetry. Pakistani media quoted a local farmer on the mountain who confirmed helicopters had been heard that night and there was evidence at least one had landed in a field of wheat. It was later reported that local residents had been tied up and guarded by the Americans while they waited in Kala Dhaka. And 'Z' smiled to himself as he had read the accounts.

Two years later Suur Gul Rafiq was standing outside his Karachi home in the spring sunshine, cradling his baby daughter to him as the gunmen approached. In an instant of realisation, he recognised this was the moment he had dreaded. Moments later he died on his doorstep in a hail of bullets. A hand grenade was thrown where his body lay before the assassins rode off on their motorbike along the busy street at high speed. His daughter and three others who had stood with him were also severely injured in the attack. It was thought the assailants were members of the Taliban who felt his work to provide education to the poor, including little girls, should be punished. They were never traced.

His friend and partner Atul Karim was one of the injured. But he was determined to continue the work he had been engaged in with his friend over many years. Yet there was a weariness in his face. He never fully overcame the loss of his friend and partner. His smile was never again so infectious and enthusiastic. Instead there was a steely, cynical determination about him as he sought to continue the fight to help the poorest in Pakistan. And he was reminded in every step he took with his walking frame of what his work had cost him and the friend he had seen murdered. It made him all the more resolute to continue, even though he knew it put his own life at risk.

The Kala Dhaka Area Development Project never did seem to fully materialise. Perhaps the Americans lost interest. Or their strategic priorities changed. Or the money disappeared. Perhaps it was an opportunity missed. The gateway which was opened by the earthquake and subsequent Relief Action distribution slowly closed. Kala Dhaka was renamed Torghar. Yet nothing really changed in the lives of its people. More recently it lost its status as a Provincially Administered Tribal Area and is now known as Khyber Pakhtunkhwa's District 25. Promises were made by the Pakistani government for improved infrastructure, education and health facilities. But the 300,000 people who live there still wait. And it would be fair to say no significant development has taken place across the Black Mountain in the years since. Its people still live their lives under the *Jirga* system as they have for centuries. And the pink opium poppy fields continue to grow and sway in the gentle breeze that blows down from the mountain.

For Cousins and Ali, the news about bin Laden's death brought back memories of their own time in Pakistan, the earthquake and the Black Mountain. The murder of Suur Gul was a shock, relayed to them by a fellow aid worker who had known him too. And it filled Cousins with sadness. He had cried as he had pictured Suur Gul's face and remembered the man's gentle humility and passion for his people. It was a further reminder, not just of their Pakistan experience, but that the country held dangers for those who hoped to create social change for its poorest elements.

The Englishman never did return to Kala Dhaka. But that is not to say he didn't sometimes think about the promise he made to Mohammed Ali Khan that day and the land he was once offered on the site of the old British garrison. Occasionally the images of the mountain would come to him in his sleep. And in those dreams, like some ethereal spirit, he would walk through the trees upon the land that lies there still, waiting for him among the thick wooded slopes of the Black Mountain in a forgotten part of Pakistan which rises up towards the Himalayan sky…

ABOUT THE AUTHOR

Andrew Goss is a former print journalist, aid worker and humanitarian reporter. His work has led him to travel extensively and for several years he lived in Pakistan, where he supported the aid and development sector. He is a passionate advocate of education for the world's poorest, and specifically girls and young women.

Andrew lives in Leicester, in the heart of England, with his partner Claire, a nurse and former aid worker, whom he says has finally shown him the true meaning of love. Between them they have six children: David, Johnathon, Emily, Ella, Lucy and Jalal.

Andrew's dream is that one day the poorest across the southern hemisphere are freed from poverty through greater equality of opportunity and fairer distribution of wealth – and that finally we learn to live as one. He hopes one day to return to Pakistan.